After studying English at university, Nell Pattison became a teacher and specialised in Deaf education. She has been teaching in the Deaf community for 14 years in both England and Scotland, working with students who use BSL, and began losing her hearing in her twenties. She lives in North Lincolnshire with her husband and son. Nell is the author of novels *The Silent House*, which was a *USA Today* bestseller, and *Silent Night*, featuring British Sign Language interpreter Paige Northwood.

By the same author:

The Silent House
Silent Night

THE SILENT SUSPECT

NELL PATTISON

Published by AVON
A division of HarperCollins*Publishers* Ltd
1 London Bridge Street
London SE1 9GF

www.harpercollins.co.uk

HarperCollins*Publishers*
1st Floor, Watermarque Building, Ringsend Road
Dublin 4, Ireland

A Paperback Original 2021
3
First published in Great Britain by HarperCollins*Publishers* 2021

A catalogue copy of this book is available from the British Library.

ISBN: 978-0-00-841854-0

This novel is entirely a work of fiction. The names, characters and
incidents portrayed in it are the work of the author's imagination.
Any resemblance to actual persons, living or dead, events or localities
is entirely coincidental.

Typeset in Sabon LT Std by Palimpsest Book Production Limited,
Falkirk, Stirlingshire
Printed and bound in UK by CPI Group (UK) Ltd, Croydon CR0 4YY

MIX
Paper from
responsible sources
FSC™ C007454

This book is produced from independently certified FSC™ paper
to ensure responsible forest management.

For more information visit: www.harpercollins.co.uk/green

For my parents, Glynis and Mark

Prologue

There was broken glass on the floor. Nadia paused in the doorway. The house felt empty, but she had to check every room before she was certain. Once she was sure she was alone, she breathed a little easier. After fetching a dustpan and brush, she cleared up the glass, straightening the furniture that had been moved. She noticed a couple of cigarette burns on the sofa but swallowed down her anger.

When she was happy the house had been returned to a more orderly state, she went through to the kitchen and flicked the kettle on. Tea was always a good idea – and making it would give her some time to think. Nadia felt better, talking to Karen and getting everything off her chest, and now hopefully something would change. It had to. She wasn't prepared to just sit back and let herself be taken advantage of, not this time. There was too much at stake. She knew that people assumed she would be a pushover, because she was deaf, and because she liked to keep herself to herself. But that didn't mean she was going to put up with this. She wasn't going to let herself be scared any more.

By the time she felt the cord begin to tighten around her neck, it was too late. The cup of tea in her hand crashed to the floor, liquid seeping into her skirt when she fell. Within a few minutes, flames were licking at the back door, creeping across the cheap vinyl flooring. Smoke began to fill the room slowly but surely, a grey cloud hanging above the body lying there. There was a cracking sound as the heat from the flames split open something on one of the shelves, then a sudden shower of glass and liquid as a bottle of vodka exploded. The small rain of alcohol fuelled the fire further, making the flames jump and spread along the worktop. Below it all, Nadia lay, unmoving, the only light in her unseeing eyes the reflection of the fire.

Chapter 1

Tuesday 16th April

I stared at Max, my mouth hanging open. The bustling sounds of the restaurant around me seemed to fade away. *What?*

He swallowed. *I asked if you would like to move in with me.* His hands shook slightly with nerves as he signed the words again. Max was profoundly deaf, and we almost always communicated in British Sign Language.

It had been a nice evening, at first. I had arranged for us to have dinner together at a fancy Italian restaurant on the outskirts of Scunthorpe. It was Max's birthday, and I'd tried to make the effort.

The meal had been fantastic, some of the best food I'd had in a long time, and the romantic atmosphere in the restaurant had been lovely. After we'd eaten dessert, we went to sit in the bar for a drink, and I had thought to myself how perfect it was – I was finally in a position where I could say I was happy with my life. I was enjoying my job, and was finally feeling financially stable with the regular salary from interpreting for Sasha, a profoundly deaf social worker. From Monday to Wednesday I worked with her, whether that was meeting hearing clients or interpreting for her in professional meetings, and sometimes supporting her deaf clients in meetings too. I had the rest of the week to take on any freelance jobs that came my way. My relationship with Max was perfect – we saw each other regularly, but still had our own separate spaces. We'd met when I first worked for the police just over a year earlier, and being with him had helped me to overcome my fear of being in a relationship, after what had happened before.

Max had reached over and taken my glass of wine from me, placing it carefully on the table.

I want all of your attention on me for a moment, he'd signed, and I'd laughed, happy to indulge him.

Do you want me to gaze into your eyes? I asked.

He sat back and pressed his lips together as if he was thinking, then gave a little nod. *I've been thinking a lot recently, about you. About us.*

I'm glad you think about me, I replied, but he held up a hand and shook his head.

Let me finish, please, he asked, and I could see from his eyes how anxious he was feeling. My heart thudded – what was wrong? Was he breaking up with me?

Max paused and looked down at the table for a moment, choosing his words, and I sat back a little in my seat. I should have known it was too good to be true, I'd thought. If this was the end of our relationship, I would be sad, but maybe not surprised that our relationship had run its course.

4

He'd looked so nervous I had almost interrupted him to put him out of his misery, but I thought it was only fair to hear him out.

It's okay, I signed to him, giving him a small smile. *Tell me whatever it is you want to tell me.*

Will you move in with me?

And now I was frozen. There was a long pause as I took it in, and I tried to force my train of thought onto a completely different track. Where had this come from? Was it a whim, or had he been building up to asking me for a while? Thinking back, I couldn't recall any signs that he wanted to move our relationship forward. He'd given me a key to his flat recently, but I thought that was just to make things more convenient, not so I could start moving my stuff in. Had I been completely naive? I tried to picture it – living in Max's flat with him – but I just couldn't conjure the image.

I was trying to think of a reply when my phone rang, and I seized the interruption like a life raft. The name that popped up on the screen wasn't one I was expecting – Lukas Nowak, one of Sasha's clients. Sasha had asked me to interpret for him at his regular meetings with the addiction support team, so I'd met him quite a few times. He was one of those small men who compensated for their size with an excess of charming personality, and I got the feeling his counsellor looked forward to the banter in their weekly meetings. But why was he calling me on a Tuesday evening?

I'm sorry, I need to take this, I told Max, trying to ignore his look of irritation. I got up and moved away from where we'd been sitting, into the entrance of the restaurant.

5

As soon as I answered the video call, I could see something was wrong. Lukas looked frantic and his signing was shaky and erratic. He was outside somewhere – I could see streetlights and a couple of parked cars in the background, and he was obviously moving.

Lukas, stay still, I signed. *I can't understand you.*

He stopped moving and the picture became a little clearer. *Paige, I need your help. Call 999 for me, please.*

What's happened? I asked. *Don't you have the emergency text number?*

I haven't set it up. Please, Paige! My house is on fire, and I don't know where Nadia is! She might be inside!

My screen went blank as Lukas hung up. I tried to process what he'd just told me, and quickly called the fire brigade and gave them his address, before trying to call Lukas back. No answer.

Looking back through the glass door into the bar I saw Max watching me. The restaurant was only a few minutes from Lukas's house – I couldn't not help. I knew Max would be cross, but I couldn't stay there, not when I knew one of Sasha's clients was in trouble. She was in Birmingham for a three-day training course and wouldn't be back until tomorrow, and Lukas would need someone to interpret for him with the emergency services.

I went back through to the bar, and my heart sank at the look of nervous anticipation on Max's face.

I'm really sorry, it's an emergency. I have to go.

Seriously? Paige, it's my birthday.

I know, but this can't wait. I'll call you as soon as I get a chance.

Max looked like he didn't believe me, but I didn't

have time to explain or argue, so I picked up my bag and left.

The heat from the blaze took my breath away and I took a couple of steps back. I hadn't expected the fire to be this bad – whatever I had been picturing in my mind, it had been minor. What I saw before me was so much worse than I had envisioned, and fear gripped my heart as I tried to get closer to the house. There was no sign of Lukas on the street outside, or in the alleyway between this and the neighbouring house. He'd been here when he called me, so where had he gone? I hoped he'd gone to a neighbour for help, and hadn't done anything stupid.

I dashed up the path and put my hand on the front door, but pulled it away again sharply. The paint was starting to blister, it was so hot, and I knew I couldn't risk opening it. Moving sideways, I tried to look through the window at the front of the house, to see if anyone was inside, but all I could see was the flickering of the flames through a sea of dark smoke.

Shouting would do no good, even if the people in the house could hear. I hadn't realised a fire would be so noisy – there was a low roar from the fire itself, as well as a myriad cracking and thumping sounds as items inside the house were engulfed by it.

I stepped back from the front of the house and looked upwards, searching for any sign of life inside. Smoke was pouring out of the upstairs windows, making me cough so hard my bones shook. I put my arm across my face but it didn't do much to shield me from the smoke. There

7

was another loud cracking noise from inside the house and I froze in fear. Was I in danger?

People had emerged from neighbouring houses and I could see the panic on their faces. A couple of them pointed at me and gesticulated for me to get away – I knew they were right, but I needed to be able to tell the fire brigade if someone was inside. Some of the onlookers started to bang on neighbours' doors, and I could see others with phones pressed to their faces. The emergency services were already on their way, but they were bound to receive a few more calls about the fire.

Where was Lukas? I looked around at the faces in doorways and on the street, but I couldn't see him. I wanted to make sure he was safe, but I didn't want to go any closer to the house. Even I knew better than to run into a burning building, whoever might be inside.

In the distance I could hear sirens, and a moment later two fire engines pulled up outside the house.

'Are you the home owner?' one firefighter asked me as the others busied themselves with their equipment.

'No, but I called you.'

'Is anyone inside?'

My mouth gaped for a moment as I panicked. Had Lukas gone inside to look for Nadia? Fear gripped me as I imagined how desperate someone would have to be to run into a burning building.

'I don't know. Maybe,' I replied, angry with myself for not being able to provide a definite answer. 'A man called Lukas lives here, and his wife, Nadia. They're both profoundly deaf.'

'Okay, anyone else?'

I nodded. 'Sometimes his son, Mariusz, I think. He's sixteen. But I don't know if he'll be here or at his mum's. I can probably find out, though.'

The man turned back to his colleagues and they huddled round to hear what I'd just told him. Looking back at the house, another ripple of fear went through me. If anyone was inside, I didn't see how they could survive that.

A police car and an ambulance pulled up and I looked over, wondering if I would know the occupants from any previous cases I'd worked, but two unfamiliar uniformed officers stepped out. I should have realised CID wouldn't have been there, not until they knew if the fire had been started deliberately. It had probably been an electrical fire, I thought. A lot of these older council houses had a backlog of maintenance issues.

One of the PCs approached me.

'You're going to have to move back,' she said with a frown. 'It's not safe.'

'Sorry,' I replied. 'I thought I could be useful.'

'How?' she asked, unable to keep the doubt from her face.

'I'm Paige Northwood,' I told her, digging my ID out of my pocket. 'I'm a British Sign Language interpreter. I had a call from the tenant, Lukas Nowak, and he asked me to call 999.'

'Why didn't he call himself?'

Now I was the one resisting the urge to roll my eyes – I would have thought my job would have given her a clue.

'He's profoundly deaf. He doesn't speak.'

It seemed like a lot more than fifteen minutes since Lukas had called me. I shivered at the memory of the terror on his face.

'Why you?' the PC asked, still suspicious of me.

'I work with his social worker, Sasha Thomas. She's profoundly deaf herself, and I'm her interpreter. Lukas has my number so I can support him if he needs an interpreter.'

She gave me a long stare, then nodded. 'Fine. But I'm going to need you to move back. It's not safe for you to be anywhere near the house.' She pointed away from the house and I obediently stepped back and into the road.

I watched as the two PCs set up a cordon to keep the neighbours away from the blaze, and comforted those whose properties adjoined Lukas's. The fire didn't seem to have spread beyond the one house yet, but I knew it was only a matter of time, unless the fire brigade managed to get it under control very quickly.

Checking my phone, I saw three missed calls from Max. I fired off a quick text to let him know I was okay and would call him later, but I didn't want to call him back in case I was needed. Lukas's call couldn't have come at a worse time, and I felt bad for leaving Max hanging. I was actually glad I had a bit of breathing space before I had to answer Max's question, but even thinking that brought a wave of guilt.

There was a shout from a firefighter and I looked over just as one of the downstairs windows shattered, sending a spray of glass out onto the pavement. I ducked instinctively, even though the glass hadn't come anywhere near me.

'Get back!' someone yelled at me, and I swiftly obeyed, moving as far back as I could whilst still being able to see the front door. Where the hell was Lukas? He hadn't been inside the house when he called me. Had he gone in, looking for Nadia or Mariusz?

Sweat dripped down my back, my proximity to the fire sending adrenaline coursing through my veins. Wasn't there anything I could do to help? There was another shout from the firefighters, and someone came out of the front door – a man kitted out in full protective gear, his tan and yellow uniform blackened by the smoke. There was a bundle over his shoulder, and as he rushed over to the waiting paramedics I could see it was Lukas.

Finally, I could be of use. I ran over to the ambulance, but pulled up when the same police officer stepped into my path, hand held out in front of her.

'You can't come any closer,' she said firmly, but I waved my ID badge at her.

'I told you before, I'm a BSL interpreter.' I went to move past her, impatient to do something useful, but she blocked my path again. 'That man is profoundly deaf,' I told her for the second time, pointing to where Lukas was lying on a gurney, two paramedics checking him over. 'Without me, it's going to be a lot harder for them to treat him if they can't communicate with him.'

The PC relented and stood back to let me past. Why were they trying to keep me away from Lukas? What was happening that they hadn't told me?

When I approached Lukas, he sat up and coughed so hard I thought he was going to be sick. Once it had passed, he lay back down again, then saw me.

Paige, he signed, his face frantic. *Where is Nadia? Did they find Nadia?*

My heart sank. *Was Nadia in the house?* I asked him.

He nodded, tears in his eyes. *Yes. I tried to call her but there was no answer. I couldn't find her in the house, though. I looked, but I couldn't get to her.*

What about Mariusz? I signed quickly. *Was Mariusz staying with you?*

A shadow passed across Lukas's face. *No, but he's not answering his phone either. Sometimes he comes round when I'm not expecting him.*

I squeezed his hand, not knowing what to say.

Will you try to call him? he asked.

I agreed, taking Lukas's phone from him and trying Mariusz's number. It rang out, but as Mariusz was hearing and his dad was deaf, I knew the sixteen-year-old was unlikely to answer a voice call from his dad's number. I sent him a text instead, from Lukas's phone, asking him to check in with his dad. A few minutes later, a reply arrived.

Dad, I'm fine. What's happened? Someone texted me something about a fire?

Lukas collapsed into sobs – even though he must have been relieved that his son was okay, he was still terrified. Sasha had been allocated as his social worker when he'd had problems in the past with alcohol and his mental health, but the sessions I'd been in showed that he'd moved on a lot. From what I'd seen, a lot of that was to do with Nadia; she was his world.

Another crash made me flinch and I turned around to look at the house. The upstairs windows had shattered this time. There were several firefighters nearby, but I didn't want to interrupt them. If they'd found Nadia, we'd know straight away.

Are you positive she was inside? I asked Lukas, and he nodded vigorously, which set off another bout of coughing.

Pulling the neck of my jumper up over my nose and mouth, I moved closer to the house, waving to attract the attention of one of the firefighters. The man I'd spoken to earlier saw me and came over.

'What is it?'

'Lukas, the man you pulled out of there, has told me his wife's inside.'

The firefighter nodded and, glancing over at Lukas, lowered his voice. 'We're aware of someone in the kitchen.'

I felt like a hole had opened up beneath me. Someone was trapped in that. Whether it was Nadia or someone else, the thought filled me with horror.

'We're currently trying to get to them. I'm not sure it's going to be good news,' he told me, then turned back to the house. The realisation of what he was saying made me catch my breath, and I blinked rapidly as a mixture of smoke and tears stung my eyes. Backing away, I went to stand by Lukas and squeezed his hand again as we saw two more firefighters bringing Nadia out of the building. They laid her lifeless body on a second gurney, and Lukas let out a howl as he tried to reach her. I did my best not to retch at the sight of her burned skin, what was left of her jeans and T-shirt clinging to her body in ragged clumps.

The paramedics rushed over to her and immediately began checking her over, blocking our view of where she lay. Lukas gripped my hand so tightly it hurt, but I didn't pull away. BSL users are good at reading body language, but anyone would have known what it meant as the paramedics' movements slowed and their shoulders sagged. Lukas let out a wail. Nadia was dead.

Chapter 2

I sat in the waiting room next to the two PCs who had been at the scene of the fire, my foot jiggling anxiously on the rubber-tiled floor. The plastic seat was incredibly uncomfortable, and I kept getting up to stretch out my back. Every few minutes I would have a coughing fit, but the paramedics had checked me over and said I was okay as I hadn't inhaled much smoke.

I had called Sasha once I'd arrived at the hospital, and explained what was happening. She was still in Birmingham, but she said she'd leave straight away, then asked me to stay with Lukas and text her updates if there was any news. Even if she hadn't asked, I had intended to stay – if Lukas needed someone to interpret for him, I didn't want him or the doctors to have to wait.

A vision of Nadia's burnt body rose up in my mind and I shuddered. There was a water cooler on the opposite side of the room so I crossed and poured myself a cup, gulping it down in two swallows, then refilled it and did the same again. How could this have happened? Was it something in the house, in the wiring? Why didn't Nadia notice the fire and get out of the house before it got too bad? Maybe she'd been asleep. But then I remembered the firefighter had told me they found her in the kitchen – I could believe she'd been asleep in a bedroom or on the sofa in the living room, but not in the kitchen. So what happened?

My phone vibrated in my pocket and I pulled it out to see that Max was calling me. For a moment I just looked at the screen then slipped it back into my pocket where it continued to ring for a few seconds. Only when it stopped did I feel how tense the muscles across my shoulders were. I leant back, resting my head against the wall.

I groaned inwardly when my phone began to vibrate again almost immediately. I couldn't ignore him forever, and he didn't deserve to be ignored. He just wanted to make sure I was okay, I was sure, but his protective nature could sometimes feel smothering. Looking around, I saw a recess in the wall at the end of the waiting area and moved over there to answer.

Hi, I signed, trying to rearrange my face into a smile.

Hi, he replied, a mixture of emotions battling for dominance on his face – relief that I'd picked up and I was okay seemed to win.

I'm so sorry, I told him.

Where are you?

I moved my phone so he could see parts of the waiting room. *The hospital. It was a house fire. They pulled Lukas out, and he's being seen by the doctors at the moment.*

16

Shit, Max replied, rubbing his face with one hand. *Are you okay?*

I nodded. *I'm fine. Well, I breathed in some smoke but it's not too bad.*

Was anyone else hurt?

I felt tears fill my eyes. *His wife. She died.*

Max hung his head. *I'm so sorry, Paige.*

Sniffing, I tried to smile again. *Thanks. I didn't know her very well, but still. It was a shock.*

I understand. I'm sorry, I shouldn't have called, he said.

No, it's fine, I insisted. *I know you wanted to make sure I was okay. And that I hadn't just run out on you for no reason.*

I could tell by the look on his face that he'd been considering this, but he shook his head. *It's okay. That conversation can wait.* He paused. *Unless you want to give me an answer now?* he asked, with a hopeful twitch of his eyebrows.

Taking a deep breath, I let it out slowly, then had to suppress a coughing fit. When I'd finished I looked back at him. *As you say, it can wait.*

He drooped slightly. *I'm sorry,* he signed again. *Terrible timing.*

Yeah. I glanced behind me to see a doctor talking to the two PCs. *I have to go,* I told Max. *I'll text you when I'm home, okay?*

I put my phone away and turned to look at the doctor who was now approaching me.

'Are you the interpreter?' she asked.

I held out a hand for her to shake. 'Paige Northwood. Do you need me?' I suppressed another cough.

'Yes, please. We need to explain to Mr Nowak the condition he's in, and the treatment we're administering.'

I nodded. 'How is he doing?'

She sighed. 'He's doing well, considering. Physically, he should heal without too many problems. Emotionally, I'm less sure. He's been cooperative, but he's in shock and hasn't tried to communicate with us. I'm told his wife died in the fire.'

Part of me had hoped there'd been a mistake, that Nadia had actually been unconscious and had survived. I couldn't imagine what Lukas was going through.

When we entered his room, there was a flicker of recognition in his eyes, but he didn't smile at me. I instinctively went to touch his shoulder, to give him some reassurance, but then pulled back – I didn't want to risk touching his burns and causing him more pain.

As I looked at him, I realised that the burns weren't his only injuries. I hadn't had a chance to look at him in decent light until now, and beneath the ash staining his skin it was clear that Lukas had numerous bruises on his face and arms. There was a gash underneath one eye that had been closed with a couple of steri-strips, and he appeared to be missing a tooth. Had this all happened to him in the fire? But how, unless he'd fallen down the stairs or something like that?

I thought back to his phone call. I had been watching his hand, the one that hadn't been holding his phone, trying to make sure I understood what he was signing to me. I'd barely paid attention to his face.

Bringing myself back to the task at hand, I interpreted as the doctor explained the situation to Lukas, but the only acknowledgement he gave that he'd understood was the occasional nod. One of his hands was burned, so signing could have been painful, I told myself. Really, I knew that Lukas couldn't bring himself to communicate. He was a shell of the man I'd met before, and Nadia's death would leave him desolate.

The doctor glanced at me, then back at Lukas. 'Mr Nowak, we noticed you have a lot of bruising on your face and chest. Can you tell me how that happened?'

Lukas watched me as I signed, but didn't respond, only turned to look towards the curtained window next to his bed. I attracted his attention and signed the question again; he shrugged, but didn't offer any explanation.

When the doctor had finished, she left the two of us alone and I sat in the chair at the side of his bed. He didn't seem to care if I stayed or not, but I didn't like the idea of leaving him there alone.

Lukas, is there anything I can bring you? Or any family or friends you want me to call? I hoped that by asking him questions I might bring him out of himself a little, but he just shook his head.

What about Mariusz? I pressed. *Have you told him what has happened?* In the panic over Nadia's body being found, I had forgotten about Mariusz's text. I hadn't replied to him, and I didn't know if Lukas had either.

He'll be worried about you, I gently pointed out to him.

Lukas's eyes widened and he focused on me properly for the first time, but he didn't make any effort to reply.

I'll ask the police to speak to Mariusz, and let them know you're okay, I continued. Lukas still didn't respond, but turned his face away from me. Was that a tacit agreement to what I'd suggested? I didn't know, and I found his lack of communication a little unnerving.

I thought about Mariusz then, a boy I'd never met, but had been told a lot about. Lukas always liked to talk about his son, how proud of him he was, and how it was being a father to Mariusz that had helped him to tackle his own issues. He had been ten years old when Lukas and his mother had split up, an impressionable age, but I got the impression that now he was sixteen there was a strong father and son bond. Hopefully getting Lukas to think about Mariusz would help, so he remembered who he still had to be strong for.

Another thought struck me, and I moved slightly so I was back in Lukas's eyeline.

Lukas, why did you call me and not Sasha? I asked. This had been bothering me earlier. Sasha would have the emergency text number on her phone, so she could have contacted the police just as easily as I had. Once again, however, Lukas didn't respond.

I wondered about asking the doctor to come back and check him over again, in case he was suffering from some sort of concussion. Was this just shock, or was there another reason he was refusing to communicate with me? Whatever it was, it felt strange.

We sat there for a few more moments in an uncomfortable silence, then the door opened behind me, and I turned.

'Hello?' I said. I didn't recognise the detective who had opened the door to Lukas's room. I'd worked for the police twice before, both times with DI Forest and DS

Singh, so I had been assuming if CID were involved it would be one of them. Part of me was disappointed; I got on well with Rav Singh. He was a brilliant detective, sharp-witted but also compassionate towards the people he dealt with. I hadn't seen him since the start of January, when we'd gone out for a drink to celebrate the start of my new job. Our friendship had run aground since then, as neither of us ever had much time, but I kept meaning to get in touch to see how he was.

'We need to speak to Mr Nowak,' the detective replied without introducing himself, his face serious. 'In private, please.'

'What's going on?' I asked.

The detective frowned at me. 'As I said, we need to speak to Mr Nowak.'

'Well, you'll need me to stay then,' I told him, explaining why. He looked uncomfortable, clearly not having been given the full information about the man he was coming to interview.

Once the detective had checked my ID and accepted the need for my presence, he turned to the figure in the bed. 'Lukas Nowak, I am arresting you on suspicion of the murder of Nadia Nowak.'

I stopped dead in the middle of what I was signing, shock rendering me motionless for a moment. Lukas frowned in confusion and I shook myself, forcing myself to continue. My hands shook as I signed while the man read Lukas his rights, tears in Lukas's eyes the only indication that he'd understood. The detective stepped forward with a pair of handcuffs and went to cuff one of Lukas's arms to the bed, but I held out a hand.

'Wait, you can't do that,' I told him.

The detective made a frustrated noise. 'I appreciate you interpreting for us, miss, but please don't interfere. He's in police custody now, so we need to secure him.'

'But how is he supposed to communicate?' I asked, anger flaring. 'Handcuffing a sign language user is like gagging a person who speaks. You can't take away his ability to communicate.' I folded my arms and glared at the detective until he eventually backed down and nodded.

'Okay, I see your point. My DI won't like it, though. There'll be a PC stationed outside the door until he's transferred to the station once he's been discharged.'

I interpreted this for Lukas, who nodded, then turned his head away from us. Taking this as my cue to leave, I followed the detective out of the room and waited for him to brief the PC. When he'd finished, he came back over to me.

'Can I ask how you know Mr Nowak?' he asked.

I explained the situation, and how I'd come to be at the scene of the fire that evening.

'So you're a witness. We'll need you to come to the station tomorrow and give a statement.'

'Fine,' I replied, still bristling a little from his attitude. 'What's happened? Do you think Lukas set the fire?'

'We're still looking into that,' he replied. 'There needs to be a full fire investigation to see how and where it started.'

'How can you arrest Lukas when you don't even know yet if the fire was deliberate?' I asked, indignantly.

The detective looked over his shoulder at the PC, then looked back at me and sighed.

Keeping his voice low, he said, 'Look, I shouldn't be telling you this, but his social worker will be informed soon enough anyway. Nadia Nowak was already dead when the fire started.'

Chapter 3

Once the detective had left, I called Sasha again, but there was no response. She was probably driving back, I told myself, so I sent her a quick text to tell her where Lukas was and that he had been arrested. Despite what he was being accused of, I didn't want to leave him on his own. In the months that I'd been working with Sasha I'd learnt not to judge a person by their circumstances, and just to be there to support them without bringing any preconceived notions about them. Attending the addiction support sessions with Lukas had been a real eye-opener for me, seeing just how many difficult situations some people had to fight against. Even if Lukas had killed Nadia, he was a vulnerable person alone in hospital after a traumatic experience. Though if he was guilty, that explained why he'd refused to communicate with me, not wanting to incriminate himself. I felt a surge of annoyance that he might have been trying to manipulate me.

Visiting hours had long since ended, but nobody had tried to throw me out yet, which surprised me until I realised the nurses assumed I was with the police. Taking advantage of this, I had a quick conversation with the PC who was stationed outside the door to Lukas's room. I wanted to give Lukas one last chance to communicate with me, to tell me what had happened, so I didn't feel like he'd been trying to use me.

'Can I go in and speak to him?' I asked in a low voice, conscious of disturbing patients and staff at this time of night.

He looked at his watch, then back at me. 'You're with social services?' he asked, and I nodded. It wasn't exactly a lie – they were the ones who paid my wages after all.

'Sure, you can go in,' he told me. The police obviously didn't consider Lukas a threat.

Cautiously, I pushed open the door a fraction and looked in, but the curtain next to the bed was pulled across a little way so I couldn't see his face. He didn't wear hearing aids, so calling out to him wouldn't help. I stepped a little further into the room and waved my hand around the curtain before I moved into his eyeline. He was awake, but he didn't turn to look at me, his eyes blank as he stared towards the window overlooking the car park.

Lukas, I signed, but he didn't seem to notice me. It's perfectly acceptable to tap a deaf person gently on the arm or shoulder to get their attention, but the only part of his body I could reach from the foot of the bed was his leg, and that didn't feel appropriate. I stepped further to my left, towards the window, in the hope that I could move into his field of vision. He sighed deeply and turned his gaze on me, his eyes puffy and full of sorrow.

Is there anyone you want me to call, who can be here with you? I asked him. *I've told Sasha what's happened,* I added. *Whatever happened, you have rights, and Sasha can help.*

He shook his head, and his eyes filled with tears.

I gave him a few moments, but he didn't respond any further. I had done all I could. It was an awkward situation; I felt responsible for him, despite the fact that he was Sasha's client, not mine. I was about to turn and leave again when his hand shot out and grabbed my wrist. The speed of his movement took me by surprise, and his grip was so tight it hurt. When I looked up at him, I could see a fire burning in his eyes, and I tried to pull away. The charming man always ready with some banter was gone, and he was scaring me slightly.

I know who did this, he told me, releasing my hand so he could sign.

If you know what happened to Nadia, you need to tell the police, I replied. He wrinkled his nose but didn't reply. *I know one of the detectives, DS Singh. He'll help you,* I added.

Nobody can help me, he replied.

Who was it? I asked. *Lukas, who killed Nadia?*

He looked at me, his eyes still bright, and he licked his lips nervously. At that moment, my phone buzzed in my pocket, making me jump. It was a message from Sasha.

Stay there, on my way up.

She must have sent it from the hospital car park. I looked back at Lukas, but he'd turned away, and the moment was lost. I tried to attract his attention to ask him again who was responsible, but he ignored me.

Accepting defeat, I left Lukas's room and went to find one of the nurses, to make sure Sasha would be allowed onto the ward at this time of night. The nurse I spoke to didn't seem happy about it, but she agreed to it anyway. Something about the presence of police officers obviously swayed her decision.

The buzzer at the door to the ward sounded a couple of minutes later, and I went up to meet Sasha. She swept through the door, her long curly hair looking a little wild as she was framed in the doorway, her eyes searching for me. Her brightly patterned quilted coat was starkly contrasted against the drab walls of the ward, and she swept up to me with the imposing air I recognised from when she was ready to fight for one of her clients.

Paige! What the hell happened? she asked as soon as she saw me. I quickly explained as much as I could – my call from Lukas, the fire, and the police arriving at the hospital to arrest him.

I need to see him, she told me, her face grave. *I want to know what he has to say about it, and I expect he'll need help to get a solicitor.*

The PC was watching our signed conversation, openly curious, and I led Sasha to him so I could make introductions. We were interrupted by a different nurse from the one I had spoken to – her uniform was a different colour, and her badge said she was the ward manager.

'I'm sorry but this is not acceptable,' she hissed at the three of us. 'We have lots of patients on this ward, sick people who need to rest, and your presence is disturbing them.'

I interpreted this for Sasha, and she nodded.

I understand, and I apologise. I'm a social worker. If you'll give me ten minutes to see my client, after that we'll leave.

The ward manager didn't look impressed, but she gave a stiff nod, then looked at the PC.

'I'll be here until he's discharged and transferred to the police station,' he said.

Sasha and I stepped back and left them to their argument.

I'm going to go in and talk to him, see what he needs, she told me.

Okay. Do you want me to wait here for you? I asked. She didn't need me to interpret as she and Lukas were both sign language users, but I didn't know if she'd want to speak to the nurses or the PC again.

She nodded. *Just in case.*

There wasn't anywhere to sit, so I stood opposite the PC, my legs aching with fatigue after the day I'd had. I'd barely had any time to think about Max, let alone whether or not I wanted to move in with him, and I was quite glad of that. I'd only spent a few seconds mentally preparing myself for him to break up with me, but even that short time was enough to completely throw me when it turned out he wanted the opposite. It was gone midnight, too late to be trying to make any decisions right now, I told myself. I would be better sleeping on it, although I had a suspicion that thinking about it would keep me awake.

I yawned widely and rubbed my eyes. I'd have to drive home carefully. I was so tired. Checking my phone, I saw

28

a message from my sister, Anna, asking when I would be home, so I let her know how I was getting on.

After about five minutes, Sasha emerged from Lukas's room. I was surprised she hadn't been in there longer. She looked pale, and gestured to me – she needed me to interpret so she could talk to the PC.

Do you know how long he's going to be here? she asked him.

He shrugged, and addressed his response to me. 'You'll have to ask the doctor. Once he's discharged, he'll be moved to the station.'

Can someone please inform me when that happens? I could see that Sasha was fighting to stay polite and not say something she'd later regret.

The PC shrugged again. 'Not my job to do things like that. You'll have to speak to the detectives in charge of the case.'

I could see Sasha was considering responding, but she thought better of it and the two of us left the ward. We walked down to the car park without a word or sign passing between us; I was too tired for meaningful communication, and she was deep in thought.

When we got outside, Sasha paused and leant against a railing.

I think he must be in shock, she told me.

I nodded. *That's likely. What did he say?*

Nothing, she replied, with a slow shake of her head as if she couldn't quite believe it. *He wouldn't communicate with me at all, except to ask me to leave.*

Nothing at all? I checked. I was surprised, assuming Lukas would be a lot more open with her than with me – maybe

29

even tell her who he thought had killed Nadia – but she shook her head.

How could this have happened? she asked me. She looked almost dazed. This wasn't the first time one of her clients had been arrested, I knew, but something about Nadia's death had obviously knocked the wind out of her. Lukas had been her client for several years and she'd got to know Nadia in that time, too.

I don't know, I replied. *We'll have to wait and see what statement he gives to the police.*

I'm sure he didn't do it, she told me firmly. *They can't hold him for long without any evidence.*

I thought of what Lukas had told me, that he knew who was responsible, and wondered again why he hadn't said the same to Sasha. As she'd said, maybe he was in shock, and was too busy trying to process it all to manage to have a conversation with anyone. But if he was deliberately withholding information, why would he do that?

He didn't say anything about Nadia, or the fire? I tried to keep my confusion from my face but Sasha must have spotted it, because she paused, her head on one side.

No, why? Did he say something to you? she asked with a frown.

He told me he knew who was responsible.

Who? she asked, and I could see her eagerness to know written all over her face.

I'm sorry, I replied with a grimace. *He wouldn't tell me. That's all he said.*

Are you sure that's what he said? You couldn't have mistaken his signs for something else? Her eyes narrowed as she questioned me, and I felt I was seeing a side to Sasha I'd never seen before.

If you don't think I can interpret accurately perhaps I should look for another job, I snapped. I was too tired for this; I just wanted to go home and sleep, and now Sasha was questioning my skills.

She put a hand on my shoulder, looking suitably chastised. *You're right. I'm sorry. I just don't understand why he'd tell you that, but refuse to say anything to me.*

I think he regretted telling me, to be honest, I told her. *By the time you arrived, he'd had a chance to think about things.* As I signed this I wondered just what it was he'd been reflecting on. Was he protecting himself, or someone else?

Yes, but . . . she signed, but then let her hands drop and shook her head. Whatever she'd been planning on saying, she decided to keep it to herself.

Sasha sighed deeply. *This is a bloody mess. He won't be able to afford a solicitor, so I hope the one he's assigned has a bit of deaf awareness.* She looked at me. *Will you be able to interpret for the police interviews?*

I doubt it, I told her with a shake of my head. *I'm a witness to the fire. I think it'd be a conflict of interest.*

She scowled, and I wondered why she wanted me to be present for the interviews. If she thought I'd give her inside information on the investigation she was wrong.

Yawning widely, I looked at my watch, and she took the hint.

You go home and get some sleep, she told me. *Hopefully the police will keep me informed of what happens next, but I won't hold my breath.*

31

I nodded, and stumbled off to my car, slapping my cheeks a few times to wake myself up before I set off. When I started the car, I put the air conditioning on, cold air blowing right in my face.

As I pulled out of the car park, I could see Sasha was still standing where I'd left her, phone in hand and texting, and I wondered what had happened in that house that Lukas wasn't telling us.

Ten hours before the fire

Caroline slammed the car door and marched up to the house. She'd checked Nadia's rota, so she knew she'd be able to get her ex alone at this time. He worked in the canteen at the steelworks, and he didn't start until midday on a Tuesday. It was no use trying to talk to him when that woman was around; she just took over and pretended to be reasonable, when Caroline knew she was smirking at her behind her back.

She hammered on the door, unable to keep her frustration from spilling out into her body language. The flick of a curtain at a neighbouring window made her scowl in the direction of that house. The neighbours around here were so bloody nosy. Well, if Lukas didn't let her in soon, there'd be a nice little scene for them all to gossip about for the rest of the week.

When there was no answer, she knocked again, looking through the window to see if there was any sign of Lukas.

She got her phone out, about to text him, when he opened the door and peered out at her.

Caroline? What are you doing here?

She didn't answer, but nudged the door further open using her shoulder, and pushed her way past him and into the living room. Once she was in, she sat down on the sofa and crossed her legs, taking off her scarf and dropping it down next to her. Lukas looked confused, but he followed her lead and sat down in a chair.

What do you need? he asked.

The question made her laugh, bitterly. 'What do I need?' she replied, speaking and signing at the same time. She'd learnt BSL when they'd first met, but she still found she couldn't switch her voice off, especially when she was mad at him. 'What do you think I need? Money, you bastard. I'm sick of waiting every month for you to pay me something for Mariusz. It's always bloody late, if I get anything at all.'

Didn't Nadia sort it out with you?

'Nadia?' she asked, incredulous. 'Why the hell should I have to deal with your tart, when you can't be arsed to do anything about it yourself? You're a lazy bastard, Lukas Nowak, and I'm not taking money off her,' she snapped, punctuating her sentence with the jab of a finger towards the kitchen, as if Nadia was in there, 'when it's your responsibility.' She finished off this pronouncement by pointing at him, her glare sharp enough to make him cower slightly.

I know, I'm sorry. Nadia knows what to do with online banking, things like that. That's all I meant.

He looked pathetic, she thought, sitting there making

excuses for why he hadn't given her any child support in three months. As if her pride would ever let her take money off Nadia. She'd die before she let her think she couldn't manage by herself. Another woman who'd fallen for his charms, not realising that she'd end up looking after him as if he was a bloody child himself.

'It's not good enough, Lukas. I've told you before, if you don't pay up I'll take you to court, and they'll take it straight off your wages.'

Please, don't, Lukas begged, and a fresh wave of anger hit her. She'd told him so many times.

'Give me one good reason why I shouldn't.'

Lukas hesitated, then hung his head. *We can't afford it.*

'What do you mean, you can't afford it?' she scoffed. 'You should have thought about that when you left me for someone else, shouldn't you! You've got a bloody job; you need to manage your money better.'

For a moment she thought he was going to make another excuse, but he just shook his head.

You don't understand.

'No,' she replied, standing up and pointing a finger at him again. 'You don't understand what it's like trying to make sure I keep a roof over our son's head, make sure he has decent clothes and plenty of food, on just my salary. If I don't have the money by the end of the week, you can see me in court. I doubt you can afford a solicitor.' She stood up, then glanced around the room, her eyes lighting on a blue and silver vase on the mantelpiece. 'And I'll be putting together a list of items I want from this house, things that you should have given me when we split up six bloody years ago.'

Caroline stormed out of the house and got back into her car, fuming all the way into work. It was only when she got there that she realised she'd left her scarf behind; it was her favourite one, but there was no way she was going back to get it. She was too angry with him. There was no reason why Lukas shouldn't be able to afford to give her the child support he owed her, unless he was spending it on something frivolous. A thought occurred to her – maybe Nadia was taking all his money and controlling their finances, and that's why he'd thought she would have sorted it out. If Caroline found out that woman was withholding money that was rightfully hers, for Mariusz, there would be hell to pay.

Chapter 4

Wednesday 17th April

The following day, I was surprised to receive a call from the police station asking me to come in. I assumed it was in order to give a witness statement, as I'd been the one to call the fire brigade in the first place, but as I'd already been told to come, I wasn't expecting a reminder.

When I arrived, I checked in at the desk.

'Oh, you're the interpreter.'

'I am,' I agreed, 'but . . .'

The woman on the desk didn't give me a chance to finish telling her that I was there to give a witness statement, but led me straight through to a room where Lukas was sitting with a couple of PCs. They would need to process him, take his fingerprints and DNA, which they couldn't do without an interpreter. It was at this point I wondered if there had been a mix-up, but I figured it couldn't hurt if I did this for them before giving my statement and leaving.

Once Lukas had been processed, the detectives turned

up to interview him and I was both pleased and surprised to see DS Singh, even if he was shortly followed by DI Forest. Singh gave me a big smile, which made up for the frown on his boss's face. Singh's broad frame was a reassuring presence in the room, and there was an openness to his face that made it easy to trust him. I could see even Lukas felt the same, by a subtle relaxation in his body language.

'Great to see you, Paige,' he said reaching out to touch my arm affectionately before he noticed Forest was watching and pulled away. 'It'd be nice to catch up but we're rushed off our feet and need to get this interview underway.'

'But I'm . . .'

'This way please, Miss Northwood,' Forest snapped, opening a door and ushering me inside, before following me. Lukas had already been brought in by the PCs and was sitting opposite us looking mournful. I wondered if he really was in a fit state for this. His skin was deathly pale, and looked almost as white as the bandages covering the burns on his arms. Another bandage was covering his shoulder, and it showed around the neckline of his T-shirt. I could see the bruises and cut on his face more clearly now that he'd been cleaned up a bit, and the blues and purples had developed a deeper hue overnight. How had he got them? Hopefully his statement would cover that.

Rather than sitting down, I hovered by the doorway, unsure of what to do. There must have been a mix-up, unless another interpreter was on their way in and Forest had just assumed that was why I was there. They must not have been told that I was a witness to the fire.

'DI Forest, I don't think I . . .' I began, but the detective shot me a look and interrupted me once again.

'Miss Northwood, would you sit down? I don't have time for this,' she snapped.

Fine, I thought. If she was going to be a bitch I'd sit here and do this interview for them, then she could deal with the consequences if it made the interview invalid.

Singh gave me a strange look; he was probably wondering what I'd been trying to say. I knew if he'd been in charge he would have at least heard me out, even if it meant wasting a bit more time.

'Mr Nowak, do you understand why you are here?' Forest asked Lukas.

Lukas watched me as I signed, but merely shrugged in response.

'Do you wish to contact a solicitor?'

He'd been asked that already this morning, but he'd refused, and he did so again now. Sasha had wanted to talk to him about a solicitor last night, but if he didn't want to communicate with her, there was only so much she could do.

'Can you tell us about what happened yesterday afternoon and evening?'

Lukas looked from me to both detectives, then shook his head, not even lifting his hands to sign.

Forest sighed, clearly frustrated.

'It's important that you give us your version of events so we can establish what happened yesterday.'

I interpreted this for Lukas, but he shook his head again.

Forest leant back in her chair and narrowed her eyes at Lukas.

'Mr Nowak, did you kill your wife?'

Still no response from Lukas, which I imagined would wind Forest up even more. I didn't understand why he wasn't trying to defend himself.

'We can sit here all day, Mr Nowak,' she said. 'If you think you're going to achieve anything by refusing to talk to us, you'll find you're sorely mistaken. Whilst your statement would be beneficial to us, it won't change the evidence we find, and if that evidence suggests to us that you killed your wife we're going to charge you, with or without a statement.'

She waited a while for it to sink in, then she opened the file that was sitting in front of her. Taking out some photos, she carefully laid them on the table in front of Lukas. His eyes briefly flicked down to the images and I saw the colour drain out of his face before he lifted his gaze again.

'These are pretty hard to stomach, I know,' Forest said, looking at the images herself. I kept my eyes on Lukas, knowing if I looked at the pictures I wouldn't ever be able to forget them. 'This is your wife, Mr Nowak. Someone killed her, and I will find out who did that, with or without your help.'

Forest leant forward, her elbows on the table, her eyes narrowed.

'What happened, Lukas? If you tell us the truth now, it might go better for you. Judges always look more favourably on people who have cooperated with us when it comes to sentencing.' She paused, but Lukas just kept his eyes on me, waiting for me to continue signing but offering nothing himself.

'Did she do something to annoy you?' Forest asked,

her voice light, but I could hear the razor-sharp undertone to it. 'Did she make you angry? Was it the final straw, and you just snapped?'

Lukas was visibly trembling, but he maintained his refusal to communicate. Whatever his reasoning, Forest was right – he wasn't doing himself any favours if he didn't even give a statement telling his side of the story.

It continued in the same way for some time, until Forest seemed to give up and turned to Singh.

'I don't have time for this,' she growled at the DS.

Singh looked down at the file in front of him, then back at Lukas. 'What about if we start at the beginning, Mr Nowak? Let's talk about yesterday afternoon. Your employer has confirmed you left work at the steelworks at six, and we have CCTV of you getting on the bus that goes past your house. Was your wife, Nadia, in the house when you got back?'

Lukas watched me as I interpreted, but then sat back and folded his arms. In the silence that followed, I thought I could hear Forest grinding her teeth.

When Singh realised he wasn't going get a response, he tried a different tack.

'Would you like to tell us how you got the bruises on your face and body?'

Lukas's face coloured, but he stayed in the same position, still refusing to be drawn.

I wondered how long he could keep this up, and if he was ever going to say anything about what had happened. When he'd told me last night that he knew who was responsible, I had assumed he was going to tell the police who they should be looking at, so this approach surprised me. He was making himself look even more guilty by refusing to defend himself.

Snatching the file from Singh, Forest pulled out a piece of paper that looked like a witness statement, and I felt as if the temperature in the room had dropped a couple of degrees.

'The police officers who were at the scene of the fire last night took some statements from other residents on your street. One of them informed us that you and Nadia had a very loud fight yesterday, shortly after you returned home. Is that how you got the bruises? Did she fight back? Is that why you killed her?'

Lukas's jaw tightened and his eyes narrowed, and I could see white patches appear on his knuckles from gripping his own arms so tightly. I couldn't imagine him ever being violent; when he was in a bad mood he became depressed, not angry, in my experience. Surely this would draw him into communicating with the detectives? For a moment, I thought he was going to sign something, but then he took a deep breath, let it out slowly, and continued staring between the two detectives.

They carried on for another ten minutes telling Lukas what they knew, and trying to provoke him into responding to them. It sounded like they'd been busy yesterday evening and this morning – they had already ascertained that Lukas left work at his usual time and took the bus home, that he and Nadia had argued at some point in the evening, and then he'd gone out to the pub, leaving her alone in the house.

'We've spoken to two people who saw you at the Frodingham Arms last night,' Forest told him. 'Hopefully they'll be a little bit more cooperative than you when we ask them about your state of mind, or if you already had these bruises when you came in.'

I noticed that Lukas had developed a slight twitch in one eye in response to a couple of questions, and I wondered if Singh and Forest had picked up on it too. Sign language users are good at communicating with their body language and facial expressions, and it wasn't easy to suppress that when it was your main mode of communication. I often found myself signing as well as speaking to hearing friends when I was particularly excited or worked up about something, and I could see Lukas was struggling to show no reaction to what the detectives were saying to him.

The crunch came when Forest pulled out the piece of information they'd been keeping back.

'Mr Nowak, your wife didn't die in the fire. The pathologist examined her body at the scene, and she said it was clear that Nadia had been strangled. We expect the post-mortem to confirm that she was dead before the fire started.'

Lukas jerked in his seat and his mouth hung open as he tried to take in this information. I felt bad that I'd known the night before, but he'd not been well enough for the police to question him, so I assumed nobody had explained the situation to him. Still, it had obviously come as a huge shock to him, as he covered his face and howled with grief, the first true display of emotion I'd seen from him that day.

The detectives gave Lukas a minute to compose himself before continuing with their questions.

'Are you sure you don't want to change your mind and cooperate with us, Mr Nowak?' Singh asked, his tone soothing, leaning towards Lukas as if to invite his confidence. 'Did you and Nadia have a fight? Did things go a bit too far?'

Lukas half jumped out of his seat and slammed his fist on the table, lifting his hands as if to sign something. The detectives and I all held our breath, expecting him to finally tell them something, but then he froze. He sat down again, his whole body trembling, then slipped his hands beneath the table and bent his head, tears running down his nose and dripping off the end.

Just at that moment there was a knock on the door. Singh got up to see who it was, and was passed a piece of paper that he put down in front of DI Forest.

'Well, this is interesting,' Forest told Lukas, scanning the paper quickly, her voice scathing. 'It seems that the preliminary examination of your house has determined that the fire was started deliberately. Did you set your house on fire because you thought we wouldn't find out you'd killed your wife?'

There was complete silence for a moment as Lukas stared at me, then looked down and slipped his hands underneath his thighs. He shook his head, over and over, continuing to sit on his hands to show his defiant refusal to answer any of their questions. He started to rock slightly in his chair, his movements getting more and more frantic, until Forest stood up suddenly. Her chair crashed to the floor behind her, making me jump.

'Mr Nowak, we have enough evidence to hold you, so I'm not going to waste any more of my time on you.

We've given you a chance to give us a statement. Next time we question you, it would be in your best interest to cooperate.' She turned and stalked out of the room, leaving Singh to sort out an officer to escort Lukas back to a cell.

'What was that all about?' he asked me quietly as we walked down the corridor a couple of minutes later.

'I have no idea.' I didn't want to tell Singh how worried I was about this turn of events. 'He wouldn't speak to Sasha last night, either.'

'Sasha?'

'Sasha Thomas,' I reminded him. He'd met her the same time I had. 'She's his social worker.'

He nodded. 'We might need to speak to her, find out some more about his background and state of mind.' He paused, then gave me a smile that almost looked a little shy. 'You look really good, Paige. I mean, well. You look really well.' He gave an embarrassed cough and I felt myself blush.

'Thanks, you're looking well yourself.'

We reached the door, when I remembered why I'd come in that morning.

'I need to give a statement,' I told Singh before he had a chance to usher me out.

'Why?' he asked, looking puzzled, but then I heard a door bang and someone yell my name, and my heart sank. Forest stamped down the corridor, brandishing a piece of paper at me.

'You're a witness! Why the hell didn't you say anything? You can't interpret for this case if you're a witness. It's a bloody good job Nowak didn't say a damn thing.'

'I tried to tell you when we went into the room,' I replied through gritted teeth. 'You kept interrupting me. I thought I'd been asked to come in to give my statement, not to interpret for an interview.'

Singh looked between me and Forest. 'You're a witness?'

I nodded. 'I was there last night.' I explained that Lukas had called me, and started to talk about what had happened, but Forest held a hand up.

'Save it for the statement,' she said. 'Rav, you sort it out. I don't have time for this,' she snarled, then turned and marched away up the corridor again.

'She gets worse,' I muttered once I was sure Forest was out of earshot. She had always seemed to resent my presence during cases involving deaf victims or suspects, and had relished the opportunity to fire me, once.

'You don't know half of it,' he replied, the look on his face making me think I shouldn't ask. 'Come on, let's go and get this statement sorted,' he continued, giving me a smile. 'Then maybe we can get a drink later?'

I nodded and returned his smile. 'That sounds nice.'

Before we started I got in touch with Sasha and explained what was happening. I checked with Singh how much I could tell her, but as Lukas himself would be able to tell her all of it, he told me I was free to keep her informed.

Being deaf herself, Sasha was naturally assigned any social work clients who were deaf, especially BSL users, because she was more likely to build up a positive rapport with someone without the need for an interpreter. I was there to interpret when she met her hearing clients, and also for regular meetings with her colleagues. I had been working for her for three days a week since January, and it was working well for both of us: I had a regular salary, as well as regular working hours, and she had the benefit of knowing when she would have access to an interpreter and could arrange her diary accordingly.

Singh looked deep in thought, and I was about to ask what was bothering him when he shook himself, and explained the procedure for giving a statement.

I went through everything that had happened, from when I'd received the phone call from Lukas, through to when he was arrested. I didn't include my conversation with Lukas in the hospital. For all I knew, he'd told me he knew who was responsible to manipulate me, to make sure I didn't think he was guilty. In reality, I didn't know what to think. Was he trying to use me to make it look like he was innocent, when all along he'd murdered his wife and set his house on fire? If he was innocent, why would he refuse to say anything to the police?

Chapter 5

This is completely ridiculous, Sasha insisted. *There is no way Lukas would have hurt Nadia. I can't believe it!*

The two of us were sitting in a meeting room with Singh, a couple of hours after Lukas's interview.

'I'm sorry, Ms Thomas,' Singh replied, indicating the file on the desk in front of him. 'A neighbour heard them arguing, and told our officers that it happens on a regular basis. Nobody else was seen entering the house, so he is the prime suspect in Nadia's murder. Lukas stormed out, probably went to show his face at the pub, had a couple of drinks to calm his nerves, then it seems he went back to set the house on fire. He's covered in bruises but won't say how he got them. The fact that he won't give a comment at all, even to protest his innocence, doesn't look good for him.'

I interpreted for Sasha and she slumped back in her chair and raised her hands to the ceiling.

This doesn't make any sense. Lukas has been doing so well, his mental health has improved dramatically, and I was going to recommend he was taken off my caseload. He didn't need my support any more. She turned to me. *You told me he looked horrified when he was told the fire was set on purpose. And that he looked shocked when he found out Nadia had been strangled.*

I nodded. 'I haven't known Lukas very long – I've just been in a few addiction support meetings with him and Sasha – but I don't think he's that good an actor.' I spoke and signed at the same time, so both Singh and Sasha could follow the conversation.

Singh shook his head. 'What do you want me to say? I have the evidence, and he won't give us anything to suggest he's innocent. Paige, you were there the whole time, you know what happened. I was as surprised as you were when he refused to comment at all, but I can't exactly take this to my DI and say I think he's innocent despite all of this. She'll want this case closed and off my desk.'

'But why would he call me, if he'd killed Nadia? And why would he go into the house when it was on fire?' I asked. 'He could have just set fire to the house and then waited until a neighbour saw it and called the fire brigade. By getting me involved, surely that would have been too big a risk?'

'Or it gave him the perfect witness,' Singh replied, looking me in the eyes. 'You believed what he told you, and he obviously thought he'd left it long enough that the fire would destroy any evidence.'

Sasha and I looked at each other and I shrugged. Singh was right – there was nothing we could do. Lukas had been given the opportunity to ask for a solicitor, had refused, and had made the choice not to respond to any of the detectives' questions. Even though I couldn't understand what Lukas was doing, I could see it from Singh's point of view.

When Sasha had arrived, she'd asked to see Lukas straight away, but Singh had asked if she wouldn't mind sitting down and speaking to him first. That's how we came to be there, in that room, all baffled by what had happened.

Paige tells me he was distraught last night when he saw the firefighters pull Nadia's body out of the house and he realised she was dead, Sasha reminded Singh.

'And plenty of murderers feel that way about their victims,' he replied gently. 'You're a social worker. You must know that domestic abuse is almost always followed by a period of remorse. That remorse doesn't last, however.'

He wasn't abusive, Sasha insisted. *There was no history of any problems, with either Nadia or his ex-wife.*

Singh sat back and put Lukas's file to one side. 'Okay. Tell me about Lukas. Why are you involved with him?'

Sasha blinked and a startled look passed across her face quickly, but a split second later it was gone. Pulling a much bigger file out of the heavy bag sitting next to her, Sasha sat it on her lap and gave Singh a searching look.

Are you just humouring me?

He sighed. 'I want to understand Lukas Nowak better. I want to know how we got here. Even with the evidence we've got, I'd like to make sure we've covered all the bases in case he changes his mind and decides to give us a statement at any point.'

Fine, Sasha replied, turning to a page in the middle of

her file. *I became involved with Lukas about five years ago. He was going through a period of deep depression following his separation from his ex-wife, Caroline, who had been very evasive regarding custody of their son, Mariusz. He became dependent on alcohol, and threatened suicide on two occasions.*

Singh turned to a page in his file. 'We have two separate reports on the system of him being found on the footpath of the Humber Bridge, late at night. I assume these are the two occasions you're referring to.'

Yes. He's been doing very well with a programme of medication and therapy, and his mental health is much more stable these days. He sees an addiction counsellor on a regular basis, and from what I've seen he's been very honest and up front when he's struggling.

'Was the alcohol a problem when he was with Caroline?'

She looked up at Singh. *No, that started after they broke up. I know what you're suggesting. There were no complaints of domestic abuse, no signs of anything physical between Lukas and Caroline. No phone calls to the police from neighbours, none of the tell-tale signs I'd normally look for. It was a bad break-up, and Lukas felt that Caroline was keeping him from seeing Mariusz.*

'Was there any truth in that?' Singh asked, picking up a pen from the desk.

Sasha grimaced. *It's a difficult one. He insisted she had told him he wouldn't be allowed any custody because he was deaf and not British, but there wasn't anything in writing. She didn't text him anything that he could show us, so we only have his word for it. However, once we were involved and trying to support them to have regular contact, she was evasive. It took a long time to make concrete arrangements, and she would find reasons to change plans at short notice.*

'Did she ever give you a reason for this?'

No, nothing that suggested she was worried about Mariusz spending time with his father. She leant forward. *You and I will have both come across a lot of manipulative people in our professional lives, and that was what it felt like, to me. Do you understand?*

Singh nodded. 'I do. So let's assume you're correct, and he has no history of violence, even unreported. How do you explain him going to the pub last night? We managed to speak to a couple of people who saw him there, and he was definitely drinking. It seems he's a regular there. I can't imagine his addiction counsellor would be supportive of that.'

I watched as Sasha's face fell. *I don't know about that. As far as I knew, Lukas hadn't had a drink in a long time, and had reached the stage where he was comfortable around other people who were drinking. Maybe he's been going to the pub to socialise? Did they actually tell you he was drinking alcohol?*

Singh took a moment to flick back through the notes of his conversation with Lukas, and his confession, then looked back at Sasha. 'They mention pints and shots. I can't imagine either of those were soft drinks. It's too late to check his blood alcohol level, unfortunately, even if he wanted to claim that alcohol was a factor. We'll be looking for other witnesses to confirm the time he arrived at and left the pub, so I'll make a note to confirm what he was drinking.'

I could see from the look on Sasha's face that she was sure the witnesses were mistaken. Over the last four months I had learnt how passionate she could be when she was standing up for her clients. She wasn't a pushover, and she would tell them exactly what she thought, handing out tough love whenever it was necessary, but she would defend them to the death if she thought they weren't being treated in the way they deserved. The clients I had met clearly respected her and felt respected by her, which had an impact on how much effort they put into helping themselves. Her caseload was huge, the whole department stretched to breaking point, but she still worked damned hard for every single one of them. Of course, some weren't grateful because they resented the interference in their lives, or because they were scared of the implications of having a social worker. It didn't help that the media had condemned social work as a profession long ago, but she and her colleagues were pretty thick-skinned, as far as I could see. Nobody went into social work thinking they were going to change the world and be showered with praise for it, but if they could change the life of one person, it was worth it.

Lukas has been so much better since he met Nadia, Sasha told Singh. *She was a very calm and supportive person, but she also didn't let him get away with anything; she wouldn't take any excuses. The medication and therapy helped to improve his mental health, but I think being with Nadia was the best therapy he could have had.*

Singh looked like he was sizing Sasha up, his brow furrowed and his lips pressed together, but then he shook his head. 'I'm sorry. I can make a note of your concerns, but it doesn't do anything to counteract our evidence. We'll continue to investigate, and if we find anything that suggests he's not responsible, of course things will change. Until then, I suggest you convince him to speak to a solicitor, and to then give us a statement.'

Sasha's eyes lit up when he said this, and a ghost of a smile crossed her face. Did that mean Singh thought there might be some truth to what we'd been saying? He was right, of course: Lukas really needed legal advice, and without a solicitor things could go very badly for him.

'Is there anything else that you think might be relevant?' Singh asked.

Sasha glanced at me, and I thought she was going to add something, but then she shook her head. *I don't think so*, she replied regretfully. *I wish I could make sense of this.*

'Well, you can go and see Lukas now, if he's willing to see you. Maybe he can explain it to you.' Singh smiled gently at Sasha, and I could see he was trying hard not to be patronising, but he thought she was deluded. I could see his point – surely nobody would keep their mouth shut about their own innocence, unless they were actually guilty. Lukas had been given plenty of opportunity to give his side, both to Sasha and the police, but had he completely clammed up due to guilt, or fear?

Rav led us through the police station and downstairs to another meeting room, this one very stark and bare. I imagined it wasn't much nicer than the cell where Lukas was being held.

'I'll bring him along. You can have about ten minutes with him, but that's all.'

We sat and stared at the heavy metal door for a moment, then Singh was back, with a shadow of the man we knew.

Lukas, Sasha signed as soon as she saw him. *Lukas, what's going on?*

He shook his head jerkily, avoiding looking straight at Sasha, but didn't reply. Sasha sat down and pointed to another chair for him to do the same. Lukas hesitated, a wary look in his eyes, and didn't sit down.

Lukas, you need to tell me what happened. Why won't you give a statement? Sasha asked him.

Instead of answering, he turned back towards the door, looking out of the tiny window as if he wanted Rav to take him back to his cell. My heart sank; Lukas still wasn't going to say anything, whether to defend himself or otherwise.

Sasha got up and walked round so he could see her again. *This doesn't look good, you know, Lukas,* she told him, gently but firmly. *You need to give the police a statement, tell them your side of the story.*

Lukas leant his head against the metal door and took a deep breath, letting it out again in a weary sigh. He turned his head to face Sasha, but I couldn't see his expression. A worried frown crossed Sasha's face and she shook her head. I assumed she was trying to tell Lukas that he couldn't continue like this; he would have to communicate with someone soon.

Sasha came back and sat down, folding her arms, watching Lukas the whole time. I'd seen her use this tactic before, giving the client space to come to her, but Lukas didn't respond in the way she'd hoped. A minute or so later, the door opened and Singh was back.

The moment the door was opened, Lukas stepped back so he didn't appear to be trying to escape, then he nodded to Singh as if to tell him he was ready to return to his cell.

Singh looked between Sasha and me before taking Lukas away.

What's going on? Sasha asked me, looking baffled. *I don't understand what's happening.*

Neither did I, but if I knew Sasha by now, she wouldn't stop until she'd found out.

Chapter 6

Twenty minutes later, we were back at the social services office. Sasha dumped her bag on her desk, and looked around at the room, which was busy with people on their computers or phones.

Wait here, she told me, then left the room for a couple of minutes, leaving me to hover awkwardly by her desk. I didn't spend much time in the office with her, as she used her time with me for meetings and other appointments as much as possible, so I didn't really know any of her colleagues very well. Most of them were friendly, although one of the managers obviously viewed me with slight suspicion and tried not to hold conversations within my hearing.

Sasha appeared at the door and gestured to me, telling me to grab her bag and follow her. Doing as I was told, I went out and through to the other side of the building, where we entered a small meeting room.

This is free for the next fifteen minutes, she told me, sliding the sign on the door across to show the room was occupied, then shutting the door. *We can talk about Lukas.*

I sat down, not sure what she wanted to talk about or why she wanted the privacy, but my role mostly involved doing what she asked so I didn't question it.

Taking the seat opposite me, Sasha leant on the table and fixed me with a piercing look. *I need to decide what's the best course of action for helping Lukas.*

I nodded. *Okay. Well, I don't know what your responsibility is, professionally speaking.*

Sasha shook her head. *Technically, none. He's in the hands of the criminal justice system now, so he's their responsibility. But that doesn't mean I'm going to give up on him.*

I didn't know what Sasha expected of me, so I sat back and waited for her to continue.

Tell me exactly what he told you, when you were in the hospital.

I'd told her several times already, but she was obviously fixated on it, so I thought back to the previous night.

He said he knew who was responsible, I told her.

Who was responsible? Did he use those exact words? She sat forward eagerly, and I felt as if I was being interrogated. *Because you can be considered responsible for something even if you didn't actually do it yourself.*

I thought again. *Er, maybe not. I think he said he knew who'd done it.*

Sasha nodded, a thin smile on her face. *Good, that's good.*

I should have included that in my statement, I told her,

58

regretting my decision to leave it out. *I thought it probably wasn't relevant, but surely they'd want to know everything he said to me? Especially as he's refusing to tell them anything now.*

You could tell them now, ask if you can add it in? Sasha suggested.

I nodded, but didn't tell her what I'd been worrying about. That maybe Lukas had told me in the first place so I would include it in my statement. If he had killed Nadia, telling someone who was a witness to the fire that he knew someone else had done it would be a good way to try and throw the police off the scent. But was Lukas that calculating? The frustrating thing was that I had no idea. I had always seen his charm and his gentle flirtation as harmless, but there was always the possibility that he was now using that in order to manipulate me.

It's worth checking, Sasha continued. *It could help him, persuade him to talk.*

I gave her a non-committal head tilt this time, neither a nod nor a shake. Unless Lukas was going to start cooperating with the detectives, and then tell them who he thought had killed Nadia and why, I didn't think it would make much difference.

Sasha stood up and walked over to the window. It afforded a rather dull view of the car park, a stretch of grass and then a fairly busy road, but she obviously wasn't interested in the scenery.

She turned back to me. *So the question is, who did kill Nadia?*

Hang on, I said with a frown. *How do you know Lukas didn't kill her?* I saw her face darken, but I pushed on anyway. *I know he's your client and you want to believe he's innocent, but you have to be open to the possibility that he might have done it.*

He told you himself that he didn't, she signed. *And he's clearly absolutely devastated about her death. Isn't that enough for you?*

No, it's not, I replied, standing my ground. *And I wouldn't have thought it was enough for you, either.*

We glared at each other for a moment, until she came back and sat down opposite me.

Fine, she conceded. *However strongly I feel that Lukas wouldn't have hurt Nadia, I can't be certain. But I think I have a responsibility, as his social worker, to at least consider all of the possibilities.*

I nodded. *Okay. What do you want to do?*

She thought for a moment. *If Lukas knows who killed Nadia, why hasn't he told the police?*

He could be scared, I replied. What I didn't add was the other idea I was mulling over, that he'd only told me that to try and manipulate me into taking his side.

Scared of being blamed? she asked.

No, I don't think so. Because otherwise he would have told the police about it, wouldn't he? I reasoned.

Okay, so not scared.

Unless he's scared of the person who killed her. That's why he's not saying anything.

Sasha's eyes lit up. *Of course, that sounds plausible. He won't admit to something he hasn't done, but he knows if he tells the police who it was they might be able to get to him.*

Could he be protecting someone? I asked. *Maybe he*

knows who killed Nadia, but doesn't want them to go to prison?

Sasha looked doubtful. *Apart from his wife and son, I can't see Lukas protecting anyone that fiercely that he'd go to jail for them. Mariusz got on well with Nadia, and he's only sixteen. No, I think you were right the first time.*

She stood up and began pacing. *So how are we going to find out who he's scared of?*

I was about to offer a suggestion, but then stopped myself. Just over a year earlier, I had been asked to interpret for the police when a deaf child had been killed. The child was Anna's goddaughter, and I'd found myself doing things that were dangerous and stupid, which ultimately led to my sister being gravely injured. When I'd first met Sasha, I was supporting the police when they investigated the murder of a teacher at Lincoln School for the Deaf, and I'd ended up trying to rescue a student from the killer. If I allowed Sasha to lead me down this route, would I end up in danger and at odds with the police yet again?

Besides that, Singh had taken me aside before we left and reminded me that as a witness I couldn't be involved with the case. He meant that I wouldn't be asked to interpret for any further interviews with Lukas, but I had a feeling he also was referring to my work with Sasha. He knew what I was like from the previous times we'd worked together, and how easily I found myself caught up in these things, but this time it had to be different. I shook my head.

Sasha, we're not the police. It's not our job to look into it, I told her, aware of my own hypocrisy, but not wanting to be drawn into something dangerous again. Besides, I trusted Singh; he was an excellent detective, and if there was more to this case than was obvious at first, I knew he'd find it.

Sasha frowned at me, then sat down again and reached for my hands. She squeezed them and looked into my eyes, before pulling away again to sign.

I don't want to let anyone down again. She looked at me knowingly and I could tell she was referring to the incident at Lincoln School for the Deaf last year. She still blamed herself for not realising what was going on, and I sympathised with her.

But, Sasha, what makes you so certain that Lukas is innocent? I knew I risked her getting angry by asking again, but I wanted to be sure myself. *He was covered in bruises. How do you know he didn't fight with Nadia and end up killing her?*

Her mouth twitched as she thought about how to respond. *I don't even know for certain myself,* she signed eventually. *But right now, I want to be certain. He hasn't confessed, and he told you it was someone else. That's enough for me.*

Sasha's reaction hadn't completely surprised me. I'd seen how passionate she could be when she fought for her clients' rights, and I knew how proud she was of the work Lukas had done to improve his life and his health over the last couple of years. She certainly wasn't a pushover, though. I remembered one time when I'd just started working for her, he'd missed a few of his addiction support meetings, and she gave him a talking-to about his responsibilities to himself and his family. Being blunt with her clients seemed to make them respect her all the more, though, and Lukas hadn't missed a meeting since.

Okay, I signed. *I'm not going to stop you, but we have to pass on anything we find out to the police,* I added.

Sasha agreed. *So we need to work out who Lukas is afraid of,* she said.

I let her go on for a while, laying out her theory and telling me what she was going to have a look at, but I didn't offer any extra suggestions. I remembered what Rav had said to me, and I intended to take it to heart and not get involved.

As I walked out of the building, I pulled out my phone and scrolled down to Singh's name, my thumb hovering over the call button. He should know what Sasha and I had been talking about, and I should tell him what Lukas told me in the hospital. But what if I was right about him trying to manipulate me, and by doing that I could be unwittingly helping a murderer? No, it could wait until I knew a few more facts. Putting my phone away, I told myself I'd give it a day or two before I spoke to Singh, and hopefully by then the police would have the answers anyway.

Chapter 7

By the time I got home that afternoon I was exhausted. I shut the door to my flat and leant against it for a minute, my head still swimming. I didn't know whether to trust Sasha's assessment of the situation. She knew Lukas better than I did; that much was true. Hopefully she would know how to persuade him to tell the police what he knew.

I went through to the kitchen and put the kettle on, and a moment later I heard keys in the door. My sister, Anna, had been living with me for around a year now. She worked at a university in Hull, running their new Deaf Studies department, and her enthusiasm for her job still shone through several months after she had started. I smiled at her as she put her head round the kitchen door, hoping she wouldn't see how stressed I was.

Hi, she signed. *Are you making tea?*

I nodded. *Want one?*

Please, I've barely stopped all day. She gave me a grin

and went off to get changed as I got her a mug out of the cupboard. By the time the drinks were made she was back, regaling me with a tale about her day. I nodded in the right places, but I found my attention drifting so I missed the point of one story and had to ask her to repeat herself.

What's wrong, Paige? she asked, with a concerned frown. *Is it about the fire? Is that man okay?*

I had told her the basics about Lukas and the fire that morning before she left for work, but not yet about Max asking me to move in with him, which was still playing on my mind. I shook my head.

The pressure of everything I'd been worrying about, Max's question and Lukas's refusal to defend himself, suddenly bore down upon me and I burst into tears. Anna jumped up from her seat and wrapped her arms around me, holding me until the flood had subsided.

Once I'd calmed down a bit, she stepped back so she could sign.

What's happened?

I swallowed, wondering what to tell her first. Anna and Max had had a mixed relationship over the last year, and the two of us had only really just got settled into living together again. I didn't want to upset her by making her worry about me moving out and leaving her alone, especially when I didn't know what my answer was going to be. But she was my sister, and I knew if anyone could help me figure out what I wanted, it would be her.

Max asked me to move in with him.

There was a pause, and I saw a range of emotions passing over Anna's face. She looked me in the eye and tilted her head on one side.

Why has that made you cry?

Because I don't know what to say, what to think, I replied, throwing my arms out to the sides. *I'm happy with the way things are. I was happy. But this has completely thrown me off guard. I wasn't expecting it.*

Really? she asked, an amused frown on her face. *Ever since Christmas he's been making little comments about how nice it would be if you didn't have to keep going between his flat and here, or how he'd like to share more things with you. And that's just what he's said in front of me. Surely in private he's floated the idea before now?*

I sat with my mouth open for a moment. Was Anna right? Had this been coming for a while now and I hadn't noticed? I shook my head.

No, he hasn't said anything about living together. I would have noticed.

She raised an eyebrow. *Would you? You've spent quite a while sticking your head in the sand in the last year or so.*

What's that supposed to mean? I asked, trying not to get wound up.

I mean you put the brakes on at the beginning of your relationship with Max, because you were scared. And that's understandable, because you hadn't been with anyone since Mike, and that ended very badly. But even after you saw Mike again and stood up to him, you didn't take on board how much you've changed. If you had, you probably would have moved in with Max ages ago.

I stopped myself from replying and tried to think about what she'd said. The first half was certainly correct – following a relationship that had been both emotionally and financially abusive, it had taken me a long time to trust anyone again, but being with Max had helped me to break down those barriers. And seeing Mike again last year had served to highlight the differences in the two relationships.

That was where my version differed from Anna's, however. In the last few months I'd really felt like I was as open with Max as I could have been, and for the first time in a long time I felt like my old self again. He cared about things that were important to me, and as a result I was finding joy in my old interests again, even when I wasn't with him. I'd worked hard to save money and pay off the last of the debts Mike had left me with, and I could finally see the light at the end of the tunnel with regard to my financial situation. Being with Max had possibly served to make me more independent and resilient, enjoying our relationship but still growing as an individual rather than defining myself as one half of a couple. I thought it was positive; I thought it was healthy. But now everything was going to change.

It wasn't that I didn't want some of the things that come with a more serious relationship, including sharing a home and maybe more, but I just couldn't picture having that with Max. I tried to explain this to Anna but I found myself going round in circles, tying my ideas in knots, until she held up a hand and asked me to stop.

Paige, do you want to move in with him? she asked, once again looking me in the eyes. I tried to hold her gaze but I felt uncomfortable with the scrutiny and soon looked away.

I don't know. I like things as they are.

Everything changes, though, she told me. *Nothing in life ever stays the same. Where do you see yourself in the future? Do you want the marriage and babies thing? Because I'm pretty sure Max does, and if you don't see yourself going down that path you need to have a conversation with him about it pretty soon.*

He's asked me to move in with him, Anna. He hasn't proposed; he hasn't mentioned having kids. Don't get ahead of yourself.

She sat back and narrowed her eyes at me. *Okay. If it's only about living together, and not about the potential future path that puts you on, what are you worried about? You know by now that he's not going to treat you like Mike did. And you know Gem and I have been watching him like hawks.*

I couldn't help but laugh at this. Gem was my best friend, and she and Anna were the ones who helped to get Mike out of my life for good. I knew they'd made things difficult for Max, because they had such high standards, but they had both warmed to him over time. Sometimes I thought Gem liked him more than I did, not that she'd ever admit to it.

The two of us sat in silence for a few moments. Part of me was starting to regret telling Anna about this, but I knew she was only asking the obvious questions. It wasn't her fault that I wanted to avoid them. Maybe she was right, and I would have preferred to stick my head in the sand and ignore the possibility of taking my relationship with Max further.

I don't really think about the future, I admitted, after a moment to get my thoughts together. *I've been so focused on building up my reputation as an interpreter, paying off my debts, and just getting by, that I haven't ever really stopped and thought about what I want next. Does that make sense?*

She leant forward and squeezed my hand. *So you have been thinking about the future,* she pointed out. *You've been building up a solid career, and you told me you'd like to start teaching BSL. That's all future planning, Paige, you just haven't mentally included Max in that future. But now he's forced your hand, and you're going to have to think about what you want. I'm sure he's happy to wait for an answer, but don't make him wait too long.*

I sighed. *I know. Okay, I'll think about it. But the whole prospect of it scares me.*

You can move in with him without selling this place, she replied. *I can take over paying the mortgage, so if things don't work out with Max you can just come straight back. It's a commitment, but that doesn't have to mean it's forever.*

You're right, I know. It was my turn to squeeze her hand. *Thank you.*

It's what I'm here for. But I do want to ask something, she signed, sitting back and giving me a mischievous smile. *Did you see DS Singh today?*

I felt my face colour slightly and looked away in an attempt to hide it. *I did, actually. Why?*

I just wondered if that might have influenced your indecision over moving in with Max.

What's that supposed to mean?

She laughed. *Oh, come on, Paige! You fancy Singh. And I know you, you feel like you can't move in with your boyfriend if you feel like that about another man.*

Don't be ridiculous, I began, but she laughed even harder, and the more I tried to deny it the worse it got. Anna had dropped hints about Singh in the past, but I had thought it was just because she found him attractive herself, not because she thought I genuinely liked him. I had been aware of my own feelings for him for a while, but every time the thought floated into my mind I pushed it out again quickly. But now Anna was teasing me about it, I worried that my feelings had been more obvious than I'd realised. Had Max noticed? Had Rav? I squirmed with embarrassment at the thought, but now Anna had directly accused me I knew I couldn't keep denying it.

Okay, fine! I gave in. *I might fancy Singh. Is that better? Are you happy now I've admitted it?*

Anna stared at me for a moment, then punched the air. *Yes! You finally said it! I thought you'd never confess.*

Look, it's no big deal, I told her. *I mean, he's a nice guy and yes, I find him attractive, but I'm with Max.*

But you still don't want to move in with Max, because you have feelings for Singh. She waggled her eyebrows at me expressively.

No, I replied, trying to stay calm and not rise to her bait. *I just don't know if I'm ready for that step yet.*

Paige, you're my sister. I know you better than anyone else, and I know there's a part of you that feels guilty for fancying Singh when you're in a relationship. And that guilt will be part of what's holding you back from moving in with Max. I started to reply but she cut me off. *No, I haven't finished. It's normal to have crushes, Paige. Nobody expects you to never be attracted to anyone else ever again. That's not how human beings work.*

I promise you, Anna, that's not the issue. I don't feel guilty about it, I lied.

Okay, if you don't feel guilty, what is it? Is it that you think you made a mistake? Do you want to break up with Max and go out with Singh? Because if that's the case, you need to do it now to avoid hurting Max too much.

I flexed my hands for a moment in a sign language equivalent of spluttering, until I realised what I was doing and stopped. Looking down at the table, I thought about my sister's probing words. On some level, she was right. Even after a year with Max, I wondered if he was the man I really wanted to be with. Until now, I was able to just carry on with our relationship, having a bit of emotional denial when I saw Singh a few months ago, but it was possible to ignore it. If I committed to Max, however, I would have to be certain it was what I wanted.

I told Anna as much. *You're right. I don't know what I want. That's why I'm wound up about Max asking me to move in with him.*

She moved round to my side of the table and gave me a big hug. *I know. I've always known. You can't hide it from me. And whatever you decide, it's okay, but you do need to make a decision now.*

Ugh. I buried my head in my arms for a moment, before looking back up at her. *I hate this.*

I know. But now you know what the real issue is, you can start thinking about what you're going to say to Max.

I nodded, knowing she was right, but also knowing it wasn't that easy.

Eight hours before the fire

Nadia took a deep, shuddering breath then let it out again slowly. The office appeared to be empty, so she could take a couple of minutes to steady herself. It was getting too much; the situation was out of hand and she needed to do something about it once and for all. Even coming into work was starting to make her feel panicky.

She was there to pick up her copy of the next week's rota after handing in her time sheet, and she scanned it to see which clients she was working with. As a carer, she knew she shouldn't have favourites, and she tried to treat all of them the same, but she still had a soft spot for certain people.

With a sigh, she realised the situation was the same as it had been last week. She'd been given completely new clients, and none of her regulars. It wasn't fair! Why should she have to change her working pattern? Any mistakes she'd made recently were to do with who she'd trusted, not what she'd done.

Feeling frustrated tears welling up behind her eyes, she left the office and went straight to the toilets, locking herself in a cubicle. She would only let herself cry when she was sure nobody was around, and if anyone else came into the office she couldn't bear them seeing.

After a few minutes, she knew she needed to get moving. She wanted to get home and do some housework, knowing everything would have been left in a terrible state again. Unlocking the door, she went to the sink and splashed some cold water on her face, then looked at her reflection. What was she doing? How had she got herself into this mess? Lukas didn't even know all of it. She should tell him, but what if he didn't agree with her about how to handle it?

She felt a tap on her shoulder and saw another face in the mirror, making her jump.

'Karen! I didn't hear you come in.'

'Are you okay?' the other carer asked, concern on her face. She manoeuvred herself into the light so Nadia could read her lips clearly, before repeating her question.

For a moment, Nadia tried to maintain her composure, but when confronted with Karen's concern, she felt the tears begin to well up behind her eyes.

'No,' she replied, shaking her head. 'No, I'm not.'

Chapter 8

Thursday 18th April

I didn't work for Sasha on a Thursday, so I had another interpreting job booked for the morning. It was a training course for an educational outreach company, and they had a couple of deaf teachers attending. Interesting as I found it, especially as it was so different from my usual fare – social work meetings, medical appointments, occasional school events – I found myself drifting a few times during the morning. I couldn't stop thinking about Lukas, and the strange chain of events that had occurred in the last couple of days.

When I thought back to the heat of the fire, I felt my pulse increase and a shot of adrenaline burst into my veins. Just the memory of it was enough to put me back into survival mode, so I could only imagine how Lukas had felt. I knew I hadn't imagined it – he was terrified, and when he realised Nadia was dead I felt like I saw his world crumble in slow motion. So why wouldn't he communicate with the police?

I knew Sasha was keen to keep me involved with this case, especially as I'd been there with Lukas as it happened, but I was reluctant. I'd told Singh I wouldn't get involved, and I meant it; I didn't want to get entangled in this. The last thing I wanted to do was make Singh mad at me, and not just because I'd finally admitted to myself that I had feelings for him.

The training had been in a small town on the banks of the Humber, about half an hour from Scunthorpe. Just before I got back in my car after my morning job, I received a phone call. Glancing at the display, I could see it was Sasha, so I pulled up and answered it.

Hi Paige, she signed as soon as her face popped up on my phone screen. *Are you busy?*

I've just left a job, I told her, wondering what she wanted.

Do you fancy meeting for lunch? I've got some stuff I'd like to talk to you about?

I was wary, but I agreed. *I'm in Barton at the moment.*

That's great. I'm not far away.

We agreed a meeting place and I set off through to the other side of Barton-upon-Humber. She'd asked me to meet her in the cafe at the nature reserve on the edge of the estuary, and I arrived before her. Choosing a seat next to the window, I looked out over the reeds and ponds. A couple of mums with young kids were feeding the ducks, toddlers clinging tightly to paper bags of seed bought at the entrance to the visitor centre, as various waterfowl converged on the area where some of the food had hit the water. My mind suddenly jumped to Max – was he thinking about this sort of future for us? If I moved in

75

with him, would I be here in a few years, feeding the ducks with my own children? Part of me could see it, but part of the picture still felt wrong. It wasn't that I didn't want a family of my own, because I'd thought about it. No matter how many times I tried to imagine it, I just couldn't see myself having that future with Max.

I sat like that for about ten minutes, before I became aware of Sasha bustling over to my table. She was dressed in denim dungarees and a retro tie-dyed T-shirt, her curly blonde hair spilling over her shoulders. Sasha was always distinctive, however she dressed, but I sometimes got the feeling she did her best to stand out, as if she was daring the world to challenge her.

Hi, sorry I'm late, she signed, pulling up a chair and sitting down.

Aren't you working today? I asked.

She shook her head. *I took a day off. I wanted to try and get my head round what's happened and work out how I can help Lukas.*

How's he doing? I asked her, getting straight to the point.

She shook her head and grimaced. *I don't know, I haven't heard anything today. Have you?*

No, I replied. *If they've interviewed him at all, they've used a different interpreter.* Singh had been clear yesterday that I couldn't be involved with the case going forward, and I'd accepted that. I would have to make sure I stayed in touch with Singh, though, so they didn't forget about me. I really valued my work with the police and I didn't like the idea of being passed over in favour of someone else, but hopefully if they needed a BSL interpreter again in future I'd still be their first choice. I certainly hoped I'd be Singh's first choice, anyway, and I resented the idea of another interpreter coming in and potentially taking over my territory.

Sasha frowned and tapped the table while she thought about Lukas and how to proceed. *It's a difficult situation, because I can't insist on seeing him, unless I have evidence that his welfare is being compromised.*

Well, if he's not had access to anyone who can communicate with him, surely that's compromising his welfare? Being isolated due to a language barrier is bad for his mental health.

You're right, she replied with a firm nod. *We'll use that as a way in. Of course, that's if he'll agree to see me.* Sasha's face fell, and she looked genuinely upset that her client wouldn't turn to her for support when he needed it. *I'm not his lawyer; I don't think I can just march in there and demand to see him.*

What about with his history of mental illness? I offered. *Surely that's another angle you could use. It's important that someone is monitoring his mental health, and ideally that should be someone who knows him and can communicate with him in his first language.*

She beamed at me. *I knew there was a reason I hired you.*

We both laughed. This was Sasha's usual response when I offered a useful suggestion. She hadn't hired me personally – we both worked for the local authority – but she'd recommended I apply for the position when it became vacant, and I'm sure she influenced the interview panel. After all, I was her interpreter and we had to spend a lot of time together; it was only right that she got a say in who was hired.

Right, Sasha continued. *Now you've had time to think about it overnight, do you think he did it?*

I was a little surprised by the direct question, but I responded immediately.

I'm not certain about anything, but now I don't think so. I didn't mention to Sasha that I'd been concerned that Lukas had been trying to manipulate me; I didn't see the point in possibly antagonising her, especially now I didn't think it was likely.

I saw him that night, Sasha, I continued. *I saw the fear and devastation when he realised Nadia was dead. There's no way he's that good an actor.* I felt a little reluctant to tell her this, knowing she might try and use it to get me further involved than I would like, but I didn't feel I could lie to her.

I know you say you don't want to get involved, Sasha signed, her expression earnest, *but I would still appreciate your advice. You've spent time with Lukas, and you know the detectives involved with this case.*

After a moment of thought, I nodded slowly. *Okay,* I told her. *But I'm going to be honest with you if I think something isn't right, or you need to go to the police.*

That's all I can ask, she replied, sitting back and looking a little relieved. *I have an idea of where to start looking, if we want to find out who really killed Nadia. Lukas was having some money problems. I don't know the full extent, because there's only so much we can get clients to discuss with us, but I know he borrowed some money, and that the person he borrowed it from wasn't exactly legitimate.*

I took a sip of my coffee, which had been growing cold as we talked. *Are you suggesting this person might be responsible for Nadia's death? Would Lukas really get involved with someone who was capable of something like that? I know he had his problems, but getting involved with organised crime seems a bit of a stretch.*

She shrugged. *I have no idea, but I do think it's something we need to look into. I'll see if I can get the name of the person he borrowed from. He told me the man was a friend, which is possible, but I do wonder if there's more to it than that.*

Okay, but what about the other possibility? I asked. *To me it seems more likely that Lukas is trying to protect someone. If he was scared of the person who'd done it, wouldn't he tell the police the truth and ask for their help?*

Sasha looked at me like I'd just asked if she was the one who killed Nadia. *Do you really think Lukas would trust the police to help him? His upbringing, the area he lives in, the experiences he's had in life . . . none of these things have left him in a position to trust many people in authority. And if whoever he borrowed this money from has a bad reputation, Lukas will feel like he's safer in jail than back on the streets.*

I paused to let this sink in, suitably chastised. I'd let my own situation influence what I thought about Lukas, and hadn't stopped to look at things from his perspective.

But there could be something in what you're saying, Sasha continued. *We have to look at the people in his life he might want to protect, and see if they had a motive for murdering Nadia.*

The people at the neighbouring table were watching

us curiously. Public conversations using sign language usually garnered attention, but in this situation I was very glad they didn't understand what we were discussing.

Other than Nadia herself, I can only think of Mariusz, I replied.

He's almost an adult, but I can't see him murdering someone. He's sweet, and small for his age, Sasha replied. *And Mariusz and Nadia got on really well.*

How's he taking it? I asked.

I've been trying to get in touch with his mother, Caroline, to find out, Sasha told me, nodding at her phone. *But she's not my client, and neither is Mariusz, so if she doesn't get back to me I don't have many other options. I suppose we could go round and see them, just to ask how they're doing.*

I'm not sure that sounds like a good idea, I replied with a frown. *The police might not be happy about it.* I had been trying to ignore the number of times she'd signed 'we' rather than 'I'. I wasn't even being paid to interpret for her today, and I didn't want her to drag me into something I wasn't keen on doing.

Sasha shrugged. *She's not my client. I'm not working today. What's wrong with knocking on the door just to check they're okay? The worst Caroline can do is refuse to talk to us.*

You can try it if you like, I told her, emphasising the first 'you' with a sharp jab of my finger in her direction, *but be prepared for it to backfire.*

She nodded slowly, then looked up and smiled at me, and I knew what was coming.

I don't know how good Caroline's signing is. I mean,

80

she must be able to sign to communicate with Lukas, but I don't want to have any miscommunication.

I shook my head before she even asked the question. *No, Sasha. I promised Singh I wouldn't get involved. This is your client, and much as I feel for him, I can't support you poking around.* Until now I'd thought Sasha just wanted to discuss alternative theories for what happened to Nadia, but it was dawning on me that she wanted to go further than that and actively investigate.

I'll sign off your overtime, if that's an issue, she replied. *Then it's no different from you interpreting for me with any of my clients or the other professionals I meet. It's me who's getting involved, not you.*

I hesitated. If Sasha found something that pointed to another suspect, I knew she'd rush to take it to the detectives, but would she be so quick to act if she unearthed evidence that incriminated Lukas? I knew I should trust her to be impartial, but it felt like she was taking this case personally.

Against my better judgement, I agreed, and a few minutes later we were on our way back to Scunthorpe. I was surprised that she knew Caroline's address, but then wondered if she'd been planning this all along and had only asked me to meet her to enlist my help before going round there. It was too late to change my mind, though.

Caroline lived in a neat little row of tiny terraced houses near the hospital, and when we rang the bell I heard movement from inside. The house opened right onto the pavement, and from our position next to the door we were very close to the front window. I tried my best not to stare, but Sasha stood and watched as the curtain twitched and a young face looked out at us for a moment.

Thirty seconds later, Caroline appeared in the doorway. She was clearly dressed for work, in a carer's uniform, and didn't look particularly pleased to see us.

'You're Lukas's social worker, aren't you?' she asked, looking Sasha up and down before turning to me. 'Who are you?'

'I'm Sasha's interpreter,' I replied, which got an eye roll from Caroline but no further comment.

'What do you want?'

We just wanted to see how you're doing, Sasha told her, putting on her best expression that managed to convey both sympathy and friendship. I interpreted for Caroline, although from her scowl I could tell her BSL was good enough that she had understood.

'I'm fine. Why wouldn't I be?' Caroline replied with a shrug, glancing over her shoulder and back into the house as she did so.

'Have you heard about the fire? At Lukas and Nadia's house?' I asked, just in case she hadn't been told about it.

'Have I heard that my ex is in jail for murdering his wife and burning his house down to cover it up?' she asked, sarcasm dripping from every syllable. 'Yeah, it's come up a couple of times. But why are you here? I don't need a fucking social worker.'

We just wanted to see if there was anything you or Mariusz needed, Sasha explained. *There are things we can do to support you in this sort of situation. If Mariusz wants to talk to anyone about it, we can arrange that.*

82

Caroline took a step forward, shoving her face into Sasha's. 'Don't you come near my boy. It has nothing to do with him. I'm just glad he was here with me that night, and not at his dad's.'

Before Sasha had a chance to respond, a figure appeared behind Caroline in the hallway.

'Mum, don't.' Mariusz put a hand on Caroline's shoulder and pulled her back, but she shook her son off. I could see what Sasha meant – for a sixteen-year-old boy, Mariusz wasn't very tall, and he was skinny. He had a mop of blond hair that fell in his eyes, and I got the feeling that he liked to hide under it. When he looked up at us I could see redness around his eyes, and he looked between us with an anguished frown.

Sasha smiled at Mariusz and was about to sign something, when Caroline stepped in between them.

'No. You're not speaking to my boy. I don't want him having anything to do with his father, not after what he's done, and you won't convince me otherwise. I know he's sent you here. Does he really think I'm going to let him see his son when he's in prison?' Her face contorted with a mixture of rage and disgust. 'It was bad enough that he shacked up with another woman and got married so quickly, but I never thought he'd do something like this.'

'Lukas hasn't sent us, Caroline,' I began, but she glared at me.

'I've told you. Leave us alone.' With that, she stepped back into the house and slammed the door. Sasha and I looked at each other, knowing we couldn't do any more, but as we turned to walk back to the car I saw Mariusz watching us from the front window. He glanced behind

83

him to check Caroline hadn't noticed, then signed *Sorry* through the window.

I miss my dad. And Nadia, he told us, then turned away. Sasha put her hand up to sign something through the window, but the curtain fell back across, and Mariusz was gone.

Chapter 9

Sasha and I sat in my car after Caroline had told us to leave.

Do you want to go home? I asked her, but she shook her head.

No. While we're here, I want to go back to Lukas's house.

My heart sank. *Sasha, I told you. I don't want to get involved.*

Look, this might not be important to you, but I need you to do this for me. I've done my best to help you out over the last few months. She gave me a pointed look. *I've given you plenty of overtime, and I know you needed it.*

I sighed. She was right, but I didn't like her throwing it back in my face like this. I'd been able to pay off the last of my debts thanks to the overtime hours she'd persuaded her boss to sign off on.

Why can't you leave it to the police? I asked.

I've seen clients in trouble with the police plenty of times before, she told me. *But that's always been for something they've actually done. I feel like because someone lives in a certain area, especially when they have a social worker for whatever reason, people will automatically assume they're guilty. If the police aren't willing to look past that, I'm going to have to do it for them.*

Okay, I'll come with you, but you're taking full responsibility for this, I told her. *What are you hoping to find out?*

Sasha explained to me that she wanted to see if any of Lukas's neighbours were in. Singh had told us that someone had reported a disturbance at Lukas and Nadia's house on the day of the fire, and it hadn't been the first time. If they were telling the truth, maybe they could tell her what that argument was about.

It was only when we pulled up in the street of terraced houses and looked at the blackened shell that was once Lukas's home, that I realised we didn't know which neighbour had given the statement. I had assumed it was one immediately next to Lukas, but that wasn't necessarily the case, and even then that left us two to choose from. Each house was a mirror image of the one next to it, so the front doors were arranged in pairs. Looking out of my car window, I realised just how lucky both immediate neighbours had been, that the fire hadn't spread to either of their houses on Tuesday night.

After a quick discussion, Sasha made the decision to start with the house whose front door nestled up to Lukas's. The next issue to surmount was what to say – she could hardly tell the occupier that she didn't believe Lukas was responsible for the fire. Nobody would appreciate a stranger coming to their door and suggesting they were lying.

We'll have to think of another story, something that would make them willing to talk to you, I said.

Perhaps you could pretend to be a journalist? she suggested.

Not everyone wants their name printed in the paper, and it could make them more reluctant to talk to us. I wondered why it was suddenly me who had to take on this role.

Okay, then we need to come up with something that would suggest there'd be some benefit to them speaking to you.

After a few minutes' discussion, we had something. The only problem was that Sasha wanted me to go and speak to the neighbours by myself – she didn't think it'd be convincing if another deaf person happened to be looking into the fire, and there was a possibility someone would recognise her from visiting Lukas at home.

I promise it will just be this, she told me. *This one thing, then I won't ask you to do anything else.*

Fine, I grumbled, *as long as it is the last thing.* Now I just had to make our story sound plausible.

As I was getting out of the car, I spotted a bright yellow notebook in the side pocket. Anna had bought it a couple of weeks ago and had left it there, so I took it with me in case I needed to make a note of anything, assuming she wouldn't miss it. I crossed the road and knocked on the door of the house next to Lukas's. I waited for a moment, listening to see if I could hear any sounds from the other side of the door. There were some doors banging in other houses, and I heard a few shouts from further up the street, but nobody came to the door. I was just deciding whether to knock again, when a woman stuck her head out from the next house, two doors down from the burnt-out one.

'He'll be at work,' the woman said, looking me up and down and wrinkling her nose. 'You want to talk to him, you'll have to come back later.'

'Okay. Thank you,' I replied, not sure what to do next. I was thinking of trying the house on the other side of Lukas's, but now this woman was standing in front of me it seemed silly to pass up the opportunity to speak to her. She seemed familiar enough with her neighbour's movements to possibly be able to tell me something about Lukas and Nadia, so I turned on my brightest smile and approached her.

'I wonder if you could help me instead,' I began. 'I'm an insurance investigator. Were you at home on Tuesday night, when the fire took place at number fourteen?'

The woman sniffed. 'I mighta been. Why you asking?'

Keeping my smile fixed, I looked around, as if I was checking to see if anyone was listening. 'Well, it's my job to make sure my company understands exactly what happened on that night. We need to be certain we're paying out to the people who deserve it, and any compensation claims are genuine.'

'Compensation?' the woman replied, her tongue flicking over her lips. She'd stood up a little straighter as I said my piece, and I knew I had her interest.

'Well, yes. In this sort of situation, we need to be sure

the policy holder isn't the only person affected by this. Neighbouring houses could well have sustained some damage.'

The woman glanced back at her house, and I wondered what sort of story she was going to concoct. I could tell her house was far enough away from Lukas's that it hadn't been damaged by the fire, but I could practically see the cogs whirring in her mind as she tried to think of a way in which she could benefit.

'I got COPD,' she said eventually. 'That's me lungs. The smoke, you know. Made me right poorly, it has.'

'Oh, I'm so sorry to hear that, Mrs . . .?' I replied, tailing off.

'Adams,' she replied. 'Jill Adams.'

'Well, Mrs Adams, would you mind telling me what you know about what happened on Tuesday?'

Jill Adams leant back against the wall that separated the front of her property from the house outside of which I was standing, and rubbed her nose.

'I don't really know,' she told me. 'I spoke to the police about it. I always knew there was summat wrong with them in that house.'

Bingo, I thought. It looked like we'd struck it lucky with the neighbour who had reported a fight between Lukas and Nadia.

'Wrong? In what way?'

'Well, you know.' She leant forward, as if she was imparting a great secret. 'They're foreign. And they're both deaf and dumb, you know.'

I cringed at the outdated and offensive phrase, but I bit my tongue. It was a good job Sasha had stayed in the car so she hadn't been faced with this sort of attitude. In my professional role, I would have corrected Jill Adams immediately, explaining the negative connotations of the word 'dumb' and suggesting she use 'mute' instead, but right now I needed to keep her onside.

'So neither of the occupants of number fourteen speak?' I asked, trying to clarify what she meant. If she was claiming that neither Lukas nor Nadia ever used their voices, she couldn't have heard them shouting at each other.

'Well, not exactly. He doesn't talk, but she does. I meant more that, you know, they're a bit simple.'

Once again, I swallowed what I wanted to say in response. I knew that Lukas had left school with several good qualifications, and he was eloquent when it came to expressing himself in BSL. He had no learning difficulties that Sasha had ever mentioned, and so I assumed this was prejudice on the part of Jill Adams. Unfortunately, some people jumped to conclusions when it came to deaf people, especially sign language users.

'They yelled at each other – I heard that sometimes,' Jill was saying, nodding to herself as if she'd proven a point. 'It was both of them, like. They each gave as good as they got.'

I knew that this could have been accurate – just because Lukas didn't use a spoken language didn't mean he couldn't make any sound, and in argument I imagined he wouldn't be silent. Still, I didn't want to lead her into talking about Tuesday night; I needed her to tell me of her own volition.

'Did they fight a lot?' I asked, trying my best to sound sympathetic, as if the rows must have disturbed her.

She shrugged. 'On and off. More when there was people in the house. Well, afterwards.'

I frowned. 'People in the house?'

'Yeah, for a few days last week there's been loads of people going in and out, at all hours of the day. I reported them to the council for antisocial behaviour,' she told me, leaning back and folding her arms. 'There's plenty of folks that could be doing with a council house like that one, and I don't think them that's causing trouble should be allowed to keep theirs.'

Sasha would definitely want to look into that, I thought, though chances were it was just a group of Mariusz's friends and Jill Adams was being oversensitive.

'And it was definitely this house, number fourteen?' I asked, pointing over my shoulder at the house behind me and making a note in the little yellow book.

'Oh yes. I'm not the only one who's noticed it. But I'm the only one who had the guts to call the council about it. Everyone else just wants to keep their head down. It doesn't last long, they say. It doesn't happen often. Well, it was too often for me, and there was obviously something dodgy about it.' She nodded firmly, as if she'd made her point exceptionally clear, but I was confused.

'I'm sorry, what do you mean, something dodgy?'

Jill spread her arms wide. 'Well, why did they have a blazing row every time it happened? You can't tell me there wasn't something going on there.'

I nodded slowly. 'What were their fights about?' I asked, hoping to get a bit more information and lead her back to Tuesday night.

She wafted a hand in front of her face. 'Oh, I haven't

a bloody clue. I can't understand a word those two say to each other. It's not like they can speak properly, is it?'

To my horror, she proceeded to do an impression of what she thought Lukas and Nadia sounded like, causing me to grind my teeth and suck in a deep breath through my nose. I felt sorry for Lukas, having to live so close to such a vile woman. I knew it was an attitude that existed, and unfortunately most deaf people came across it occasionally, but it was still shocking to bear witness to.

'They were at it on Tuesday, though, I remember that. There'd been people round on Monday night, right into the early morning, then they were rowing during the day on Tuesday.'

'And you're sure it was Tuesday?' I asked. The fake smile had gone now; I couldn't keep up the charade in the face of this awful woman.

Her lip curled. 'What's that supposed to mean? Of course it was Tuesday. I'd been out to do me shopping, and when I was walking back from the bus stop I could hear them. It was mostly her, wailing about something or other. Didn't give him a chance to answer back, she didn't.'

I perked up at this bit of information. 'So, you heard her side of the argument, but no sounds from him?'

She shuffled uncomfortably on the wall. 'Well. Not exactly. But he was there; it were him she were shouting at. I saw him go past my house later, off to the pub I bet.'

That was exactly what I needed to hear: she couldn't be certain Lukas had even been in the house. All she'd heard was Nadia shouting, or maybe crying, the way she'd described it.

'Thank you, Mrs Adams, you've been very helpful,' I

said, forcing my lips into something close to a smile. 'I'll be in touch.'

'Wait, but what about my compensation? For my COPD, the smoke?'

I should have known she wouldn't have forgotten about that.

'As I say, we'll be in touch if we think there's anything due to you.'

I was seething by the time I got back in the car and related what she'd told me to Sasha. She was still standing outside her house, watching my car.

So she told the police they were both in the house when she only heard Nadia? That's good, Sasha told me with a nod. *Hopefully the police will double-check her statement before putting too much stock in anything she says.*

I agreed with her, but didn't voice my concern that the police still didn't know how Lukas had come by the bruises all over his body – and if there was an innocent explanation, why had he kept quiet about it?

Chapter 10

We sat in my car and discussed what to do next. My first instinct was to go to DS Singh and tell him everything we'd been thinking – even if they're weren't looking for an alternative suspect, I'd still feel better if we shared information. Keeping it from him made me feel like I was getting involved in exactly the way he'd warned me against. Sasha, however, wasn't keen.

If we want to convince them they have the wrong man, we're going to need to find something stronger than our gut feelings, and hearsay from Lukas's neighbour.

If we can find something that the police should look at, then we'll go and speak to them, Sasha reassured me. *It's not that I don't want to involve them – of course I do. We're not vigilantes. It's just that I think we might only get one opportunity to convince them of Lukas's innocence, and, based on what you've told me about DI Forest, if we mess it up then it's gone for good.*

So, what do you want to do next? I asked her.

She stared out of the windscreen for a moment, then frowned. *Who's that?*

I followed her gaze to where a middle-aged man in an expensive grey suit was standing outside Lukas and Nadia's house. As we watched, he stepped back and rubbed his chin, looking up at the smoke-blackened windows.

Journalist, maybe, I replied.

That or an ambulance chaser. A cheap lawyer. Maybe one of the neighbours is hoping for compensation, Sasha suggested, a dark look on her face. I felt a pang of guilt for the lie I'd told Jill Adams – maybe there really were people looking to cash in on the tragedy.

Let's go and find out, she signed, already moving to get out of the car. I would have refused, but she wasn't paying any attention to me, already moving towards the stranger.

I got out of the car and followed her up to the house. The man turned to look at us as we approached, a confused frown on his face.

'Can we help you?' I asked, keeping my face and voice neutral until we found out who he was and why he was there.

'I . . . I'm looking for Nadia,' the man said, looking back at the house. 'She didn't turn up to work this morning. What happened?'

'You work with Nadia?' My heart sank at the realisation that I would have to break the news to this man.

'Paul Ilford,' he said, holding out a hand for me to shake. 'Nadia's a carer, and I run the care agency she works for. I'm not just her boss though, I'm friends with her and Lukas, too. Where are they? What happened?' he asked again.

Sasha and I introduced ourselves, and Paul didn't seem fazed by the use of sign language. Sometimes people would stare awkwardly when they weren't used to having an interpreter around, but if this man was friends with Lukas then he was probably used to signed conversations.

He turned to Sasha. 'You're Lukas's social worker? Where is he? Are he and Nadia okay?'

Sasha and I looked at each other and I took a deep breath, signing as I spoke, for Sasha's benefit. 'I'm really sorry, Mr Ilford. There was a fire on Tuesday night, and I'm afraid Nadia died.'

Paul's face paled and he took a step backwards, as if the enormity of what I'd told him had knocked him off balance. He ran a hand over his face and looked at the ground for a moment, before looking back at me.

'Are you sure? It was definitely Nadia? Where's Lukas? Is he okay?'

I looked at Sasha again, unsure how much we should tell him. 'Lukas is okay. He was in hospital for a short time. But he's been arrested. The police think he's responsible for Nadia's death.'

'What?' A mixture of confusion and anguish played across Paul's face. 'That's insane. How could Lukas hurt Nadia? He's devoted to her.' He shook his head and looked between me and Sasha. 'This doesn't make any sense.'

Paul stepped back onto the pavement and ran a hand across his face again. I felt terrible for having to break the news to him but we couldn't have left him there and pretended we didn't know what had happened.

'Look, I need to get back to my office. Do you have some time to come along, tell me what happened? I want to help Lukas if I can.'

I interpreted his request for Sasha, who shrugged.

Sure, she replied to me. *He might be able to tell us something that can help.*

Paul's care agency was only round the corner, so ten minutes later we found ourselves sitting in his office while he paced restlessly.

'I don't understand. It must have been an accident. Surely?'

We don't know exactly what happened, Sasha told him. *The police are investigating the cause of the fire.*

He paused in his repetitive journey across the office floor. 'What were you doing at the house? You already knew Lukas was in jail, so why were you there?' He looked between us as he spoke, seeming unsure of who to address his questions to.

'Mr Ilford, why don't you sit down?' I suggested, interpreting for Sasha as I spoke. His constant motion was making me feel queasy.

'Call me Paul, please,' he replied, sinking down into a chair.

'Okay, Paul,' I said gently. 'We're trying to help Lukas. We agree with you; we don't think Lukas could have hurt Nadia. But the police do, so unless we can find something that proves otherwise, there's nothing that any of us can do.'

'What do you need me to do?' he asked.

Do you know of anyone else who might want to hurt Nadia? She worked for you, so you probably knew her better than I did, Sasha told him.

Paul nodded. 'I knew her pretty well, yes. I can sign, and I think she was more comfortable with me than she was with some of the other carers. She always spoke very clearly, but there was some . . . unkindness,' he said, grimacing. 'Because she was deaf,' he added.

What happened? Sasha asked, sitting up a bit straighter. Paul looked awkward, as if he didn't want to tell us, but Sasha shook her head. *Keeping it from us won't help Nadia now. If you don't think Lukas killed her, it must have been someone else, and anything you know could help us get closer to the truth.*

'But wasn't the fire an accident?'

Sasha looked like she was about to respond but I gave her a look and quickly shook my head. We shouldn't be giving out any information that the police hadn't made public.

'They're treating it as suspicious at the moment,' I told him, hoping that was neutral enough.

Paul's face fell, and he looked down at his hands for a long time, before sighing. 'Okay. Nadia was accused of stealing from a couple of her clients. One of them made a complaint about things going missing, but I followed it up and it turned out the items had just been moved, probably by the client herself. Some of them are in the early stages of dementia,' he explained, 'so I would always give my staff the benefit of the doubt until I'd looked into it.'

He frowned. 'But then suddenly a couple of other clients complained about thefts, and they were all people that Nadia had been caring for. She was the only carer they had in common, so of course I had to look into it further.'

What did you find out? Sasha asked.

'It was their word against hers, and it definitely did seem as though things had gone missing that time. But with numerous people going in and out of these clients' houses, they also couldn't prove it was Nadia.' Paul chewed his lip for a moment. 'Sometimes people get a bit annoyed with her, because she's deaf. They think she's stupid, or not as good at her job as some of the others, which was completely untrue. She was my best carer – she was always my first choice for my own mum, before she passed away. I wouldn't have let her care for Mum if I didn't think she was up to the job. But some people's prejudices aren't so easily dealt with. I changed the rotas around so Nadia didn't go to any of those clients again, and it seemed to stop. But I know it bothered her. She thought I didn't trust her,' he said sadly, shaking his head.

'When you changed her client list, were there any more problems?'

'No, but that was only a couple of weeks ago. I haven't had any more complaints, anyway.'

Was there anything particularly valuable or sentimental in the items that went missing? Sasha asked. I knew she was wondering if there was anything worth killing for, but if Nadia's clients were mostly elderly I couldn't imagine any of them being viable suspects in her murder. It was worth looking into though, in case a family heirloom had gone missing and a relative of one of her clients felt cheated out of their inheritance.

But Paul was shaking his head again. 'No, nothing like that. It was mostly cash that the client said they had kept in a drawer or a handbag, and there's no way we can prove it even existed. One woman said her jewellery box had been rifled, but then she couldn't say if anything was missing. It was all very circumstantial.'

Sasha looked thoughtful, her brows pulled together as she processed this information. *And you're sure Nadia was the only one it could have been?*

'Well, she was the only carer who visited all of the clients who complained, but I don't believe she could have done anything like that. She was very conscientious; a hard worker and she valued her job. I feel like some of my staff only do this job because they need something to pay the bills, not because they actually care about the clients. But Nadia was different – she genuinely cared. She enjoyed their company, and in turn they enjoyed hers. I know my mum always asked for her first.' A wistful look came into Paul's eyes, and he looked away for a moment. I wondered how long it was since his mum had passed away. If it was recent, the shock of losing a friend and colleague would be even harder to bear when he was already grieving.

'Can I go and see Lukas?' he asked us a moment later, after swallowing hard.

'That depends if he'll see you. You'll have to speak to the police and see if he's allowed visitors,' I said. 'I don't know anything about that side of things.' I wondered if there was any point, as Lukas had refused to communicate with everyone else he'd seen, but it couldn't hurt for a friend to go and see him.

He nodded, then stood up. 'Thank you for taking the time to speak to me, both of you. I'll need to contact the rest of my staff and let them know what's happened, as well as deal with the practicalities of reallocating Nadia's shifts. Sorry, that makes me sound callous, but I can't have clients being missed out.'

Sasha and I nodded our understanding. On our way out, I stopped to look at some of the photographs on the wall and spotted one of Nadia with an elderly lady. Was that Paul's mother? I turned back to ask him, but he was picking up the phone and gave me a dismissive wave.

Do you think any of that could provide a motive for Nadia's murder? Sasha asked me once we were outside.

That depends on a lot of things. Did she steal something valuable that someone wanted back? Or was she framed for the thefts, and found out who the real thief was? I hadn't really known Nadia, but I was inclined to believe Paul's assessment of her as honest – it wouldn't be in the interests of his professional reputation to cover up something like that.

We definitely need to find out more, but I think we've outstayed our welcome for today.

As we were driving away, I noticed a familiar figure walking towards the office: Caroline. Of course, how could I have missed that? Caroline had been wearing a carer's uniform when we spoke to her earlier. I hadn't realised that she and Nadia worked together, but perhaps Caroline's reluctance to talk to us was connected to the accusations against Nadia. Whatever she was hiding, we now had another reason to talk to her, if she'd let us in the door.

Chapter 11

I spent the rest of the afternoon brooding over what I'd learnt and discussed with Sasha. Despite not wanting to get sucked into the investigation, I really wanted to know exactly what Jill Adams had said in her statement to the police. Had they delved deeper and discovered the ambiguity in what she was saying, or had they just taken her assertion that Lukas and Nadia were fighting at face value? I thought it was unlikely that Singh would give me that information, but I could ask him to look at what she'd said more closely, or maybe get a uniformed officer to interview her again.

Then, a worrying thought struck me. What if she realised that I'd found a hole in her story, and she changed it? What if she now told the police she'd definitely heard Lukas's voice too? From what she'd told me about reporting them to the council to try and get them evicted, I wouldn't be surprised if she did something like that just to be spiteful, not realising the devastating consequences for Lukas.

Sitting down at the table in the kitchen, I pulled out the yellow notebook, reminding myself that I'd have to get Anna a new one at some point. I found the page where I'd noted down the date and time I'd spoken to Jill Adams, and read back the notes I'd made, adding in anything else I remembered. Below that, I added what Paul Ilford had told us about Nadia and the accusations of theft. I hadn't been able to make notes at the time because I'd been signing for Sasha.

There were so many questions going round in my mind, things I wanted to discuss with Sasha as well as things I wanted to ask Singh, that I knew I needed to write them down to try and get my thoughts in order. I supposed I couldn't really blame the detectives for their attitude – after all, Lukas was the most obvious suspect and wouldn't defend himself. What else were they expected to do, other than arrest him? I felt sure they were missing something, though, something big, and I hoped they would continue investigating until they were certain they had the right man.

As I was making some notes and writing down every question that came into my mind, my phone vibrated with an incoming text. It was Max. Usually, his messages would cheer me up, but since Tuesday night I felt a sense of dread when I saw his name on the screen. I knew he was going to want an answer about moving in together soon, but I'd been avoiding even thinking about it, let alone had made up my mind.

Do you want to come over tonight? xx his message read.

I thought for a moment before typing my reply. *Sure. Pizza?*

Of course xx

Thursday night pizza was a regular habit of ours, and it was comforting to see he still wanted to stick with our usual routine. I would have to think about what I wanted to say to him before I saw him, though.

That evening, I sat in my car outside Max's flat for about ten minutes before I plucked up the courage to go in. He'd given me a key a few weeks earlier, and with hindsight I should have realised what he was building up to ask me. I still felt the urge to ring the bell, as if letting myself in would indicate that I'd made up my mind to move in with him, but I shook it off.

He was in the kitchen when I walked in, and I hesitated before stepping forward into his outstretched arms. If he noticed, he didn't comment. I tried to remind myself that I wasn't questioning my relationship with Max, just whether I wanted to live with him or not. But now that I was feeling resistant to moving our relationship further forward, a little voice at the back of my mind kept making itself heard – was this what I really wanted? I quietened it for now, determined to relax and enjoy my evening with him.

You're later than I expected, he signed. *Busy day?*

I nodded. *I was trying to get some emails sorted, jobs for next week,* I replied. It wasn't completely untrue. Before I left the flat, I'd decided to make a start on organising my taxes. Of course, my tax return didn't have to be submitted until January next year, but there was nothing wrong with being prepared. I definitely wasn't finding things to do in order to delay coming over to his flat. Absolutely not.

Well, it's time to put your feet up, he said with a grin, opening the fridge and pulling out a beer for himself and pouring me a glass of wine. I took it from him and clinked my glass against his, then put it down on the table.

I'm working tomorrow, and driving home tonight, I reminded him. *But one glass will be okay.*

He held his hands up. *You're right, I'm sorry. What are you doing tomorrow?*

Something for Sasha, I told him. *One of her clients is in a bit of a tight spot.*

I stopped short of telling him I'd let myself get tangled up in another police investigation, though. We'd met when he was linked to the first case I'd worked on for the police. I'd become too involved, with Anna ending up getting hurt, and ever since then he bristled at the idea of me being caught up with another investigation.

I thought they only paid you to interpret for Sasha from Monday to Wednesday? he replied, a slight frown tugging at his eyebrows. I resisted the urge to sigh.

They do, but this client needs support, and it can't wait until Monday.

He nodded. *Okay. Just make sure they're not taking advantage of you.*

I can look after myself, I told him, my signing a bit sharper than usual, and he held up his hands again.

Okay, I'm sorry. I'm just trying to look after you.

I nodded, and didn't reply. He'd been doing this a lot recently, and I understood that he meant well, but

105

it was starting to feel claustrophobic. Having been in a controlling relationship before, I was constantly on the alert for signs of manipulation, but Max's attitude didn't feel at all like gaslighting, it just felt a little patronising.

Stepping forward, Max pulled me into a hug. For a very brief moment I resisted, but then let myself relax into it. If he hadn't asked me to move in, I wouldn't have an issue right now, I told myself. Sure, some of the things he said irritated me a little, but he meant well, and he cared about me. But if they were irritating me so much I didn't want to move in with him, the little voice in the back of my mind said, maybe they were bigger issues than I thought? Once again I ignored the voice and smiled up at Max.

How is your week going?

He nodded. *Pretty good. It's going to be an intense few weeks until the summer, though. We've got a couple of kids doing their SATs, and the revision has already put a lot of pressure on our team.*

Max worked as a teaching assistant at a school in Hull that had a specialist unit for deaf children, and he was passionate about his job. I let him tell me all about his week, trying hard to concentrate on what he was signing, but my mind kept drifting back to the huge elephant in the corner of the room. Once he'd finished, we went through to the living room and sat on the sofa. He shifted round so his back was against the arm of the sofa, and gave me a searching look.

So, are we going to talk about the other night? He was obviously trying to keep it light-hearted, but the way his eyes roved across my face, trying to read my expression, I could tell he'd been thinking about nothing else.

Of course we can talk about it, I replied, trying to give him a smile that would make him relax. *I think it's important that we do talk about it. It was a big question, and it's not something I want to answer without having given it a lot of careful thought.*

He gave me a wry smile. *Here was me hoping you wouldn't have to give it any thought at all, or that you'd already been thinking about it and were just waiting for me to ask.*

I shook my head. *You know my history, Max. You know why the idea of living with you, with any partner, is a difficult one for me to process. I need to separate my feelings for you from my fears, and sometimes that's really hard, even now.*

For a moment, I searched for the right words to explain how I felt. For four years I'd lived with a man who gambled away all of his own money, then started making his way through mine. He gradually took control of my finances, without me even noticing until it was too late, but by then he'd worn down my self-esteem so far that I didn't have the fight left in me to challenge him. It all came to a head when he went out on a three-day casino bender, locking me in the flat without a phone or any other means to communicate with the outside world. I'd broken a window to get out, in the end, leaving me with a jagged scar on my left forearm.

Now, as I looked at Max, my other hand was drawn to touch my scar, but I forced myself to resist the impulse. I knew he was sensitive about being compared to my ex, and I understood why, but sometimes I couldn't help it. It was automatic that my past experiences would play a role in my decision-making in this relationship.

I understand that, Paige, I do. But at some point I feel like we need to move past that. You need to move on and remember that I'm completely different from him. To me it seems like the logical next step in our relationship. He sat forward, his knee touching mine. *I love you, Paige. I want to wake up next to you every morning, and go to sleep next to you every night. I don't want to take away any of your independence, I just want to spend my life with you.*

I love you too, I replied. *I just need a bit of time to decide what I want.*

Max took a deep breath, and I could tell that he was trying not to get cross. Maybe it was something he'd been thinking about for months, but I hadn't. Whenever thoughts about our future drifted into my mind, I'd deliberately pushed them away again. Now that strategy was coming back to bite me, but I didn't think I was being unfair by asking for a few days to make my decision.

It's a big commitment, I reminded him, *and neither of us should go into it without thinking carefully about it first. That's all I'm asking for.* I looked down at my hands for a moment while I thought. *Can I give you an answer by Saturday?* I asked.

Max nodded, and I tried not to let the sadness in his eyes get to me. Part of me wanted to say yes and agree to whatever he wanted, just to please him, but that was the part of me that had acquiesced to everything with my ex and got me into such a difficult situation. I wasn't going back there, and if that meant being selfish and always putting myself before Max, so be it.

We settled down on the sofa, and I put my feet up on the coffee table, dislodging a couple of papers. Picking them up, I noticed my name on one of them, so I had a closer look.

What's this? I asked him. I had a pretty good idea what it was, but I needed to make sure.

Oh, I got it from the leisure centre, Max replied, taking the papers off me.

You applied for a joint membership?

I haven't applied yet, I just got the form.

I paused. *And you filled the form in. Without asking me.*

Max sat up a bit, realising I wasn't happy. *I thought it would be nice, if you moved in. It would be something for us to do together.*

My head swam with all of the potential responses. *Are you serious?*

What? he asked, looking hurt.

Have I ever expressed any interest in going to the gym? I asked him slowly, trying not to get angry.

Well, no, but I thought it would be good for us to try and share each other's interests, he began, but I held up a hand and shook my head.

Are you trying to tell me something? That you don't think I'm fit enough, that my body isn't good enough? I snapped.

He rolled his eyes, which was probably the worst thing he could have done at that point. *No, Paige, of course not. I thought it would be a bit of fun. Just forget about it.*

I sat back on the sofa, my arms folded and my stomach

churning. Had he really thought that I would appreciate a gesture like that? Going to the gym was not my idea of fun, but if I ever did decide I wanted to work out it would be me making that decision, not whoever I was in a relationship with. How could he have thought I would be happy about it? Didn't he know me at all?

I didn't bring it up again but there was tension between us for the rest of the evening. I was meeting Sasha at the office the following morning, so I didn't stay over, and as I got in my car Max watched me from the doorway, his face blank. I knew he was deep in thought, but perhaps I didn't want to know what he was thinking.

Six hours before the fire

The gym was quiet, but Nadia could still feel eyes on her as she crossed the floor towards the door marked 'Private'. Feeling her resolve start to trickle away, she took a deep breath and pushed the door open without knocking. Inside, there was a short corridor with a door to either side and one at the end. The office was quite easy to find, and she found the man she was looking for sitting at a desk with three computer monitors.

'Can I help you?' he asked, his smile charming, but she wasn't fooled. She knew about his reputation, and would have to be on her guard. Even if he accepted her offer, she was prepared to find herself in a dangerous situation.

'I'm Nadia Nowak,' she replied, willing herself to hold his gaze. This statement earned her a raised eyebrow, and she knew she had caught his interest.

'And what can I do for you, Nadia Nowak?' he asked,

his voice silky. He enunciated clearly, and she was relieved that she'd be able to understand him. Hearing aids weren't much use against mumblers.

She came into the office and perched herself on the edge of his desk, so she was looking down at him. This position had the added benefit that she could see his face clearly in order to lip-read as he spoke.

'I've come here to talk to you, to see if we can renegotiate the arrangement.' She'd practised what she was going to say in the hope that it would make her sound more confident than she felt, but her voice still shook slightly.

He stretched out, looking at her legs appreciatively, clasping his hands across his taut stomach.

'Renegotiate? That sounds interesting. I might be willing to hear your proposal.'

She swallowed, and looked down at the floor before realising her mistake. The moment she dropped her gaze, he knew how nervous she was. When she looked up again, his grin was that of a wolf looking at a lamb.

'Before we begin our, ah, negotiations,' he said, enunciating the word very carefully, 'I have a question. Does Lukas know you're here?'

'No. But if he's not willing to do what needs to be done for the good of his family, I am.'

He laughed, throwing his head back so she got a glimpse of his smooth neck. How she wished she had the strength to reach out and throttle him, but she knew if she even tried to lay a finger on him he'd overpower her in seconds. Muscles rippled beneath his well-tailored shirt, his outfit a little over the top for a seedy boxing gym in the middle of Scunthorpe. A treacherous part of her mind said that if she felt this was her only option, at least he had a great body.

'Well,' he said, standing up and approaching the desk. 'I'm always interested in a bit of, what was it? Negotiation.' He placed one of his feet between hers, forcing her legs apart slightly, and tilted his pelvis forwards, pinning her to the desk. He put his weight on his left hand while his right traced a line from her jawline, down to her shoulder, around the curve of her breast and down to her waist. She recoiled a little from his touch, which made him laugh, and his hand slipped lower, gripping one of her buttocks.

'Did you really think that this would work?' he asked her quietly, looking her in the eyes, his wolfish grin still there. 'You're lucky that I'm not really in the mood right now, or I might have taken full advantage of your attempts to screw me over, pun very much intended. Why don't you trot along home like the good little wifey you are, and tell Lukas that I want my money, and there's nothing that will make me reduce the figure.' On the last word, he ran his hand back up her side again, making her squirm uncomfortably.

'Fine,' she replied, pushing him away from her. As she went to leave, he grabbed her wrist.

'What would Lukas think if he found out about this?' The blush that crept up her face answered for her, and she didn't like the expression that appeared on his face.

'Oh, well now. I bet he'd be interested to know how his wife tries to meddle in his business affairs, wouldn't he?'

She pulled away from him and hurried out of the office,

anger and fear spurring her on. If he told Lukas . . . No, she didn't want to think about that. She'd hoped she could make things better, but it was possible she had just made them a lot worse.

Chapter 12

Friday 19th April

Sasha's office was busy when I arrived the following morning. She normally spent Fridays at Lincoln School for the Deaf, but she'd rearranged things in order to devote more time to helping Lukas, whether he wanted that help or not.

Sasha was already sitting at her desk with her emails open, and she gave me a wave as soon as she saw me.

Morning. We've got a busy day today. Do you mind calling the police station to see if we can arrange to speak to Lukas?

Part of my job sometimes involved making calls for Sasha, when it was something that might take too long over email. The job was interesting, so I was happy to be part-interpreter, part-PA. Every day felt very busy, but the pressure of Lukas's situation presumably added to Sasha's workload.

Do you think he'll be willing to see you? I asked.

I don't know, but this time I've got some information I need to talk to him about.

I raised my eyebrows in question.

I've found out who he owes money to, she told me. *If he can tell us a bit more about this friend of his, it might explain what's gone on.*

Once I'd made the call, Sasha told me a bit more of what she'd found out.

The man's called Roy Chapman, and he owns a gym near to where Lukas lives. It's called Worx, she told me, spelling it out on her fingers. *The business appears to be above board, on the surface at least, but there have been rumours for quite a while about Chapman being dodgy.*

Dodgy in what way? I asked.

Drugs, maybe prostitution, but the one I've heard the most about is his extortionate loans. He preys on vulnerable people, and lends them money at rates they'll never be able to pay back.

I shook my head. *And Lukas borrowed money from him?*

So I believe, but I need him to confirm it.

I could tell Sasha was on edge, because her leg jiggled under the desk the entire time we were discussing it. It got worse the longer we waited to hear back from the police. To try and take her mind off it, I showed her my notebook and the questions I'd written down. She suggested I make a new page about Lukas's debt to jot down anything we found out today. Before I did, I noticed her frowning at one of the notes I'd made: it was just one word, 'bruises', followed by several question marks.

I'm sure there's an explanation, she told me.

I nodded, but didn't answer. Unless Lukas actually broke

116

his silence and told the police how he came to be black and blue on the night his wife had been murdered, I didn't think it looked good for him.

Eventually, the phone rang. I answered and spoke to the officer on the other end; it wasn't good news.

Lukas won't see you, I told her.

What? The emotions on her face ranged from annoyed to confused, then she sighed. *I had hoped he would have seen sense by now. I don't think he's doing himself any favours if he keeps this up.*

I didn't know what to say; I agreed with her, but there was no way to force him to cooperate with the police, and he didn't have to see her if he didn't want to. I was trying to think of a response when one of the frazzled-looking reception staff came into the room and trotted over to us.

'There's someone here to see Sasha,' she told me. 'A kid. I told him she was busy but he said he'd wait.'

'A kid?' My mind immediately went to Mariusz, and when I interpreted this for Sasha she agreed with me.

'Yeah, a teenager. He's in the family room,' she told me, nodding in the direction of a little side room before hurrying back into the office, following the sound of a ringing phone.

Sasha and I went straight through; if Mariusz had come to see Sasha about his father, it must be important.

We were right about who the visitor was. When he saw us, Mariusz jumped slightly and sat up straight in his chair. Before then, he'd been lounging with his legs stretched out, feet up on the little table in the middle of the room. Even when he tried to pull himself up to his full height he didn't look his age, and I wondered how often he had to prove he was sixteen.

Sorry, he signed, looking awkwardly between me and Sasha. *I want to talk to you about my dad.*

His signing was slow and a little jerky. I knew he must be used to communicating with Lukas this way, but nerves and unfamiliarity were probably affecting his signing with Sasha.

'Do you want me to sign for Sasha, then you can concentrate on what you want to say?' I asked him gently. I didn't want him to think he wasn't good enough, but it's always easier to express yourself in your first language.

He nodded. 'Okay.' He looked back at Sasha and swallowed hard. 'I want to help my dad. Mum says I can't see him, and that I mustn't talk to you or the police about him. She says I'm too young to understand it, but she doesn't know what she's talking about.' His voice rose, and I could see a mixture of anger and frustration behind his eyes. 'Maybe I can find out something, find out what happened to Nadia. It wasn't Dad, I know it wasn't.'

Sasha and I exchanged a look before either of us responded. We knew this was going to be a difficult task, giving Mariusz the space he needed to talk without leading him. I felt a bit uncomfortable talking to him in the first place, without a parent here. It was important that we let Mariusz talk, and then if he told us anything useful that we passed it on to the police straight away, so they could interview him formally. Of course, that was if Sasha was willing to talk to the police. I was starting to worry that she would do her best to prevent me sharing what

118

we'd learnt with DS Singh, which was making me all the more inclined to talk to him myself.

Sitting forward in her chair and giving Mariusz a reassuring smile, Sasha tried her best to put him at ease.

Mariusz, you can tell us anything you know that you think is important, okay? But you know we'll need to tell the police. They're the only ones who can catch the person who killed Nadia, and get your dad out of prison.

Mariusz looked to me as Sasha was signing, so I interpreted for him. I thought the way Sasha worded it was a smart move – hopefully Mariusz would trust her enough to tell her what was on his mind.

The boy shuffled so he was sitting on his hands, and started rocking slightly, shaking his head.

'I don't know anything. My mum told me Nadia died before the fire started. I don't know who killed her, but it wasn't my dad. It can't have been him; he loved her. He'd never hurt her. And he'd never leave me by going to jail.' His voice was on the edge of breaking, and it cracked at the end of his sentence.

I understand you're upset, Sasha told him. *We want to help him too.*

Mariusz's eyes darted around the room and he started to bite his nails, before sitting on his hands again.

'What if there's someone who knows something, but they haven't told anyone about it?'

Sasha paused before she replied. *What do you mean? Do you know something, Mariusz?*

He shook his head violently. 'No, I told you, I don't know anything. But what if someone did?'

Well, they should tell the police, Sasha replied, her

eyes narrowing in suspicion. It was clear she didn't believe him.

'But, what if they don't want to tell the police? What if they're worried they'll get in trouble too, and Dad'll still be locked up?' His eyes were wide as he asked these questions, and I could see how scared he was. But was he scared of Lukas being charged with murder, or was there something else?

'Mariusz, if you know something that could help your dad, you should tell us,' I told him, signing at the same time for Sasha's benefit. 'We can help you, if you do.'

He shook his head vehemently. 'No, I don't know anything. Why would I know anything? I was at home with Mum that night.' But his eyes were still shifting all over, and I instinctively knew he was lying. Sasha and I shared a look, but I couldn't tell if she was thinking the same thing as me.

Do you know anyone who might have hurt Nadia? Sasha asked, trying a different angle. At the mention of her name, Mariusz shook his head again.

'I told you, I don't know anything. I just want to be able to help my dad, and I thought you could help me.'

I could tell Sasha felt as exasperated as me by this conversation; there was obviously something the boy wanted to tell us, but he was scared to say it, and we were just going round in circles. If he was this afraid, though, it must be worth hearing, so we had to persevere.

'How do you want to help him?' I asked, but he looked at me blankly. 'You say you don't know what happened the night Nadia died, so you don't have any useful information for the police. So, in what way do you think you

120

can help your dad?' I gave him an encouraging smile and touched him gently on the arm, in the hope he'd open up to us.

'I don't know, I thought you could tell me that,' he said. 'Maybe, I could give the police some information about a different crime, to show my family's honest, and then they'd let Dad go.' His eyes widened as he spoke and his hands were clenched so tightly they trembled.

I didn't know if this was naivety or just a poorly thought-up story, but I shook my head. What other crime, though? Was that something he'd thought up on the spot, or was there something else going on?

'It doesn't work like that, Mariusz, I'm sorry. But if you know something about a different crime, you should still tell the police.'

He hung his head and his shoulders drooped, and he stayed in this position for a moment or two, before standing up.

'I need to get back to school.'

It was like a mask had dropped over his face. The fear and anxiety we'd seen a moment ago had gone, hidden behind a toughened exterior. He went towards the door and I stood up to open it for him. As he left, he glanced at me and I caught a flash of anguish in his eyes again. He muttered something I didn't quite catch, then bolted for the door.

After he'd gone, Sasha looked at me.

What was all that about?

I have no idea. I think he knows something, but I don't know what.

Do you think he might have been there that night, and

he's lying about being at Caroline's? Sasha asked with a frown.

I shrugged. *Maybe. But if he had any evidence that someone else had killed Nadia, why wouldn't he tell us? He's hardly going to get in trouble with the police for being out when his mum thought he was at home.*

Sasha nodded, deep in thought. *He knows something, though.*

Maybe he saw something else, I suggested. *Something that he thinks might be connected, but not Nadia's murder?*

Sasha shook her head and gave me a tight smile.

Whatever it is, he's clearly not ready to talk about it. Chances are that it's not relevant, and he's just a scared kid wanting to do something to help his dad.

I nodded, but I didn't entirely agree. Something had made Mariusz come all the way here and wait to speak to us, and I didn't think he'd do that unless it was important. Before I could put this point forward, though, Sasha had left the room and was heading to her desk.

We spent the next forty-five minutes discussing what we had achieved so far, which seemed to be very little. I tried to bring up the subject of what Mariusz might know, but Sasha brushed it off again, so I left it.

Roy Chapman seems to be our most obvious suspect, she insisted. *He has a bad reputation for getting his own way using violent means, and it's almost certain that his businesses aren't a hundred per cent legitimate.*

But what would he get out of killing Nadia? I asked, still stuck on this aspect. *I can't see that Lukas owing him money is enough of a motive. It means he's less likely to get his money back.*

Sasha frowned at me. *If Lukas didn't respond to his threats, it's only natural that he'd escalate them.*

Threats, yes, but stretching as far as murder? I don't know about that one. I don't know how much Lukas owes him, but surely it can't be enough to warrant murdering someone.

She sat back in her chair and folded her arms, looking down at her desk. I could tell she wanted to disagree with me, but I was prepared to keep pressing her on this matter. If she was so convinced that Lukas was innocent, she'd have to come up with something more solid than Roy's reputation.

What other motive do you suggest? she asked, her face impassive.

I thought for a moment, then picked up my notebook and flicked to a page, pointing to one of my scribbles.

The thefts. I wasn't prepared to back down on this one. *Paul Ilford told us he had to change her shifts because several clients accused her of theft. Maybe she knew who the real thief was, and they killed her to keep her quiet.*

You're assuming Nadia wasn't the thief, Sasha replied, with a tilt of her head. *Maybe she was.*

I wasn't going to be deterred. *In which case, maybe she took something that was far more valuable than she realised – either monetary value, or sentimental – and someone was desperate to get it back.*

They wouldn't kill her then, would they? Sasha reasoned.

They might, if she'd sold it on and they couldn't find it. Or once they'd got it back, they could have just killed her in a rage. I sighed. *All I'm saying is that we're speculating, we don't have any evidence, so we can't fixate on* one suspect. *I have no problem with speculation, but if we don't keep an open mind about it then we risk being as blinkered as you think the police are.*

From the look on Sasha's face I was sure she was going to argue with me again, but eventually she nodded.

Fine, we'll consider all angles for now. But that means still looking further into Roy's connection to Lukas and his movements on the day Nadia was murdered, as well as seeing what we can find out about the thefts.

I nodded, knowing that this compromise was the best I could hope for, but I was still uneasy. I wanted to help Sasha and Lukas, but I was mindful of Singh's warning not to get involved. What Sasha was suggesting would involve more digging, and I didn't know where to draw the line.

I have an idea, she continued, *but I'm going to need your help. I think it's best if a hearing person does it, and if he figures out who I am it could look bad for me.*

She outlined her plan and I felt my heart sink. I wasn't keen to do it, but if it meant we could rule out Roy as a suspect it was probably worth it. We spent a while discussing what I was going to do the following day, before I left Sasha to her emails.

On my way out of the door, I sent a quick text. I knew Sasha had her own way of going about this, but I had a nagging feeling that there was something she wasn't telling me. Even though she had dismissed Mariusz's visit, I wondered if there had been something he couldn't bring himself to tell us. As he'd left, the words he'd muttered had been so quiet I might have misheard him, but I thought he'd said, 'It's all my fault.'

Chapter 13

Fifteen minutes later, my car door opened and DS Singh got into the passenger seat. I'd sent him a message asking if we could talk, and he'd told me to meet him outside the police station.

'Aren't we going in?' I asked.

'No, Forest's in a foul mood for some reason. Better if we go somewhere else.'

'Fine by me. Where to?'

In the end, we drove a few minutes round the corner to Scunthorpe's Central Park. The old civic building had been closed down and was being converted into a new university campus and the car park was blocked off, so we drove round and parked by the children's playground before getting out and going for a walk.

'What did you want to talk to me about?' Singh asked. I was surprised by the lack of small talk; I appreciated that he'd taken time out of his day to see me, but it would have been nice to catch up a bit with him. When we'd been sitting close to each other in the car I'd tried not to notice how nice he smelled, or the slight tingle I felt in my skin when he looked at me.

'Lukas Nowak,' I replied, and he nodded to show that he'd assumed that much by himself. I thought for a moment about where was best to begin, then stopped and faced him.

'On the night he was arrested, I went into his room to see him, before Sasha arrived. He told me that he knew who was responsible for Nadia's murder.'

Singh frowned. 'Who?'

'He didn't say who, just that he knew who it was,' I explained. 'But then when Sasha arrived, he didn't say the same thing to her.'

Singh folded his arms and looked away for a moment, up the path towards the fountain. 'Paige, why didn't you tell me this? When we were questioning him, or when you gave your statement?'

I grimaced, feeling stupid, and knowing I deserved the annoyance I could see written all over his face. 'I'm sorry. I had this idea in my head that maybe he'd deliberately told me that to manipulate me, but I realise now I should have told you. I'm sorry,' I repeated.

He nodded to show that I was forgiven. 'I mean, I know it's not evidence,' I continued. 'I might have been right, and he could have just been saying that to try and convince me he's innocent, but then why wouldn't he say the same thing to you?'

We'd come to a bench so I stopped and sat down, resting my elbows on my knees. He sat next to me, stretching his

126

arm along the back of the bench for a moment before he caught my eye. He gave a shy little laugh, then pulled his arm back and clasped his hands together.

'You're right, it's not evidence, and if he'd told us he knew who killed his wife but then wouldn't say who it was, I don't think I would have believed him. Have you any idea why he'd tell you that, then refuse to speak to us? Has he said anything to you and Sasha when you've visited him?'

I shook my head. 'No, we wanted to see him this morning but he refused. Sasha was annoyed. I think she'd hoped Lukas would speak to her once he realised the severity of the situation. She particularly wanted to talk to him about his financial situation. I assume you're looking into that?' I asked, with a quizzical look.

'We know about him owing money to Chapman, if that's what you mean,' he replied. 'We are actually quite good at finding this sort of information, you know.' I knew that was a playful dig at me, so I raised an eyebrow at him.

'What's that supposed to mean?'

He chuckled. 'You know full well.'

I folded my arms and adopted an expression of injured innocence, making him laugh.

'Fine, it had absolutely nothing to do with you, and your habit of poking your nose in because you think we can't solve things on our own.'

'Hey, I never said that,' I protested. 'I never intend to get mixed up in things. It just sort of happens.'

'Well, don't let it happen this time, or I'll set Forest on you,' he joked. I kicked him lightly on the ankle and he pretended to clutch it in pain, then sat back and looked at me.

'Anyway,' I said, going back to our original conversation. 'That's what Sasha wanted to discuss with Lukas today, his debts.'

'What about yesterday?'

'We didn't see him yesterday,' I told him, after thinking for a moment. I could sometimes lose track of days when my job changed from week to week, but I knew we'd only seen Lukas on Wednesday and then again today.

Singh sat back and put his arm back along the bench again. 'You might not have been to see him yesterday, but Sasha did.'

I stared at him uncomprehendingly for a moment, wondering if I'd misheard him. He was watching me, obviously interested in my reaction.

'Didn't she tell you she'd been to see him yesterday morning?'

I shook my head slowly. 'No, she hasn't mentioned it. In fact, I saw her yesterday afternoon and when I asked her how Lukas was, she told me she hadn't had any information since Wednesday.' Staring down at the grass, I went over our recent conversations in my mind. Could she have thought she'd told me about it, but actually she hadn't? No, that didn't make sense, because why would she have said she didn't know how Lukas was doing? Maybe there was something they'd discussed that she couldn't share with me, for confidentiality reasons.

Singh put his hand on my shoulder to get my attention back, making me jump.

'Sorry, you were miles away there. I'm sure it's nothing – I just assumed that she would have talked to you about it.'

'No. She'll have her reasons,' I said, trying to brush it off, though I was feeling quite hurt. I thought Sasha trusted me, and I thought she genuinely wanted my help to try to prove Lukas's innocence. But if she wasn't sharing everything with me, maybe I couldn't help her in the way she wanted. Could it even be possible that Lukas was guilty after all, and she knew? But then why would she want him to be released? I couldn't think of a logical answer to any of these questions, and every route my brain went down came to a dead end.

'Maybe she just went to see him to arrange his solicitor,' Singh said, obviously concerned that he'd said something he shouldn't, but once again I looked at him in confusion.

'I didn't know he even had a solicitor,' I replied. 'If he does, surely you arranged it?'

Singh shook his head. 'No, we didn't. We would have arranged for a duty solicitor to be assigned to him, but he's got one who's been hired for him. We were told that Sasha Thomas had arranged it.'

I frowned. Lukas had refused legal advice just as he'd refused to give a statement, so I didn't know when this had changed. Sasha hadn't told me that she'd done this, and frankly I was surprised that social services had the budget for a solicitor for one of their clients if they were entitled to legal aid. Unless . . . No, surely Sasha wouldn't have paid for it herself?

I turned these thoughts over for a few moments, then pushed them to the back of my mind. It didn't make sense, but I didn't have all the information yet. When I next saw Sasha, I'd ask her to explain why she'd felt the need to hide these things from me, and hopefully she'd have a reasonable explanation.

'Did Lukas speak to the solicitor?' I asked.

Singh shook his head. 'No, he brought an interpreter with him, but he sent them away.'

So it hadn't been Lukas's decision to hire him, presumably. It all seemed very strange, and I wondered what I was missing.

As we sat, I became increasingly aware of Singh's presence next to me, and my mind went back to the conversation I'd had with Anna the other day. Until I'd said it to her, I hadn't really admitted to myself how strong my attraction was to Singh, but now I'd said it out loud I couldn't deny it. But I was in a relationship so I'd never really allowed myself to think about it before.

I still didn't know what I was going to say to Max. Would he accept that I was happy with things the way they were, and wasn't in any hurry to change them? I could imagine what Anna would say to me, if she could read my thoughts – would I be so reticent if it was Singh who had asked me? He was so different from Max; I always felt like he took the time to remember little things that were important to me, he was considerate of boundaries and didn't behave as if I needed constant protection. But I couldn't start thinking like that, and I gave myself a small shake.

Stealing a sideways glance at Singh, I saw him watching me curiously.

'Are you okay? I think we lost you again for a minute there.'

'Sorry,' I said, shaking myself once more.

'Anything I can help with?'

I fervently hoped my face wouldn't betray me as I gave a short laugh. 'No, I don't think so. Personal stuff.' He definitely couldn't help with my confused feelings about him and Max, and I didn't think I should tell Singh just how much Sasha had kept from me, in case it jeopardised her relationship with the police. Whatever she'd done, it wouldn't do her clients any good if she antagonised the people she was supposed to be allied with. Telling Singh that she'd lied to me would hardly encourage him to trust her. I thought about what Sasha and I had been planning, too. If Singh knew what I would be doing tomorrow, I didn't think he'd be very happy with me.

'Everything okay with Max? I assume you're still seeing each other?' There was a forced casual tone to his voice, which intrigued me, but now wasn't the time to start reading anything into it.

'Yeah, fine. He's, er, asked me to move in with him.' I groaned inwardly, regretting the words the instant they were out of my mouth. Why? Why did I tell him?

'Oh. Well, congratulations.' He looked down at the grass rather than at me when he said this.

'Maybe,' I replied with a shrug. He looked up at me then, his eyebrows raised. 'I don't know . . .'

'You don't know what?' he asked quietly. I looked him in the eye and for a moment I felt like something passed between us, something that we both should have put into words a long time ago. I was thinking of what to say, when his phone rang, making him wince.

He stood up and walked a short distance away to

answer it, and I used the time to look at him carefully. Ever since I'd first met him, Rav had been a reassuring presence whenever I worked for the police, but we'd rarely seen each other outside of a professional capacity. Maybe we should try and spend some time together socially, to see if I still felt the same when we weren't discussing strictly work matters. It might give me a chance to see how he felt, too.

I shook myself. What was I thinking? I was with Max, and I was happy with him. I was. I just didn't really see us living together, that was all. A small voice in the back of my mind asked me if that meant I wasn't in fact happy, but I silenced it straight away. Whatever the situation between me and Max, it wasn't right to be thinking about spending more time with Singh.

Singh was walking back towards me, a rueful expression on his face. 'That was DI Forest,' he said. 'I need to get back to the station. Do you mind dropping me off?'

'No, that's fine. I should be getting home anyway.'

We didn't speak as we walked back to my car, and I tried to keep my mind on Lukas and what Sasha and I could do to help him. I wasn't looking forward to meeting Roy Chapman the following morning, but it could definitely get us some answers, and as Sasha continued to point out, I owed her this. The overtime she'd given me had helped me to pay off the last of the debts my ex-boyfriend had left me with, but I was starting to wonder if that assistance from Sasha was worth what she was asking me to do. And from what Singh had said, should I really be trusting Sasha as much as I had been doing? She obviously didn't trust me enough to keep me fully in the loop. In which case, should I be doing the things she asked?

I agonised over it all the way back to the police station. Singh could obviously tell there was something bothering me, but he didn't press me on it this time. After he got out, he leant back in and gave me a quick smile.

'It was nice to sit and have a chat, if only briefly,' he said. I was busy thinking of a reply when he waved a goodbye, shut the door and jogged into the station. Hopefully he wouldn't be in trouble for being away from his desk in the middle of the afternoon.

On the drive home, my mind kept flitting between Lukas and Sasha, Singh and Max. I had too many things going on in my life at the moment, and my head couldn't cope with it all. Sooner or later I was going to have to stop being passive and letting things just happen around me, and take some decisive action. The problem was that the thought of any particular action left me paralysed with anxiety about whether or not it was the right thing to do. Anna and I had planned an evening out tonight, so hopefully that would help to distract me and give me the perspective I needed to make a decision once and for all.

Chapter 14

The music and lights of the funfair were overwhelming after the confusing day I'd had, but right now it provided exactly the distraction I needed.

Do you want some candyfloss? I asked Anna, pointing to a stall that was festooned with plastic bags of bright pink and blue confectionery.

My sister shook her head. *Not yet. I want to go on the Waltzer!*

I groaned. The funfair came to our village every year and set up on the green, but I usually found a way to avoid going on any of the rides. I didn't like rides in general; a day out to a theme park was always pretty dull for me, because I was the one hanging around on a bench holding everyone else's bags while my friends queued for two hours for some monstrosity that flung them upside down seventeen times.

You'll be going on it on your own, I told her. *You know I hate those things.*

Anna pulled a face and signed *Chicken,* but I didn't rise to the bait. I was intending to have a fun evening with my sister, and that didn't include throwing up on my own shoes.

Fine, we'll go and play some games then. She grabbed my hand and dragged me to the Hook-A-Duck stall, digging in her pockets for change. I knew these things were all rigged, but I pushed the logical side of myself to the back of my mind and had a go anyway. After that, it was the coconut shy and one that involved hitting plastic frogs with a rubber mallet, all of which Anna bested me at. By the end of it she was clutching three different stuffed toys, all slightly sad-looking replicas of Disney characters.

Here, you should have Elsa, she told me, thrusting a doll into my hands. *You're Anna's sister,* she added with a grin.

I laughed, and steered her towards the food carts. My stomach was rumbling with the aromas wafting from the grill van, and a few minutes later we were wolfing down hot dogs, trying not to drip ketchup on our clothes. When we'd finished, we got a selection from the sweet stall and sat down on a patch of grass for a little while.

Have you decided if you're going to move in with Max? Anna asked me, before popping some marshmallows into her mouth.

I sighed and looked down at the grass. We'd been having a really nice evening, and I'd somehow managed to stop thinking about Max, or Lukas, and for a while it had felt as if my life wasn't full of confusion and stress.

I don't know, I replied, hoping to fob her off. *I haven't decided yet.*

Anna raised one eyebrow. *Don't lie to me, Paige. I know you said you'd give him an answer tomorrow, and I know you. You'll have made your mind up a couple of days ago; you're just putting it off until the last minute.* She tilted her head on one side. *I know you're worried about hurting someone, but I can't tell if you're worried about upsetting me by moving in with him, or Max by saying no.*

Leaning back on my elbows, I stretched my legs out in front of me and looked up at the evening sky. It was that gorgeous dark blue that comes right before the sun goes down, and I could just see a couple of stars beyond the glow of the fairground attractions. The sounds of people talking and laughing mingled with the music from the rides, and the occasional scream of a teenager.

I have decided, I told her eventually, and finally admitting it to myself. *But I don't really want to think about it right now. I feel like it's such a big decision, I can't really process it properly. So you're right, I am putting it off, but it's more selfish than you think.* I turned onto my side and started pulling at a clump of grass. Anna was watching me carefully while chewing the edge of one of her fingernails and I realised she was nervous. It had taken her a while to recover from the brain injury she'd suffered last year, and I knew she was doing so much better now, but living with me was a big part of the stability she'd rebuilt for herself. I realised she was scared I was going to leave her.

I reached across and squeezed her arm. *Hey. It's going to be okay, I promise.*

She gave me a small smile. *I know I shouldn't be worried about living alone at the age of twenty-nine, but I am. In London I always had several flatmates, and now I've got you. I don't know how I'll manage on my own.*

Let me talk to Max tomorrow, I told her. *Then we can talk about you and me.* I didn't want to start talking about it in too much depth with Anna right now, because I felt I should talk to Max first. Whatever happened between us from now on, I owed him that at least. He'd given me a few days to think about the question, and I thought it was a bit unfair to be essentially discussing his future with someone else before him.

Anna nodded her understanding, though I knew she was desperate to ask me more.

How's work? I asked her, hoping that a change of subject might perk her up a bit. Anna had been increasingly busy over the last few months, devising modules and planning lectures for her Deaf Studies classes. She only had a few students at the moment, with a bigger cohort due to be taken on in September, but it seemed like she was finally feeling satisfied with her work and her decision to leave London.

She gave me a look, aware that I was trying to steer the conversation away from myself, but she didn't push it any further.

Work is going pretty well. There's more to do than I expected, because there's always some more paperwork to fill in, or another bit of admin that needs to be completed. But I'm still enjoying it, which is the important thing.

Do you know how many students you'll be getting in September?

She shook her head. *Not yet. Some of it depends on funding, though we've had a lot more applicants than we expected, so that's positive.*

That's great, I told her, genuinely pleased for her. I think she was worried that her academic career would suffer once she left London, but so far it looked like her fears were unfounded. And the cost of living was drastically different in North Lincolnshire, which was a big advantage.

I've been thinking about leaving my injury support group, she told me suddenly, and I wondered if this was another thing that had been bothering her recently as well as the possibility I would be moving in with Max. *I'm not sure I'm getting any benefit from it any more.*

Okay, I replied, unsure what to ask. I'd fought hard for her to be able to access the brain injury support group – at first they'd said she was welcome to attend but that I would have to act as interpreter for her, which we both refused point blank. Family shouldn't be fulfilling that role, and I knew Anna would never open up about her experience with me there. It had taken a few meetings and strongly worded emails, but in the end some funding was made available for an interpreter, and Anna started attending the group just after Christmas.

Do you think it's been beneficial? I asked her, not wanting to pry too much but also interested in her reasons for wanting to stop going.

She shrugged but didn't look me in the eye. *I think so. I think it's helped to go over what happened, and to talk about the things I've found difficult while I've been* recovering. But a lot of them just go over the same thing repeatedly, and I'm finding that part difficult to deal with.

Do you mean some of the other members?

She nodded. Yeah, I think a couple of them are a bit stuck, for want of a better word. They either haven't dealt with whatever happened to them, whether it was an illness or an injury, or they can't cope with the changes in their life. I understand, I really do, because I've been there. But I'm worried the more time I spend with people who can't move on, the harder it will be for me to move on. Does that make sense?

It does, I replied, giving her hand a squeeze. Do you feel like you've come to terms with what happened?

I think so, she said, and a dark look passed over her face. I wondered if she was remembering the day she was hit by a van and left for dead at the side of the road. The memory of coming home and finding the police outside my door was one I wouldn't forget any time soon.

It's taken a while to get used to my own limitations, she continued, sitting up a bit straighter, but I think I'm getting there. I get tired more easily, and I know my emotions are a bit more volatile than they were before, she added with an apologetic smile. But I'm making a new life for myself, and I don't feel like the group needs to be part of that now.

That makes sense, I told her. But maybe you should think about giving it another couple of weeks, I suggested.

Why? she asked, and I could see the suggestion irritated her slightly so I held up a hand in defence.

I'm not telling you to go, I quickly clarified. If you don't want to go I can't make you. I just meant you

139

shouldn't make a decision too quickly, that's all. I knew she could be impulsive, and I wondered if something else had happened in her group to make her wary of going.

Paige, will you accept that I know what I'm doing, for once? she asked, getting up off the grass. *At least I know what I want and I'm prepared to own my decisions, unlike you.*

Her comment stung, but I knew I couldn't argue with her. I stood up too, and she glared at me with her arms folded. *I just want to move on without being constantly reminded of what's wrong with me,* she signed. She was more defensive than I'd expected, and I knew there was something else going on, but she clearly didn't want to tell me.

In my pocket, I felt my phone vibrate, and when I pulled it out I saw it was Max. I'd missed a couple of calls from him earlier when I'd been talking to Singh and I felt a pang of guilt that I hadn't returned them, so I knew I really had to answer this one.

Hi, I signed, my smile feeling a little forced.

Hi, I've been worried about you, Max said straight away. *What have you been up to?*

I had some work to do this morning, I replied, not going into any details in the hope he wouldn't push it. *How are you?*

I'm good thanks, better for seeing you, he added with a grin. *I was wondering what you fancied doing tomorrow?*

I thought I'd just come over to yours, I replied, mindful of the conversation we needed to have and not really wanting to have it in a public place.

Okay. I wondered if you'd like to go up to the funfair, he said with a hopeful tilt to his eyebrows.

I winced, then turned my phone around so he could see where I was. *Sorry,* I told him. *I came up tonight with Anna. We can still come tomorrow if you like, though.*

He shook his head. *No, it's fine. We'll do something else.* I could tell he was annoyed but he was trying to hide it, and I felt a pang of guilt for not telling him we were going. One of our first dates had been to the funfair a year earlier, and I should have realised the significance. If I was honest, though, it hadn't occurred to me to let him know.

Once I'd hung up, I went to find Anna, wondering if I'd be able to get any sleep tonight, or if I'd lie awake rehearsing what I wanted to say to Max tomorrow.

Four hours before the fire

The car door slammed as Mariusz flung himself into the passenger seat and huddled down, his face glued to his mobile.

'What was it this time?' Caroline asked as she pulled out of the school car park. Her son ignored her and put his headphones in, but she reached over and pulled them out again with a deft flick of her wrist.

'Don't try that with me; I'm not beyond grounding you.'

Mariusz let out a snort. 'How would you manage that? You're never in.'

'Oh, I'm so sorry for going to work,' she snapped. 'Who do you think pays for your phone?'

The boy muttered something unintelligible.

'Anyway, what was the detention for? You know I can just call your head of year and ask, if you won't tell me the truth.'

'Ugh, why does it matter? I've done it now. It's all bullshit anyway.'

'Watch your language.'

'Why? You never do.'

Caroline sighed. She didn't have the energy for these conversations. Where had her cheerful boy gone? It seemed like he'd turned into some sort of Neanderthal in the space of a few weeks. She waited to see if he would eventually cough up the information she was looking for.

'Fighting, all right?' he mumbled.

'Fighting? Oh, love. What made you get into a fight?' That was so out of character for Mariusz, she knew there must have been something seriously wrong for him to lash out at another kid.

'He started it,' he said defensively, and she could feel the tension radiating off him in the cramped car.

'I believe you,' she replied quietly. 'What happened?'

'Nothing.' His voice had dropped to a mutter again.

'Mariusz, I want to help you with this. I know you must have had a good reason for reacting to this person, but fighting isn't usually the best solution.' Caroline was of the opinion that sometimes giving someone a swift punch was the best way to sort out an issue, but she didn't think it was a good idea to tell him that at this point.

'He called my dad a retard,' the boy said, turning to look out of the window. Caroline winced. She knew Mariusz was sensitive about his dad, whom he worshipped, and she could understand why that sort of comment had made him snap.

'Oh, love,' she said, not knowing how else to respond. 'It's fine.'

'It's not fine, obviously. That boy should never have said such a vile thing about your dad.'

'Why do you care? You hate him.'

Caroline sighed. 'I don't hate him. It's complicated – you understand that. Do you want me to talk to him about your fight?'

Mariusz shook his head. 'He wouldn't care. I feel like he doesn't notice me much these days.'

'Nadia then?' she suggested. The idea of having a chat with her ex's new wife made her clench her hands tight on the steering wheel, but Caroline would be willing to do anything to help Mariusz.

'She's just as bad,' he muttered. 'She's been different lately . . .' His voice tailed off.

As she pulled into a space in front of their house, Caroline turned to her son, hoping to try and comfort him and delve a little deeper into how he was feeling, but he was out of the car before she'd even turned the engine off. She followed him into the house, but by the time she'd shut the front door she heard his bedroom door slam, shortly followed by loud music. She sat down on the bottom stair, feeling like she'd let him down yet again.

Chapter 15

Saturday 20th April

That morning, I left home with some trepidation. I'd gone over the plan I'd made with Sasha the day before, and I didn't think it would be too difficult to do what she'd asked, but I was still concerned. There was a possibility that I'd be putting myself in harm's way, or at least making myself known to someone with a dubious reputation. Still, if I didn't do it I knew Sasha would be annoyed with me, and I didn't want to wind her up, at least until I could work out why she'd been so secretive with me.

Just before ten that morning, I got in my car and headed up to Frodingham Road, to Worx gym. I'd packed a bag with the nearest things I could find to gym gear – a T-shirt and some leggings – and made an appointment online for a tour. If any of my friends had seen me they would have suspected that I was up to something, because I hadn't set foot in a gym in at least ten years. The whole environment was my idea of a nightmare, but I needed to look

145

like I was there for a reason other than finding out more about Roy.

After getting home from the funfair the previous evening, I'd spent some time looking up Roy online. I'd started with the local paper, but the only mentions I could find of him were focused on the gym – a couple of articles about it opening, and one about the members contributing to a local fundraising project. The most promising story was about a drugs raid eight months earlier: one of his employees had been bringing drugs back from regular trips to Europe and then selling them from the gym, but it looked like the police hadn't found any connection to Roy himself. Was that because he hadn't known anything about it, or because he was good at keeping his hands clean? I couldn't imagine that a business owner wouldn't notice someone dealing right under their nose, but without any evidence I couldn't go very far down that route. I wanted to ask Singh if he'd be looking into it, but I knew my interference wouldn't be appreciated.

My next avenue of investigation had been social media. Worx had its own Instagram account, Facebook page and a private group for members, but I wouldn't be able to access that without joining the gym myself. Instead, I searched for references to the gym and Roy. On Instagram it was all positive, usually people's workout photos, mirror selfies with muscles on display, or occasionally photos of the outside of the gym. Facebook was a different story, however. There was a group for the local area that I joined without needing to be approved by an admin, and after a quick search I found a couple of posts from last year about the drugs raid. It seemed that some people weren't surprised by it, and said they'd suspected the owner of dodgy dealings for a while. One person expressed surprise that Roy hadn't been arrested and said they'd often seen people going in and out of the gym late at night when it was supposed to be closed.

There was no reference to violence of any kind, though. I didn't imagine someone like him could go from no criminal record to murder, but whatever search terms I tried, there wasn't anything to suggest he'd so much as had a parking ticket. Pulling up a photo of him from the gym's website, I tried a reverse image search, but it only brought me references to Worx. It had been a long shot. If I was going to be visiting the gym in person I wanted to have as much information about Roy as possible before I went.

As soon as I walked in I realised I was out of my depth. This wasn't the sort of gym I was expecting, the sort with rows of identical cross-trainers and rowing machines, and a small free weights section in the corner. This was completely different. The centre of the room was dominated by a red and black boxing ring, two men sparring while a couple of others stood at the edge shouting advice. There were several punch bags and rows of boxing gloves on one side of the room, while two of the other sides were taken up with weights and ropes hanging from the ceiling. Glancing around, I couldn't see another woman in the room, and I immediately wanted to turn around and run.

A huge, muscled man wearing a tank top with 'WORX' in capital letters across the front saw me and began heading in my direction. I barely had a moment to make a decision, and I froze. As he approached me, I could see a couple of men in other parts of the room stop what they were doing and turn to stare at me. I'd never felt more out of place anywhere in my life; even if I'd been an exercise fanatic I don't think I would have felt welcome, but as it was I wondered if this was the last mistake I'd make. The threat in the air was palpable and I knew if one of those men turned on me I wouldn't be able to get myself out. Why hadn't Sasha warned me about what it was like? I thought about the things Sasha had been keeping from me and instantly regretted putting myself in danger for someone who hadn't even been honest with me.

'You Paige?' the huge bloke asked me when he was within earshot.

I nodded, unsure if I could make my voice work or if it would come out at a strangely high pitch. I was also regretting using my real name when I signed up for a trial session online.

'You here for a look around?' He looked me up and down, clearly wondering what the hell a woman like me would be interested in this gym for. 'You know the Best Western's got a gym, right? Got a pool and sauna and everything. Might be more your thing.'

Part of me wanted to agree with him, but then there was the part that refused to be spoken to as if I was a silly little girl who'd wandered into a man's world. If he wanted to intimidate me he was doing a good job, but I was damned if I'd let it show.

'I don't really like saunas,' I replied coolly. 'If I'm going to sweat I want some muscles to show for it.'

He raised his eyebrows and inclined his head slightly,

though clearly wasn't fooled by my bravado. Another scan of my body made me feel uncomfortable, but I tried not to flinch. He was obviously wondering where the hell my muscles were.

'Right, well, I can show you around,' he said with a slight shrug. I knew he thought I was wasting his time, but I had to keep up the pretence if I wanted to speak to Roy.

'You wanna get changed, have a workout now?' he asked, with a suggestive leer.

'No, I'll just have a look round first,' I said, gritting my teeth to stop my disgust from showing on my face.

He shrugged. 'Suit yourself.'

As he led me over to the other side of the room, I glanced around to check if I could see Roy. I'd studied his photograph on the website so I thought I'd recognise him if I saw him, but there was no sign of him. I spotted a door in the far corner marked 'Private', and I assumed it led to Roy's office and the staff area.

For ten minutes, the huge guy pointed out different bits of equipment and explained the day-to-day rules for members. He didn't make any effort to hide his boredom, throwing the odd expletive at his mates on the other side of the room when they heckled him.

Wanting to get out of there, I decided to try a different tactic.

'Is Roy in today?' I asked. The guy frowned at me.

'Why do you want to know?'

'I just wondered if I could see him.'

There was a pause while he looked at me, then looked over his shoulder at the door to the office.

'Nah, you can't see him. Does he know you?'

I shook my head. 'No, but we have a mutual friend.'

'Who would that be?' he asked with a sneer.

'Lukas Nowak.'

A look of understanding passed across the guy's face and he laughed, though there was no humour in it. 'That why you're here, to argue Lukas's case for him?' Another harsh laugh. 'Roy wants his money and he's going to get it, one way or another. He doesn't give a shit that Lukas has got himself banged up. He can hide in there for as long as he likes, but he's still got a debt to pay. Now, if that's all . . .' He pointed towards the door, still smirking.

I stood frozen to the spot for a moment, until he made a move towards me and I flinched. He laughed, and I picked up my bag and hurried back out of the building, cursing myself for being so stupid. Getting in my car, I rested my head on the steering wheel and felt tears welling up behind my eyes. This made me even angrier with myself; if it wasn't bad enough that I'd put myself in a difficult situation, now I was crying about it like a child.

Taking a deep breath and scrubbing the heel of my hand across my eyes, I reached into the glove compartment and pulled out my notebook. On the page where I'd written about the gym and the drugs raid I made some notes about what I'd seen inside, and what the man had told me. Sasha would want to know that part, even though I hadn't been able to speak to Roy himself. I was partway through a sentence when someone knocked on my window, scaring the hell out of me.

I blinked at the man on the other side of the glass: it was Roy. My instincts told me to drive away without speaking to him, but I had to know what he wanted. I wasn't going to open the door, but I rolled the window down a little so I could hear him.

'Hi. Paige, is it?'

I nodded, wondering again why I'd been stupid enough to use my real name.

'I wanted to apologise for the rudeness of one of my employees just now. He doesn't really understand boundaries, at times.' He flashed me a bright white smile that had definitely had some cosmetic enhancement. 'Would you like to come into my office and we can chat about Lukas?'

His eyes dropped to the notebook sitting open on my lap, and I hurriedly pushed it onto the passenger seat, but not before he'd had time to see that his name was written across the top of the page. I saw a shadow cross his face as he realised what he'd read and I had to swallow a lump in my throat.

Struggling to find my voice, I said, 'I'm sorry, I have an appointment I need to get to.'

He raised his eyebrows, obviously unused to people saying no to him. 'You came into my place of business on false pretences. I think it's only polite if you give you me five minutes of your time to explain.'

Swallowing the hard lump that had appeared in my throat, I thought about my options. I really didn't want to go back inside that gym; if Roy Chapman wanted to harm me, he would have no problem doing so. But if I refused, what would he do to me? I didn't want to risk

151

putting anyone else I cared about in danger, so I reluctantly agreed.

I got out of the car and followed him back through the gym, keeping my head high but avoiding meeting the gaze of any of the patrons. Roy led me through the door at the back of the room and into what I assumed was his office.

'Please, take a seat,' he said, indicating a low chair to the side of his desk. If I sat on it, it would put me at a lower level than him, and I saw the power play straight away.

'I'll stand, thanks,' I replied. If he was bothered by my defiance he didn't show it, but sat down at his desk and leant back casually, stretching his legs in front of him.

'What can I do for you?' he asked. He was well spoken, but his words had a hard edge to them that I knew I shouldn't ignore.

'Tell me about your connection to Lukas.'

He raised his eyebrows in amusement at my command, but chose to humour me.

'Last year, Nadia's father became ill. Lukas wanted to send money back to Poland to help with his medical care, but the bills were far more than he could keep up with. He tried to get a loan from the bank but his credit rating was too poor. I offered to help him out.' Chapman spread his hands to suggest he'd done it out of the goodness of his own heart.

'How much does he owe you?'

He laughed, a sharp bark that made me want to get out of there as soon as possible.

'He sent you to talk to me and you don't even know that?'

'How much?' I repeated. I wasn't going to give him the satisfaction of explaining who I was or what I wanted to achieve.

'Fifteen.'

'Thousand?'

Chapman rolled his eyes at me. 'I'm a generous man, but I'm hardly going to be lending a friend fifteen million.'

I felt my face flush but tried to hide my embarrassment at my own question. 'How much had he repaid?'

'A little over three thousand.'

I nodded, thinking. There wasn't much more information I could get out of Chapman, I knew; I could hardly ask him where he was at the time Nadia was murdered. He sensed my hesitation and gave me a wolfish grin, his teeth perfectly straight and gleaming.

'Is there anything else I can help you with?'

I shook my head, so he stood and took me by the elbow. I tried to pull my arm out of his grip but it was like a vice. He steered me back through the door, across the gym and to my car, then watched as I got in.

'Please, let Lukas know that if there's anything I can do to help him out, I'll do it. Yeah, he owes me a bit of money but that can wait. It's awful, what happened to Nadia.' He shook his head sadly.

'I will, thank you.' I tried not to choke on the words, forcing myself to be polite to him out of a sense of self-preservation.

'If you want to talk more, you're always welcome here,' Roy replied, glancing at the yellow notebook I'd left on the passenger seat before taking a step back and walking away. Without wasting any time, I put my car into gear and drove away. Glancing in my rear-view mirror, I saw him standing in the gym entrance watching me leave.

Chapter 16

I was nearly home when my phone rang. Sasha. She probably wanted to find out what happened with Roy, but I was still shaking slightly from my encounter with him. I did consider ignoring the call, but I knew I'd have to speak to her eventually.

Even though I wasn't far from my flat, I pulled over in a lay-by. I wanted to get the conversation over with. Answering the video call, I sat up a bit so I could sign clearly.

Hi, Paige, Sasha said once her face popped up on my screen. *How's it going?*

I winced. *It didn't go well at the gym.* I briefly described what it had been like and she pulled a face.

Well, at least we tried. There's another reason I'm calling though, she told me. *One of the other social workers has let me know about an incident that happened last night.*

What is it? I asked, concerned that something had happened to Lukas, or another of Sasha's clients.

There was another fire, one street over from Lukas and Nadia's house. I don't know many details, but I'm going to go over there and see what I can find out. Do you want to come?

After my experience at the gym I really wanted to go home and curl up in a ball, but I saw an opportunity to find out why Sasha had been keeping things from me. *Sure,* I replied. *Text me the address and I'll meet you there.*

Before I turned my car around, I sent a brief text to Singh, asking what he knew about the fire. I wasn't sure if he'd give me any information, but if I brought the latest fire to his attention it might give him second thoughts about Lukas's guilt.

The house I was looking for was obvious as soon as I pulled onto the street. There were plenty of people milling around, including a Police Community Support Officer who was talking to someone wearing one of those white paper suits. I assumed they were investigating the cause of the fire, and I wondered if we'd be able to speak to either of them or if they'd tell us to get lost.

Sasha was already there, leaning against a wall a few houses down from the one that had caught fire. I joined her and saw she was watching the people hanging around being nosy.

Do you have any clients on this street? I asked her, wondering who she was looking for.

No. I just thought I'd have a look at who was around, see if any of them might be willing to speak to us. She looked back at the gathered crowd. *I think they're all just here for the gossip, but one of them might know something, or they might have seen something.*

Do you think this fire is linked to the one at Lukas's house, then? I asked, and she sighed.

I have no idea, but it seems a bit strange to me. Two house fires so close to each other in less than a week? It doesn't seem like a coincidence.

I looked back at the house and the PCSO posted outside.

Was anyone hurt? I asked Sasha.

She shook her head. *No, thankfully. Nobody was at home when the fire started.*

What makes you think they might be connected, then?

She started ticking off points on her fingers. *Both houses had council tenants who were on social services' caseload, both fires were extinguished before they caused damage to neighbouring houses, and they happened at almost exactly the same time of night.*

That's a bit tenuous, isn't it? I asked, not wanting to question her but also wondering if she was grasping at straws a little.

I can't explain, but something feels off. It won't hurt to talk to some of the people in the street and see what they know.

I agreed, and we walked closer to the house. I nodded at a young woman who had been keeping her eye on us, and we went over to talk to her.

'What do you want?' she asked as soon as we were within earshot.

'Do you know anything about what happened here?' I asked her, getting straight to the point.

She sniffed. 'Who's asking?'

I explained who Sasha and I were. 'One of her clients

had his house set on fire just a few days ago. We were wondering if they were connected.'

The woman turned away slightly. 'I haven't a clue. It's nothing to do with me.' She took a step away from us and looked over her shoulder. 'Someone probably left the gas burning. Or fell asleep with a fag on.'

I signed this for Sasha, but by the time I'd finished the woman had walked away. An older man had been watching us from the other side of the street, but when I caught his eye he too walked away. I wondered if he'd overheard me talking to the young woman. Clearly, questions weren't welcomed in this area, particularly from strangers.

I grimaced when I realised my own stupidity. *I shouldn't have told them you were a social worker,* I explained to Sasha.

She nodded slowly. *You're right, that might mean people don't trust us.* She turned back to the house. *Let's see if she'll talk to us, then,* she signed, indicating the PCSO.

I'd been hoping to build up to asking Sasha about her visiting Lukas without telling me, and about the solicitor, but I felt like I'd missed my opportunity now. We crossed over the road and were approaching the house when I heard someone calling my name. Turning round, I saw Singh walking towards us. I smiled in greeting, but he didn't return it and I felt my heart sink.

'I thought I'd find you here,' he said, annoyance written all over his face. 'Is there something I can help you two with?'

We heard about this fire and we thought it might be

158

connected to the one at Lukas's house, Sasha explained, standing shoulder to shoulder with me. I was grateful that she didn't leave me to answer the question, but I really didn't want to antagonise Singh – I would be crushed if we fell out and besides, he was my one friendly contact in the police.

'How can it possibly be connected, when the person who set that fire is currently in custody?' Singh asked quietly. He was keeping his voice low to avoid us being overheard, but I could still hear the tension underlying his words: he was angry with us for being there.

We don't believe Lukas did it. You know that. If we can find another explanation, perhaps that will help him. Sasha folded her arms, refusing to back down.

'Come on, Rav,' I added, hoping to appease him. 'You can't blame Sasha for wanting to help one of her clients.'

Singh tensed his jaw, and I wondered if he was going to shout at me. 'Can we talk? In private?'

I looked at Sasha and she shrugged. *I should go, anyway,* she signed to me. *Nobody here is going to talk to me.*

Singh and I watched her walk to her car, then he looked back at me.

'Come with me,' he said, shoving his hands in his pockets and striding off down the pavement before I had a chance to reply. He walked to the end of the road, turned right, then crossed over to a small, scrubby patch of grass with a children's playground behind it. Here he turned to me and looked me in the eyes.

'Paige, you know I respect you as a professional, and I like you personally. But you need to drop this now. When we've worked together before you've been invaluable to our investigation. Now, you seem determined to undermine us. You're a witness, and meddling like this isn't going to look good for Lukas.'

I shook my head. 'That's not what I'm trying to do, Rav. I told Sasha I didn't want to get involved, but I can't stop her doing it, and I'm her interpreter. Anything I've done, I've done to support Sasha because it's my job.' This wasn't strictly true when I thought about my trip to Worx gym that morning, but I knew he'd be fuming if I told him about that. And I didn't feel that I could tell him my concerns about Sasha lying to me until I'd given her the chance to explain herself. 'She doesn't believe Lukas did it.'

'He won't defend himself, Paige! How can she keep insisting he's innocent when he won't even do that himself?'

Trying to stay calm, I thought carefully before I spoke. I'd been mulling over Lukas's reaction for a while, and I'd had some time to come up with a theory based on my experience. 'My parents were always scared of anyone in authority. Even people like the staff at the bank. The communication barrier always made them feel like they were doing something wrong. Deaf people are routinely ignored or mistreated because of the difficulties in communication, and if they find it hard to stand up for themselves they can end up agreeing to things just because they think it's what the person in authority expects of them. I once interpreted for a lady who went to Citizens Advice because she was struggling to pay her bills, and when they looked into it they found she had dozens of direct debits going out to charities every month. People would come to her door and ask her to sign up to something for three pounds a month, and she couldn't understand what they wanted. She realised that signing their bits of paper made them go away, so she did it, not realising exactly what they were asking.'

I made a frustrated noise. 'I sound like I'm saying she was stupid – she wasn't, but she'd grown up being afraid of people in authority, in case she was taken away or locked up in an institution, or in case she had something blamed on her because she couldn't communicate properly with the hearing people around her. I'm worried the same thing is happening with Lukas.'

Singh scowled at me. 'You think we've manipulated him? Scared him somehow, so he won't tell us anything in case we use it against him? You were there, Paige. That didn't happen.'

'You know that's not what I'm saying!' I threw my hands up and tried to lower my voice. 'Lukas is scared of you. He's scared of the police. He's scared of something worse happening to him if he tells the truth. So he won't tell you anything because he's worried what will happen to him if he protests his innocence.' I thought back to Tuesday night and the fire and my eyes filled with tears. I tried to blink them away but it was too late – Singh's face fell, and I knew he thought he'd upset me.

'I saw the look in Lukas's eyes when he thought Nadia was trapped in that burning house,' I told him, my voice cracking slightly. 'I saw the utter horror and devastation on his face when they pulled her body out. There is no way you can convince me that he's responsible for her death. He was broken by it.'

161

We stood in silence for a moment, before Singh turned away from me and kicked a clump of grass.

'Shit. Shit, shit, shit.'

'What?' I asked.

He walked away from me and sat down on a bench, leaning back with his hands linked behind his head. I joined him, wondering what had caused this sudden shift in his attitude.

'Forest knows Sasha thinks he's innocent. We talked about it yesterday, after I saw you, and she thinks you're driving it, that you've got it into your head that you're some sort of amateur detective now.'

'Wow,' I replied, stung by his words. 'I wish you hadn't told me that.'

'Sorry. But what I mean is that she actually had me convinced for a few hours. That's why I came down here to talk to you. But what you just said . . .' He looked at me searchingly, and after a moment I felt uncomfortable, as if he was looking right into my mind. 'I think I know you well enough that you wouldn't be so emotionally involved if you didn't genuinely believe what you're saying. And if you believe it that fiercely, I really don't know what to think any more.'

I rubbed my face and took a couple of deep breaths. 'All I'm asking is that you keep an open mind. I understand that the evidence points towards Lukas being the one responsible, but can you at least consider the fact that someone else might have had a motive to kill Nadia?'

'We're still investigating, but I can't push it too far,' he replied with a frown.

'Fine, but don't stop us from talking to people,' I replied, my tone sharper than I'd intended. 'I've been doing my best not to get involved, like you told me, but if Sasha and I find something that could prove his innocence, tell me you'll take it seriously.'

He glanced over his shoulder, back in the direction of the most recent fire, then turned back to me. 'They think it was kids messing around,' he told me. 'One of the neighbours said there's been a gang of teenagers hanging around outside for a few days, coming and going on bikes. They haven't been seen since last night when the fire started.'

I nodded. 'Thank you.'

He gave me a small smile. 'I meant what I said, Paige. I respect you.' His eyes flicked up to mine. 'And I like you. But I also worry about you. Don't do anything stupid.'

I opened my mouth to respond, but he cut me off. 'Don't argue with me. You know you tend to act before you've thought about the consequences. I can't stop you from talking to people, so please promise me you'll be careful.'

'I will,' I told him. He stood up and gave my shoulder a quick squeeze before walking back towards where he'd left his car. I didn't follow him immediately, because I wanted to think about what he'd said, and I needed a bit of time to gather my own thoughts.

When I'd told Singh about Lukas's reaction to Nadia's death, I knew he thought I'd become emotional because we were arguing, but really it had made me realise something – I had never had that sort of love in my life, not even with Max. And that scared me, because the answer to his question was becoming more and more clear.

Chapter 17

After my conversation with Singh, I didn't want to go straight home. I hadn't heard from Sasha, and I wondered if she was annoyed with me for talking to Singh. She'd probably be digging for information when I saw her on Monday.

Rather than being discouraged from digging any further, I found myself wondering what else I could do to help Lukas. I was even more certain that he hadn't killed Nadia, and I felt I had a duty to act on that; my job involved supporting and empowering members of the Deaf community, and here was someone who was especially vulnerable. I drove around for a little while, eventually deciding to pay a visit to the office for the care agency both Nadia and Caroline worked for. Even if the break-up between Lukas and Caroline had been amicable, I imagined it would be difficult to work with your ex's new wife, and I wondered if that had led to any animosity between

Caroline and Nadia at work. I assumed it wasn't a coincidence that they worked together, and that was how Lukas and Nadia had met. That was one thing I was hoping to ask Paul about.

As it was Saturday I wasn't sure if he'd be in, but I didn't have to wait long before I was shown into his office by the receptionist, and he offered me a broad smile along with a firm handshake.

'How's Lukas?' he asked me as soon as I'd sat down. 'I was wondering if I should go and visit him, but I didn't know if he'd be happy to see me.'

'You can ask,' I replied. 'Seeing a friendly face might be good for him. But don't be offended if he refuses to see you,' I added. 'He's not in a good way at the moment.'

Paul looked concerned and leant forward, resting his elbows on his desk. 'Is there anything I can do to help him?'

'Well, that's partly why I'm here,' I explained. 'I'm trying to find out a bit more information about Nadia, just to see if I can work out a way to help Lukas. In case there's something the police have missed. I can't believe he'd do this to her.'

He shook his head, and for a moment I thought he was disagreeing with me, but then he said, 'You're absolutely right. Lukas would never hurt Nadia; she meant everything to him. I know he's had problems with alcohol in the past, but even then he wasn't a violent man. He's always been a depressed drunk, not an angry one.'

'I understand,' I replied. 'How is that you and Lukas became friends?'

'We knew each other from down the pub, before Caroline worked for me. He was always sitting on his

165

own, so I learnt a bit of sign language. We used to chat about the football. When he told me his wife was looking for a new job, I offered her a position, including training.'

'That was Caroline?' I asked, double-checking.

He nodded. 'We stayed friends even after they got divorced. He went through a rough time, but things improved so much when he started seeing Nadia.'

'Do you know of any problems the two of them might have had recently? Anything that might give someone a motive to do something like this?'

He grimaced. 'Possibly. But I don't really know how much I should be telling you. I mean, Lukas is my friend, and I want to help him, but I don't know how he'd feel about me discussing his private business with a relative stranger.'

'There are some things I already know,' I told him, hoping it would help him to trust me. 'For instance, I know he had a large loan from a friend.'

Paul let out a snort. 'Friend? I wouldn't call Roy Chapman a friend. Oh, I know, he and Lukas are drinking buddies, but all that means to Roy is that Lukas is someone he can use in some way.'

'Do you know Roy, then?' I asked, and I realised my eagerness had shown in my voice, because he crossed his arms defensively.

'I know of him. He's not the sort of man I associate with.' A frown had creased his forehead and darkened his expression. 'I'm a legitimate businessman, and people like Roy Chapman give this town a bad reputation. I'd happily see the back of him, and if I'd known Lukas was going to him for a loan I would have warned him off.'

'What sort of bad reputation?' I asked, digging to see what Paul knew.

'Well, let's just say that not all of his business is above board, and he seems proud of that fact. He's a swaggering lout who thinks he's a cut above others because he's always one step ahead of the taxman or any other authorities who might be wanting to take a closer look at his businesses, but one day soon that will all come crashing down around his ears, I'm sure.' Paul's tone of voice was measured, but I could see his neck reddening as he spoke; he clearly had a great dislike of Roy.

'Why did Lukas go to him, then?' I asked. 'Doesn't he know that Roy has a shady reputation?'

Paul spread his palms wide, a look of exasperation on his face. 'I have no idea. Lukas can sometimes be a little too trusting, but I would have thought he'd have enough sense to be able to see through Roy. Nadia spoke to me about it, because she was concerned that they wouldn't be able to afford to repay the loan. If Lukas had gone to a bank, they could have negotiated their repayments and made sure they could pay it back, but someone like Roy . . .' He tailed off.

'What?' I asked, urging him to continue.

'Well, I can't imagine him being too flexible. And I doubt his interest rates are fewer than three figures. Nadia was worried they'd end up being in debt to Roy for the rest of their lives.'

I paused for a moment and thought about what he was saying. 'Did Nadia know Roy? Do you think she could have gone to him to discuss the loan, without telling Lukas?'

Paul raised his eyebrows. 'I hadn't thought about that.' He tapped his fingers on his desk, thinking. 'I suppose it's possible. She would have done anything to protect Lukas. She was working extra shifts so they could overpay each month, and I always offered her overtime where possible. I mean, if they'd come to me I could have helped them, especially as they needed the money for Nadia's family,' he added, his frustration evident. He sat back and folded his arms. 'Do you think Roy had something to do with Nadia's death?'

I thought before I answered, not wanting to commit myself or give him too much information. 'I don't know about that. I do think the police need to look a little further into different avenues. Sasha also doesn't think Lukas would ever have hurt Nadia.'

'I agree with her,' Paul replied. 'But I don't think Roy is the type to get his hands dirty.'

I didn't answer him, instead pulling my notebook out of my bag. I turned to a page where I'd made notes about Nadia and the people she might have seen on the day she died.

'How can we find out if Nadia spoke to Roy?' I asked him.

'I don't know. It's unlikely she would have told anyone about it. She didn't want her friends knowing how much debt they were in.'

'Why did she confide in you, then?'

He laughed. 'She needed to convince me to give her extra shifts instead of sharing them out. Some of the others had started to notice, though, so I wouldn't have been able to keep it up. There was already some tension between

Nadia and the other carers because of the unfounded rumours about thefts. But I wanted to help them out if I could.' I jotted this down in my notebook, as he continued speaking. 'I did offer to give her the money myself, but she refused. She didn't want to complicate things by shifting the debt around, and she was worried Roy would find another way to get some sort of hold over Lukas.'

'Why would he do that? Lukas was pretty insignificant, in Roy's world.'

'Just because he liked to have power over others, I suppose,' Paul replied with a shrug. 'I don't profess to know how a man like that thinks.'

I nodded again, thinking about what he'd said. 'But he wouldn't benefit from it, would he?' I pointed out. 'With Nadia dead and Lukas in prison, Roy won't be getting the rest of his money.'

'He probably didn't think Lukas would take the blame for it,' Paul reasoned. 'Why would he, if he's innocent?'

'Good point,' I replied, and went to write that in my book. Paul looked interested, so I tapped it with my pen and explained. 'I'm trying to help Sasha, and she wants to get Lukas out of prison. I want to make sure anything relevant is written down, then if I find something that we can take to the police, I won't forget anything.'

He nodded and glanced away, checking his watch as he did. 'I'm sorry, Paige, I need to go. Please let me know if there's anything else I can do to help.'

'Of course. And do try and see Lukas, if you can. It might do him some good to know a friend is thinking about him.'

He agreed and showed me out. As I walked to the car

I tucked my notebook back in my handbag, frustrated that I hadn't had time to ask him about Caroline and Nadia's relationship at work. It would have to wait; I had other things on my mind today.

I let myself in to Max's flat, and found him in the kitchen. We hugged, but I could feel the tension across his shoulders as we did. I was nervous; part of me wanted to run out of there and put the conversation off for another day, or week, or maybe even a month. But I knew it was time, and I forced myself to take a deep breath.

Come on, I said, beckoning him into the living room. *We need to talk.*

He nodded and followed me in, sitting down on the sofa next to me.

You promised you'd give me an answer today, he reminded me. His leg jiggled up and down and he couldn't seem to sit still.

I know, and I will. I took a couple of deep breaths. *Thank you for being patient with me. I know it's been hard for you to do that.*

He nodded, but let me continue.

I have thought about it a lot, all week, I told him. *I've thought about the pros and cons of both sides, until I could barely sleep. But I think right now, the fairest thing is for me to say no. I'm sorry, I'm not ready to move in with you.*

Max sat back against the sofa cushions and ran a hand through his hair. *Why?* he signed, without looking at me.

I'm not ready for that sort of life change yet, I told him. *I like things the way they are. I like having my own flat and my independence.*

170

He looked anguished. *I would never take away your independence. Why would you say something like that?*

If I lived with you it would be different, I told him. *Our lives would be different, and our relationship would change.*

In a good way! Don't you want to spend more time with me? He leant forward, his elbows on his knees. *Paige, I love you. I want to wake up with you every morning. I want to see you every evening, and ask how your day went. I want us to plan holidays together – we've never even been away for a weekend together.*

Exactly, I pointed out. *So moving in together would be too big a step right now.*

Max shook his head again, exasperated. *That's not what I'm saying. You're always stalling, Paige. Whenever I try to suggest we go away, there's a reason why you can't, or don't want to.* He looked me in the eyes. *Don't you want a serious relationship, Paige? Don't you want to live with the person you love, maybe even get married, have children? Have a life together?*

I didn't know what to say. I couldn't tell him that there had been many times when I'd imagined having that in my life, and I knew there was a big part of me that wanted it. But I'd never been able to see that happening with Max. But if I didn't want it with Max, should I even be with him at all?

As these thoughts bounced around my mind, my hesitation must have given Max a clue.

Shit, he signed, standing up and walking over to the other side of the room. *Shit, shit, shit. Are we breaking up? Is that what's happening?*

I hesitated again, and that was all the answer he needed. *What the hell, Paige? I thought you loved me? I thought we loved each other?*

Standing up, I approached him but he backed away from me. *Is there someone else?*

No, you know I'd never do that to you, I told him, hurt that he'd even ask. *I didn't intend to come here and break up with you.* I paused, trying to gather my thoughts. *But if I don't feel ready to move in with you, and can't see that sort of a future for us, maybe you're better off without me.*

Don't you dare do that, he said, pointing a finger at me. *Don't you dare suggest you're doing this because it's the best thing for me. It's not what I want. None of this is what I want. I want you to move in with me and spend the rest of your life with me, but that's obviously not going to happen.*

He buried his face in his hands, his shoulders trembling. Tears sprang into my eyes and I wanted to wrap my arms around him, but I knew it wouldn't be welcome. I waited until he looked up at me again, a complex mixture of anger, hurt and confusion in his eyes.

I'm sorry, I signed. *I don't want to hurt you.* It felt empty, but what else could I say?

He shook his head. *Just go.*

Swallowing hard, I did as he asked, but once I was in my car I rested my head on the steering wheel and sobbed.

Chapter 18

I wasn't known for my exceptional cooking skills, but my speciality was my lasagne, and by the time Anna got home I had one ready to go in the oven. One of the ingredients for the sauce was red wine, and whilst a generous slug had gone in the pan while I was cooking, the majority had gone in me. My sister saw my glass and reached for the bottle to pour herself some and raised an eyebrow when she saw it was nearly gone.

You started early, she joked.

I'd told myself I'd keep it together when she arrived home, and tell her matter-of-factly that I'd broken up with Max but didn't want to talk about it. Of course, as soon as she looked at me my face crumpled and I burst into tears. She wrapped her arms around me and let me sob; every time I tried to lift my hands up to tell her what had happened they shook too much for me to sign clearly.

Is it Max? she asked.

I nodded.

You told him you didn't want to move in with him?

I nodded again.

And he broke up with you?

This set off more tears. *No,* I signed eventually. *I broke up with him. When I went there I wasn't sure exactly what I wanted; I just knew I didn't want to take that step yet. But then, when I was there, it seemed so obvious, because I don't think I ever want that serious a relationship with Max.*

Anna brushed my hair away from my face and kissed my forehead, like our mum used to do when we were young.

I know it hurts, but it sounds like you did the right thing. It wouldn't be fair to him to carry on in a relationship if you didn't want to commit to him.

But what if there's something wrong with me? I asked her. *What if I'm damaged from my relationship with Mike, and I'll never be able to commit to anyone? Maybe I should have just pushed through, given it a go. I could move in with him and see what happens.*

Your relationship with Mike has affected you, of course it has, but you're not damaged. He controlled you, Paige, and now that you're free to make decisions for yourself it's going to seem strange. Anna squeezed me tight for a moment, then stepped back and looked at me. *I don't know what's going on in your head at the moment, but I don't think you can make any decisions right now. You've got too many emotions fighting for attention, and I don't think you'll be able to make a rational decision.* She nodded at my phone sitting on the table. *Do you want me to delete his number, then you're not tempted to call him?*

174

I shook my head. *No, it's fine.* I paused for a minute. *Do you think I've made a mistake?* I asked, searching her face for signs of what she was thinking.

Slowly, she shook her head. *I don't know, Paige. I've thought you haven't been happy for a few months now. Well . . .* She paused. *I didn't think you were unhappy, exactly. I just thought maybe your relationship with Max had run its course. The gym membership thing wasn't the only time he's got it completely wrong – he kept pushing you to go away for a weekend when you didn't want to, and don't forget the massage voucher.* She gave me a look with raised eyebrows and I gave a little laugh. I hated massages, wasn't comfortable with strangers touching me, but Max had given me the voucher for Christmas anyway. He'd insisted it would be relaxing and I'd enjoy it eventually. I'd given the voucher to Anna.

So I did the right thing?

Only you can answer that, she told me, squeezing my hand. *And you're clearly not in a fit state to do that right now.*

Why would I be this upset if it's the right thing to do though? I asked her, staring into my glass of wine.

Oh, Paige. She gave me another hug. *You're upset because you're not a robot. Max is hurt, and you don't want to be the person who causes another human being to be upset. Plus, it's bound to be emotional, making such a big decision about your life, and change is scary.*

I nodded, trying to believe her. I'd been telling myself the same things since I left his flat, but I hadn't managed to convince myself.

I care about Max a lot, I told her. *I enjoyed spending*

175

time with him, but I don't think I want anything more. I think I just want to be friends, but he won't want anything to do with me now.

Anna got up. *Right. We're putting this lasagne in the oven, because I'm starving, and you need something to soak up the wine. Then we're going to open another bottle, you can tell me exactly what happened and how you feel, but you're not allowed to ask me any more if you did the right thing. Deal?*

Deal, I agreed, opening the oven while she reached for the corkscrew.

By the time we'd eaten, another bottle of red wine was empty, and I'd poured my heart out to Anna. I felt surprisingly lighter after sharing it with her, and I was glad I hadn't been able to keep it to myself as I'd originally intended. One eye had been on my phone the whole time, but there were no calls or texts from Max. He would be too proud to try calling me so soon.

Should I call him? I asked Anna. *I want to know how he's doing.*

She shook her head. *I don't think it would be a good idea just yet. You're both going to be very emotional, and neither of you want to say anything you don't mean.*

I nodded. *I know you're right. I just feel terrible.*

That's natural, she said, *but that doesn't mean it's the right thing to do. He has other friends who will support him right now; if you call him it'll only confuse both of you. Sit on it for a couple of days then see how you feel.* She spread her palms. *Maybe after a few days you'll decide you want to try again, or maybe you'll realise it was definitely the right decision. Either way, if you call him now you risk having a knee-jerk reaction that could make things worse.*

I stood up and took her plate, thinking about what she'd said as I stacked the dishwasher. Anna took the remains of the bottle of wine and our glasses through to the living room, where I joined her a few minutes later, sinking down onto the floor in front of the sofa.

You're really tense, she told me. *I can see it in your shoulders.*

There's a lot going on, I told her. *It's not just Max; it's work as well.*

The house fire? she asked. *I thought the police must have ruled it an accident.*

I shook my head. *It's a murder investigation.*

Her eyes widened, but to her credit she didn't ask me for any more details.

It's a confusing situation, I told her, wanting to share without giving her too much information. *They've arrested someone, but I don't think he did it. I don't even know this guy very well, but Sasha's convinced me he's innocent and we need to help him.*

Why don't you think he did it? Anna asked.

He told me he didn't do it, before he was arrested, and he was telling the truth. I'm sure of it.

She seemed to be choosing her words carefully before she replied. *Do you think it's because you've worked for the police before?*

What do you mean?

Well . . . She paused. *Being involved with the police as an interpreter, maybe you've started thinking a bit like one of them, if you see what I mean.*

I frowned. *I'm not trying to be a detective, Anna. Just because I've been involved in a couple of cases doesn't mean I think I know better than them.* Her words smarted, especially because they echoed what Forest had been saying about me.

What does Singh think? she asked, and I wondered if this was connected or if she was changing the subject.

I thought for a moment. *I really don't know. I think he's not sure about Lukas's guilt, but he's not convinced there's any evidence to point towards another suspect either.*

Well, you can help him find it, she replied, as if it was the most obvious thing in the world.

I didn't reply straight away. What could I say? I knew I shouldn't be getting involved, but I'd been talking to people and sticking my nose in, exactly what Singh had warned me against.

Maybe I should just leave it, I told her. *You're right, I'm getting carried away because I like having a mystery to solve. Maybe there isn't a mystery this time, and I'm just looking for something that isn't there.*

She nodded, obviously satisfied with my answer.

Have you told Gem about Max? she asked. Gem was my oldest friend – she was the only deaf person in her family and I was the only hearing one in mine, and when we were children our respective families took us to the Deaf club in Scunthorpe. Opposites attracted, and we'd been close ever since.

Not yet. I wanted to tell you first. I didn't tell her that telling my friends my relationship was over almost felt like admitting failure, as if my inability to maintain a stable relationship was a character flaw. In reality, this was rubbish, because a couple of my friends were happily single, including Gem herself, but I judged myself in the way I expected other people to judge me. But telling people also meant accepting it myself and I didn't know if I was ready for that.

Go on, you should tell her, Anna told me. *She'll want to take you out.*

That's the last thing I want right now, I replied, but she was right, so I spent the next ten minutes texting my friends to tell them what had happened, then another fifteen fielding their replies and assuring them all I was okay.

When Anna went to bed, I spent some time toying with the idea of calling Max, but I knew she was right and it wasn't the right time. My mind drifted to my conversations with Singh and Paul earlier that day. The more people I talked to, the more complicated the case seemed to be. I remembered I'd never actually asked Paul about the relationship between Caroline and Nadia, so made a note to find out more about them and how well they'd got on. I thought it was important to find out more about these thefts too, and see if it really had been Nadia.

I sat in the living room for ages, rereading my notebook, looking for a pattern to jump out at me, but nothing came. Giving up, I went to bed but tossed and turned for ages, struggling to sleep as everything whirred round in my head, until finally the exhaustion won.

Three hours before the fire

Lukas closed the front door carefully and took off his shoes and jacket. He knew Nadia didn't like him tracking dirt from outside into the house. She had tried to train him out of a lot of his bad habits in the time they'd been together, not that he thought there was anything wrong with half of the stuff she was bothered by. He knew if she weren't there he'd be straight back to his old ways and it wouldn't do him any harm. Right now, though, he wasn't in the mood for being nagged yet again, so it was easiest just to do what she wanted. He thought he knew Nadia inside and out, but ever since she'd been accused of taking things from her clients he wondered if there was a different side to her he hadn't realised was there. Paul insisted he thought she was innocent, but Lukas didn't know what to think.

He was relieved to see the house was empty, apart from Nadia. The people who had been hanging around for the last couple of days had frightened him, and he knew Nadia hated having them there. But he also knew they had him backed into a corner – he couldn't get rid of them without exposing himself and his family to more danger, and he wouldn't do that.

There was a delicious smell wafting from the kitchen, so he poked his head around the door to see what Nadia was cooking. She was standing over the hob, stirring a large pot of some sort of stew or soup, and the steam coming off it had made the hair around her face go a little frizzy. So engrossed in what she was doing, she didn't notice Lukas, so he took the time to look at his wife for a moment and appreciate her. She was dressed very nicely, in something more low cut than she usually wore, he noticed, and he wondered if she had plans to go out this evening, or if she'd just put on something she knew he'd like.

He crept up behind her and put a hand on her hip, startling her. When she turned round and smiled at him, he thought he saw a glimmer of sadness in her eyes, but it quickly disappeared. She put down the wooden spoon she was holding, and turned to wrap her arms around him, holding him tightly.

When they separated, he smiled at her. *What was that for?*

Can't I greet my husband when he comes home from work?

He leant forward and kissed her, pleased that she was in a good mood with him for once. *Of course. How was your day?*

Fine, she replied, turning back to the pot of stew. When

she didn't add anything else he frowned. Nadia always told him about her day, in the smallest detail, and it was usually boring as hell. The fact that she didn't today made him wonder why.

Is something wrong? he asked, moving around to her side so she could see him. He knew she'd been furious with him recently, blaming him for the way their lives had been invaded.

No, I'm just tired, she told him with another smile.

She did look worn out, he realised, and for a moment he was reminded of those first few months when Caroline was pregnant with Mariusz. She couldn't be, could she? No, he didn't think so. They weren't too old to think about it, though, and he'd been considering broaching the subject soon.

It occupied his mind all through their meal, and he knew he must seem distracted. Once they'd both finished eating, he put his fork down by the side of his plate and looked at Nadia. She was truly beautiful, and she was so caring, even if that did sometimes manifest itself as nagging. She would be a good mother, he knew.

Would you like to have children? he asked her directly, needing to express the thoughts that had been filling his mind. Perhaps it was something they should have discussed before they got married, but it had been a bit of a whirlwind.

She frowned. *I would. But we can't afford a baby right now, not with our debts.*

Lukas's heart sank. That debt would be hanging over them for the rest of their lives if he wasn't careful.

I will sort out the money, he told her firmly. *You were right about Roy. I should never have taken his money. I'll* find a way to repay him, then we can have a family of our own. Mariusz can be a big brother.

He'd be a wonderful brother, she replied, her expression wistful, but then she shook her head. *We can't think about that at the moment. Whatever made you suggest it?*

I thought it might be something you want, he said.

I did, but I don't want to think about things that can't happen.

Lukas bristled slightly. *You don't believe me, do you? I said I would sort out the money, and I will.*

Nadia sighed and stood up, reaching over to collect his plate. Before she could pick it up, Lukas grabbed her wrist.

Answer me.

'Let go of me!' she shouted, taking him by surprise, so he did as she asked. He saw her eyes flash with a mixture of fear and anger before she turned away from him, grabbed the plates and stalked into the kitchen without giving him the satisfaction of a response.

Her reaction strengthened his resolve. Whatever it took, he'd find a way to get Roy Chapman out of their lives for good.

Chapter 19

Sunday 21st April

I was woken by the door buzzer, and groaned as I dragged myself out of bed. My head felt like it was stuffed with cotton wool after my overindulgence in red wine the previous evening. Who the hell was at my door at this time in the morning? A quick glance at my phone surprised me – it was already well past ten o'clock. It had taken me so long to get to sleep last night that I'd slept in far later than usual. The buzzer went again and I went to answer it.

I was about to press the button to answer it when I stopped. What if it was Max, coming to beg me to change my mind? Or worse, to have a go at me for letting him down like that? As I was debating whether to ignore the door, my phone vibrated in my hand. It was a message from Sasha.

Are you in? I need to see you. Urgent.

I buzzed her in straight away, and a moment later she hurried into my flat, dropping her bag in the hall before turning to me, her face frantic.

They've charged him.

What? I was still half asleep and it took me a moment to process what she'd said.

Lukas. They've charged him with murder. He'll be in court for a hearing in the morning.

My heart sank. I could see tears in Sasha's eyes, which surprised me. I knew she felt strongly about this, but I hadn't realised just how much it was affecting her.

Go through and sit down, I told her. *I'll make coffee.*

I had assumed Anna was still asleep, but I found a note in the kitchen saying she'd gone out. I must have slept even better than I'd thought, because Anna was notorious for making a hell of a lot of noise when she got up. She said it was because she couldn't hear things like cupboard doors banging, but I'd complained about it often enough that she knew by now. I thought she just did it to wind me up.

A few minutes later I joined Sasha in the living room. I'd made the coffee pretty strong, because I needed it to wake me up and she looked like she could do with it too.

What happened? I asked.

She shook her head slowly. *I don't know. I just got an email informing me that they'd charged him with Nadia's murder first thing this morning.* She hung her head. *I knew they were getting towards their limit for how long they could hold him. They'd already applied for the full ninety-six hours; they had to charge him or release him. But I suppose I thought they would have to release him without evidence that he's guilty.*

I rubbed my face. *That's it then,* I signed. *There's nothing else we can do.*

185

She stared at me fiercely, her eyes bright. *What? Of course that's not it! This doesn't change anything.*

I hesitated. *But they must have some more evidence, Sasha. Something we don't know about. They wouldn't charge him if they thought there was any room for doubt.* I spread my palms wide. *What about the bruises? We still have no idea how he got those. Maybe they found evidence that he got them when he killed Nadia.*

Well, what do you know about it that you're not telling me? she snapped. *You're the one who's been having cosy little chats with one of the detectives. What have you told him?*

Hang on, that's not fair, I replied, holding up my hands defensively.

No, what's not fair is you not sharing things with me, Sasha replied. *What have you been telling DS Singh?*

Nothing that he didn't already know! I stood up and walked over to the window. I wasn't in the mood for this from Sasha, especially when I knew she'd been keeping more from me than I'd kept from her. *I don't want to do this right now. Maybe you should go, and we can talk tomorrow.*

Sasha's face fell and she stood up, crossing the room to join me. *Paige, I need your help. I'm sorry. I just don't know what to do. How are we going to help Lukas now?*

I let out an exasperated noise. *I don't know, Sasha. We're looking into things, but there's nothing obvious. I can't deal with this right now.*

Why, what have you got going on that's more important than an innocent man going to jail? she snapped.

Well, I split up with Max yesterday, if you must know, I retorted, scowling at her.

There was a pause while she took in what I'd just said, as I glared at her, my hands trembling and tears threatening to spill again. I knew she cared about Lukas, but she needed to understand that he wasn't the only person in the world, and that helping her wasn't my sole goal in life.

A moment later, she bit her lip and shook her head. *I'm sorry, Paige. I've been so caught up with what's going on with Lukas that I've barely noticed anything else that's going on in the world. I should have realised. Do you want to talk about it?*

I sat down again. *Not really.* I gave her the bare bones of the story – that he'd asked me to move in with him and I'd realised I didn't want our relationship to progress any further – and to her credit she listened without inter-rupting.

Is there anything I can do? she asked once I'd finished.

No, I'm fine. But I think you need to take a step back from this, I told her, meaning Lukas and the murder investigation. *I think it's not good for you.*

I understand why you're saying that, she signed slowly, carefully choosing her words, *but I can't do that. I have a responsibility towards him.*

Have you ever stopped to think he might have done it? I asked, knowing I might risk her wrath again, but also knowing that I had to ask the question.

She blinked rapidly, and for a moment I didn't know if she was going to cry or explode at me again, but in the end she did neither. *I don't need to think about it,* she replied eventually. *Because I know there's no way he could have done it. I don't expect you to believe it, and if you don't want to help me with this any more that's fine. But*

I know he's innocent, and I'm not going to stop trying to prove it. Even if he's convicted and I need to fund an appeal myself, I'll do it.

I thought for a minute, taking her words in. I trusted her judgement, but I also trusted Singh and his ability to do his job correctly, and in this instance one of them must be wrong. For the first time I started to think that perhaps Lukas was guilty, and Sasha was being swayed by her personal connection to him. I knew I couldn't say that to her, though, without risking another fight, and I didn't have the energy for it. Her comment about paying for his appeal reminded me of what Singh had told me about the solicitor, and I needed answers before I was willing to trust her further.

Why didn't you tell me that you'd been to see Lukas on your own?

Sasha's eyes widened and I thought she might be about to deny it, but she swallowed and nodded.

Okay, you're right. I should have told you about that. I suppose DS Singh told you?

I nodded, waiting for her to answer the question.

I don't know, if I'm honest, she signed with a shrug. *I went on a whim, thinking I might be able to talk Lukas into speaking to the police, to professing his innocence. But it didn't work and he still refused to speak to me. I hoped he might have changed his mind the next day; that's why I asked you to call.*

But why wouldn't you tell me about it? I pressed.

I thought you'd say I was getting too obsessed with the case, she replied. *I didn't want anyone to know just how much of my time I've been putting into trying to find a way to prove his innocence. If my manager knew, she wouldn't be impressed. Supporting a client through the criminal justice system is one thing, but I know I've neglected a few of my other clients this week because I've prioritised Lukas.*

You paid for his solicitor, too, I said. This wasn't a question, it was a statement, and she knew there was no point denying it.

I did. I wanted to make sure he had someone decent to defend him, and you don't know who you're going to get with legal aid.

I nodded. *All of this is stuff you could have told me, Sasha. If you want me to help you, you need to trust me.*

She hesitated for a moment, and I wondered if there was something else she'd been keeping from me, something that even Singh didn't know about.

I promise to be honest with you from now on, she told me. *But please, Paige, I need your help.*

Do you really think there's a chance of you finding evidence against someone else? I asked her. I thought about my conversations with Jill Adams and Roy Chapman, and the second house fire. *We haven't got anywhere so far.*

The fierce light came back into her eyes as she nodded. *I do.*

I took a deep breath. *Okay. In which case, I want you to come with me tomorrow to speak to DI Forest.* It went against all my own instincts, to voluntarily talk to the DI when she had always wanted to see the back of me in the past, but I thought that might be the only way to convince Sasha to give up on this idea. It was obvious that I wasn't going to change her mind, so maybe the detective inspector in charge of the case would be able to.

Sasha looked unsure. *I don't see what that will achieve.*

Maybe there will be an avenue they haven't looked into, that you can tell them about, I suggested. *And maybe they can share with us what evidence they have against Lukas.*

Do you think they'd be willing to do that?

Knowing Forest, possibly not, but it can't hurt to ask. You'll be there in a professional capacity, as Lukas's social worker, and maybe she'll do you the courtesy of answering your questions.

Sasha nodded slowly, not completely convinced but obviously willing to agree to it if it meant I'd continue to help her. All I could hope was that Forest would lay things out clearly to show Sasha it was futile, rather than just throwing us out of her office.

Make an appointment to see the DI tomorrow, I suggested. *Have we got some free time in the diary?*

She pulled out her phone to check, and we moved on to discussing which clients she would need to see over the next few days, some of whom she'd cancelled appointments with last week, in order to see Lukas. Whilst I didn't relish talking about work on a Sunday, I thought it was a good idea to help Sasha focus on the rest of her caseload, instead of devoting all her energy to just one man.

When she'd gone, I stood by the window for a while, watching people coming and going. My chat with her had kept my mind off Max for a while, but now the flat was empty again I couldn't avoid the thoughts that were cropping up. Now I had time to think about it, I was sure it had been coming for a while, my desire to end our relationship, but that didn't stop me from feeling as if a rug had been pulled out from under me.

Checking my phone, I noticed a message from Gem, telling me that we were going out that evening. I didn't protest, knowing she wouldn't accept any excuses, even though I would rather hide away from the world for a while. As I stood and thought about it, my phone rang in my hand. It was Max. After a brief inward battle, I decided to ignore it. I put my phone down on the table and watched it until it stopped ringing.

Perhaps a night out with my best friend was exactly what I needed.

Chapter 20

I felt like I needed some fresh air, so I walked up into the village and went to sit on the green, near the children's play area. Any evidence that the funfair had been there had been cleared away, except for some patches of grass that had been churned to mud. The sun was warm and there was a slight breeze, and something about it lifted my spirits a little. There were some children playing on the climbing frame, and their excited chatter drifted over to me as I tried to clear my mind a little.

Checking my phone, I found myself thinking about Max's call. Did I want him to rant at me and call me a heartless bitch? Or did I want complete radio silence, suggesting he hadn't thought about me at all? I didn't know the answer to that question. Should I call him back? If he wanted to talk I should at least let him say whatever it was he wanted to say, but if it was going to be an angry rant I didn't think I could take that right now. I wanted to be able to judge his emotional state before talking to him, in order to take my own feelings into account. A small part of me thought I deserved to be called every name under the sun, but then I had never intended to upset him. If his feelings were stronger than mine, there was no way to end it without hurting him.

Even though we'd only been together for just over a year I was now used to being in a relationship, and the idea of being single again was uncomfortable. Before Max, I'd been single for three years, and it hadn't done me any harm. I could do it again now, without a problem, and I'd always rolled my eyes at people who couldn't cope if they weren't in a relationship. But right now I wanted to stay with the familiar, and I knew it was going to be a difficult adjustment. Change was terrifying.

Deciding against calling him back, I put my phone back into my bag. He could wait. At least until I'd got my head round this situation myself, then maybe I'd feel up to getting in touch with him.

I shook myself and stood up. Wallowing wasn't going to do me any good, so I needed something to take my mind off Max. I didn't know if Anna would be home yet, and I didn't want to go home and sit in an empty flat until I went out that evening, so I walked back towards home, got in my car and drove into Scunthorpe. Before I realised which direction I was heading in, I found myself approaching the end of Lukas and Nadia's street. The case was the perfect distraction right now, and my subconscious had taken me back to where it started.

There was a space right outside the blackened shell of a house, so I pulled up there and got out. Before I had a chance to decide what I was going to do next, the front door of the house opposite opened.

'You don't want to park there.' An elderly man stood in the doorway, glaring at me and my car.

'Is this someone's space?' I asked, doing my best to sound innocent.

The old man snorted. 'Nobody got their own space round here. I were just trying to help you. That house is trouble.'

'This one?' I replied, pointing at Lukas's house behind me.

He nodded. 'Leave it there if you want, but don't expect it to be in one piece when you come back.'

He turned and was about to go back into his house.

'Wait!' I called, and jogged across the road so I could speak to him more easily. He looked me up and down suspiciously, but clearly decided I wasn't going to mug him or anything like that.

'What do you want?'

I pointed at the house again. 'Did you see what happened, the night of the fire?'

'Why do you want to know?'

'I'm friends with the couple who lived there,' I told him, stretching the truth as far as I dared. 'I'm worried the police aren't going to find out what really happened.'

'What's your name?'

'Paige.'

He paused for a moment. 'I'm Eric. I don't go out much any more, and I spend most of my days sitting in my front window watching the world go by. So happen as I did see some things on that night, yes.'

I tried to hide my excitement, wondering how I could

194

get this man to talk to me, but a moment later he was already ushering me inside his house. The hallway was dark, with woodchip wallpaper that was browning at the edges, and a dark red carpet that had worn through in patches. The decor in the front room was similar, and a slight smell of rising damp added to the effect. There was a large recliner chair next to the window, which was clearly Eric's seat, so I perched gingerly on an elderly sofa that sagged in the middle.

'Cup of tea.' It was a statement rather than a question, and I waited while he clattered around in the kitchen. I had offered my help before he left the room, but he just glared at me and didn't reply, so I'd taken that as a refusal.

While he was making tea, I got up and stood behind his chair, looking out over the street. The angle of the window meant you could see people approaching on the opposite side of the road from several houses down in both directions, and if you stood right in the bay you could see the front doors of Eric's neighbours' houses too. I wondered whether there was much that went on at this end of the street that Eric didn't know about, even if he rarely went out.

'Here you go.' He appeared in the doorway behind me with a tray in his hands, which I took off him and carefully placed on the low table at the side of the room. He seemed to have no objection to me pouring the tea even though I hadn't been allowed to help make it, and he settled himself in the recliner while I busied myself with the milk and sugar.

Once we both had a drink and were seated, he nodded out of the window.

'You see what I mean, love. I don't miss much. And I know you've been back a couple of times in the last week. Saw you talking to her ladyship the other day.' He pointed over at Jill Adams's house, and I felt my face flush. I should have realised that in an area like this someone would have been bound to notice me poking my nose in and asking questions. Perhaps I shouldn't have come into a stranger's house when nobody knew where I was, but Eric must have been in his eighties and didn't look like he meant me any harm.

'I'm sorry,' I said. 'I just want to find out what happened. I don't think the police really care.'

He sighed. 'They often don't care about folks who live round here. I've reported all sorts, but you never see anyone actually coming out to investigate. They say they'll send someone round when they can, but it never happens. Or they say it's an issue for the council, not the police. Riotous parties, bottles being smashed in the street, people screaming at each other, but no no, nothing to do with the police.' He shook his head. 'I remember the days when you'd always see a copper on the streets, and there was never any of this trouble like we get nowadays.'

'Who is it that has the parties?' I asked, wondering if there was another reason the neighbours might have disliked Nadia and Lukas, but Eric pointed over his shoulder at the house next door to his.

'Don't know how I'm supposed to sleep with that happening. Music that shakes the walls, people running up and down stairs. Happens regular like, at the weekends.'

'Do you have any family who could help you report them to the council?' I asked. 'They can install something in your house that records the noise, to prove how bad it is.'

Eric perked up a bit. 'My granddaughter comes over once a week, cleans for me and does some shopping. I could ask her.'

'You really should. It's not fair on you, having to live with that.'

He nodded thoughtfully, then pointed over at Lukas's house. 'They were never no trouble, them two, not until recently. I don't know what happened on the night of the fire, though. Must have fallen asleep in my chair, because I woke up and there was all these flashing lights and a huge fire engine outside my window.' Looking at me, a thought seemed to occur to him. 'Are they okay?'

Clearly, he didn't get all the local news. I shook my head. 'I'm sorry, but Nadia died, and Lukas is in prison.'

'In prison?' he asked, looking genuinely puzzled. 'What for? He didn't start that fire. I saw him go out.'

My ears pricked up at this: here was another eye witness to confirm that Lukas went out that night before the fire started. I made a mental note to suggest that Singh interviewed Eric, although as he'd already admitted to falling asleep in his chair I didn't think he'd be considered very reliable. I didn't know how much the police had made public yet, and Singh would kill me if I got the local rumour mill working, so I didn't answer his question.

Luckily, Eric didn't seem to notice and was still muttering to himself. 'Bollocks. It will have been all those kids who were hanging around.'

'Which kids?'

Eric jabbed a finger in the direction of the house. 'The

197

last week before that fire, there was all sorts of people coming in and out of the house at odd hours. No idea who they were, or why they were there, but I'd never seen any of them before. And there were loads of kids hanging around outside on bikes. Not a lot of kids on this street, just a couple down the other end, and it weren't any of them.' He looked at me triumphantly, as if he'd solved the crime himself.

I remembered Singh's comment about kids hanging around outside the other house that had been damaged in a fire, and I wondered if it was the same group. Were they responsible for the fires? But what did that have to do with Nadia being murdered?

I spent another hour with Eric, listening to the gossip about the people whose houses he could see from his window. He was especially vicious about Jill Adams, but, honestly, I didn't blame him.

As I left, he stood in the window to wave me off, and I returned the gesture. Turning back towards Lukas's house, I looked up at the blackened walls, and the boards that had been nailed over the windows to keep the house secure. It looked like one of the boards had been prised off. Moving closer, I pulled it back, peering into the gloom of the living room, but the lack of natural light coming in meant I couldn't see much. Just as I was about to go back to my car, I thought I heard a noise coming from inside the house. I froze, my breath catching in my throat. I was about to call out and see if anyone was there, but instinct stopped me. I'd been in too many dangerous situations in the last year or so, and I couldn't risk walking into another, certainly not alone.

After stepping away quietly, I got back in my car and went home, knowing I wouldn't be able to stop thinking about what I'd heard: it had sounded like someone crying.

Chapter 21

Anna was still out when I got back and Eric's words had got me thinking, so I spent the time sorting through my notebook again, which prompted me to go over my thoughts about Roy. The way the muscled guy had spoken to me the previous day had made me instantly suspect that Roy had killed Nadia and burned down Lukas's house as a threat, and whilst Roy himself had seemed genuinely sympathetic to Lukas's situation he could have just been covering his tracks. If Sasha was right that Lukas was innocent, I wasn't sure if Roy was as obvious a suspect as she first thought.

Adding some more bits to my notebook, I thought about what Roy could gain from Nadia's death. If Lukas had the money and was withholding it from Roy, it would make sense to threaten him, but to go so far as to murder his wife? That seemed pretty extreme. Unless Nadia had money that we didn't know about, or if she had life insurance, in which case her death could benefit Roy financially. If Lukas was convicted of Nadia's murder, however, the life insurance policy would be void, so that wouldn't do either of them any good. Then, of course, there was the matter of the thefts – was Nadia responsible, or was she framed? And I still needed to find out more about how she and Caroline got on at work. I couldn't imagine they were playing happy families.

It was too confusing, and I knew I needed to stop thinking about it for a little while if I was going to make any sense of it. I often found that if I did something different to take my mind off a case, my brain would carry on working away at it in the background.

I arrived at the Deaf club before Gem – she had a seven-year-old daughter called Petra, and I knew she would be making sure she was in bed and settled before leaving her with whoever was babysitting. The club was housed in a tiny old building near the steelworks, and provided the local Deaf community with opportunities to socialise. Some nights had organised activities, from yoga to bingo, but mostly people just met up for a drink and a chat. It wasn't busy as it was mid-week, but I glanced around to see if I knew anyone before choosing a seat.

Ten minutes later, Gem came through the door looking flustered.

Sorry, sorry, she signed. *I never seem to leave the house when I mean to.*

I laughed. *It's fine, don't worry. Do you want a drink?*

I'd deliberately driven that evening to avoid a repeat of the previous night. Red wine wasn't my friend the

201

morning after, especially with how much I'd drunk, and I'd been dealing with a fuzzy headache all day. Gem got us a lemonade each and sat down opposite me, fixing me with a searching look.

How are you?

I grimaced. *I've been better. But I'll be okay.*

Of course you will be, she replied, *but I need to work out how I can help you to get to being okay.*

I squeezed her hand briefly across the table. *Thank you, I appreciate it.*

What are friends for? I picked you up after the disaster that was Mike. You picked me up after Peter died. I can pick you up again this time.

I nodded my agreement. Sometimes I needed reminding that I had been there to support my friends as much as they'd been there for me. Peter, Gem's husband, had been killed in a car crash when she was pregnant with Petra. It had been a devastating time, but I had pulled together with a couple of her other friends to make sure we kept her going, through the rest of her pregnancy and those first few months of navigating parenting on her own. Petra had a lot of aunties whom she'd spent time with in her formative years, and we made sure Gem was able to rebuild herself and her life.

This won't be as difficult as my experience with Mike, I told her with a wry smile. *After all, I was the one who ended it.*

That doesn't mean you're not hurting, she replied. *It's a big decision to make, ending a relationship, and it's scary. I'm proud of you, though.*

Why? I asked, confused. *I thought you liked Max?*

Oh I did, I do. He's a nice guy, even if it didn't work out. No, what I mean is I'm proud of you for knowing your own mind and acting on it, even when it's hard.

I nodded, knowing what she meant. When I was with Mike, I thought about ending it so many times over the years, but I could never bring myself to do it. Partly, it was because I was scared of him, scared of what he would do, either to me or to himself. But it was also the fear that he'd planted in my mind that I wouldn't cope on my own, that I wouldn't be able to look after myself or maintain the flat by myself. Of course, now I knew that it was rubbish, and he'd spent years gaslighting me and making me doubt my own abilities, but at the time I hadn't been able to see past that. My friends had noticed what was going on though, and it was Gem and Anna who had cleared Mike's belongings out of the flat while I was in hospital, recovering from my ordeal of being locked in by Mike.

I'd seen Mike again last year and it had brought back a lot of bad memories. One thing it had shown me, though, was how much I'd changed, how much stronger I was now. I wasn't going to stay in a relationship that wasn't right for me any more, however hard it was to end it, because I knew it would only make things worse in the long run.

I explained all of this to Gem, and she let me talk for as long as I needed to. I poured out all the things that had been going round in my head all day – whether I'd made the right decision about Max, as well as my fears of being single forever and missing out on things like marriage and children.

You can have children when you're single, Gem signed with a pointed look.

I know, and I'm not knocking what you've achieved, but you know what I mean.

She nodded. *I do. But you're only thirty-one, Paige. You have plenty of time to meet someone else and settle down. There's no rush, and panicking about it is only more likely to cause you to end up with the wrong person.* I wondered if she'd always thought of Max as the wrong person for me, and what the right person would look like. An image of Singh rose unbidden in my mind and I felt a strange churning sensation in my stomach, but I tried to ignore it. Right now I couldn't work out what my feelings were for Rav; there was too much going on and my head was all over the place.

You'll get there, Gem told me with a smile. *The first few days after a break-up are always hard.*

I'm so used to texting him, I told her, nodding at where my phone sat on the table, noticeably silent. *I keep thinking of things I should tell him. I read an article this morning and automatically went to send him the link before I remembered.*

You'll get used to it soon. And maybe you'll be able to form some sort of friendship, once you're both used to it.

I grimaced. *I don't know. He was so upset yesterday. I really didn't want to hurt him; he didn't deserve it, but there wasn't an alternative.*

Give him time. Have you talked to him since then? I shook my head, and she nodded. *Good, probably best to leave it a bit longer.* She was about to sign something else when she grimaced at something over my shoulder.

I went to turn round, but she put a hand on my arm to stop me.

I groaned inwardly as I realised what, or rather who, she'd seen.

Max has just walked in, hasn't he?

She nodded. *Shall we go somewhere else?*

I thought for a moment, then shook my head. *No, we need to get used to seeing each other occasionally. It might as well start now.*

We sat for a moment, Gem carefully watching over my shoulder, me resisting the urge to turn round. I racked my brains for something to talk about, but my mind had gone blank.

I think he's coming over, she signed, her nose wrinkling to show she obviously thought it was a bad idea for me to talk to him. *Do you want me to head him off?*

No, it's fine, I told her, standing up. *If he wants to talk, I'll talk.*

Turning around, I saw Max approaching and gave him a small smile. I had no idea what sort of mood he'd be in, but I really didn't want to make a scene in the middle of the Deaf club.

Hi, he signed, his face twitching between a smile and a frown. He glanced at Gem, who took the hint and went off to chat with someone else. I sat back down at the table and Max joined me, pulling his chair out a little so he wasn't within arm's reach of me.

How are you? he asked.

I'm okay, I replied cautiously. *You?*

He nodded, then shook his head immediately after. *I don't know. I can't get my head round it at the moment.*

I called you this morning, he added, giving me a searching look.

I know, I'm sorry. I was busy with something for work. It wasn't strictly the truth, but I didn't want to explain why I'd felt the need to ignore him.

Okay. But you didn't call me back.

I sighed. *Because I didn't know why you'd called, Max. I didn't know if you wanted to have a go at me, and I wasn't in the right head space for an argument.*

He frowned. *Why would I have a go at you? I just wanted to talk.*

Okay. I'm sorry. But if you'd sent me a text I would have known why you were calling. I ran a hand over my face. *What was it you wanted to talk about?*

He looked down at the floor for a moment, clasping and unclasping his hands as he sat there. When he looked up I could see in his eyes that he was hoping for a reconciliation, and my heart sank. Even though I'd had a few moments of panic during the day, wondering if I wanted things to change, I knew I'd made the right decision.

Are you sure, Paige? he asked eventually. *Are you sure this is what you want? I understand why you're wary of us moving in together, because of what happened with Mike, and I completely respect that. If you're not ready, that's fine. Can't we just carry on as we were?*

I took a moment to decide what I wanted to say to him.

I don't think that would be fair to you, Max. I care about you, a lot, but I don't think I'll ever want that future with you. Would you really want to waste time with me, hoping I'd change my mind, and then miss out on the possibility of meeting someone else? Someone who could be the person you want to spend the rest of your life with?

He stood up abruptly, and rubbed his hands on his jeans, his mouth set in a firm line. *Okay. Fine. I just wanted to make sure.*

I started to sign *I'm sorry*, but he turned and walked away. Closing my eyes, I wondered if I could have done that any differently. Not that it mattered now.

Gem slipped back into her seat and reached over to get my attention. *Want to ditch our cars and go and get drunk?*

Before I had a chance to reply, my phone buzzed. It was a text message from Max.

You were the person I wanted to spend the rest of my life with.

I nodded at Gem. *Yes please.*

Chapter 22

What had been planned as a quiet evening out with Gem turned into a late-night drinking session. From the Deaf club we went to the nearest pub and had polished off a couple of bottles of wine before they called last orders. I wasn't finished, and Gem was following my lead, so we found another pub with a later licence, which was when we started on the shots.

By the time I half-stepped, half-fell out of the taxi outside my flat I'd had far too much to drink, but I didn't care. I couldn't handle the emotions I was feeling – blaming myself for hurting Max, but also anger with him for blaming me, confusion over my own feelings, frustration with myself for looking stupid in front of Singh when that was the last thing I wanted him to think of me – it went on and on. I'd needed something to numb me and distract from everything that was happening in my life, and for a few hours it had worked.

My phone screen seemed blurry as I checked it for messages before going inside. Anna had got in touch when I hadn't come home by eleven, but I expected she'd have been in bed ages ago. Nothing from Max, which was to be expected. I'd half hoped for something from Singh, not least because he was now the only significant man in my life, but it was probably a good job he hadn't been in touch. Drunk as I was, I couldn't trust myself not to say or do something that would embarrass us both, particularly as I was newly single and very aware of it.

Whilst we were out, Gem had tried to cheer me up by getting me to look at other men and rate their attractiveness, but I felt uncomfortable doing it. Max had come into my life by pure chance. I hadn't been looking for anyone to be with, in fact had actively sworn off dating, but he won me over with his charm and his easy-going manner. Now that was over, I couldn't see myself wanting to meet someone new any time soon. It was all too messy and painful and confusing.

Putting my phone away, I rooted in my bag for my keys. I could hear something jangling, but in my drunken haze they seemed determine to evade my searching hand. Frustrated, I put my bag down on the low wall outside the block of flats and started to take things out. I looked up at the bank of buttons that would ring the bells in each of the flats, and wondered if it was worth risking it. There were flashing lights connected to my doorbell, for Anna, but not in her bedroom, so if she was asleep it wouldn't wake her. I decided to risk it and, forgetting that I'd scattered half of the contents of my handbag along the wall, rang the doorbell to my flat.

I waited for a moment, then remembered my bag. Turning back, I caught sight of movement out of the corner of my eye, but before I could work out what it was I was slammed against the wall.

'Get off me! What the hell? Who are you?' I yelled loudly. I didn't care if I woke anyone. 'Get off me!' I shouted again, before a large, calloused hand was pressed firmly across my mouth.

I don't know if the sheer amount of alcohol I had in my bloodstream made me brave or stupid, but I kicked back against him – I was sure it was a man, with the size and strength of him. When I did, he didn't even twitch; it was like kicking a brick wall.

'Stop being so fucking stupid and listen to me.' Definitely a man. At that point it occurred to me just how much danger I could be in, and I froze. Would anyone have heard me shouting? Or was this man going to be able to do anything he wanted to me without anyone coming to my aid? My heart thundered and I felt my breath catching in my throat as I fought off the rising panic. Please just let him take my purse and my phone, I thought. Please, let him be a thief and nothing more.

'You need to learn what's good for you,' he growled. 'I've got a message to deliver.'

A message? What the hell was he talking about? I managed to control my breathing, and the roar of blood pounding in my ears subsided a little.

'Back off. Stop sticking your nose into other people's business, or you might find it gets cut off.'

I held my breath. Was this about me going to the gym

yesterday? He was certainly built like someone who spent time there.

'Who sent you?' I demanded, my drunkenness disabling my sense of self-preservation.

In response, he leant harder against me, mashing my face into the brick wall and pressing hard on my lower back. The sharp pain in my face was followed by the warmth of blood seeping out of my damaged skin. His hand crept up my side and under my arm, and I braced myself for what was coming next when the front door to the block of flats flew open.

Almost immediately I was released, and I sagged to the ground. I looked behind me but all I could see was a large figure dressed in black, running in the opposite direction. Gathering my knees to my chest, I started to shake, not even noticing that it was Anna who had opened the door.

God, what happened? she asked me, looking at my belongings scattered on the ground next to me. She put a hand to the side of my face.

Paige, you're bleeding. What happened? Who was that?

I couldn't answer; I was shaking too hard. All I wanted to do was curl up in a ball and close my eyes. A moment later, however, I pulled myself up, leant over the wall and was sick in the gutter. Anna held my hair back, then helped me up before guiding me inside and up to our flat.

She bustled around me, taking off my shoes and wrapping a blanket around my shoulders as I continued to shiver. A couple of minutes later, a cup of tea was pushed into my hands and I took a sip, then recoiled at the sweetness of it.

Mum always said you should have sweet tea when

you've had a shock, Anna said, nodding at the cup. *Did he take anything?*

I put the cup down so I could reply. *No, I don't think so.* My signing wasn't clear, with the alcohol and the shaking, but she understood.

Did he . . . do anything to you?

I shook my head. *He was threatening me. I don't know what he would have done if you hadn't come out . . .* The realisation of what had happened hit me and I burst into tears.

I'm so stupid, I told her. *This is all my fault. Everything in my life is going wrong, and it's all my own stupid fault.*

Anna sat down next to me, hugged me and let me cry for a couple of minutes, then pulled away from me.

I need to get you something for your face, she told me. *Wait here.*

A moment later she was back with the box we used as a first aid kit. She got some wet cotton wool and dabbed at my cheekbone, and it was only when a searing pain shot through me that I realised it was more than just a scratch. I got up to check it in the bathroom mirror before she could stop me: a large patch of the right side of my face was grazed, scarlet drops of blood oozing out from the dozens of thin scratches in my skin. There was going to be no way of hiding it, and I dreaded to think how much it was going to hurt when the booze wore off.

I went back through to the living room and threw myself down on the sofa, wincing as Anna tried to clean it and apply antiseptic cream.

Stop squirming. You don't want it to get infected.

She was right, so I forced myself to sit still until she'd finished.

Right, tell me what happened, she instructed.

Anna, please, can I just go to bed?

No, you need more fluid in you first, or you're going to have the mother of all hangovers. And you might as well tell me what happened first, because you're going to need to repeat it for the police report.

It hadn't even occurred to me to call the police. I was so busy blaming myself for getting involved with Lukas's case and thinking it served me right that someone had done this to me, I didn't think it was something I should report. If I reported it, though, I'd probably have to tell them what Sasha and I had been doing. Rav would be furious if he found out I'd put myself in danger. With how shit the last week of my life had been, having him mad at me too would probably be about par for the course. I knew there was no way Anna would accept me saying I wasn't going to report it, however, so I just let her comment pass without replying.

She went to the kitchen and got me a pint of water, and I obediently drank half of it before putting it down on the coffee table.

Come on, she signed, watching me carefully. *Tell me what's been going on.*

After considering for a moment how much I should tell her, I gave her a very brief summary of Lukas's case – that he'd been charged with a crime Sasha didn't think he'd committed, and that she and I had been talking to a few people to try and find any witnesses who might be able to tell the police what had really happened. I made it clear that Sasha was the one spearheading it, and that she had a lot more faith in the theory than I did.

So who was the man that attacked you? she asked.

I grimaced. *I expect he works for the guy Lukas owes money to. I spoke to him yesterday, so maybe he's warning me off.*

Is he a viable suspect? Her eyes lit up with interest, and I shook my head.

I don't know, but that's not the important thing.

Of course it is, she replied. *Come on, tell me who your suspects are and what you've got on each of them so far. I can help you organise everything. Then maybe you can figure out exactly who this guy was, for when you report him.*

No, Anna, I told her firmly. *I'm doing this to help Sasha support one of her clients. I'm not going to get you involved.*

She rolled her eyes. *It's a bit late for that, Paige. If you're going to be looking into the sorts of people who loiter outside your front door and attack you in the middle of the night, you need as much help as you can get.*

I knew she was trying to protect me just as much as fulfil her curiosity about the case, but I didn't let her argument sway me.

No. Honestly, we'll be passing it all over to the police soon anyway. We're seeing Forest about it tomorrow.

Anna was slightly appeased by the mention of the DI, but I could tell she was still annoyed with me for not including her. As she forced me to drink another glass of water, I couldn't help but wonder if we were already out of our depth, but I knew I wouldn't be able to give up on this until Sasha knew exactly what had happened to Nadia.

Two hours before the fire

Mariusz crept down the stairs with his shoes in his hand and his rucksack already on his back. His mum was in the living room watching some crap on the TV, so he hoped she wouldn't notice he'd gone. She never checked on him much these days anyway. He'd left his music playing, so she probably wouldn't even bother looking in before she went to bed.

They'd told him to meet them later, but he wanted to get out of the house already. Unchaining his bike from the fence at the side of the house, he hopped on it and rode up the road. He cycled around the streets aimlessly for a little while, not wanting to go anywhere in particular, but enjoying the freedom of being out on his own. The group of friends he'd made recently would be waiting for him soon, but he was near his dad's house and decided to go past.

As he slowed down, he saw a car parked at the end of

the road that looked familiar. There was no one inside, so he carried on past, glancing back a couple of times. He knew he'd seen that car before, and he was sure who it belonged to. What was it doing outside his dad's and Nadia's house? Mariusz didn't like it. He looped round a couple of times, but nobody returned to the car.

Checking his watch, he knew he needed to go and meet his friends soon, but he made a mental note to tell his dad about it later. In recent weeks he'd been feeling pretty defensive of his dad, and he didn't want to find out someone was taking advantage of him.

Chapter 23

Monday 22nd April

There was a dull ache in my head when I finally opened my eyes the following morning, but it was nothing compared to the burning pain in the side of my face. I took a gulp of water from the glass on my bedside table then dragged myself out of bed, squinting in the bright morning sunlight filtering through my curtains. A glance in the mirror told me there was going to be no hiding my wounds from the attack, so I'd better come up with a decent cover story. Would people believe I'd fallen and landed on my face? It was possible, I decided, especially if I took the self-deprecating route and suggested that I'd had a bit too much to drink.

Sasha and I had a busy day ahead, so I was going to have to grin and bear it. I hoped that we would only see Forest when we were in the police station, though, and not any of the other officers. She probably wouldn't even be that bothered about the mark on my face.

Sasha was surprised to find me a bit more keen to help

her than she did yesterday: far from warning me off, the events of the previous evening had spurred me on further to find out what had happened the night of the fire. After all, if we were completely missing the mark, why would someone feel the need to threaten me? No, I had obviously hit a nerve somewhere, so I needed to push and find out where.

Sasha had a couple of client meetings that morning, and she'd managed to get an appointment with Forest around lunchtime, so I was kept occupied driving to different parts of Scunthorpe and interpreting while we were there. One of them was a woman who could sometimes be aggressive, but I think she sensed something was wrong this morning and was unusually compliant. Sasha certainly didn't complain, though I could see her giving me sideways looks a couple of times. I had told her the truth about how I grazed my face, and I could tell she was wondering how I felt about being threatened by someone related to Lukas's case. She knew I'd talk about it if I wanted to, and right now I didn't.

My phone had stayed resolutely silent all night, and I found myself wishing for a message – not from Max, but from Singh. This longing to connect with him surprised me slightly, but of all the people I felt I could rely on at the moment he was the one I really wanted to talk to. Should I tell him that I'd split up with Max? But if I started down that path and found that he wasn't interested in me, then I didn't know if I could take it.

After we left the second meeting, Sasha looked at me searchingly. *Fancy going for a coffee?* she asked.

Sure, I replied, because agreeing was the easiest course

of action. We found a little coffee shop with a couple of tables outside and I ordered for the two of us, wondering what Sasha wanted to talk about.

Do you want to talk about last night? she asked me once we both had our drinks.

I shook my head, taking a sip. She nodded.

Okay then. But I'm here for you, if you need anything. I feel bad that I've put you in this position, she signed, indicating the graze on my face.

I nodded, unsure of what to say, but before I had a chance to think, Sasha had moved on.

Anyway, I've been thinking about Lukas, she began. I tried not to feel annoyed that she'd changed the subject so quickly. *I wondered if we should mention Nadia being accused of stealing when we see Forest this afternoon. Maybe it's not something they've been looking into.*

Okay. I nodded my assent. If I knew DI Forest, she wouldn't let us know much about her investigation, but it was worth a try, though I wondered why Sasha had suddenly switched her focus to the thefts. The attack the previous evening had lifted Roy to the top of my suspect list, and I didn't think much could move him off the top spot. I was surprised that Sasha didn't feel the same, but her lack of sympathy about what had happened to me kept me from saying anything about it.

Even though Lukas was Sasha's client, and I hadn't had much contact with him before this, I now felt a strong desire to help him. When I'd interpreted for him at his addiction support meetings he'd always been both polite and friendly, trying to charm me with compliments and witty stories. Now, though, he had begun to remind me of my dad, and the times when he would just let something slide because it was easier than trying to make his point understood when the communication barrier became too much.

Despite the fact that Lukas's situation was far more serious than anything my dad had experienced, there was still something about his attitude that reminded me of the way my dad had been, that resignation to being misunderstood because you couldn't communicate well enough with the other person. There was obviously something else going on, though. Even if he felt like his life wasn't worth anything without Nadia, that wasn't a good reason to go to jail for someone else's crime. He had a son, for one, and I knew he'd talked to Sasha in the past about wanting to be a good role model for Mariusz. Something wasn't right, and I realised that for the first time since Lukas was arrested I didn't completely trust Singh to get to the bottom of it, because he was limited by his unfamiliarity with the Deaf community and how Lukas could be feeling, as well as by Forest.

Right, we'd better get moving, Sasha signed, pulling me out of my thoughts. She screwed up the paper cup from her coffee and put it in the bin. *Miriam gets stroppy if I'm late.*

I smiled. Miriam was one of Sasha's favourite clients, even if she would never admit to it. They both enjoyed Sasha's regular visits, whatever either of them might say, and however much they might grumble about each other. Miriam was a model client – she always kept her appointments, called Sasha if she needed help with something but didn't monopolise her time, and was always receptive to whatever Sasha suggested. She had learning difficulties that impacted on her ability to look after herself, and she lived in an assisted living facility in the middle of Scunthorpe.

When we arrived, Miriam made a show of checking her watch, but she was clearly pleased to see us. The meeting itself was uneventful, but her cheerfulness helped to take my mind off the dull ache coming from the graze on my face, and thinking about whoever it was who had attacked me.

The time for us to leave seemed to come round quite quickly even though we had been with Miriam for over an hour, and we were crossing the lobby when Sasha's phone rang.

I need to take this, she signed, indicating that she was going to step outside for some privacy. Before I went out to my car, someone else came into the lobby, walking in the direction of the outer door, and I paused to watch her. Her uniform looked familiar, and I realised that she worked for the same care agency as Nadia.

'Excuse me?'

She stopped and turned to look at me, with a half-smile that suggested she didn't want to be rude, but she also wasn't in the mood to talk to strangers.

'I'm sorry,' I continued, 'but I just noticed your uniform. Did you know Nadia? Nadia Nowak?'

The woman's face softened and she nodded. 'I did. Horrible, what happened to her.'

'I know, I can't believe it myself,' I replied, hoping she would stay and talk to me for a moment. 'I know her husband, Lukas,' I explained, but didn't give her any

221

further information. People were often reluctant to talk to anyone connected to social services and I'd learnt my lesson from the other day with the people hanging around outside the scene of the second fire.

The woman's face darkened slightly, and I knew she'd heard that Lukas was in prison for Nadia's murder. Would she still want to talk to me?

'It's awful. They say he killed her. I can't believe it myself – they always seemed so much in love. But then you never know what's going on behind closed doors, do you?'

I shook my head and took a step closer to her, willing her not to leave before I could ask her a couple of questions. 'No, you don't. But the police will be looking into it.'

She made a noise that sounded like 'huh'.

'I heard Nadia had some trouble at work, a little while ago,' I said. 'Did they ever get to the bottom of it?'

'Oh, the thing with the thefts?' She waved a hand dismissively. 'That was nothing. It was all a misunderstanding. The old woman hadn't lost anything after all; she just didn't know where anything was.'

'That's a relief,' I replied, deciding to follow her lead in order to keep her talking. 'I didn't think she was the type of person to steal anything.'

'No, not Nadia. She was lovely, and she was always great to work with. Some of the others, they don't do their share, and if you're paired up then you know you're going to have a hard day of it while they fanny about and leave the crap jobs to you. But not Nadia – you could rely on her to work hard. I always liked working with her.'

The woman had leant back against the wall, and I could see the sadness in her eyes as she talked about Nadia.

'I'm glad she had friends at work,' I replied with a smile. 'That makes all the difference.'

She nodded, and I thought she was going to say something else, but then she closed her mouth. I wanted to push her a bit more about these theft rumours – I was sure Paul had mentioned there being more than one accusation.

'What happened about those other thefts, then?' I asked. 'It all seemed a bit strange, coming after the one where she was accused.'

A dark look crossed the woman's face, and she looked out of the door as if she was checking that nobody else was coming into the building. When she looked back at me, she leant forward slightly and kept her voice low.

'That wasn't Nadia. They weren't even proper thefts. Everything turned up eventually, after a week or two.'

I frowned. 'What do you mean, weren't proper thefts?'

'I mean nothing was actually taken. All of the people who made complaints were convinced something had gone missing, when it hadn't.'

'Really?' I tried not to sound too excited by this revelation, but it sounded like something I wanted to know.

She nodded. 'And I'm pretty sure I know who it was. But Paul, the boss, won't listen to rumours; gets really cross if we go to him with petty stories, and I can't prove it. But she looked pretty smug when the rotas all got changed. She knew it was because of these alleged thefts, and them thinking it was Nadia, although I think she really hoped Nadia was going to lose her job.'

'Who was it?' I asked, trying to sound casual.

'Caroline Nowak, Lukas's ex. He and Nadia met

through Caroline's work, and that's always pissed her off. I don't know why she suddenly decided to try and mess up Nadia's life now, but I'd swear it was her.'

I stood looking at her for a moment, before I realised my mouth was open, and swiftly shut it. She must have noticed my shock, because she nodded.

'I know, it surprised me that she'd stoop that low too, but you know what they say about a woman scorned. Lukas and Nadia got together after the two of them had split up, so I can't see that Nadia deserved any of it, but you never know how people feel in these situations. I reckon Paul had an idea it was Caroline, too, but he couldn't prove it either.'

This caught my attention; Paul hadn't mentioned anything about suspecting one of his other employees, and I wondered why he'd left that part out of his story. I was about to respond when the woman checked her watch and grimaced.

'I've got to go. Don't get much time between jobs these days.' She gave me a nod, along with a searching look, probably realising she'd just opened up to me without knowing who I was, then left.

Glancing up, I could see Sasha standing by her car watching me, so I hurried out to join her, my mind reeling. No wonder Caroline didn't want to talk to us. If her attempts to get revenge on Nadia at work hadn't been successful, how far would she have been willing to go to try again?

Chapter 24

'Absolutely not,' Forest snapped. 'This isn't an episode of *Midsomer Murders*. We're not sitting around twiddling our thumbs in the hopes that some interfering amateurs will come along and solve our cases for us.'

She glared at me, and I knew she was wishing she'd seen the back of me the last time I interpreted for a police investigation. Our appointment hadn't gone as well as I'd hoped, and Forest had not been pleased with Sasha asking for information regarding the evidence against Lukas. Sasha had tried offering her the things we'd found out about Lukas being in debt to Roy, and about Nadia being accused of theft, but that just seemed to make Forest even angrier.

Sasha refused to be cowed by the DI, however, and she stood her ground.

Lukas is innocent, and if he ends up in prison for the rest of his life that will be on you. We're bringing you some information about him that might be useful, and it's up to you what you do with it. If you choose to ignore it, that's your choice, but I won't stand by and watch one of my clients be convicted of a crime he didn't commit.

'Admirable,' Forest replied drily. 'If I decide we need your help, I will ask for it, Ms Thomas. For now, I'll respectfully ask that you leave my office.'

I could see that Sasha wanted to argue, but I could have told her it was futile; I'd had arguments with DI Forest in the past, and I knew it wasn't worth it, even when you were convinced you were the one in the right.

Forest was standing by the door, holding it open expectantly. Sasha looked at me but I gave her a quick shake of my head, so we both stood to leave. On our way out I caught a glimpse of Singh coming down the corridor and our eyes met for a brief moment, but Sasha and I were ushered out before I got a chance to say anything to him.

Once we were in the car park, Sasha leant against the side of my car and frowned at me.

That was a waste of time. Why are they so reluctant to listen to us? You'd have thought they'd want to avoid sending an innocent man to prison.

I think they do, I replied, *but I think they don't feel that we know what we're talking about. And you can understand their point of view – Lukas is in court today, so they must have built up plenty of evidence against him.*

It's not right, Sasha snapped. *I don't believe they can prove he did it.*

I don't know any more than you do, I told her, holding my hands up. *I think the only way we're going to get them to look into it further is if Lukas actually makes a statement and tells them who he thinks is responsible, and why.*

Sasha let out a hollow laugh. *Do you think that's likely? You saw him the last time we visited. How am I going to get him to make a statement now? It would be easier if he'd told me exactly what had happened, but we don't even know which parts are true. Did he and Nadia have a row, or not? Did he go out to the pub when he said he did? What about the time he came home? How did he get the bruises?* She made a frustrated noise in her throat.

I know, I signed, putting my hand on her shoulder. *We'll work something out. Right now we need to think about where we go from here, now we know that Forest has no interest in talking to us.*

I was about to continue when my phone rang. Pulling it out, I frowned and turned to look at the police station behind me. Singh's name had flashed up on the screen; why was he calling me from inside the station?

'Hello?'

'Hi,' he said, his voice low. 'I can't talk for long. Can you meet me in about half an hour?' He named a coffee shop about five minutes' walk from the police station.

'Sure. What do you want to talk about?' I asked, but by the time I'd finished the question he'd hung up. I was puzzled, but told Sasha what Singh had asked.

I have a client meeting in an hour and a half, she reminded me. *I can't cancel it – I'm catching up from last week. What do you think he wants?*

I don't know, I replied. From what he'd said when I

227

last saw him, and Forest's reaction today, I was worried he'd tell us we were wasting our time, or even worse, to back off.

If it's another telling-off from his boss, I'll be pissed off, she warned me, and I nodded my agreement. A nervous sensation churned in the pit of my stomach; I liked Rav a lot and I didn't want to find myself in a position where I'd lost his respect. Having said that, I also didn't think I could sit back while a man I believed was innocent was sent to jail.

It was nearly forty minutes later when Singh met us in the coffee shop. Sasha had been getting ready to leave, and she wasted no time in telling him that she couldn't be late for her next appointment. He looked a little put out, and I wondered if maybe he wasn't here to have a go at us.

When he looked at me, he did a double take, and his hand automatically went out to touch my face. His fingers brushed my jaw as he took a look at the large graze on my cheek, and I felt a small shiver at the gentleness of his touch. His hand was warm, and I found myself holding my breath until he slowly pulled away.

'What the hell happened?' he asked.

'It's nothing,' I said, shaking my head. 'I fell.'

'You fell,' he repeated, his tone sceptical. 'Paige, tell me the truth.'

'That is the truth. I had a bit too much to drink and I stumbled, crashed into a wall.'

He looked at me for a moment and I felt uncomfortable.

'That's what happened,' I added, and instantly regretted

228

it. The more I insisted it was true, the less honest I sounded. I knew Anna would kill me if she found out I hadn't reported the attack to the police, but there was still a part of me that felt it was my own fault for digging too far into the case.

Singh glanced at Sasha, then looked back at me, pulling me aside and lowering his voice.

'Look, if this was something to do with Max, I can help you report it and make sure he doesn't hurt you again.'

The idea of Max laying a finger on me was so ridiculous that I couldn't help but laugh, which made Singh look even more confused.

'I promise, it wasn't Max. In fact . . .' I wondered if I should tell him, but I'd already started speaking, so it seemed as good a time as any. 'Max and I broke up.'

'Oh. Well. Okay. I'm sorry.' Singh didn't seem to know what to say. He almost looked stunned, and I could see him trying to process it. Was he pleased? Or did I only recognise that emotion in his eyes because that's what I wanted to see?

Remembering why we were there, I turned back to Sasha, who was getting impatient. Singh got the hint and sat down with us, though I noticed his eyes kept straying back to my face.

'I won't keep you long, but this is important,' he told us, a look on his face that suggested what he was going to say was quite difficult for him. 'I've had a look back at the evidence we've compiled against Lukas, and I'm wondering if there's something in what you've been saying, Paige.'

I raised my eyebrows in surprise as I interpreted his words for Sasha.

'We've interviewed him twice since his arrest,' Singh continued, 'and he's still refused to cooperate. He hasn't given us any details about that night, and hasn't told us anything that suggests he's innocent.'

I knew they had to employ a different interpreter for those interviews because I was a witness, but it still stung a little.

'So do you have enough evidence, or not?' I asked.

Singh shook his head. 'In my opinion, no.'

Sasha and I looked at each other in shock.

You believe he didn't kill Nadia? she asked.

'He might have done,' Singh said quickly. 'I'm not saying that I agree with you that he's innocent. I do think there's a chance he'll be released, at least until we can find further evidence.'

'Why are you telling us this?' I asked.

'Because I think you might be right. I'm going to put together a case to ask Forest to let me look into this a bit further. His refusal to cooperate with us may or may not be a sign of his guilt. It might be that there's something else going on, and he did kill Nadia but doesn't want us to find out about another crime,' he warned us, looking between me and Sasha. I didn't know what he meant, but it echoed something Mariusz had said to us. Was there something else going on that Sasha and I didn't know about?

'And if I find something that points in that direction, I'll follow it,' Singh continued. 'My job is to find out what really happened, whether that's exonerating this man or not.'

Sasha nodded enthusiastically. *That's all we can ask.*

'Is that why you asked us to meet you here?' I asked.

He nodded. 'I don't know what Forest is going to make of this. It might be something I have to do on my own time. But if you tell me what you know, if Lukas has said anything else to you, then it could help.'

Biting her lip, Sasha shook her head. *This is what's so frustrating. He won't tell us anything. I know there's no way he could have killed Nadia, but I don't have any evidence I can show you. We've talked to a few people, so we can give you an idea of where to look, but that's all.*

'Okay. Paige, I've read your statement from the night of the fire, but is there anything else you haven't put in?'

I shrugged. 'I included how Lukas looked and behaved, but I knew I wasn't meant to speculate on what that meant so it doesn't include my opinions. But that's all.'

It took another fifteen minutes for Sasha and me to go through what we'd discussed, including my impressions of Lukas on the night Nadia had died, and the conversations I'd had with Jill Adams and Eric. We also told Singh about the accusations of theft, and the suggestion that Caroline had fabricated the whole thing. When I added this last detail, Sasha gave me a strange look – I hadn't had time to tell her about it before we went to see Forest.

'I'll have a look at the statement Jill Adams gave us the first time, and go back to speak to her, as well as Eric. I'm not sure how we missed him when we went door-to-door. If Jill lied to us the first time it could have very serious consequences, both for her and for Lukas.'

'I don't think you'll consider her to be a reliable witness,' I replied. I knew how Singh operated; I'd worked with him during two past murder investigations, and when you spent that much time with another professional you began to understand how they worked.

'Fair enough, I'll see what I think,' he said, giving me a look that told me not to get ahead of myself. I got it – he was the professional detective; I was the interpreter. Still, I was confident he'd agree with me.

'Okay, this has been really useful, thank you,' he told us once we'd finished telling him everything we knew, or thought we knew. 'For now, I think it's a good idea if you stop trying to convince DI Forest of Lukas Nowak's innocence and leave the police work to us. If you carry on, you risk jeopardising our case, which could be worse for him in the long run.' There was a warning note in his voice, and I wondered if Forest actually knew he was here with us. Was this just an attempt to get us to back off, by making us think they were looking further into it? I couldn't see Singh doing that to us, although I wouldn't have put it past DI Forest.

As we were leaving, Singh pulled me aside again.

'I mean it, Paige. If you want to talk about what happened,' he said, looking pointedly at my grazed cheek, 'then give me a call.'

I knew it didn't make any sense to keep it from him, especially now he was going to be looking further into other potential suspects and motives, but I still didn't tell him. For a start, I had no idea who had attacked me the previous night, or who might have sent them. It might not even have anything to do with Lukas, though it seemed that it was connected to him somehow. And if I was honest, I was embarrassed, because it was my own actions that brought it on myself.

'Are you okay?' he added. 'With the thing with Max, I mean?' He looked a bit shy as he asked, and I smiled.

'I'm okay,' I said with a nod. 'It's strange, but I think I'm okay.'

He nodded and smiled, then turned to leave. A moment later, he glanced back at me, then looked embarrassed when he realised I'd noticed.

Chapter 25

Sasha's meeting was with one of her deaf clients and she told me she wouldn't need me, so after we'd seen Singh we went our separate ways. On my way home, I found myself sitting in traffic for ages due to roadworks on Brigg Road. It gave me time to think, although that wasn't necessarily a positive thing at the moment.

I hadn't checked my phone much all day, not really wanting to hear from Anna, who would be checking up that I'd made the police report. I was also trying very hard not to think about Max and our chance encounter in the Deaf club yesterday. Unless I was going to start socialising in completely different places, it was inevitable that I was going to bump into him sooner or later, but I hadn't expected it to be so soon. I had hoped we both would have had a chance to get used to the situation, to our change in circumstances, before we had to face each other again.

The more I thought about Max, the more anxious I felt. I couldn't stop second-guessing myself, wondering if I'd done the right thing. The change was still too new for me to be happy with it, and I knew I was in danger of going back on what I'd said, just to find some stability again. I took a deep breath and reminded myself that even positive change could be very uncomfortable to begin with, and that I just needed to ride it out.

As I crawled through the traffic queue, I drove level with a side road, and made a split-second decision to turn off. I could find a short cut and avoid the worst of the traffic. It took me on a winding route, but it was better than sitting still for ages. One side street I turned down was parked up with cars on both sides, so there was only room for one vehicle to pass between them at a time. Seeing a car at the other end of the road, I pulled in when I saw a gap, to let them pass. As I waited for the road to be clear again, I glanced at one of the houses to my left, where I could see a lot of activity.

The house was set back a little from the pavement, with a messy front garden surrounded by a rotting wooden fence. Several people were hanging around outside the house, and I could see they were mostly teenagers, with a couple of young adults. Two of the lads were sitting on bikes, and another was on the ground, his back against the front wall. In his hand, his phone blared loud music. I assumed it was some sort of party, but then as I watched the front door opened and a man in his thirties stuck his head out and spoke to one of the lads on bikes. The boy nodded, took something from the man and slipped it into his pocket, then set off on his bike. I watched him leave, zipping down the pavement, weaving around a lamp-post then disappearing round the corner. The others at the front of the house hadn't moved from their positions.

It seemed a little strange, but I didn't really think anything of it until the teenager who was sitting on the ground stood up, brushing down his tracksuit bottoms and taking a cigarette off the boy next to him. It was Mariusz. What was he doing hanging around outside a house in a dodgy area of Scunthorpe during the day? Shouldn't he be at school? He might have taken some time off, considering what had happened to his dad and stepmum, but this probably wasn't how his school thought he was spending his time.

The other bike had now been handed over to one of the young adults, who was riding it round the front yard of the house, standing up on the pedals and yelling something at a woman who was walking past. She kept her head down and scurried past as quickly as she could, and for a moment I thought the man on the bike was going to follow her, but he obviously thought better of it and carried on doing his laps.

I glanced at the houses on either side, and the twitch of a curtain caught my eye in the house nearest to me. An elderly Asian woman in a colourful dress was watching the gang from her window – because they did appear to be a gang of some sort.

The lad who had cycled off was back, one of his mates giving him a fist bump as he skidded into the front yard. A playful shove from the youth on the other bike soon turned into a bit of posturing, and before I knew it a fight had broken out. Within seconds, the front door had been pulled open and the same man appeared. He marched in between the two throwing punches at each other and forcibly separated them, snarling something at them as he did so. They fell back, glowering at each other, but they obviously didn't dare argue with the older man.

By now I'd parked up at the side of the road, interested to see what happened next. Would I be able to get Mariusz on his own to ask him what it was he wanted to say when he came to visit Sasha the other day? With everything that had gone on with Roy, the man who'd attacked me, and my break-up with Max I'd almost forgotten about Mariusz. Would he even talk to me in front of his friends?

A man was walking up the other side of the road, glancing over at the house occasionally, until he crossed in front of my car and went up the path. His clothes were filthy, his hair straggly and unwashed, and I was glad I couldn't smell him as he went past. Rubbing his hands together nervously, he approached the front door, watched the whole time by the group out the front. A moment later, he disappeared inside the house. None of the gang moved until, about ninety seconds later, the door opened again and the man was ejected into the street. A couple of the teenagers heckled him, and he looked like he was going to go for them, but his emaciated frame would have been no match for their youth and he shied away, ducking back out onto the path and scuttling away up the street.

Making my mind up, I got out of the car, taking no chances and locking it behind me. As I approached the house, my heart was in my mouth; I told myself a group of mostly kids was no threat to me, but I knew that age had nothing to do with it. It was clear I didn't fit in in this environment, and the look one or two of them gave me was almost predatory.

'Mariusz?' I said, trying to get his attention. He didn't look up, so I cleared my throat and tried again. 'Mariusz, can I speak to you?'

When the boy didn't look up, one of his friends kicked him on the shin. 'Oi, Mac. Your mum's 'ere.' This sent a snigger around the group, but I ignored them.

Eventually, Mariusz looked up at me. The recognition in his eyes darkened almost instantly, and he looked down at the ground again. He muttered something that I didn't catch.

'I need to talk to you about your father,' I said quietly, hoping he'd respond.

He looked up again, his expression furious. 'I said, piss off. I don't want to talk to you.'

At that, a couple of his mates sidled closer to me. I could see the movement out of the corner of my eye, and I felt the atmosphere shift. It was only subtle, but I suddenly didn't feel very safe at all.

Taking a step back, I nodded, admitting defeat. 'Okay. Get in touch with Sasha if you want to talk.'

I turned around and walked back to my car, willing myself to walk slowly and not respond to the unspoken threat the boys posed. Before I got in, I heard a voice. The elderly Asian lady was standing with her door open, sheltering behind it and beckoning me over.

'They're terrible boys,' she said softly once I'd moved nearer.

Her English was heavily accented, but I knew what she was telling me.

'Are they here often?' I asked.

'No. Only two days. I called the police.'

'You've called them today?'

She shook her head. 'I call yesterday. Boys very loud, shouting at people, break a window in that house.' She pointed to the house they were gathered outside. 'Police come, speak to my neighbour, but do nothing. Boys come back.' She gave a little shrug, as if to say she had tried but there was nothing else she could do.

'Who lives there?' I asked, pointing at the house.

'An old man. Bill. His name is Bill.'

'On his own?'

She nodded. The man who came to the door wasn't old, so I was sure he wasn't the owner she'd just described. So where was Bill? I looked at the gang, who were swaggering and talking loudly, but I knew they were keeping an eye on me.

'Does he invite these people round?' I asked, unsure how an elderly man who lived alone could be connected to this group of teenagers.

The old lady shrugged, and I could see her backing away. She didn't want to be seen talking to me, so I thanked her and walked back to my car.

As I drove away I was reminded of the gang of teenagers who had been seen outside the house that had caught fire a few days after Lukas's. Could it be the same gang? And Eric, Lukas's neighbour, had told me he'd seen a lot of people coming and going from there a couple of days before Nadia died. There had to be some connection, but

I couldn't work out what it might be. What was going on in these houses? One thing I did know was that Mariusz knew something, and somehow one of us was going to have to find a way to get him to talk.

Chapter 26

I drove away from the house without looking back, half expecting a missile of some sort to land on my bonnet as I passed, but my car remained unscathed. Instead of going home I headed into town, parking at the cafe where Singh had talked to me and Sasha barely an hour earlier. I needed to think, and that seemed like a good place to do it.

After ordering myself a coffee, I chose a table in the far corner and checked my phone. As I'd expected, there were a couple of messages from Anna. I replied, reassuring her that I was okay, then pulled out my notebook. Unsure of how to link things, I started a whole new page and added everything I'd heard about a group of teenagers hanging around outside the two houses that had then been set on fire, as well as what I'd seen today. Part of me had hoped that writing it all down would suddenly make everything become clear, but I was still as confused as I had been before, if not more so. What was I missing?

My food arrived and I ate in the hope that doing something else would let my brain work on the problem, but my thoughts kept drifting back to Mariusz. When he'd come to see Sasha at work he'd seemed genuinely concerned about his dad, and he'd obviously cared about Nadia. I'd been surprised to see him hanging round with a gang like that, and whilst rudeness from a teenage boy wasn't always unusual I hadn't expected it. What had changed? What were we missing? Frustrated, I put my notebook away and pulled out my phone, knowing I needed to talk to someone who could help me make sense of everything.

'Hi, Paige, how can I help you?' Singh was straight to the point when he answered the phone. I wondered if he was too busy to speak to me.

'I can call back later if that would be better?'

'No, it's fine,' he replied, then I heard a noise that sounded like a door shutting, and suddenly his voice was clearer. I hadn't noticed the level of background noise until it had stopped; he must have stepped into another room.

'Is this about our conversation earlier?' he asked. 'Do you want to tell me what really happened?'

'No, it's nothing to do with that.' I thought it was best to be open with him, so I told him about passing the house and noticing the gang outside, including Mariusz.

'I remembered you'd said that there were kids hanging around outside the other house that caught fire, so I wondered whether Mariusz might know something about it.'

There was a pause on the end of the line, and for a moment I thought we'd been cut off.

'Where are you?' he asked.

'I'm in town, why?'

'Can you come into the station?'

'Sure, I'm only round the corner,' I told him, puzzled.

'Good, I'll see you soon, then. Ask for me when you come in, and for God's sake, don't talk to Forest.'

He hung up before I had a chance to ask him anything else.

When I got to the station I did as Singh had told me and asked for him directly. A few minutes later, a door opened and he appeared, beckoning me to follow him.

'Come on, we'll go through this way,' he said, leading me to an interview room. I sat down, and he sat opposite me, leaning forward and resting his elbows on his knees.

'The things you just told me on the phone,' he said, his face serious, 'would you be willing to give a formal statement?'

'A statement?' I frowned, confused. 'Why?'

He tapped his fingers together before replying, seeming to choose his words carefully. 'The case with Lukas Nowak has potentially been linked to another case. An ongoing investigation across a couple of different teams. It sounds like you might be able to provide us with some important information.'

'Sure, okay,' I replied. This must have been what he was alluding to earlier, and I was keen to help if I could. Singh had spent plenty of time defending me and my ideas to his superiors, so if I could help in any way I'd gladly do it. 'What do you need me to do?'

'I want you to take me through what you saw and heard today, and I want to record it. If you could tell me exactly where you were, and try to remember everything in order, that would be really helpful.'

I nodded, thinking before I began, then I took him through what I'd seen that afternoon. I tried not to add any of my own speculations, though it was difficult. Singh interrupted me a couple of times with questions.

'Are you certain the boy you saw was Mariusz Nowak?'

I nodded, then realised I needed to speak for the recording. 'Yes, it was definitely him. I've met him before, and it was clear that he knew I was speaking to him when I said his name.'

He also asked me for detailed descriptions of the people I'd seen, particularly the man who had been inside the house. I struggled with that one, and felt a sinking sensation when I saw a look of disappointment flash across his face. I desperately tried to remember more detail, but the more I forced myself the less sure I was that my memory was accurate.

'I'm sorry,' I told him, hanging my head. 'I was concentrating on Mariusz.'

He gave me a small smile. 'Don't worry, this is all really useful. Thank you.'

Singh double-checked that there was nothing else I could add before turning off the tape.

'What's this all about?' I asked him. 'Is it something to do with Lukas?'

He looked at the door, then back at me. I knew I shouldn't be asking the question, and he was well within his rights to refuse to answer me, but I also knew he trusted my judgement of Lukas.

'Paige, I think it would be a good idea if you stopped

looking into this,' he began, his voice level. 'There's more going on here than you realise.'

I took a moment before I answered, trying to make sure I didn't snap at him. 'I'm not going to do anything stupid, but I want to help Lukas. Have you even interviewed Mariusz? The guy who went into the house while I was there looked like a drug addict, and the one who was inside the house passed something to the kid who rode off on his bike. Maybe Mariusz is mixed up in something with this gang, and Lukas found out about it?' He looked like he was about to speak but I leant forward and cut him off. 'What if this gang are connected to Nadia's death, and the fire, and Lukas lied about it in order to protect his son? I can't think of anyone else that he'd be willing to go to prison for. I don't know if Mariusz had anything to do with his stepmum's murder, but maybe Lukas thinks he did.'

I sat back triumphantly, sure that Singh would be happy to talk to me about it, but to my dismay he shook his head.

'You need to stop doing this, Paige. I can't give you details about an ongoing investigation – you know that. You're not interpreting for us this time, and I can't justify talking to you about it.' His tone was firm and I knew he meant it. I felt my face colour.

'I'm just trying to help an innocent man,' I replied, louder than I had intended. 'How can you carry on with your job knowing he shouldn't be in jail? Or if you think he should, why don't you believe me?'

Singh frowned, and for a moment I thought he was angry with me but then I realised he was confused.

'Paige, Lukas has been released. One of the witnesses changed their statement earlier today, probably while I was speaking to you and Sasha, and as a result the CPS decided the evidence against him was too circumstantial to hold him.' He must have seen the delight on my face at being proved right, because he continued. 'This doesn't mean we don't think he's responsible,' he warned me. 'It means that we no longer feel we can prove our case. What we're going to be doing now is continuing our investigation, gathering more evidence, and then we'll arrest the person we believe is responsible. That might still be Lukas.'

I didn't know what to think. I was elated that Lukas had been released, and that the police investigation would be looking at all the angles I'd been considering, but I was also aware of the look on Singh's face. Something had changed since our earlier chat, and now he wasn't convinced that Lukas was innocent; I'd been wrong about him trusting my judgement. That hurt, but I tried not to let it show.

'Where can I find Lukas?' I asked. 'His house isn't habitable right now.'

'A friend came to collect him. I don't know who, and don't bother trying to ask another officer because we can't give out that sort of information.' He sat back and looked at me. 'It's good that you're doing your best to fight for what you think is right, but can't you find yourself a different cause?' He laughed, but it was with exasperation rather than humour. 'I like you, Paige, but you're your own worst enemy.'

I opened my mouth to reply, then shut it again. I thought of the notebook in my bag, and the people I'd been speaking to. With a slight shiver, I remembered the bulky man waiting outside my flat, shoving me roughly against a wall and threatening me. My pride would take me too far one day, and perhaps I should listen to Singh for once. After all, he did have my best interests at heart.

He glanced at the door again. 'Look, I need to be getting back, but I just need to ask. Are you okay? You seem really on edge about this, more so than I would have expected from you.'

Swallowing hard, I nodded. 'I'm fine. Honestly.'

'Is Anna okay?'

'She's fine, yeah. Loves her new job, and it's been good for her.'

'Good.' He looked down at his hands. 'You haven't had any problems from your ex again, have you? Mike, I mean,' he added, obviously remembering that Max was now my ex, too.

I smiled at his efforts to hide his concern. 'No, nothing like that. I . . .' I let my voice tail off. I'd been about to tell him what had happened with Max, but then thought better of it. It wasn't the time or the place.

Tilting his head on one side, he gave me a quizzical look, but when he realised I wasn't going to continue he smiled and stood up.

'Okay, I've got some criminals to catch,' he said lightly, holding the door open for me.

I was still burning with curiosity about the gang Mariusz had been hanging around with, and whether they were linked to Nadia's death, but he'd made it clear that he wouldn't be telling me anything else. Saying goodbye, I went back to my car and called Sasha straight away. She

247

picked up, and I could see from the background that she was still at the office.

Paige? What's wrong?

I'll get straight to the point – do you know that Lukas has been released?

A look of confusion turned to a look of delight. *No, I didn't know. Sometimes it takes a while for that sort of information to filter through to us. Oh, I'm so pleased for him. How did you know? Have you seen him?*

I shook my head. *I've just been speaking to Singh again.* I gave her a brief explanation of seeing Mariusz with the gang of lads, and I could see her thinking as she took it all in.

That does seem very strange. I wonder if it's his way of acting out following Nadia's death? I know they had a good relationship. Well, I'll see if I can get hold of Lukas and see him tomorrow, check up on him. Did they say where he's staying?

No, a friend came to pick him up, they said, I told her. *That's all I know.*

Okay, I'll see what I can find out. Thanks for letting me know.

Sasha? I asked. *If you go to see him tomorrow, do you mind if I come too?*

She nodded to show she understood. *Of course. I'll call you once I've got hold of him.*

I thanked her and we both hung up. I knew that Singh had told me to back off, but all I was going to do was see that Lukas was okay. After that, I'd leave it to the police, I told myself, though I wasn't very convincing.

Ninety minutes before the fire

Lukas rounded the corner on his way to the pub, when he saw someone crossing the road towards him. He looked over his shoulder to check there was nobody around who he recognised.

What are you doing here? he asked the woman as she came close to him, slipping her arm through his.

I wanted to see you, she replied, leaning up to kiss him. He shied away, checking around him again.

Not here.

She looked annoyed but he didn't care. He wasn't going to risk Nadia finding out about them, especially when they'd just had a conversation about starting a family. Anyway, this was just a fling, nothing serious.

There was a small alleyway ahead of them on the left, so he pulled her in there, out of sight of the road and the curtain-twitching of the local residents. Just because he didn't know anyone who lived on that street didn't mean it couldn't get back to Nadia.

She reached up to kiss him again and this time he didn't resist her, enjoying the sensation of her body pressed against his for a few moments. Why did he do this? He loved Nadia with all his heart, and he desperately tried to be faithful, but he couldn't resist women. Women, of all shapes and sizes, skin colours and ages, were beautiful creatures, and he wanted to please them. When a woman showed interest in him, he knew he should tell them no, he was married, but they were so enticing.

This has to stop, he told her, once he'd pulled away. *I can't do this any more.*

Don't you want this? she asked, pouting.

I want you, but I love my wife. I want to be faithful to her.

With a frown, she stepped back. *What do you mean?*

I mean what I said. It has to stop. I can't see you any more.

He saw her eyes narrow and wondered if he'd made a mistake. She had the power to make his life incredibly difficult if he made her mad.

Where has this come from? You didn't seem to object to being with me just a few days ago, she said. He flushed as he remembered that afternoon, hot and sweaty in her bed. She'd had more energy than he had expected and he could barely keep up.

The memory made his resolve waver, and she could see it in his eyes. With a smirk, she stepped closer again and pressed her lips to his neck, her hand reaching for his belt buckle. Before she could slip her hand inside his jeans, however, he grabbed her by the wrist and shook his head.

No.

What's wrong? Too risky for you? Her grin told him that she didn't care.

No, I meant what I said, he told her. *I love my wife. I can't see you any more.*

Her anger was quick to spark, and she slapped him across the face.

Fuck you, then.

He pressed a hand to his stinging cheek as he watched her march away, turning back to sign to him.

You're going to regret this.

Chapter 27

Tuesday 23rd April

Sasha had texted me the address to meet her and Lukas at the following morning, in an area of Scunthorpe I hadn't been to very often. I used Google maps to navigate my way there, passing Silica Country Park and turning off into an area that any respectable estate agent would describe as 'set in woodland'. Trees lined the streets, providing privacy to the large houses that were well spaced out along my route.

I turned into a cul-de-sac and found the right number, quietly impressed at the imposing gateposts at the end of the drive. The gate itself was wrought iron – fancy enough to suggest that the homeowner could afford nice things, and strong enough to serve a purpose. It swung open as I approached, and I drove a little way towards the house before parking my car behind Sasha's. The drive itself swept round a neatly tended front lawn, which had a silver birch in the far corner, and had space for at least half a dozen cars. The tree must have been at least twenty metres tall and the top branches were swaying constantly in the breeze.

Sasha was getting out of her car as I parked, and together we looked up at the house. Judging by the number of windows, and the length of the house, it must have had at least six bedrooms and a large amount of living space on the ground floor. I took a couple of steps to the side and peered round the back, but there was another gate and a couple of trees blocking my view.

Whose house is this? I asked Sasha, feeling seriously envious. When she'd messaged me the night before, she hadn't told me which friend Lukas was staying with. For a moment I had a heart-stopping thought – what if it was Roy Chapman? If it was Roy who sent the man to threaten me the other night, I had no idea how he'd react if I walked into his house, or what the repercussions might be. I looked to Sasha for confirmation, but I needn't have worried.

Paul Ilford, Nadia's boss, Sasha told me. *Apparently he's the friend who collected Lukas yesterday, and he's letting him stay here with him for a while.*

I raised my eyebrows. Clearly owning a care agency was a lucrative business, if this was the house he lived in. Of course, a house this size in a big city would be worth a lot more than it was in Scunthorpe, but I estimated it was still worth more than half a million.

We rang the bell and waited. Behind us, I heard the gate clang shut, then a moment later the door opened. Paul smiled at us, but he looked tired.

'Morning, thank you for coming,' he told us. 'Lukas is just getting dressed. We stayed up quite late last night.'

How is he? Sasha asked. I expected she wanted to hear someone else's assessment of him before she saw Lukas himself.

Paul grimaced. He talked as we went through a wide hallway into the enormous dine-in kitchen that seemed to run the full length of the back of the house. 'He's been better. There's a lot going on – he's grieving for Nadia, of course, but he's also dealing with his emotions around being arrested.'

He indicated some stools at the breakfast bar where we could sit, and offered us tea or coffee. The kitchen was immaculate, with gleaming surfaces and smooth finishes to the units. I imagined he didn't have children, to keep it that clean; I found it hard enough with only two adults living in my flat. The dining area had patio doors leading out to a beautifully landscaped garden, and I could see a long extension that ran down the side of the garden. The way the light was reflected onto the part of the interior wall I could see made me realise this was an indoor swimming pool.

'He's had a tough time of it.' I knew Paul could sign, but as I was there I interpreted his words for Sasha and he seemed grateful. I wondered how much sleep he'd managed to get.

'Has Lukas said anything about what happened to Nadia?' I asked.

Paul shook his head. 'I asked him a couple of times, but he just said he didn't want to talk about it. I didn't want to push him.'

Sasha patted him on the arm. *Don't worry, you've been a good friend to him. Is he going to stay with you for now?*

'I've given him a choice,' Paul said, busying himself with the kettle. 'He can stay here, or if he'd rather have some privacy, I still have my mum's old house. I'd be happy to let him kip down there for a while, at least until the council can get him something. I haven't got around to putting it on the market yet,' he added with a shrug. I remembered Paul saying that Nadia had been his mother's carer, and I wondered if he thought Lukas might like to be somewhere he could feel close to her. Perhaps Paul was still grieving for his mother and couldn't bring himself to sell the house yet, so this gave him a good excuse to delay the sale further.

There was a creak from upstairs and I heard footsteps in the hall, then a moment later Lukas appeared in the doorway. He was dressed in jeans and a shirt that were clearly a size or two too big for him, and I realised they must be Paul's – Lukas had lost all his belongings in the fire as well as his wife. His skin looked grey and he had the gaunt look of someone who has lost weight quickly due to stress or illness. When he saw Sasha, he attempted a smile, but it didn't reach his eyes.

Good morning, he signed, his gaze flicking back and forth between the two of us. *Sorry, I overslept.*

Hi, Lukas. Sasha stood and put a hand out towards his shoulder, but he flinched away so she pulled back. *I'm so glad you're here.* I knew what she meant was 'I'm glad you were released', but she obviously didn't want to mention the police or prison at the moment.

How are you feeling? she continued.

Lukas glanced over to where Paul was pouring coffee and took a cup, sitting down opposite me and taking a sip before replying.

I am very tired. I have nightmares.

Sasha and I looked at each other, and I could see my surprise mirrored on her face. Even though Lukas had been released, I had expected it to take more effort to get him to open up to us.

Sasha gave Lukas a sympathetic smile. *That's understandable. If you want me to help you arrange some counselling, I can do that.*

Lukas shrugged.

You don't have to make a decision straight away. Even if you want to see someone in a month, or six months, I can help you with that.

Lukas sniffed, and glanced over at Paul. I could smell stale alcohol on him, and I wondered if Sasha had noticed it as well. I wouldn't have been at all surprised if the first thing he did as soon as he was released was drown his sorrows, especially with his history with alcohol, but I knew it was something Sasha would need to be watchful for.

For a few minutes, Sasha talked to Lukas about the situation he was in now – how it was important for him to stay away from anyone who might cause trouble, as the police would be watching him, and his options for housing. Lukas didn't respond the whole time, which made me worry he was going to clam up completely again. Paul had walked off to make a phone call, so I sat and looked out of the back window at the huge garden, in the hope that Sasha could get something out of him on her own. I really wanted to jump in there and ask Lukas what he'd meant when he talked to me in the hospital, and said he knew who had done it. Would he tell me with Sasha here, or would I have to try and get him on his own? I knew I couldn't push it, because Lukas would probably be feeling pretty vulnerable straight after being released from prison, but I was anxious to find out what he'd been thinking that night.

Turning back to see if Sasha had got anywhere with him, I saw Lukas shift in his seat and begin to sign, so I moved closer in the hope that I could join the conversation.

There is something I need to show you, Lukas signed, pulling out his phone. He scrolled through, then held it out to Sasha. She frowned, then passed it over to me. It was a text message.

That's your only warning.

I felt cold just reading it, and looked back at Sasha.

When did you get this? she asked him.

On the night Nadia died, he replied, hanging his head in despair. *Someone killed her as a warning to me.*

Why didn't you tell the police about this? Lukas, this is evidence you didn't do it.

I wasn't as convinced as Sasha that it automatically proved his innocence, but I didn't say anything. It certainly looked like Lukas was right, and that someone was trying to get to him.

Sasha started to ask him more questions, but I could see that Lukas was ready to shut down again. I put a hand on her arm to get her to slow down, and she took the hint.

Okay, Lukas, I just need to know one thing, she said. *Do you know who sent it?*

He shook his head, then turned to look out of the window. I could see tears in his eyes, and his hands were trembling. I didn't know if I believed him, but I knew we couldn't push him right now.

I need you to help me with something. Lukas turned back to Sasha suddenly, keen to change the subject. *Caroline. She says I cannot see Mariusz. That I am a bad influence.*

What does Mariusz say? Sasha asked. *He's old enough now that his opinion needs to be taken into account.*

Lukas shrugged. *She won't let me talk to him. Told him not to answer my calls.*

I wondered if Mariusz was ignoring his dad for another reason, and I watched Lukas for signs that he might be lying.

Has Mariusz been in any trouble himself recently? I asked. Sasha shot me a sideways look, but I thought it was a good time to try and find out how much Lukas knew.

Trouble? Lukas frowned at me. *What sort of trouble? He is a good boy; he's not getting into trouble.*

I paused before I replied, wondering how best to word it, and how much to tell him. *I've seen him hanging out with a gang of older lads, some of them adults, outside a house in Scunthorpe. During the day, when he should be at school. Does he do things like that a lot?*

At this, Lukas's eyes widened and I thought I saw a trace of panic in his eyes.

Why are you watching my boy? He hasn't done anything.

Sasha put out a hand to calm him down. *Nobody has been watching Mariusz; Paige just happened to drive past and see him. She was worried about him, with you being held by the police and not being there to support him.*

Lukas hung his head. *I am a bad father, not looking*

after my son properly. I should have been there for him.
He looked up at me, determination in his eyes. *I will speak
to him, ask him about missing school. We'll have a chat,
father and son. If there is something he needs help with,
I will help him.*

I glanced over at Sasha, but I couldn't read her expression. I didn't want to upset Lukas, but equally I wanted
to ask some of the questions that I'd been turning over
in my mind. Knowing I might not get another chance, I
went for it.

*Lukas, someone told me that there were a lot of people
hanging around outside your house for the couple of days
before the fire,* I began, deciding it was better to refer to
the fire rather than Nadia's murder. *Who were they?*

He shifted on his stool, avoiding eye contact with either
of us. *I don't know. We have friends round sometimes.
Maybe that was who.*

The person I spoke to said they were mostly kids, teenagers. He looked uncomfortable but I pushed on. *I
wondered if it might have been the gang that Mariusz is
hanging around with?*

He shrugged. *I don't know who he hangs around with.
I don't meet all my son's friends. Maybe some of them
came by, but he was at Caroline's house that week. If they
came to look for Mariusz, he wouldn't have been there.*
He looked away again, and I could tell there was something he was keeping back from us.

Did you know there was another fire? I asked. Lukas's
eyebrows went up, and I saw genuine surprise.

Where? he asked.

A house near yours, just a couple of streets away.

Witnesses said there had been a group of kids hanging around outside that house, too. I paused and waited for Lukas's reaction. I had half expected him to act puzzled, or perhaps get angry with me, but when he leant forward and grabbed my hand I could see fear in his eyes.

You must stop, he told me firmly. *Stop this. Please. This has nothing to do with Mariusz.*

Lukas, if this gang of his had something to do with the fire at your house, you need to tell the police.

No! He jumped up off his stool and came round the breakfast bar towards us, and I shied away from him. *I will not tell the police. There is nothing to tell.*

He looked towards Sasha, his expression imploring now. *Please. You must stop.*

Sasha looked at me, then back at Lukas, and she nodded. *Paige, I think it's time we left Lukas to rest, now.*

Yes. Go, he signed, looking at me, and now I could see the anger starting to build. I wanted to explain that I was only trying to find out the truth, to protect him and his family, but I knew it would only add fuel to the flames of his anger. Knowing when I was beaten, I nodded.

You're right. I'm sorry.

Lukas looked slightly appeased, but stood with his arms folded until we left the room. There was no sign of Paul, so we showed ourselves out.

I'm going to go and see Caroline, Sasha told me once we were outside, with her back to the house so Lukas wouldn't be able to see if he was looking out of a window. *I'll see if I can sort out some mediation between her and Lukas, at least as far as Mariusz is concerned. Are you happy to come with me and interpret?*

Of course, I told her. *Maybe she'll know something about this gang.*

I went to get into my car, but Sasha put out a hand to stop me.

Paige, I understand you want to help, but you can't do this. I can't let you upset my clients, when you're talking about something that goes beyond the scope of my role. Okay? Let me talk to Caroline. Don't get yourself involved.

I felt my face flush, and I nodded, feeling suitably chastised. I wanted to defend myself – couldn't she see I was only trying to help him? Why had Sasha suddenly changed her tune now that Lukas had been released? Maybe she didn't realise that there was still a good chance he'd be arrested again, and all the police were doing was buying time to gather more evidence. Whatever happened, I was determined that Lukas Nowak wouldn't go to jail for a crime he didn't commit.

Chapter 28

Caroline was wearing her work uniform when she opened the door to us. She sighed deeply.

'What do you two want?'

We want to talk to you about Lukas and Mariusz, Sasha told her. I interpreted for Caroline and she rolled her eyes at me.

'I understand well enough,' she snapped at me, then turned to Sasha, signing as she spoke. 'I have nothing to talk about. I'll talk to Lukas if I need to, though I'd rather not.'

Sasha looked at her for a moment, and something obviously wavered in Caroline's resolve, because she let out a loud huffing sound and stepped back into the hall, leaving the door wide open.

'Fine, come in. But you won't change my mind about anything.'

We followed her into a small living room that was neat

but cluttered. A large TV dominated the wall opposite the sofa, and there were clothes piled up on the armchair that stood to the side. The coffee table in the centre was scattered with remotes and a couple of games console handsets, as well as a pile of magazines and a couple of schoolbooks.

'I keep telling him he needs to keep all his school stuff together,' Caroline muttered as she neatened a few things. 'It ends up all over the house, then when he needs it he can't find it.'

'I did the same thing when I was a teenager,' I told her, hoping to lighten the mood, but she just shot me a dark look, as if to say nobody had asked me.

Caroline nodded to the sofa, and Sasha and I both sat down. She didn't offer us a drink – I imagined she didn't want to encourage us to stay any longer than was necessary.

'You've seen him, then?' she asked, and I knew she must mean Lukas. 'I can't believe they let him out,' she added, with a shake of her head. 'What if he does it again?'

The police don't have enough evidence to hold Lukas, Sasha said. *He's innocent until proven guilty.*

Caroline let out a harsh laugh. 'That's bollocks and you know it. They'll arrest him again soon enough, I bet.'

In her anger, Caroline had stopped signing so I took over interpreting, which was probably a good thing because it prevented me from jumping in myself. Sasha was right, I needed to leave it to her – if I'd been there on my own it would be different, but I didn't want to damage her professional reputation just to satisfy my own curiosity.

Is that why you don't want him to see Mariusz? Sasha asked. *Because you think Lukas killed Nadia?*

Caroline looked at Sasha as if she was stupid. 'Obviously. The police wouldn't have arrested him in the first place if they weren't pretty fucking certain he'd killed her, would they? I don't care what they say – they had to let him out on some technicality, not because he didn't do it. It's a good job I don't know where he's staying, or I would have gone round there and told him what I think of him.' She sat down on the arm of the chair, a disgusted look on her face. 'And to think I let Mariusz go round there every other week. It's a bloody good job he was here with me when it happened, or God knows what Lukas would have done to him.'

Sasha wore a frown of concern as she took in Caroline's words. *Do you think that Lukas has the potential to harm Mariusz?*

'He's a murderer,' Caroline snapped. 'He's got the potential to harm anyone. If he'd do that to his wife, of course he'd do it to his son.' She shook her head and grimaced. 'He was a pretty useless husband, but I always thought he was good with Mariusz, even though it's a nightmare trying to get money out of him. I can't believe I trusted him for so long.'

She folded her arms and gave us a defiant look, and I wondered if she was waiting for us to try and convince her of Lukas's innocence.

'Is Mariusz here?' I asked.

'No, he's at school,' she replied, this time looking at me as if I were the stupid one.

How does he feel about not seeing his father? Sasha asked. *Have you talked to him about it?*

Caroline shook her head. 'I told him last night that his

264

dad was out, but that he shouldn't talk to him, that he's dangerous. When I said that, he stormed out, and when he came back a few hours later he didn't speak to me, just went straight to bed.' She gave a sharp shrug. 'Teenage boys, they're not great at communication. He'll do what I tell him, though.'

Don't you think you should give him the opportunity to talk about how he feels? Sasha suggested. *He's sixteen, old enough to be involved in these sorts of discussions.*

'That boy thinks the sun shines out of his dad's arsehole, so no, I don't think he should be involved. He's not mature enough to think sensibly about it.'

I understand your reservations, Sasha began, but Caroline didn't give her a chance to finish, speaking over me as I interpreted Sasha's words.

'Do you? You've obviously come here to try and persuade me to let Lukas see Mariusz, so it's clear you don't care about whether or not he's guilty.' She stood up again and started pacing the room in front of us. It felt strange to still be sitting down, as if she was trying to unbalance us, but Sasha stayed calm so I followed her lead.

'When we were together, Lukas was volatile,' Caroline was saying. 'I never knew what mood he was going to be in, how much he would have been drinking, or how he was going to behave.' She stopped pacing for a moment and seemed to be thinking deeply about something before shaking herself and turning back to us. 'I don't doubt that he was exactly the same with Nadia. Maybe she pushed him a little bit too far one day, and he snapped. I don't know. All I know is that it didn't surprise me when he was arrested for her murder.'

I thought his drinking started after you split up, Sasha signed, her eyebrows drawn together in confusion. I'd thought the same, and that was always the reasoning he gave at his addiction support meetings too.

Caroline gave a hollow laugh. 'Oh, that was his excuse: poor Lukas, everything fell apart for him when we split up. No, he's always been a drinker. It's the social side, for him. He loved it, being down the pub, making friends, flirting. He could always charm women, even when they didn't know a single bit of sign language.' She sighed deeply and I wondered if she was remembering when he'd first charmed her.

Was he ever violent when he wasn't drinking? Sasha asked.

'When was he ever not drinking?' Caroline asked, a sour twist to her face. 'I don't think I ever saw him sober. Even when we were first dating, we went to the pub all the time.' She glared at Sasha. 'Are you going to try and tell me that suddenly he was a completely different person once he was sober? Because I don't believe that bullshit for a minute.'

Sasha raised her hands slightly in a gesture of defeat to show she wasn't going to try and convince Caroline of anything.

'He wasn't sober, anyway. I know he tried to make out that he'd changed, that his relationship with alcohol was completely different. He says he can go to the pub for a couple of pints now and that's it, he can stop there. I don't believe a damn word of it. He's an alcoholic and he'll always be an alcoholic.'

What did he do to you? Sasha asked gently. *Was he physically abusive?*

'Well . . . not as such, no, but I knew he had the potential to be,' Caroline replied defensively. 'He always stopped short of raising a hand to me, but that doesn't mean he didn't hurt Nadia. She wasn't as tough as I am,' she said with a sneer. 'I imagine she pandered to him more than I did, but if she refused to stand up to him it might have just made him more angry.'

It was at this point that I realised Caroline was talking herself round in circles. I wasn't sure if she wanted to believe that Lukas had killed Nadia or not, but she obviously thought Nadia wasn't as good for Lukas as she'd been. Had Caroline been jealous of their relationship? Was that why she'd tried to frame Nadia for theft?

'Did you get on well with Nadia?' I asked. 'The two of you worked together, didn't you?'

She gave me a sideways look, obviously wondering where I was going with this. 'We worked for the same company, but we didn't actually spend much time together. Paul's not that stupid – he wouldn't stick us together on the rota if he could avoid it.'

'So you didn't have a good relationship, then?'

Caroline let out a bitter laugh. 'The woman my husband left me for? No, I didn't like her much, surprisingly.'

We were told you'd already separated when Lukas and Nadia met, Sasha interjected.

'Whoever told you that doesn't know shit. He'd met Nadia plenty of times before we split up, and I bet he was shagging her before they let people know they were together. He's always had a hard time with being faithful, has Lukas.' She shot Sasha a pointed look that I couldn't interpret.

Did you resent Nadia? Sasha asked, her expression blank.

'Resent her? No, she was welcome to him,' Caroline spat, though she wasn't very convincing.

'So why did you frame her for those thefts?' I asked quietly, hoping such a brazen question would take her by surprise. Caroline gaped at me for a moment. I could feel Sasha's annoyed gaze on me but I didn't make eye contact with her. I knew she didn't want me to get involved in this conversation, but I wanted to confront Caroline with this and see how she reacted for myself.

'I don't know who you've been talking to, but your information isn't correct,' she said through gritted teeth. There was a long pause, then Caroline began walking up and down again, appearing to be deep in thought. She glanced at me but I refused to give in, giving her a hard stare that made her turn away again. It was clear she was wrestling with something internally, before she stopped and turned back to us, her arms folded defensively.

'Okay, maybe a couple of the old dears occasionally fretted about things going missing, when really they were just in another room, or they were thinking about trinkets they'd thrown out years ago. And maybe I might have wound a couple of them up to think that Nadia might have pinched them. But it was just a bit of fun, something for me to take out my irritation at her.' She looked up and glanced between me and Sasha. 'It was nothing. Paul only changed the rotas to show he'd done something.'

I didn't think we were going to get anything else out of her about the thefts. Was she telling the truth? Was it just a malicious prank? Or had she been hoping for a more serious outcome, and taken matters into her own hands when Nadia hadn't been punished?

Caroline was still pacing when Sasha changed the subject.

How has Mariusz reacted to his father being arrested?

Caroline put her hands on her hips and stopped pacing to glare at Sasha. 'How do you think he's reacted? He's angry. Teenage boys are angry at the world anyway, but now he's got something substantial to be angry about.'

Was he angry with his father, or angry with the police?

'I don't think he's even sure himself,' she replied sadly, and her shoulders drooped all of a sudden. 'I don't see him much at the moment. Between my work shifts and him going out with his mates, we're barely in the house at the same time. I only know he's been here because the fridge has been emptied.'

The change in Caroline's body language made me realise that here was our chance to get her to open up further. The fight seemed to have gone out of her, so I hoped she might be more cooperative now. I looked over at Sasha and she gave a quick nod, granting me permission to ask a couple of questions.

'Do you know the friends he's going out with in the evenings?' I asked.

She shrugged. 'Just lads from his school, I think. Why?'

'I saw him the other day, with a group of older lads. It was during the day, when he should have been at school.'

She shook her head. 'He hasn't skipped school, they would have told me. It must have been someone else.'

I was surprised that Mariusz's school hadn't picked up on the fact that he was absent, but it was always possible he'd forged an appointment letter or something like that. Or, was Caroline lying to cover up what Mariusz had been doing? Either way, this time I decided not to push it.

To my surprise, Sasha didn't change the subject. *He wouldn't be the first teenage boy to act out following such a major upheaval in his life,* she pointed out.

Caroline's face reddened. 'Are you suggesting I don't know what my boy's up to?'

You told us yourself that you barely see him.

'Yeah, because I'm working stupid shifts every goddamn day. How else am I supposed to put food on the table, if I don't go out to work? You bloody social workers think we should all be magic, in two places at once – I'm a single parent and I'm working my arse off to provide for my son. My alternative would be to claim benefits and sit around with my feet up, but you'd frown on that too, wouldn't you?'

Caroline, I'm not blaming you, Sasha replied gently, and I tried to put the same feeling into my tone of voice as I interpreted. *You're right, Lukas asked if I could help him, because he really wants to see Mariusz. I'm not going to try and force you, or him, to do anything you don't want to do. I came here to ask if you'd consider it, and if the answer is no then I can suggest mediation.*

'Ha!' Caroline let out a brittle laugh. 'No way am I wasting my time with mediation. If he wants to see Mariusz he can bloody well take me to court. See what they say about the suitability of a father who's been arrested for murder.' She folded her arms and glared at us. I could see we weren't going to get any further, and Sasha obviously

270

agreed, because she thanked Caroline for speaking to us and stood up to leave.

Caroline shut the door firmly behind us, and Sasha and I walked away from the house. We were both taking a minute to process everything Caroline had told us, about Lukas's behaviour and how she'd framed Nadia.

That answered some questions, but I don't know if we're any closer to the truth, Sasha signed to me when we reached her car.

I nodded and was about to reply when I heard Caroline calling my name. Turning around, I saw she was holding something out to me, and my heart dropped into my boots.

'You dropped this,' she said, her expression stony. It was my notebook, where I'd written everything we'd found out, everyone we'd spoken to and all our suspicions. Had she had time to read any of it before she came out to hand it back to me? I hoped not, but the way her gaze bored into me I suspected I was out of luck.

I thanked her, took my notebook and walked back to my car, expecting her to say something else, but she remained silent, staring at the pair of us for a moment before she slammed the front door again. Sasha said goodbye to me and set off, but I sat in my car for a couple of minutes, thinking. Nobody wanted to listen to me about Mariusz and this gang – Singh had told me to back off, Lukas didn't believe his boy could ever get mixed up in any trouble, and Caroline clearly had her head in the sand. Even Sasha didn't seem interested now that Lukas had been released. I wanted to find out what the boy had been up to, and what the group he was hanging around with were involved in. If I could find some way of linking them

271

back to Lukas and Nadia, then perhaps I could get Mariusz off the hook.

An idea came to me. It was reckless, I knew that, but it would hopefully answer some of my questions. Looking at the street around me, I worked out a plan.

Chapter 29

It was dark by the time I returned to Caroline's street that night. I parked a couple of minutes' walk away, because she would easily recognise my car if I left it outside her house. I'd worn dark clothes, but nothing to suggest I was trying not to be seen – I thought that would make me look more suspicious.

It was too mild an evening for a hat or scarf, but I had a dark jacket that zipped up to my chin, dark blue jeans and black shoes. I'd left my mousy brown hair hanging loose rather than tying it back, in the hope it could hide my face from some angles.

The front window glowed blue with the light of the television, but that was the only light coming from their house. I didn't want to go too close, in case Caroline or Mariusz saw me and confronted me, but I wanted to know who was in. Caroline's car was parked outside, so I assumed she was there, but there was no way of knowing if her son was at home or if I was too late and I'd already missed him. The only thing I could do was wait.

Most of the houses along the road had their curtains shut, but I still didn't feel comfortable sitting in one place and watching the house. You never knew which of the neighbours was a curtain-twitcher, and the last thing I needed was a police car pulling up and asking what I was doing there. Rav had got me out of a few scrapes in the last year or so, but I knew he wouldn't do it this time, not after he'd warned me himself to stop digging.

I walked slowly up the road, keeping an eye on Caroline's house for as long as I could before it became uncomfortable to crane my head round, then kept walking for a short distance, before pausing, checking my phone then walking back the other way. I did this a couple of times, but I knew it wasn't sustainable, so I cast around for something else to do while I waited. For a few minutes, I stood at the end of the road, making a pretend phone call, until I ran out of things to say to myself, then I began my slow walk back up the road again.

When I reached the end of the road, I saw a small shop just round the corner. Glancing back over my shoulder, I didn't see anyone coming up the road, so thought I could chance it. I ducked my head in, browsed the magazines for a moment, bought myself a chocolate bar and a drink then turned to leave. As I did, I saw someone pass the window, and I hurried out onto the street – the figure was about the same height as me, slight, and wearing a dark hoodie with a design I recognised from the other day. It was Mariusz.

Berating myself for nearly missing him, I followed him

along the road. He'd had a head start, so I was far enough behind him that he wouldn't notice me. I only hoped he wasn't going to catch a bus or something like that, because there was no way I could stand at a bus stop next to him without him recognising me. For now, though, we kept on walking.

I assumed he was off to meet the gang he'd been hanging around with yesterday, which was precisely why I was following him. I needed to know who they were and what they were doing. They had to be connected to the fires, but I couldn't quite make it all add up in my head. Nobody had been hurt in the second fire, so I wasn't convinced they were responsible for Nadia's murder, but I wanted to learn more and understand what they were doing.

It was Tuesday night, when I thought most teenagers should be at home doing their homework, but that didn't seem to be a priority for Mariusz. I followed him along a couple of residential streets, until we came out on Frodingham Road. It was busier than some of the other roads, with numerous takeaways and off-licences still open at this time and doing decent business, by the looks of things.

To my dismay, Mariusz suddenly stopped and went into a kebab shop. I couldn't follow him in there without being noticed, so I would have to hang around outside and hope he wasn't in there for long. There were a couple of tables inside by the window, but I doubted many customers stayed and ate their food there. Then there was the issue of which way he would walk once he left the kebab shop – if he came back the same way then he'd walk right into me. To be safe, I crossed the road and lingered outside an empty unit. I could watch the kebab shop from there, then follow Mariusz when he came out, without risking him seeing me.

As I stood there I wondered if I was doing the right thing. If I was caught following one of Sasha's clients' children around Scunthorpe after dark there would be a lot of questions asked. Maybe I should have told Sasha what I was planning to do, but I knew she'd tell me I was being ridiculous, though before Lukas was released she would have probably encouraged me to do it.

I was mulling over this when Mariusz left the kebab shop, and I was left with a split-second decision about what to do. As I was already there, I realised it was stupid to give up now and I might as well carry on, but if things looked like they were going to get risky I wouldn't hesitate to duck out and go home. My desire to find out what was going on only stretched so far.

A little way down the road, Mariusz turned off and I followed him. The streets became quieter as we moved back into a residential area from the main road, so I kept my distance again to avoid him noticing me. He stopped outside a house, its windows dark, so I stopped too. I didn't get any closer to him, but crossed the road to give me a better view of the house.

Mariusz walked up and down the pavement outside the house a couple of times, then turned round to see if anyone was watching him. There was a van parked on the pavement near where I was standing, so I ducked behind it. When I peered out again a couple of seconds later, Mariusz had vaulted over the gate and was slipping down the side of the house.

I don't know what I'd been expecting, but a silent house wasn't it. Were his friends round the back? There was no evidence from the front of the house that anyone was in, and the curtains were open, so light from a back room would have been visible from the road. No, the house looked completely empty. My heart sank. Was Mariusz breaking in? If so, where did that leave me? Should I call the police and report it, then have to explain what I was doing here in the first place, or should I pretend I'd never been here?

Ducking behind the van again, I thought about my options. If he was committing a crime, I knew I needed to call the police, but I didn't want to give them my name. The obvious answer was to do it anonymously, but I didn't know where I'd find a phone that couldn't be easily traced back to me. Public payphones weren't exactly common in Scunthorpe, and I wasn't sure how to call 999 and block my number.

I was debating with myself over what to do when I saw a movement out of the corner of my eye. Mariusz was on the move again. I hadn't noticed him come from round the back of the house, because I'd been expecting him to be there for longer. He didn't have a bag with him, and there was no noticeable bulge in his pockets, so it didn't look like he'd stolen something. Had he met someone there? Was it something to do with drugs? I left my hiding place behind the van and followed him in the direction of the main road again.

As I walked, I realised we weren't far from Lukas's house. The two fires and now this – whatever it was – were all within walking distance of one another, and I wondered if it was a territory thing. I didn't claim to be an expert on drug gangs, but from what I knew they tended to only work in certain areas to avoid stepping on each other's toes. Part of me wanted to believe I was being ridiculous, that Mariusz had just been hanging out with a group of friends and had nothing to do with drugs, but what other explanation was there for the strange interactions yesterday between the lads outside, the man inside, and the people visiting the house? The lad who'd ridden off on the bike had been carrying a package given to him by the man inside, so the most obvious answer was that he was acting as a courier.

Five minutes later, Mariusz had stopped outside another house. This one wasn't dark – the curtains were closed, but a glow from an upstairs window showed a light was on in one of the bedrooms. It was a terrace, with a small passageway leading round the back, which was shared with the neighbouring house. Mariusz looked like he was about to head round there when the gate belonging to the next house opened and a man came out, shortly followed by a Staffordshire bull terrier on a chain.

I jumped out of the way as Mariusz ran straight past me, but he paid me no attention as he pelted away from the house. By the time I'd caught up with what was happening, he was at the end of the street and I only just glimpsed which way he turned. I set off after him, walking quickly because I was afraid running would attract attention, but by the time I reached the end of the road there was no sign of him.

'Shit,' I muttered to myself as I turned into the next street. There was a scattering of alleyways Mariusz could have ducked into, as well as a couple of other roads that met this one. I walked to the next crossroads and looked up and down in both directions, wondering where he could have gone.

As I looked, I realised that the road to my left was where I'd seen Mariusz the previous day. I had well and truly lost him now, so I thought my best bet was to go in that direction, in case he was meeting someone at the same house. I wanted to see with my own eyes what they were up to, so I had something concrete to prove my theory, and then tell Singh about. The street was empty and eerily quiet. A dog barking made me jump and I thought I saw someone watching me out of a window, but when I looked again whoever it was had gone. I told myself that as soon as I'd checked out this house I would go back to my car and go home – I'd had enough of this.

The house was near the end of the street, so I put my head down and hurried up, not looking to either side as I walked, in case I attracted someone's attention. As I got closer to the house, I couldn't see anyone hanging around outside it, nor could I see any lights coming from inside. In fact, where the front window had been yesterday, there was now a sheet of plywood boarding it up. Puzzled, I stopped by the lamp-post next to the house. The front door was still in place, but in the orange glow I could see the white paint had bubbled and was covered in a layer of black soot. There was more soot around the window upstairs, which was also boarded up, and the yard in front of the house was piled with damaged furniture and covered in filthy boot prints.

I stepped back so I could get a better view of the house.

This confirmed everything I'd suspected, and I was starting to think Sasha and I were in over our heads. Another fire, at a house linked to a gang hanging around outside. But what did the fires have to do with Nadia's death?

To my right, a group of people rounded the corner so I quickly turned and walked away. I didn't want anyone to see me outside that house. Picking up the pace, I kept walking with my head down, hoping I wouldn't draw any attention to myself that way. Keeping my attention focused in front of me meant I didn't notice someone approaching me from behind until it was too late. Something hit me in the middle of my back and I fell, cracking my head on the pavement. The pain was like a small explosion, overwhelming me with agony until everything went black.

Chapter 30

When I came round, I wasn't alone. I could hear voices but couldn't make sense of what they were saying, and when I opened my eyes I could see some people hovering over me.

'You all right, love?' one of them asked me, and I blinked a few times before he came into focus. He was a middle-aged bloke, wearing a branded polo shirt – he worked for the chippy over the road, and must have seen me lying on the ground.

'Someone knocked into her,' another voice said. 'They ran off up that way.'

I tried to open my mouth to ask which way she meant, but I couldn't quite coordinate myself.

'Should I call an ambulance?' the woman asked.

'Nah, give her a minute,' the man replied. 'She might just be pissed.'

Gee, thanks, I thought, but then I remembered the state

I'd been in when I got home from my night out with Gem on Sunday, and thought I probably didn't have the right to be offended.

Taking a few deep breaths of the cool night air, I pushed myself up to sitting, holding my head as it throbbed. The man was crouching down next to me, but the woman was standing up. I couldn't bring myself to tilt my head back to look at her, thinking I might be sick if I tried it.

'My car,' I muttered. 'My car's not far away.' While following Mariusz I'd doubled back on myself and I was only a couple of streets away from where I'd parked. I patted my pockets, finding my phone, but no keys. I groaned.

'Don't think you're in any fit state to drive, love,' the man said with a chuckle. 'Think you'll need a few coffees first!'

'Not drunk,' I told him. 'I hit my head.'

He frowned and looked at me, peering at my head in the darkness. 'Yeah, you do have a bit of an egg on your temple there. Maybe we should call an ambulance.'

'No, I'll call someone,' I told him. 'Can you help me up?'

It took a minute or two, but I eventually managed to get to my feet with assistance and a lot of nausea. The woman was still watching – she looked to be around the same age as me, and she was shifting nervously from one foot to the other.

'I told him someone pushed you over, but he wouldn't listen to me,' she said. 'I think they stopped to check on you before they ran off, though.'

'I think they stole my car keys,' I replied, after another search of my pockets turned up empty. The pair of them had a look around where I'd landed on the pavement, but there was no sign of my keys. Shit. Who had taken them? Did they know which car was mine? Had they been following me, while I was following Mariusz? Or had Mariusz spotted me and looped around to get behind me?

'I'd better go and see if it's where I left it,' I told the two people who were helping me. I was feeling steadier on my feet now, so I thanked them for their help and turned up the road where Caroline lived. At least the mugger had left me my phone, so I could call someone for help, although I had no idea who to call – Anna was the obvious choice, but I didn't want to completely freak her out. I'd lied to her when I went out, telling her I had an evening interpreting job. Sasha, maybe? Though then I would have to explain what I'd been doing.

To my utter shock, my car was still sitting where I'd left it, in the road adjacent to Caroline's. As I approached, I could see that the door was open, and the interior light was on. My bag had been upended on the passenger seat, and whoever it was had rifled through the glove compartment and the pockets in the doors, too. Instantly, I knew what was missing. Strangely, the mugger had also dropped my keys on the front seat. Had they been hoping it would be stolen before I came back to it, to cover up their crime? I sighed and pulled my phone out, knowing who I needed to call.

Singh arrived in just under fifteen minutes, parking behind my car and jumping out.

'How are you doing?' he asked straight away, taking me by the elbow and leading me to his car. He opened the passenger door and made me sit down so he could look at the bump on my head. I'd sat on the pavement while I was waiting for him, knowing I shouldn't touch my car but not wanting to leave it, and I was glad of somewhere comfy to sit down now.

'I feel a bit sick,' I confessed. His face was very close to mine as he examined my head, then looked back at me. I felt a swooping sensation in my stomach, then everything went a bit blurry and I leant back in the seat, waiting for the head rush to pass.

'I'm taking you to the hospital,' Singh said, standing up and folding his arms. 'No arguments.'

'Wait. Look at my car, first.' On the phone I had just told him I'd been mugged and needed his help. To his credit, he didn't ask what I'd been doing there, although I knew he was just filing the question away to ask later.

'Right, I'll get someone to come down here and secure your car. We can fingerprint it, see if we can get anything that way. Is anything missing?'

I nodded sheepishly. 'I'd been writing down things about the case in a notebook. It was in the pocket in the driver's side door, but I think it's gone.'

Singh rolled his eyes at me, but didn't say anything, just pulled out his phone and requested for someone to meet us there. Once he'd done that, he pulled out a small torch and shone it in my eyes.

'Hey, what are you doing that for?' I pulled away, blinking, then clutched my head after the sharp movement made it throb again.

'Checking to see if you've got concussion,' he said.

'I'm fine, honestly. Just take me home, please.'

'No,' he said firmly. 'You might not have any regard

for your own welfare, but I do.' Something in his tone flooded me with a warm sensation and set my head spinning again.

As he looked me over, he gently took one of my hands in his to reassure me. Before I knew what I was doing, I leant in and kissed him.

For a split second it was perfect; the touch of his lips on mine was warm and gentle, sending a little spark of electricity through me. But then he pulled away and shook his head, giving a little nervous laugh.

'Oh God, I'm sorry,' I said, sitting back and drawing my hands into my lap away from him. 'I don't know what I . . . I just . . .' I didn't know how to finish the sentence.

'It's okay,' he said quietly. 'You've had a bump on the head.' He said this with a little self-deprecating smile, and I wanted to tell him that didn't mean anything, but I was too embarrassed. He'd pulled away, so it obviously wasn't something he wanted.

'Come on, we need to get you checked over.'

I could tell there was no arguing with him, so I sat quietly while we waited for someone to arrive. When a police car pulled up a few minutes later, Singh had a quick chat with the PC who was there to have a look at my car. Once that was out of the way, Singh got in the driving seat.

'Right, hospital next,' he said, and I didn't protest. I was grateful to him for picking me up and still helping me even after I'd kissed him, and started to say so, but a wave of tiredness washed over me. Leaning my head back, I was tempted to let it take me, but Singh shouted my name a couple of times.

'What?'

'Paige, I need you to try and stay awake until we get to the hospital, okay?'

'Okay,' I mumbled, though I couldn't see why it mattered.

We were only a couple of minutes away from Scunthorpe General, and once we were there he parked as close as he could get to A&E without blocking an ambulance bay.

'Come on, let's get you inside,' he said, reaching into the car to help me out.

'I'm fine,' I told him, just before my legs gave way.

'Yeah, I can see that,' he said sarcastically. 'Come on.' He pulled my arm across his shoulders and helped me inside, propping me up on a chair as he got me booked in. I don't know if it was because I had a head injury, or because he was a police officer, but within a few minutes I was taken through and helped up onto a bed in a small bay. I was reminded of when I'd been here only a week ago, with Lukas, and I felt like bursting into tears.

'I'm sorry,' I said to Singh, my voice shaking. 'Thank you for helping me.'

'Hey, it's okay,' he said, giving me a hug as I started to cry. 'You know I'll always help you, Paige.'

The doctor appeared then, so Singh sat down and let her get on with examining me. After a while, she decided it was safest to keep me in for the night under observation, then I could have tests in the morning if they thought it was necessary, much to my distress.

'I don't want to stay here,' I told Singh when the doctor had gone to arrange for me to be transferred to a ward. 'Can you get them to send me home?'

'No way. If the doctor thinks you need to stay in, then you need to stay in.'

'I have to call Anna,' I said, looking around for my phone.

'I've already texted her,' he told me. 'She's worried about you, but I told her you'd call when you felt up to it.'

I looked at him in surprise. 'You have my sister's number?'

He nodded. 'She texted me when we last worked together, don't you remember?'

I was still surprised that he'd saved her number, but I didn't question it.

'Will you come up to the ward with me?' I asked, suddenly not wanting to be left alone. I knew I was pushing it, especially after he'd pulled away from my kiss earlier, but I still wanted him there. Tentatively, I reached for his hand, needing the reassurance and comfort of having him there with me. He gave my hand a gentle squeeze and didn't let go.

'Of course, but then you'll need to get some sleep.'

It was another hour until the bed was arranged, and Singh pushed me up there in a wheelchair. I insisted I could walk, but the doctor wouldn't let me even attempt it, pointing out that if I passed out on the floor and hit my head again it would take me even longer to get discharged. Keeping my mouth shut, I let myself be wheeled into the lift and along to a ward, then into a side room.

I was surprised not to be in a communal bay, but maybe Singh's presence had made them find me a private room. Whatever the reason, I was grateful to have the room to myself. Once I was settled, he looked at me. I felt my face flush, wondering if he was going to mention the kiss, or if he was going to ignore it.

'Are you going to tell me what you were doing there?' His voice was gentle, but there was a firmness to it, and I knew he wasn't going to be happy with the answer, but I told him anyway. I thought he would be annoyed with me, but his reaction went well beyond what I was expecting.

'Are you serious?' He took a step back and ran a hand through his hair. 'Paige, what the hell did you think you were doing?'

'I wanted to see what Mariusz was up to with this gang of his.' I was too tired to defend myself properly.

'When I told you it was probably connected to an ongoing investigation, didn't you consider that maybe you should have just left it well alone?' His voice was rising, and I felt my breath catch in my throat. I'd never seen him this angry before, and what made it worse was that it was directed at me and I knew I deserved it.

'You have absolutely no idea the sort of danger you've put yourself in, have you?' he snapped at me. 'Every time our paths cross, you do something dangerous, but this is the worst. Do you get that? You're dealing with something you don't understand. I'm trying to keep you safe!'

'Well, if you told me what the hell was going on, maybe I would understand,' I replied, but he just shook his head and made a sort of frustrated growling noise.

'You're not a police officer, I don't have to tell you anything.' He shook his head and turned away from me. 'I wish you could understand . . .' He tailed off.

'Understand what? What are you not telling me?'

288

He rubbed his face and turned round, but then the door opened and a nurse came in.

'What's going on in here?' She had a face like thunder, and I was glad she was glaring at Singh and not me. 'Are you the police officer who escorted her here?' she asked, looking him up and down.

'I am,' he snapped. 'And I'm leaving.'

'I should think so too.' She stood back, holding the door open for him, and he stormed out without looking back at me. I pressed my head into the pillow, trying to stop myself from bursting into tears. The nurse fussed around me, checking my blood pressure and my pupils, but she soon left me in peace. When the door shut behind me, I wondered for a moment where everything had gone wrong. Within an hour I'd gone from kissing him to him shouting at me and storming out, and what was worse was that I knew it was all my own fault. I hadn't intended to kiss him – it had just sort of happened – but it had felt right. I didn't regret it, but now I might have ruined everything anyway. The tears came then, before the fatigue washed over me and I fell asleep.

One hour before the fire

Lukas was still feeling out of sorts by the time he arrived in the pub. He ordered himself his usual pint and a whisky, then went to sit at the end of the bar, where he could see everyone else and try to get an idea of the conversations that were happening.

His pint disappeared pretty quickly, and he ordered a second. He used to have problems with alcohol, and he knew Sasha and Nadia would both have a go at him if they knew how much he liked to have at the pub some nights, but it wasn't a problem. He could handle it.

Over the next hour he got through a third pint, nodded to a few people and watched others come and go. The regulars he was friendly with had all picked up a bit of sign language over the last couple of years, and between that and basic gestures they managed to have a conversation with him. He was starting to think he'd go home to Nadia, continue their conversation about starting a family,

290

when Roy walked in. Lukas's eyes narrowed when he saw him.

Roy came in and worked the room as he usually did, shaking hands and making jokes with the other regulars, flirting with the girl who was serving, despite the fact that she was easily young enough to be his daughter. If he wanted to sit and have a serious conversation with Roy he'd do best to wait until he'd finished his ritual and was ready to sit down with a drink. It meant he had to wait about fifteen minutes, but he could be patient.

Lukas, Roy declared, smacking him on the shoulder as he sat down next to him. *How are you?*

Roy wasn't as good a signer as he thought he was, but Lukas had to give him credit for his efforts. Of course, recently he'd come to realise that Roy had only put the effort in because he felt it could benefit him somehow. They'd built up a friendship over several years of sitting at the bar together, but the dynamic had changed ever since Lukas had accepted Roy's offer of a loan. He should have known at the time that it was a bad idea, that he should have gone to the bank instead, but he thought they might turn him down. Now he was racking up a huge amount of interest every day, interest Roy had somehow never thought to mention before the money was in Lukas's possession, and there was no clear way that he'd ever be able to repay it.

I'm okay, Lukas replied, wary of Roy's intentions. There was a gleam in his eye tonight that Lukas didn't like.

Good. And what about that lovely wife of yours? Has she been working hard?

Lukas noticed a smirk on Roy's face. *What's that supposed to mean?*

Roy let out an unpleasant laugh. *Oh, you know. Nadia is obviously very interested in helping you pay back your debt. It's . . .* Roy paused for a moment and switched to fingerspelling the next word: *admirable. But I wouldn't let my woman go around doing what she's doing, just to earn some money. I wouldn't feel like a man if she had to do that.*

Do what? What do you mean? Lukas had no idea what Roy was talking about, but he got a sinking sensation in the pit of his stomach as he thought about what he might mean.

Where were you this afternoon? Roy asked, his face a picture of innocence.

I was at work. Why?

Maybe you should ask your wife why she felt the need to dress herself up like a tart after she'd finished work.

Lukas thought about the nice dress Nadia had been wearing when he'd got home, then looked at the smug expression on Roy's face. Oh no, she wouldn't. Would she? He felt a sickening mixture of horror and anger at the idea. How could he have let it get to the stage where Nadia felt that was their only option? He knew things had been difficult recently, especially with the disruption in their home, but he hadn't expected her to be that desperate to change things.

Getting to his feet so quickly that he knocked over his stool, Lukas jabbed a finger towards Roy's face.

Don't you dare say a word about my wife!

Roy laughed again, and Lukas saw red, throwing a punch before he even stopped to think. A moment later, two other men were pulling him off. They dragged him over to the door and threw him out onto the street. Seething, Lukas kicked the wall a couple of times. Should he wait outside for Roy to emerge and then finish what he'd started? Even through his rage, Lukas knew that wasn't a good idea. Roy ran a gym, and he had plenty of strong blokes who would help him out, so Lukas wouldn't stand a chance.

Letting out a roar of fury and frustration, Lukas turned away from the pub, intending to head home. Before he got very far, however, he felt a hand on his shoulder and he was spun around, a punch landing in his gut before he could even see his attacker. He fell to the ground and automatically curled up, arms covering his head as kicks and blows rained down on him.

As soon as the attack had started, it ended, and Lukas found himself lying on the pavement panting, alone. It was a warning, he realised. If they'd wanted to put him in the hospital, or even to kill him, they wouldn't have found it difficult.

Hauling himself to his feet, he winced as a pain shot through his ribs. He would go home and talk to Nadia and find out what had really happened before he did anything else. But then, Roy Chapman would pay.

Chapter 31

Wednesday 24th April

I spent a strange night in the hospital. In the wall opposite my bed was a pane of glass covered in an opaque film; presumably it used to be a window, and then the ward was rearranged. There was another private room on the other side, and I could see the glow of the other patient's bedside lamp through the glass, and a shadow crossing it whenever they moved around the room.

I slept fitfully, dreaming about being chased by faceless men on bikes, and Singh telling me I had to set the hospital on fire to save Lukas. Twice during the night, nurses came to check my blood pressure and other vitals, which didn't help. I was relieved when I heard the trolley of tea and coffee coming round, because I felt like it was an acceptable time to give up on the idea of sleeping and attempt to get out of bed.

The moment visiting hours began, Anna was shown into my room and threw her arms around me. Little more than a year ago our positions had been reversed, when

Anna had been the one in hospital with a head injury, and the significance of this wasn't lost on me. Thankfully, I was in nowhere near as serious a condition as she'd been, but that probably didn't make a difference to how much she had been worrying about me. I could see tears in her eyes as she pulled away from me, and I spent several minutes reassuring her that I was okay, and I'd only been kept in as a precaution.

What the hell happened? she asked, sinking down into the chair next to my bed.

I frowned. *I thought Singh explained everything to you yesterday?*

She rolled her eyes. *He only gave me the basics, said that it was better if you told me. What were you doing? Was it just a random mugging, or was it something else? I know you and Sasha have been digging into this case.*

Groaning, I laid my head back on my pillow. I really didn't want to have to go through everything again, but I knew Anna wouldn't let me relax until I answered her questions. I took her through what had happened, ignoring her every time she tried to interrupt, much to her annoyance.

I need to call Sasha, I told Anna once I'd finished my story. *She'll be expecting me in work today.* She had brought me a bag of things, including my phone charger, which I plugged in next to my bed.

I can do that, she told me, snatching my phone from the bedside table and scrolling through to get Sasha's number. I was going to protest, but I realised I might as well let Anna do this for me, so that she could feel like she'd helped. While she called Sasha, I dragged myself to the bathroom, my head throbbing as soon as I stood up. She had also brought me a change of clothes and a towel, so I stepped into the shower in the hope that hot water would help to relieve some aches and pains, but the pathetic trickle I managed to conjure up was only lukewarm.

Better? Anna asked me when I emerged from the bathroom.

I nodded, then winced at the movement. *Yes, a little bit.*

Have you seen a doctor yet today? she asked, helping me back over to the bed.

Not yet. The nurse said they'd probably be round late morning. Then they'll decide if I need any scans. I scowled at the thought of having to stay in hospital any longer. I understood why Singh had brought me to A&E instead of taking me home like I'd asked, but I was still annoyed about it.

The thought of Singh gave me a hollow feeling in the pit of my stomach. I'd never seen him as angry as he was last night, and the fact that it had been levelled at me made me feel sick. The one thing I didn't tell Anna about was my stupid, impulsive moment where I had kissed Singh. I hoped that hadn't contributed to his anger. I still felt absolutely mortified about it, and I was worried he would avoid me from now on. There was also a big hard lump of disappointment in my throat when I thought about it – I was realising more and more that I had feelings for Singh and the rejection hurt. I knew it had been the wrong time and place, but it had felt so right, and I was sure I hadn't imagined him kissing me back for a moment before he pulled away.

But then, I'd had a bump on the head, so maybe it was

just wishful thinking. The last thing I needed right now was to fall out with him, after everything I'd been through recently. Should I call him and apologise? Or would he still be too angry to speak to me?

Anna was watching me intently, and I wondered if she had an idea of what I was thinking.

Is Rav coming back to see you today? she asked, and I could see in her eyes that there were dozens of other questions she wanted to ask, but I just shook my head.

No. I left it at that, despite the disappointment on her face. *What did Sasha say?* I asked, trying to move the conversation away from Singh.

She gave me a look, telling me she knew I was changing the subject and would be asking her questions soon enough. *Well, obviously, she was very worried about you and wanted to make sure you're okay. She said she'd come down to visit you.*

She doesn't need to, I replied, but Anna made a gesture to show it was out of her hands now. I could call Sasha myself and tell her not to come, but it might be a good opportunity to tell her what I had seen Mariusz doing, and that my notebook had been taken from my car. I'd left out that last detail when I told Anna what had happened, just saying that my car had been rifled. I was starting to panic about the information in there and who might have got their hands on it. Someone must have realised that Sasha and I were getting close to the truth and wanted to find out how much we knew. But which of the potential suspects could have taken it?

Where were you last night? I asked Anna, trying to steer the conversation away from me and why someone mugged me and ransacked my car. *You've been out a lot recently.*

Her face coloured slightly, and I thought she was going to avoid answering, but then a small smile crept across her face.

I was on a date, she told me.

Ooh, tell me more, I replied, shifting slightly on the bed so I could see her better.

He's called Jonathan. She went on to describe his looks and personality, the few dates they'd been on and her excitement at meeting someone, and I was thrilled to see genuine happiness lighting her up from the inside.

So what does he do? How did you meet?

At this question, she looked at the floor, embarrassed.

What? I asked. *Oh God, he's not your student, is he?*

No! Nothing like that. He's . . . well, actually, he's an interpreter.

I slotted a couple of pieces of the puzzle together in my mind. *He's been your interpreter for your support group, hasn't he? That's why you don't want to go any more, because you can't date him while he's interpreting for you.*

Anna blushed a deep scarlet and I laughed, which made her laugh too.

You know you can just request a different interpreter?

She shrugged. *I know, but I meant what I said the other day. I don't feel like I'm getting anything from the group now. And Jon is so supportive. He's been there with me for every session, and it got to the stage where I felt like I was talking to him about everything, not the rest of the group. Does that make sense?*

I nodded. *I think so. Well, as long as you're happy.*

I am, I really am.

I smiled, but still felt a little pang of jealousy that she'd found happiness just as I'd thrown my own love life under the bus.

Do you want me to call Max? Anna asked gently, correctly interpreting the look on my face.

No. I don't want to confuse things. It would have been nice to have someone there for me the way that Singh was last night, and I knew if I hadn't broken up with him, Max would have been pacing the corridor until he was allowed in to see me, but the fact remained that we weren't together any more. If Anna called him, it would muddy the waters.

He would want to know that you're in hospital, she persisted. *I know you've broken up, but he still cares about you.*

I know, but I don't want to call him. I'll be home soon, anyway. I looked up at the clock on the wall. *Don't you need to go to work?*

Yeah, probably, she replied. *I moved my tutorials this morning, but I need to go into the department. Are you sure you're going to be okay?*

I was about to reassure her when the door opened and Sasha walked in. She and Anna greeted each other, then my sister said her goodbyes as Sasha settled herself in the chair by my bed.

Tell me everything, she said. *And I mean everything.*

I could see her trying to keep her annoyance from showing as I told her about my plan to follow Mariusz, but once I explained his behaviour around the two houses I'd seen him looking at, her interest took precedence.

So whoever mugged you knew exactly what they were looking for, she signed. *I'm surprised your DS Singh didn't give you some police protection.*

He's not my anything, I told her, earning a pair of raised eyebrows from Sasha. *I'm fine. I don't need protecting. If they'd wanted to hurt me more they could have done. They wanted that notebook, and now they've got it.*

But why would someone want it?

To see how much we know, I suppose. Someone must be worried that we're getting close to the truth. I'd been thinking about this while I'd lain awake in the early hours of the morning, but I couldn't pinpoint exactly what might have made someone scared enough to attack me. If we'd found out something that someone didn't want us to know about, neither Sasha nor I had made the connection yet.

How much can you remember of what was in the notebook?

I screwed up my face and looked up at the ceiling, then shook my head. *I don't know. I think I can remember all of it, but I'm not completely confident.*

Tell me as much as you can remember, then, she said.

For the next fifteen minutes we went over what we'd talked about over the last week, including the conversations we'd had with people like Lukas's neighbour, Jill Adams, and Caroline.

What are we missing? she asked, giving me a searching look, as if I was keeping something from her. *Why did someone want that notebook so badly?*

I don't know, I told her. *I honestly don't. Someone must have thought there was something in it that would*

300

incriminate them, or they wouldn't have gone to all that trouble to get it.

Could it have been Mariusz? she asked.

I don't think so. I was following him and he ran past me before it happened. I don't see how he could have crept up behind me. As I told her this, something niggled at the back of my mind, but I couldn't work out what it was. Had I seen someone, and now I couldn't remember? Did I get a glimpse of the person rifling through my pockets for my keys before I lost consciousness?

What do you think he was doing? Sasha was now sitting forward in the chair, her brows knitted in thought.

Who, Mariusz? I have no idea. I was worried at first that he was breaking into those houses, but I couldn't see any evidence that he'd taken anything, unless whatever it was was so small it fitted in the pocket of his jeans.

Mariusz doesn't strike me as the kind of kid who'd be breaking into houses, she said, shaking her head. *Could it be something to do with Lukas, and Nadia's death?*

I don't see how, I replied.

Can you remember where the houses were?

I made a note of the addresses on my phone last night when I couldn't sleep, I told her, pulling up the document and emailing it to her. *Do you think they could be significant?*

Well, there must be some connection between them if Mariusz was at both houses last night. I'll have a look for the addresses on our databases, see if anything pops up. I had a message from Lukas this morning, she continued. *He's moved into Paul's mum's old house. I think he wanted some privacy, after everything that's happened, but I am worried about him being on his own.*

Where is the house? I asked, thinking it was important that we kept an eye on where he was. She pulled out her phone and brought the address up on the screen, showing it to me. I paused for a moment; I knew exactly where that road was. It was in the same area as Lukas's house, and the two other houses that had had fires.

Nice for him that he's back in the same area, I said, but Sasha looked sceptical.

Quite a few people round there know him, and think that he killed Nadia, she pointed out. *I don't think they'll be too happy to see him back. And of course now there's been another fire,* she said. *I don't want him to be blamed for that too. There's obviously some connection between the gang hanging around outside these houses and the fires. But if they're setting the fires, why are they doing it? And what does it have to do with Nadia?*

Maybe you should ask Lukas, I pointed out. *He obviously knows more than he's telling us.*

Why do you say that? she snapped.

Because he kept avoiding our questions about who had been hanging around outside his house. I wasn't going to let Sasha keep protecting Lukas when I knew there was more he could tell us. *If he told us everything he knew, maybe we could make sense of this. If he'd actually spoken to the police to defend himself, they might be a lot further on.*

Sasha bristled at this. *I thought you understood, Paige? I thought you knew what it was like for someone like Lukas to find himself in that position, badgered by the police until he was too scared to say anything in his own defence? Taken advantage of because of the communication barrier?*

I hadn't seen any evidence of the police treating him like that, but I didn't say as much. Sasha obviously had her own reasons for being so defensive, and I wondered if she also knew more than she was telling me.

She shook her head. *I think maybe you need to rest. Let me know if you'll be back at work on Monday or if you need more time off.*

With that she stood up and walked out of the room, leaving me confused. What had I said? What was she hiding from me?

Chapter 32

'Well, Paige, I think you've been quite lucky,' the doctor told me as she looked at my notes. 'I don't think we need a CT scan. The nurse will give you a leaflet with your discharge letter about the warning signs to look out for following concussion, but you're fine to go home.'

I breathed a sigh of relief, before wondering how I was going to get home. My car was still parked a few streets away, but I didn't have any keys, having left mine with Singh so he could lock it after they'd taken fingerprints. I needed my car, so I was going to have to swallow my pride.

Hi, where can I pick up my keys?

I sent the message quickly before I could overthink what to say and change my mind. I was worried he'd be too annoyed with me to answer, but I got a quick response.

Are you still in the hospital?

Yes.

Stay there.

I sat on my bed and waited. A nurse had come to tell me it could be a couple of hours before I was officially discharged, so I had nothing else to do until then.

About half an hour later I heard a conversation outside my room, recognising one of the voices as Singh's. I felt a flutter of nerves – how was he going to be with me after everything that happened yesterday? Maybe he was just dropping my keys off with a nurse so he didn't have to see me. I bit my lip and waited.

There was a knock on the door and I opened it to see Singh looking a bit rumpled.

'They really don't like anyone coming onto the ward outside of visiting hours, do they? I had to point out that I'm a detective and you were the victim of a mugging before they'd even consider letting me in.'

'I'm sorry,' I blurted out, stepping back to let him into the room.

'It's not your fault – they're just strict about visiting times,' he replied with a smile.

I blinked, then realised he was trying to make a joke and had known exactly what I was talking about. Relieved that he was the one to break the tension between us, I returned his smile. Moving past me, he reached into his pocket and handed me my keys.

'Have you been discharged?'

'Not yet, but it shouldn't be long,' I said, gesturing at the door to indicate that I was waiting for someone to tell me I could go.

'How are you getting home?'

I looked down at the keys in my hand, then back up at him, and he rolled his eyes.

'Paige, you can't drive yourself home less than twenty-four hours after being hospitalised with a head injury.' He sat down on the edge of the bed and ran a hand through his hair. 'I meant it when I said you were your own worst enemy.'

'Well, Anna and Gem are both at work, and I'm not calling Max to give me a lift home, seeing as I broke his heart a few days ago,' I said, my words coming out a bit sharper than I'd intended. 'I don't have any money on me to pay for a taxi or a bus. So what do you suggest?'

He mimed looking over his shoulder, then checking under the bed, then sat back. 'No, you're right. There's absolutely nobody else who could give you a lift home.'

I folded my arms, feeling my face redden. 'I think I took up too much of your time yesterday to impose on you again.' I had decided when he walked in that I wasn't going to mention the kiss unless he did.

'Well, I can be the judge of that.' He looked at me seriously. 'I'm sorry I left it the way I did last night. I was frustrated that you keep putting yourself in dangerous situations. It's not nice for the people who care about you to see you get hurt.'

I felt a little flush of pleasure that he was obviously including himself in that group of people, and moved to sit next to him on the bed.

'You're right that I don't always think before I do something. But I was being careful yesterday, I promise.' He raised his eyebrows, but I continued. 'I know you think I'm reckless, but I don't deliberately set out to get myself into these situations.' I'd had plenty of time to think overnight, and it was true that I had just wanted to help Sasha, to begin with. I'd only found myself getting carried away when I became sure that there was something else going on.

He rubbed his chin. 'Maybe you need to leave these things to us,' he replied. 'Sometimes when you try and help someone, they're not telling you the full story.'

I frowned. Was he talking about Sasha?

'What do you know that I don't?' I asked him.

He grimaced. 'You know I'm not meant to talk to you about these things. It's an ongoing investigation.'

'Oh for God's sake, Rav. You can't just make these cryptic comments then suddenly decide you're not going to say anything else. It's not fair.'

He still looked torn, so I put my hand on his arm.

'Please, Rav. Tell me what's going on.'

'Okay, you make a good point,' he agreed. 'Let's just say, we've had access to Lukas Nowak's phone for the purposes of the investigation, and there's one number that appears far more than any other.'

'Whose?'

'Sasha Thomas's.'

'She's his social worker, of course he called her,' I replied, brushing it off. 'Surely that's nothing particularly interesting?'

'We have the texts between them, Paige. They're not exactly professional.'

I paused, taking in what he was saying. 'They were having an affair?' I asked, incredulous.

He raised his eyebrows again. I knew he wasn't going to say anything else, but he'd said enough. I felt like someone had smacked me in the face. How could that have been going on right under my nose? After everything I'd believed about Lukas being completely devoted to Nadia, I felt like a complete idiot.

'How long for?' I asked, my voice sounding hollow.

'A few months.'

'No wonder she was so desperate for my help to get him out of jail,' I said. 'I can't believe I didn't work it out. I've been so bloody stupid!'

Singh shook his head. 'Don't blame yourself. People who are having affairs are good at hiding it.'

'But she pushed me so much to help her prove he was innocent, then as soon as he was released she didn't seem to be that bothered about the evidence or anything else I had found out. This is obviously why, because her main concern was to have him back with her.' I smacked my hand down on the bed next to me. 'I should have seen it.' I thought back to the way Caroline had looked at Sasha when she was telling us how Lukas couldn't resist flirting with other women. Had she known?

'Hey, you trusted her – there's nothing wrong with that,' he said.

'I'm gullible,' I muttered.

He laughed and shook his head.

'Wait, text messages,' I said, and he raised an eyebrow. 'You must have seen the text that Lukas got, on the night of the fire. The one threatening him, saying that was his only warning.'

Singh nodded. 'We did. Why?'

'Sasha insisted it proved Lukas's innocence. He could hardly have sent it to himself.'

'No, but he could have asked someone else to send it, in order to give him an alibi.' Singh shook his head. 'We couldn't trace it. It was an unregistered pay-as-you-go SIM, bought with cash. If we find the phone on a suspect, then maybe the text can be used as evidence, but as it is there's no way of knowing if it's genuine or not.'

At that moment, a nurse walked in with my discharge letter. Once all the paperwork was handed over, I gathered my things in the bag Anna had brought that morning and followed Singh to his car. I had planned to drive myself home, but I was so tired I was glad I didn't have to navigate the busy roads and could just leave it to him.

When we got to my flat I invited him in, expecting him to refuse, but he didn't. He could see how tired I was, so in the end he made us both a cup of tea while I curled up on the sofa. I was glad Anna had brought me a change of clothes and that I'd been able to have a shower that morning, so I didn't feel too unattractive in front of him.

'I've been thinking about something,' I told him, and I could see him take a deep breath in anticipation of what I was going to say. 'Hear me out for a minute. I have a theory.'

Singh let out the breath he'd been holding and visibly relaxed, and I realised he'd been expecting me to say something about the kiss.

'Okay, I'll humour you, as you've had a bang on the head,' he said, with a wry smile.

'I'm serious. What if whoever murdered Nadia didn't set fire to the house?'

I was expecting Singh to roll his eyes and tell me I was being ridiculous, but he nodded.

'That's certainly something we've been considering.'

'Really?' I couldn't conceal my surprise. 'So you think I'm right?'

'I don't know if you're right, because we haven't got all the details clear just yet, but the evidence is pointing in that direction.'

I sat back and thought for a moment. I had been expecting to have to work to convince Singh of my theory, but it turned out that the police were thinking the same thing as me. I knew I should trust him to do his job, and I did, but I also wanted to know what they were investigating.

'Is that all?' he asked, leaning forward, his hands clasped round his cup of tea.

'Well, no. I wondered if Mariusz might have set the fire.'

'Why would he have done that?' Singh's expression was unreadable, and I wondered if he'd been practising his poker face.

'Okay, what if Caroline killed Nadia?' I said. 'She obviously held a grudge against her, and her attempts to get Nadia sacked had failed, so what if she took things too far? If Mariusz knew about it, he might have set fire to the house in order to cover up any evidence against his mother.'

Singh smiled. 'I'll give you something, you've certainly thought it through.'

I waited for him to continue, but he just looked at me. 'What?'

'What about the other fires?' he asked. 'You've connected them, same as we have. How do they fit into your theory?'

I could tell he was just teasing me now, but I'd considered that. 'Have you ever read *The ABC Murders* by Agatha Christie? The killer hides the one murder they really want to commit in a string of murders connected by letters of the alphabet.'

Singh frowned as he tried to unravel my comparison. 'So you think Mariusz set fire to other houses to make it look like they were connected, so we were less focused on the fire at Lukas's house?'

'Exactly! So if you thought it was just a spate of arson attacks, you wouldn't consider it might be someone wanting to conceal evidence about Nadia's murder.'

He gave me an appreciative nod. 'I like that idea, I do. But we think the fires are linked to something else.'

'What?' I sat forward, eager to learn more. 'Is this the connected case you told me about the other day?'

'Paige,' he said, in an exasperated tone. 'You know I can't talk to you about things like that.'

'Oh, come on, Rav.' I was annoyed that he kept dropping hints without actually confirming anything. 'Who exactly am I going to tell?'

'Sasha,' he answered immediately. 'Anna. I don't know.'

'I'm certainly not giving Sasha any information about this,' I replied bitterly. 'Not after she's lied to me.'

Singh looked like he was hesitating, and I put a hand on top of his, feeling the warmth of his mug through his fingers. 'Please, just tell me the basics.'

'Fine,' he said, giving me a look that was half amused, half annoyed. 'It'll all be made public in the next day or so anyway. Arrests are imminent.' He sat back in his chair. 'The group of young men who have been seen hanging around outside a few houses are working for a drug dealer who has been trying to mark his territory quite clearly. He's cuckooing.'

I frowned at him. It wasn't a term I was familiar with. 'What's that?'

'It's when a criminal, usually a drug dealer, uses the home of a vulnerable person as their temporary base of operations. They find someone who's an addict, or someone who's socially isolated, and either they force their way in or they befriend them, get invited into their home. Once they've got access, they come and go as they please for a short time, using the house to store and deal drugs. They move around regularly, finding new victims to prey on, and they've often got a couple of houses on the go at once. Do you know what county lines is?'

I shook my head, so he continued. 'It's when drug dealers from cities branch out into smaller towns, like Scunthorpe. Cuckooing means they can keep moving around and they're less likely to get caught. And they often use teen-agers, hooking them in with gifts of designer trainers and new bikes, then asking them to deliver packages, and eventually sell drugs. It's becoming a big problem across Lincolnshire. As I say, it's usually drugs, but we've had some cases of sex traffickers operating in this way too.'

I was horrified at the idea. I thought I knew a lot about the world, but occasionally I learnt about something that made me realise my upbringing had been quite sheltered. 'So all of these houses that have been set on fire have been used for this cuckooing?'

'We believe so. Some of the victims refuse to give us statements, because they've been threatened or coerced into allowing these people into their house and they're afraid of the repercussions, either legally or from the criminals. Others don't even know if it happened – these are usually elderly people with some level of dementia, who probably shouldn't still be living alone but are just coping well enough to prevent their relatives moving them into a home.'

I was quiet for a couple of minutes, trying to process all of this and thinking about Bill, the elderly man who I'd been told lived in the house I'd seen Mariusz and the gang outside.

'Hang on, does this mean Lukas and Nadia had it happen to them, too? The neighbours, Jill Adams and Eric, both said there'd been people going in and out of the house, as well as kids on bikes hanging round outside, a day or two before Nadia died.'

Singh nodded. 'We think so, but Lukas wouldn't speak to us. If we can get him to testify to what happened, perhaps that will go well for him if any other charges are brought.'

I took the hint. 'I'll get Sasha to speak to him about it, see if she can get him to open up. Even if she's been behaving unprofessionally, I still think she has his best interests at heart.'

'You can tell her that he needs to cooperate with us, but don't give her any details,' Singh warned me. 'As I say, we're hoping to make arrests very soon. We've been working with the council on this, they've got someone specifically working on this sort of manipulation of council tenants, and nearly every one of the victims we've got on our list is living in a council property.'

A thought popped into my head. 'But why are they setting fire to the properties after they've used them?' I asked. 'That doesn't make sense. Surely that would just draw attention to them?'

'We haven't figured that part out yet. It could be a territory thing, if there are two rival gangs operating in the same area.'

'And how is Nadia's murder connected?'

Singh grimaced and shook his head. 'We don't know that, either. It might not be connected at all. Lukas is still our main suspect,' he said, giving me a look that told me I shouldn't get involved.

I was about to ask another question when he looked at his watch. 'Give me your car keys, and I'll get your car back to you in the next few hours,' he said. 'I don't want you trying to drive for a couple of days, though.'

I rolled my eyes, but handed my keys over anyway. He said his goodbyes and walked to the door, then turned and took one of my hands.

'Paige, you know, yesterday . . .' His voice tailed off and I knew straight away he was referring to when I kissed him. 'I hope I didn't offend you. It wasn't the right time or place, that's all.'

Swallowing hard, I suddenly found I'd lost my voice. It all seemed obvious now: I knew that I wanted it to happen again, and I wanted to be with Singh. Did this mean he felt the same? Before I found the right words, he gave me a soft kiss on the cheek and left. I closed the door behind him, then leant on it for a moment, taking a deep breath to try and slow my hammering heart.

Much as I wanted to lose myself in a daydream about

314

going on a date with Singh and kissing him again, my mind kept coming back to what he'd told me about the other investigation. How had Mariusz got himself involved with a drug dealer who was cuckooing? Did Lukas know about it? There were so many unanswered questions.

A wave of tiredness washed over me as I went back into the living room and curled up on the sofa. I tried to keep my eyes open, to try and make some connections and work out what we were all missing, but before I knew it I was asleep, my cheek still tingling from Singh's kiss.

Chapter 33

A loud noise penetrated my consciousness and I sat up, bleary-eyed and confused. I rubbed my face, and as the sound came again I realised it was my door buzzer. How long had I been asleep? It was still light outside, and Anna must not be home from work yet. Perhaps it was Singh, leaving my car keys?

'Hello?' I said into the intercom. The only thing I heard in return was static. Fear started to bubble, and I said, 'Hello?' again. Still no response.

After checking the door was locked I backed away slowly, then went into the living room. I peered out of the window, down to the front door of the building, but my view was obscured by the roof of the small porch. Whoever was pressing my buzzer would be underneath it.

I had just made my mind up not to answer the door, when someone stepped back and looked up at me. It was Max.

A wave of relief flooded through me, shortly followed by another twinge of anxiety. What was he doing here? He smiled and waved, so I couldn't leave him on the doorstep; he knew I was in, and he knew I'd seen him.

Reluctantly, I pressed the button that would unlock the exterior door, and waited for him to climb the stairs. I hadn't checked my phone since Singh had brought me home from the hospital, so maybe Max had tried texting or calling before he came round. If he wanted to have a go at me for the way I'd ended things I didn't think I could cope.

Hi, he signed, hovering outside the door, obviously waiting for me to invite him in. I stood back and held the door open, so he stepped inside awkwardly. Without responding, I went back into the living room and sat down rigidly on the sofa again, so he followed me and sat on the chair opposite. I could tell that he wanted to come and sit next to me on the sofa, but I lifted my legs up and stretched them out, making it clear that he should stay where he was.

How are you? he asked eventually.

Anna called you, I assume, I replied wearily. I should have known she would have done something like that. Even though she'd understood why I'd broken up with Max, and even told me she thought I was doing the right thing, she assumed I'd want him there to lean on when things went wrong. What the last twenty-four hours had shown me, however, was that he wasn't the one I wanted to comfort me in my hour of need.

She thought you might need some support, Max explained. He still looked awkward, almost perching on the chair as if he thought I'd throw him out at any moment. *Your face looks pretty painful.*

My hand automatically went to my cheek. Of course, Max hadn't seen me since Sunday night. Was it worth explaining to him that that injury had been sustained at a different time? I thought not. I didn't want to activate his 'knight in shining armour' mode by telling him I'd been injured by unknown people twice in the space of a few days.

I'm fine, I told him. I knew I was being cold but I couldn't help it. I was tired and in pain, I was trying to make sense of everything Singh had told me, both about the case and about our kiss. The last thing I needed right now was Max trying to offer a shoulder to cry on when I just wanted to be on my own.

You don't look it.

I closed my eyes, took a deep breath and counted to ten. I wanted to shout at him, to tell him to stop patronising me and treating me like I couldn't cope without him, but I knew those feelings stemmed from how Mike used to treat me. Still, if he wanted to use this as a chance to reconnect with me, or however he might put it, that wasn't going to happen. I didn't want to see or talk to anyone; I felt like Anna had let me down by calling Max when I'd asked her not to, and Sasha, well . . . I didn't want to think about Sasha just yet.

Max, what do you want? I asked.

I wanted to make sure you were okay, and see if you needed anything. There was a little crease between his eyebrows from the frown of concern he was wearing, and something about the sight of it made me burst into tears.

318

He came over immediately and knelt in front of me, putting his arms around me, but I pushed him away.

Don't. Please, just don't.

Paige, you've been through a lot, he signed, still on his knees. *You don't have to do everything on your own, you know. I still love you.*

Max, please, don't, I signed. *This hasn't changed anything.*

I know, but I'm worried about you being here on your own. Anna said she didn't think it was a random mugging, that someone must have been following you.

I frowned. I hadn't told her the full truth about what had happened, so I didn't know where she'd got that information from, unless she was just making assumptions yet again.

Shaking my head, I brushed off Max's concerns. *I'm fine, there's nobody out to get me.*

But I couldn't sit at home and do nothing when I knew what had happened to you. If it had been something worse, I don't know what I would have done. He paused, clearly choosing his words. *Why don't we give things another go?* he asked me, out of the blue. *I won't push you to commit to anything until you're absolutely ready. I'll be guided by you.*

I wanted to tell him that what happened to me wasn't any of his business any more, but I stopped myself. It was hard to say what I wanted to say without being rude, because I was too tired to word it in a way that didn't sound bitchy.

I'm not your responsibility any more, I signed eventually.

319

I'm not going to stop caring about you, Paige. I can't just switch off my feelings. After I saw you in the Deaf club the other night I thought I needed to move on and forget about you, but I've realised I don't want to do that. I want to fight for you. I want to fight for our relationship. I'm not willing to sit back and give up on what has been the best relationship of my life, simply because you've got cold feet.

Do I get a say in this? I asked him. He looked confused, and I didn't think he'd even realised what he was doing. *You're talking about not giving up, as if it's a one-sided choice, not a decision that both of us have to agree to. Or did you just assume I'd agree to it because I've been mugged and I'm feeling vulnerable?*

That's not what I said. He sat back on his heels, looking slightly offended. *What I mean is that I'm willing to put the effort in to try and convince you to give us another go.*

I stood up and walked away from him, shaking my head. *I'm not trying to be some sort of martyr,* I told him. *I'm not saying that I want to be on my own because I think I have to battle through, or something like that. I don't understand why you're here, why you're saying all of this.*

Well, I came round because I wanted to make sure you're okay, he began, but I cut him off.

But why, Max? We split up. I know it's horrible, and I know I hurt you. Please believe me when I say I never wanted to. But I'm not going to change my mind about that. If you came here hoping that I'd fall into your arms because I'm tired and emotional then I'm sorry, you're here under false pretences.

There was a horrible pause as I watched several different emotions cross Max's face. I wished I could take my words back; I hadn't meant to be so harsh, but even if I blamed the head injury I couldn't change what I'd just said.

Fine, he signed, getting up off the floor. *Fine. I had hoped we could talk about this, but maybe now isn't the right time.*

There won't be a right time! We've already talked about it. I'm sorry that you're not happy with my decision, I really am, but I can't do anything to change that. And you saying you're not going to give up just fills me with dread, because I can't keep having the same conversation over and over, just because you hope my side of it is going to change.

There was a pause in which I wasn't sure if he was going to yell at me or burst into tears, but in the end he did neither. He shook his head, then turned away from me and moved towards the door.

As he pushed past me, the door buzzer went again. I followed Max out into the hallway and down the stairs, hoping to apologise before he stormed out, but when he flung open the front door of the building he came face to face with Singh, who was passing my car keys from hand to hand.

'Er, hi,' Singh said, looking between me and Max, his expression puzzled. 'Paige, I brought your car back.'

Max looked Singh up and down, noticing my keys in his hand, then turned to me.

What the hell is this?

Rav picked me up from the hospital, then went to get

my car for me, I hastily explained, not wanting Max to get the wrong idea. Even though we weren't together any longer, I didn't want him thinking I'd replaced him quite so quickly. There was a keyring in the shape of a little yellow duck attached to my car keys – it was the first gift Max had bought me when we started dating, and I could see him looking at it.

Singh watched us signing, clearly wondering if he'd interrupted something. 'I'll just leave you your keys. I've got to get back to the station.' He looked between me and Max again, gave me a quick smile, then jogged up the road to where a police car was obviously waiting for him. I watched him climb into the passenger seat, then turned back to Max, whose expression had turned sour.

Whatever I thought, Paige, I didn't think you'd found someone else. I believed you when you said that. Maybe I shouldn't have bothered.

I sighed. *Max, I was telling the truth. Rav is a friend, he took me to the hospital after I was mugged and he brought me home today.* I threw my hands up. *Why am I even explaining myself to you?*

You're right, you don't owe me anything, he replied, turning and walking out of the door. I watched him go, and for a moment considered going after him, but I didn't have the energy. He didn't glance back, and when he was out of sight I shut the door and dragged myself back up to the flat.

My phone beeped. It was a text from Singh.
Is everything okay?

I started typing out a reply, deleted it, then repeated this another three times before throwing my phone down on the sofa in frustration. I couldn't answer him because I didn't know.

Fifteen minutes before the fire

Mariusz pedalled furiously in his desperation to get away from there, away from that house. He'd been so fucking stupid, to think that these guys were his friends. They were just using him; he could see that now. And he'd let them into his dad's house! Stupid. Stupid, stupid, stupid. They'd told him some story about needing somewhere to leave some stock for a few days; he'd assumed the guy had a shop. He'd given Mariusz some absolutely sick trainers and said there was plenty more where they came from. What a fucking idiot he'd been.

Once he was far enough away from that house, he stopped and got his breath back, leaning his bike up against a wall. He burned with anger and embarrassment when he thought of all their faces as they laughed at him, making fun of him for not realising what they'd been doing. Drugs! His dad was going to kill him. He'd never touched the stuff himself, but even being around them was bad enough.

He started walking, pushing his bike. He was too full of adrenaline to stay still for long. Was there a way to fix it? All those people, whose houses they'd been in . . . He felt sick just thinking about it.

I'm not a bad person, he told himself. *I didn't know what they were doing.* They'd told him they knew these people, that they were mates or relatives. He thought it was a bit strange hanging round someone's grandad's house last week, but he never asked any questions. He should have done.

But that didn't make him feel any better about it. He knew he had got involved with these people willingly, when the lads had approached him in the park three weeks ago. Why had they picked him? Did he look that pissed off with the world that they thought he'd be a good prospect to groom for a life of crime?

His feet took him back to his dad's house, and he found himself standing on the other side of the street, looking at the front door. He'd been fighting with his mum so much recently, he'd considered moving in with his dad and Nadia full time, but he didn't want to leave his mum on her own. She'd be devastated if he did that, and even though he knew he was a shit to her a lot of the time, he still didn't want to hurt her. Maybe he could spend a bit more time with his dad, though. If he told him about what had happened, would he be able to help him? Nadia had seemed uncomfortable being around the lads when they were in the house, but Mariusz had made sure they only usually went there when she was at work. She'd been so nice to him recently, as well, trying to spend more time with him, and he felt like he'd thrown it all back in her face.

Mariusz thought about it for a moment, but then realised it wouldn't work. His dad would tell him to go to the police, and he couldn't do that. He'd watched enough TV to know that drug dealers didn't take kindly to people who ratted them out, and he felt like he'd put his family at risk enough already.

He watched the house for a few minutes. He could see someone moving around in the kitchen – he couldn't see who it was, but it must be Nadia, because he knew his dad would be at the pub at this time of night. He didn't let his mum know just how much his dad was drinking again; she'd throw a fit, and she'd probably stop him going round there. Putting his hand in his pocket, he suddenly came up with an idea. It was a crazy one, even he knew that, but it might be a way of stopping these people he'd thought were his friends.

Hanging around, he heard the front door of the house open and close, so he ducked down behind a car. He didn't want Nadia to see him. If she'd gone out, that meant the house would be empty. Well, no time like the present.

Pulling out his key, he let himself into the house. Looking around him, he spotted a couple of sentimental items, including some photos of his dad and Nadia, so took them and shoved them into his bag. He didn't bother going into the kitchen, because there wouldn't be anything in there that he wanted, so he went upstairs to his room and took a few of his belongings.

Once his bag was full, he went back into the living room for a moment and took a last look at it before pulling up his hood and slipping out of the door again. With the deed done, he grabbed his bike and raced home, refusing to look back at the house.

Chapter 34

Thursday 25th April

Despite what Singh had said about not driving for a few more days, I knew I had to get out of the flat. There were things I needed to do, and say, and I couldn't do them by sitting alone at home, brooding. Anna fussed around me before she went to work, asking if I needed anything or if I wanted her to finish work early, but I managed to get her out of the door on time.

When I arrived at the social work offices, I sat outside for a few minutes, working out exactly what I wanted to say. I enjoyed interpreting for Sasha, and it had given me some much-needed stability in my working life over the last six months, but my trust in her had been destroyed. I had to talk to her and hear her side of things.

Her car was in the car park, so I knew she was in. At first, she didn't notice me when I walked into the office, because she was absorbed in something on her computer. I didn't know how she'd react to seeing me, after she'd walked out of my hospital room yesterday, so I waited for a moment rather than interrupt her.

She looked up, and the first emotion on her face was surprise, with a brief flicker of something else – was it guilt? Eventually she gave me a quick smile.

Paige, I wasn't expecting to see you today. How are you feeling?

I'm okay, I told her, my hand automatically finding the tender spot on the side of my head. *Can we talk?*

Sasha looked around at the busy desks surrounding hers, then nodded towards the door. *Let's see if there's a meeting room free.*

There was, which was a relief, because I didn't want to have this conversation in front of any of her colleagues, even if none of them could understand what we were signing. She settled herself in a chair opposite me, keeping an eye on the door, then looked at me. I couldn't quite read her expression – was she still angry with me for suggesting Lukas was keeping secrets? I knew now that that anger had only been covering up what she herself was hiding.

What do you want to talk about? she asked, her smile bright, making it look more than a little fake.

I know, I told her.

She paused. *What do you know?*

I know about you and Lukas.

She blinked rapidly, then swallowed. *What are you talking about?*

Don't try that, Sasha. Just don't. I can't believe you've been lying to me this entire time.

I don't know what you're talking about, she signed

329

again. I could see the tightness of the muscles in her jaw.

You have been having an affair with Lukas Nowak, I signed, slowly and clearly to emphasise the fact that I was happy to spell it out for her, and I wouldn't be fobbed off with her lies or protestations of innocence.

I thought she was going to try and deny it, but she didn't.

How did you find out?

That doesn't matter, I replied. I wasn't going to drop Singh in it, because I had no doubt Sasha would put in a complaint against him if she could. *What matters is that I know exactly why you've been so desperate to get him out of jail. It wasn't for his sake, it was so you could be with him, and so nobody would find out what you've been doing.*

She sat and stared at a poster on the wall for a moment before turning back to me. *I knew if he was held for long enough, the police would get access to his phone records. I'd thought we'd been discreet, but if someone could read our text messages then . . .* She shrugged. *Obviously I was right. I assume that's how you know? Your DS friend told you?*

I kept my face neutral, refusing to rise to it, and she scowled at me.

Of course it was him, it must have been. I can report him for giving you information, you know. She waved a hand dismissively. *Anyway, I'm sorry I lied to you, but you wouldn't have understood.*

I shook my head. *You're right, I don't understand. One of the reasons I like working with you is that you're so*

330

good at what you do. You always seem to strike just the right balance between professionalism and caring for your clients. But then it turns out you've crossed this line, and I feel like I don't know you at all now.

Who are you to judge me? she snapped. *You have no idea what my relationship is like with Lukas. And you don't know what it's like to do my job, either. You're my interpreter; you're not a social worker.*

You're right, I don't, and I'm not. But a big part of your defence of Lukas has been that he loved Nadia so deeply he could never have hurt her. How can I believe that now, when I know he was cheating on her with you?

Sasha's expression changed, and I could now see the sadness in her eyes. *I wasn't lying about that, Paige. Lukas did love Nadia, far more than he ever could have loved me.* She sighed, and I was reminded of a love-struck teenager. *He's the sort of man who will always struggle to commit himself to one woman. He likes the attention, and he likes having people to spoil, to romance. With me, I think he enjoyed the clandestine nature of our relationship.*

The rueful smile on her face made me feel sorry for her at first. It was clear she'd been hoping for more from Lukas, but had settled for what she could get. Maybe since he'd been released from prison he'd decided he couldn't be with her any more, or maybe he was just grieving too deeply for Nadia, but I got the feeling she hadn't received the reaction she'd hoped for when they'd seen each other again. Then, however, my mind jumped to another possibility: had Sasha been so besotted with Lukas that she would do anything to be with him, including getting rid of anyone who stood in her way? I looked at her with fresh eyes, then, and wondered if I could have missed the prime suspect staring me in the face all along. She'd hidden crucial information from the police, and I couldn't overlook that.

She glanced over my shoulder at the door. *Are you going to report me?*

I'd asked myself the same question over and over since I'd found out. In the end, I'd decided against it. It was highly likely that the truth would come out eventually, seeing as the police knew, but I didn't have to be the one to reveal it, especially as Singh had told me about it in confidence. I was furious with her for lying to me, but I didn't want to be the one to ruin her life because of it. I knew she'd have to deal with the consequences of her actions eventually.

No, I told her. *But I haven't decided yet if I'm going to hand in my notice.*

She nodded. *That's fair.*

My problem now is trust, I told her. *I've been basing everything on my assumption that you knew what you were talking about, that Lukas couldn't have killed Nadia, but now how am I supposed to know what's true and what's a lie? I've been helping you all this time, when really Lukas is probably the one who killed Nadia, because she found out he was cheating on her.*

No, Paige. Sasha's eyes were wide and she leant forward in her chair to appeal to me. *Please don't say that. You can't believe he did it, because he didn't. I wouldn't have lied to you about that, even with our affair. If he belonged in jail, I would have sat back and let the police get on with it.*

I didn't trust her, and her insistence that he was innocent made me suspect her even more. Could she have killed Nadia? Or had Lukas done it, and she was protecting him? Whichever it was, I knew I didn't want to be associated with her any more.

How do you know, Sasha? I asked. *He's refused to defend himself, and he won't say anything about the people who were hanging around his house the day before Nadia died. The police are looking into that, you know. They think the gang are connected to the fires, and I've seen Mariusz hanging around with them. Lukas needs to talk to the police. You need to make him.*

She was shaking her head as I signed, but I didn't know if she was telling me I was wrong or saying she couldn't do it. *Can't you see, he's refused to speak to the police because he knows the only person who can confirm his alibi is me?*

You?

She nodded. *I saw him on that night, before he went to the pub. I was waiting outside his house, and Nadia was inside. I saw her through the window, alive and well.*

I was confused. If Sasha was telling the truth, she was the only person who could confirm that Nadia was still alive after Lukas had gone to the pub. She was able to provide Lukas with an alibi. *But you were in Birmingham. You were there for the conference. You drove back when I called you about the fire.*

No, I came back earlier in the day, and went straight to Lukas's house. I wanted to see him. So if he'd told the police that I could give him an alibi, it would have come out that we were having an affair, and that would be the end of my career. I could see the weight of the last week bearing down on her as her shoulders sagged. *Nadia was dead, so there was nothing he could do for her any more. He thought he could at least protect me. That's why he refused to say anything to the police.*

He could have still defended himself, I told her. *He told me he knew who was responsible. Why didn't he tell the police who that was?*

A thought dawned on me, and I saw Sasha's face go pale. *Oh God. Does he think you killed Nadia?*

Sasha pressed her lips together tightly, and I could see she was trying to keep her composure. *I don't know. He's refused to see me alone or talk to me since we saw him at Paul's the other day. But it's possible.*

For a moment, a feeling of panic rose in my chest. Could Sasha have killed Nadia? If she was jealous, knowing Lukas would never leave her, could she have lashed out? After all, if she saw Lukas before he went to the pub, it would have been easy for her to knock on the door and ask to speak to Nadia about something.

As I processed these thoughts, I must have failed to keep them from showing on my face, because Sasha looked panicked.

Paige, I didn't kill Nadia! I didn't think I'd have to tell you that, I thought you'd know I could never hurt anyone. She stood up and backed away so she was up against the wall of the meeting room. *Yes, I fell in love with Lukas, and I shouldn't have acted on it, should have passed his case on to another social worker, but that's where my mistakes end. I know I've lied to you, but you can't possibly believe I'm a murderer?*

334

She sat back down and clasped her hands together, as if she were begging me. I didn't know what to think. Surely either of them could have killed Nadia? Sasha claimed to be Lukas's alibi, but what if that was a lie and they'd committed the crime together? I felt like I'd been taken for a fool, and that the pair of them had been using me the whole time. I'd been attacked twice, and all because I'd agreed to help her prove that Lukas was innocent and I felt I owed her a favour after she'd helped to get me extra work.

Taking a deep breath, I tried to push down the anger that was building. I didn't know what had happened that night, but I knew I was going to be telling Singh that Sasha had been there. Even though I'd said I wouldn't report her affair with Lukas to her superiors, I wasn't going to keep that sort of information from the police. It might finally convince Singh that I was being sensible and leaving the work to him, too.

I stood up. *Sasha, I don't know what the hell has gone on, but I don't want to be a part of it any more. You'll have my resignation letter in the morning. I'll work out my notice, but you need to find yourself a new interpreter.*

Paige, please. She grabbed my arm. *I still need your help.*

I shook my head. *No. I'm not helping you any more. I'm sick of getting involved in other people's problems and ending up being the one in danger. You can sort out your own mess.*

With that, I turned on my heel and marched out of the door.

Chapter 35

I was so angry I didn't know what to do. It felt like I was back at square one. My theory about Mariusz setting the house on fire to cover up for Caroline didn't seem very likely any more. I was no longer convinced of Lukas's innocence, or even Sasha's. I tried calling Singh, but there was no answer on his mobile and I didn't leave a message because I didn't know where to begin. My head still throbbed from where I'd hit the pavement and I just wanted to go home and sleep and forget about the whole sorry mess.

On my way home I took a shortcut through some side streets, and recognised one of the roads I had followed Mariusz down a couple of nights ago. I was curious about my theory concerning Mariusz and the fires, so I slowed down and kept an eye out for the first house I'd seen him checking out, where he'd gone round the back. The road looked different in daylight, however, and I had to check the address on my phone so I knew exactly which house it had been.

As I approached the house I was looking for, I couldn't see any signs of a fire, so it looked like my theory was wrong. I was about to drive away when I saw the front door of the house open and someone familiar emerge. At first I couldn't place her, but then I recognised her uniform. She was the carer I'd spoken to a few days ago, when Sasha and I had been to visit Miriam. On impulse, I pulled up and jumped out of the car, managing to reach her before she got into her own.

'Hi!' I called, and she turned to look at me. I could see the same look of recognition pass across her face. 'We met a few days ago, at the assisted living facility. We talked about Nadia.'

'Oh, yes! Hi.'

We looked at each other awkwardly for a moment, before I pointed at the house she'd just come out of. 'I take it one of your clients lives here?'

She raised her eyebrow, but didn't reply.

'I mean, it's not your house,' I said.

'No, it's not my house,' she replied warily, clearly not willing to give me any more information than that.

I rubbed my face. I must look a mess – huge graze on the side of my face, exhausted and a bit dishevelled. No wonder she was looking at me like I might be dangerous.

'Sorry, I really should explain myself. My name's Paige, and I know Lukas, Nadia's husband. I saw his son hanging around this house, and I wondered what he might have been doing here, if one of his friends lived here.'

'There are no kids here,' she said, still wary. 'Just an old lady. Maybe you got the wrong house.'

I nodded. 'Maybe you're right, yes. She hasn't had any break-ins lately? Nothing like that?'

She shook her head. 'I don't think so. I'm sure she would have said.'

Relieved, I glanced at the house. What had Mariusz been doing, then? Was it connected to the cuckooing? An elderly lady would definitely be a prime victim for that sort of crime. If Mariusz had got himself mixed up with this gang, maybe he was being expected to scout out houses of potential victims.

The carer was still watching me, obviously curious about why I was asking these questions.

'They let him out then,' she said after a pause. 'Her husband.'

'Lukas?' I said, getting my brain back on track in the conversation. 'Yes, he's been released. Insufficient evidence, I think.'

She fiddled with her car keys, obviously wanting to ask something else. 'Do you think he did it?'

'I honestly don't know,' I told her, shaking my head. 'I did think he was innocent, but since then . . .' I let my voice tail off, knowing I couldn't tell this stranger everything that was going round in my mind.

'I thought of something else, after we spoke the other day,' she began. I could see that she was torn between talking to me and getting in her car. I didn't blame her for not trusting me when I'd just been asking questions about one of her clients, when many of the people she worked with would be vulnerable.

'Something else about Nadia?' I asked.

She nodded, a quick, sharp single nod, but remained silent.

'Do you think it might have something to do with her death?' I probed.

'I don't know about that,' she said hastily. 'It might be nothing. It's just something she said to me the other week. It would have been the last time I saw her.'

I waited, wondering if patience was the key to getting this woman to open up to me. After a long pause, I was rewarded for waiting. She glanced over her shoulder, as if to check nobody was watching her.

'She'd just finished a shift and she'd come into the office to hand in some paperwork, I think. Anyway, we were in the loos, and I could tell she was really distracted. She was just standing there, looking at herself in the mirror, as if she was in her own little world. I asked her what was wrong, and she didn't hear me at first. She spoke well, did Nadia, but she had to be looking at you to understand you. So I tapped her on the shoulder and she jumped, like she hadn't even noticed I was there.'

'Did she tell you what was wrong?' I asked, wanting to hurry the woman up but also not wanting to risk asking any leading questions.

'Sort of,' she said with a frown. 'She was obviously really worked up about it. She started trying to tell me about something, but she couldn't quite find the right words. It all ended up a bit muddled. I offered to make her a cup of tea so she could talk to me about it properly, and she agreed, but a couple of minutes later she got up and said she had to get home.' She shrugged. 'That was the last time I saw her.'

'Do you remember what day that was?' I wondered if this had happened on the day Nadia died, and if whatever she'd been anxious about had been the motive for someone to kill her.

'I've been thinking about that and trying to remember. I think it was the Monday.'

'The day before she died?'

She nodded. 'I think so. But it might have been the Tuesday.'

I bit my lip and thought for a moment, not realising that I was leaning on the woman's car. 'What was it that got her that worked up, do you think?'

The woman glanced over her shoulder again, then lowered her voice. 'It was something to do with one of her clients. She said that one of them had died, and she wasn't happy about it. I mean, she thought there was something dodgy going on, that whoever it was hadn't died of natural causes. She kept saying, "He's been lying."'

'Who was she talking about?' I asked, unable to keep the eagerness from my voice.

'That's what I don't know,' she replied, clearly as frustrated as I was. 'She didn't say. Whoever it was, she just kept saying "he", "him".'

I folded my arms as I thought about who it could have been. I knew Lukas had been lying to her. Had she found out about his relationship with Sasha? Was that why she was flustered and making no sense? Because she'd found out that her seemingly devoted husband was having an affair with his social worker? But that had nothing to do with her work.

Mariusz was another possibility. I imagined none of his

parents or step-parents had known about the gang he'd been hanging around with, and the crimes that he was now linked to. If Nadia had found out about that, though, surely she would have told Lukas and Caroline, rather than keeping it to herself. Roy Chapman was another man she could have been referring to. But what did any of these people have to do with one of her clients dying in suspicious circumstances?

'Do you know which client she was talking about?' I asked, hoping that that would make the identity of Nadia's killer more obvious. There couldn't have been many who died recently, but the woman shook her head.

'I don't know who Nadia had been working with. We support a lot of elderly people, so deaths aren't that unusual. I asked around, but I couldn't work out which client it might have been. Nobody that Nadia had been assigned to has passed away in the last couple of months, so it must have been something that happened a while ago, and she'd just found out something about it. That's what I thought, anyway,' she added defensively.

'Thank you,' I told her, because she looked as if she was getting ready to leave, already regretting having told me so much. 'I appreciate you speaking to me.'

She nodded. 'I hope he rots in jail, whoever killed her. She didn't deserve it.'

'You're right,' I agreed. 'She didn't.'

After giving me another strange look, she got in her car and left, leaving me standing on the pavement, wondering what on earth it all meant.

I drove home, all the time trying out different theories in my mind. I'd forgotten my promise to Singh to leave it alone; there was something about the puzzle that kept drawing me back in. I was missing something, something that was probably obvious.

When I got home, I grabbed my tablet and started looking at the local obituaries, and any newspaper stories about recent deaths. From what the carer had said, the death itself might not have been treated as suspicious, even though it was clearly bothering Nadia. I scrolled through dozens and dozens of names until something caught my eye: a familiar name. The obituary was about six weeks old, but that could fit with the time frame.

Within about fifteen minutes, I had a plausible theory. It all fitted, even the cuckooing. Grabbing my phone, I called Singh, but there was no answer from his mobile, so I called the police station and was put on hold. When someone finally came to the phone I was almost bursting.

'Yes?' My heart sank at the sound of the voice. It wasn't Singh, it was DI Forest.

'Er, hi. It's Paige. I was trying to reach DS Singh.'

'He's not available right now. Is there something I can help you with?'

I hesitated for a moment, wondering if I shouldn't tell her and should wait to speak to Singh, but I knew I needed to pass on my thoughts as soon as possible. Forest already had a low opinion of me, so it didn't really matter if she got annoyed with me for sticking my nose in, as long as she actually listened to me.

I related the conversation I'd had with the carer that morning, and told her about the obituary I'd found, and why I believed it was the person Nadia had been referring to. To my surprise, Forest didn't interrupt me while I was speaking, but waited for me to finish.

'That's potentially new information. We'll look into it,' she said, and I smiled to myself that she couldn't even bring herself to thank me.

Emboldened by the lack of hostility from her, I told her how I thought it fitted with the cuckooing and how they'd managed to choose their victims and keep it under the radar for so long. At this, there was a frosty silence on the end of the line.

'How do you know about the cuckooing?' Forest's voice was cold enough to make me shiver.

I swallowed and made a couple of incoherent noises before she interrupted me.

'As if I need to ask. And what other details of police investigations has DS Singh been sharing with you?'

'It wasn't Rav, I mean, DS Singh,' I spluttered, but she knew I was lying. The damage had already been done, and she hung up.

'Shit,' I said to myself, hurriedly calling Singh. He still didn't answer, and I didn't know how to tell him I'd just dropped him in it with his boss, so I didn't leave a message.

I paced around my flat for a while after I spoke to Forest, wondering what I should do. I knew that in the past she'd completely ignored anything I'd said, but would she do that this time when she'd told me herself that I'd given her some new information? She wasn't the type to cut off her own nose to spite her face, so I was sure she would at least follow it up. I couldn't sit around at home doing nothing, however, so I decided to pay one last visit.

Chapter 36

Turning off Frodingham Road, I followed the directions on my phone until I reached the house where Lukas was staying. Sasha had given me the address the previous day when she'd come to see me in hospital – it felt like that had happened weeks ago. Before Lukas called me on the night of the fire at his house, I had barely spent any time in this area of Scunthorpe, yet now I was finding myself there on an almost daily basis.

The house itself looked like it could do with some attention. Paint was peeling from the front wall of the red-brick terrace, and the wooden window frames were starting to rot. Most of the other houses in the row had been extended slightly, with a bay window added at the front, but this one didn't look like it had had anything done to it for a long time. I could see a yellowing net curtain hanging in the front window, and the front doorstep had cracked right down the middle.

I knocked, then realised Lukas wouldn't be able to hear me. I doubted he'd had time or opportunity to install any sort of adaptations for himself, so I'd need to find another way of alerting him to my presence. Moving to the side, I pressed my face against the front window, wondering if I would be able to see anything through the ancient polyester on the other side of the glass.

'Hello?'

I jumped. Someone had opened the door, but it wasn't Lukas.

'Paul, hi. I came to see Lukas. Is he here?' I shouldn't have been surprised that Paul was there – after all, the house belonged to him, and had been his mother's before he let Lukas use it. I'd hoped to have a conversation with Lukas alone, and Paul's presence immediately put me on my guard.

'Paige, isn't it?'

I nodded and Paul held the door open wide.

'Why don't you come in?'

I hesitated for a moment, but I didn't want to make a scene on the doorstep, so I followed him inside.

The smell of damp hit me as we walked in. I knew the house had probably been lying empty for a few weeks, but the intensity of the smell suggested it had been neglected for a long time prior to Mrs Ilford's death. I picked my way across the filthy carpet and into the room to the right.

'Take a seat,' Paul said cheerfully, pointing at an armchair in the corner. The leather was worn, but it was definitely a better choice than the sofa, whose upholstery had worn right through to the stuffing in a couple of patches.

'Where's Lukas?' I asked.

'He's just popped out to get a couple of things,' he told me. 'He should be back soon, though. Do you want a cup of tea while you wait?'

I had two choices – I could make my excuses and leave, and try to talk to Lukas another time, or I could suck it up and wait. I don't know what pushed me towards the latter, but I was already there so I thought I could sit it out.

While Paul busied himself in the kitchen, I stuck my head into the hallway and had a quick look around. There were only two rooms downstairs – the kitchen and the sitting room Paul had shown me into – so I assumed upstairs had two bedrooms and probably a very small bathroom. The carpet on the stairs was the same murky shade of dirt as the one in the hall, and I shuddered to think just what had been ground into it over the years.

'Tea.' Paul appeared from the kitchen, with a tray in his hands. I hoped the mugs hadn't been here as long as the carpet, but the one he handed me looked relatively clean, so I risked it and took a drink.

'How long did your mother live here?' I asked him, stuck for conversation topics.

'Most of her life,' he replied. 'I grew up in this house.'

Maybe nostalgia kept him from changing anything, but that still didn't excuse him allowing his mum to live in squalor.

We drank our tea in an awkward silence; I was itching to say something about the state of the house, but I knew there was a chance I could get myself into trouble, so I kept my mouth shut. After finishing my tea, I put my mug on a low table by the side of my chair and stood up to have a look at the pictures on the wall. They all appeared to be of Scunthorpe in the 1950s, and I took a few minutes trying to identify the different locations.

'Do you mind if I just use the toilet?' I asked, pointing to the door and moving towards it. There was no way I actually wanted to use the facilities in a house that was in this state, but it would give me an excuse to poke around a little bit before Lukas got back. I wondered where he'd gone, because he was taking a while.

Paul jumped up out of his seat and followed me into the hallway, where I already had my foot on the bottom stair.

'No!' he said sharply, making me jump. His eyes were narrowed and there was a tightness in his jaw that made me uncomfortable. 'No, the bathroom isn't upstairs,' he continued, his voice now returned to a more even tone. 'It's an old house, used to just have an outside privy when it was built. The bathroom's off the back of the kitchen.'

I nodded and stepped back, skirting round him carefully and going into the kitchen. I could feel his eyes on me as I walked across the tatty lino to the door at the back. Pushing it closed behind me, I leant on it and pulled my phone out of my pocket. Something was telling me that wherever Lukas was, he wasn't at the shops. I sent a text to Singh, telling him where I was and that I might need some help, fervently hoping he read it quickly.

I waited in the bathroom for as long as I felt was decent, then flushed the creaking toilet and splashed some water in the sink, drying my hands on my clothes rather than touch anything else in there. When I stepped out, Paul was standing in the kitchen, rubbing his arms, obviously waiting for me.

'Is Lukas back yet?' I asked brightly, and Paul's eyes narrowed slightly. I glanced past him, wondering if I could make a break for the door, but I wasn't certain, and I didn't want it to seem like I was in a hurry to get out of there.

When Paul didn't reply, I shrugged. 'Maybe I should come back another time. I'm quite busy. I need to get to work.'

'Why are you here?' he asked, moving himself so he was positioned between me and the door.

'I came to see Lukas,' I said evenly.

'Why? What did you need to talk to him about?'

I opened my mouth to reply, then my eyes went to his hand. I hadn't noticed what he was holding until then. It was my notebook, the one that had been stolen from my car on the night I was mugged.

He saw where I was looking and brandished it at me.

'Looking for this? It wasn't hard to get hold of.'

When I'd come here, I'd been certain that Paul Ilford had killed Nadia, either because she suspected him of killing his mother, or because she was threatening to expose him as the man behind the cuckooing gang operating in that area of Scunthorpe. But I had had no intention of confronting him – I had wanted to talk to Lukas, to find out how much of it he knew, how much Nadia had told him. Now I found myself in a situation I really didn't want to be in, and I wasn't sure how I was going to get out of it. Even if Singh had read my message, how quickly would he get here?

'How did you get that?' I asked him quietly, wondering if I could manage to pretend to be clueless about the whole thing. The look on his face told me he wasn't buying it, however.

A sneer pulled at the corner of his mouth. 'I've got a few people who are willing to do little jobs for me. Breaking into a car isn't much to any of them, but I had him take your keys from your pocket in case we needed to search your flat too. Of course, in the end he didn't need them.'

I gave a shudder at the idea of one of Paul's unsavoury associates in my flat, particularly if Anna had been home, and was thankful that I'd taken my notebook with me that night and left it in my car.

'I thought you'd be easier to scare off,' he said with a glance at where the graze on my cheek was still healing.

'That was you too?' I asked in surprise. I had assumed from the size and shape of my attacker that it had been a patron of Roy's gym.

'You and that social worker were asking a few too many questions,' he replied. 'I couldn't have you fucking everything up for me, not now that I'm getting properly established.'

'You used your care business to find vulnerable victims, people who you knew wouldn't say anything about strange people coming in and out of their house.'

'And it worked,' he said with a smug grin. 'Nobody suspected a thing, until Mariusz Nowak got involved. I should never have pulled him in.'

'Why Mariusz?' I asked. If I could keep him talking, hopefully Singh would arrive, with back-up.

Paul glared at me. 'What does it matter?'

'I'm trying to work out why you killed Nadia,' I replied. 'I think it started with your mother. The obituary said she passed away peacefully in her sleep, but Nadia didn't think that was true, did she?'

'Stupid woman,' Paul spat, and there was rage in his voice. 'She should have left well alone! She came to me a couple of weeks afterwards, when she finally plucked up the courage to say something. She'd noticed that there was a lot of my mother's medication missing, that the packs and bottles had been much fuller when she was there the day before my mother died.' He stepped back and flung my notebook down on the worktop. 'That didn't end up in your little book, did it?' he jeered. 'No, she stuck her nose in where it didn't belong. She could have just ignored it, forgotten all about it.' He looked up at me, his eyes blazing. 'Mum did have a peaceful end, I made sure of that. Yes, I helped her along a little bit, but she was old and in pain. It was the kindest thing.'

'Why did you do it?' I asked, but I don't think he heard me.

'I liked Nadia, I actually fancied her. Was a bit pissed off when she went out with Lukas. I mean, what could he offer her compared to me?' He held his hands out, as if to suggest the house we were in would impress anyone. I remembered the size and luxury of his own house, and was once again appalled that he'd been living like that while leaving his mother in these conditions.

'So when she kept pushing you about how your mother died, is that when you lured Mariusz into your little gang?'

Paul laughed, an unpleasant sound that echoed in the

kitchen. 'He didn't need much luring. That kid was always going to be open to a bad influence.'

'You thought you could use him to threaten Nadia. But even that didn't work, did it?'

Paul shook his head. 'She was persistent. I even used her house for my business dealings for a couple of days, with Mariusz's help, to show her what hell I could make her life. But she was a stubborn bitch. Told me she would give me one last chance to admit what I'd done before she went to the police.'

'So you went round there when Lukas was out at the pub, and killed her,' I said softly. 'Then you set fire to the house to cover up what you'd done.'

He gave me an incredulous look. 'You think I set those fires? Why the hell would I do that? Every time I pick a new house to use as a base, I keep finding someone sets fire to it just after I move in. Some even before.' He made a low noise in the back of his throat. 'Never mind – it'll work in my favour. When they find your body and Lukas's in the remains of this house, they'll assume it was the same person.'

That was when I smelled the smoke. At the same time Paul swung a fist at my head.

After

Paul looked down at Nadia's lifeless body, the cord he had used still held tightly in one fist. She had been one of his best workers, but she'd been unable to keep her nose out of things. He'd thought that she'd be easy to fool, and to control, because she was deaf. In fact, she'd been completely the opposite.

When he'd picked her to be his mother's carer, he'd already known what he was going to do. He needed the old hag out of the way, but he didn't want anyone to spot what had happened, which was why he'd used one of his own carers but run it off the books. Nadia hadn't minded. She'd thought she was just doing him a favour, and he'd offered her some extra cash, which he knew she was desperate for.

She had actually thought that by talking to him, he'd see the error of his ways and turn himself in to the police. He shook his head as he thought about it. Killing her had been too easy. He'd just waited until her back was turned and slipped the cord round her neck. He was stronger than her – easy to overpower her.

Should he try and get her body out of the house and hide it somewhere? If he did that, it might be a while until anyone realised she was dead. Lukas would come back from the pub, drunk of course, and find that she wasn't there, but he might not report her missing until tomorrow, if he thought she'd gone out. He peered out of the front window and noticed an old man over the road sitting in his chair, looking out at the street. No, there was no way he'd be able to get her body out of the house without someone like that old bastard seeing him. She'd have to stay there.

He went back into the living room and pulled a cloth from his pocket, using it to wipe down any surfaces he might have touched, including door handles. He'd slipped on a pair of gloves before killing her, and he kept them on until he was in the car. The front door closed quite loudly behind him, but he didn't care. He just wanted to get away from there as quickly as possible. If anyone had seen him, he'd tell them he was dropping off Nadia's new rota.

As he drove away, he pictured the police coming to the office the next day to tell him one of his employees had died. He practised his best shocked and sad faces, then reminded himself to tell them just how drunk Lukas could get some nights. Yes, that should be enough to do it.

Chapter 37

Paul swung for me but I dodged his punch and he caught me on the shoulder, which sent us both sprawling onto the floor. I had no idea where he'd set the fire, but the smell of smoke was getting stronger, so I needed to find a way out of there as quickly as I could.

My mind went back to something Paul had said: that they'd find Lukas's body after the fire as well as mine. Was Lukas already dead, or was he still alive and somewhere in the house? My flight instincts were telling me to get out of the house, but if there was a possibility that Lukas was alive I had to try and find him.

I scrambled forwards on my knees, but Paul was quicker than me. He grabbed one of my ankles and hauled me backwards, my jaw crunching as it hit the floor. I cried out, but a moment later his hand was across my mouth, cutting off my airway. Struggling against him, I tried to push him off me but he was stronger than he looked. The edges of my vision started to darken as I fought to breathe, so I let my body go limp. This tactic worked – Paul thought I'd passed out, and released the pressure on my face, allowing me to breathe again. As soon as I felt his weight lift from me, I made another dash for the kitchen door and into the hallway.

Paul obviously expected me to go for the front door, but instead I raced up the stairs. Smoke was curling out from underneath the door of the living room, and I could already see it starting to fill the hallway. I pulled my top up to cover my nose and mouth as I ran up the stairs, tripping on a bit of loose carpet halfway up. Part of me expected to feel Paul's hand on my ankle again, dragging me back down the stairs, but there was nothing. I picked myself up and hurried to the top, checking the two rooms for any sign of Lukas.

The back bedroom was piled floor to ceiling with cardboard boxes, and a quick glance told me a person couldn't fit in the spaces between them, so I went into the other bedroom. It was still furnished with Paul's mum's things, down to the open powder puff on the dressing table, and I felt a small shiver. Lukas was lying on the bed, tied up but conscious and alert. He stared at me, struggling against his bonds, as I came into the room.

Paul's set fire to the house, I signed quickly, before attempting to untie him. The knots were tight and it took me too long just to pick at them and work an end loose. I looked around the room for something I could use to cut the cords binding his hands, but there was nothing, and by the time I'd freed his hands I was coughing. When he had use of his hands I thought Lukas would help to untie his feet, but he just lay there staring at me.

Paul killed her. He killed Nadia, he signed to me, looking dazed.

I know, and he's trying to kill us!

Lukas just looked at me, as if he had no idea what I was talking about, and I wondered if he hadn't even noticed the smell of smoke as it drifted through the house.

Fire! I signed again, and this seemed to galvanise him into action. Between us we got the ropes off his ankles and rushed out onto the landing. I got to the top of the stairs and felt the panic in my chest reach up to my throat, nearly suffocating me. I could see now why Paul hadn't bothered to follow me up there. The fire had spread out from the front room into the hallway, and the flames were licking at the carpet at least three steps up from the ground floor. We were trapped.

Lukas pushed against me from behind and I stumbled, my foot slipping down off the top step. I fell to my knees and grabbed on to the banister rail to stop myself from falling down the full flight of stairs.

Go back! I hastily signed to Lukas, and he looked past me at the fire. Pushing me out of the way, he looked like he was going to try and get down, but I knew there was no way he'd make it. I grabbed the back of his shirt and dragged him back onto the landing, then into the smaller bedroom, which was the furthest away from the fire.

Help me move these boxes, I told him, pulling them away from the window.

What are you trying to do?

I pointed at the window. *It's our only way out of this house.*

He shook his head. *We can't jump. We'll be killed.*

I shook my head at him in frustration. *It's only a few feet, we'll be fine.* I didn't have time to argue with him, so I just ignored him and carried on lugging the boxes out of the way. They were heavy, so it would have been easier if he'd helped me, but the next time I looked round he'd disappeared. I was about to see where he'd gone, but the smoke was getting thicker and I could feel the heat of the fire coming up through the floor, and I knew I no longer had time to think about anything other than my own survival.

A moment later, however, Lukas was back at my side, grabbing me by the arm. I tried to shake him off but he was persistent, forcing me to look at him.

Police, he signed.

Where?

Outside. He pointed to the front bedroom, and I left the box I was trying to manoeuvre and dashed back through to the other room. Sure enough, there were blue flashing lights outside the window, and I saw a familiar figure standing next to a couple of uniformed officers, shouting orders and pointing at the house – it was Singh. He must have got my message. I felt a rush of emotion at the sight of him, knowing he had come to help me when I needed him most.

My hand went to the window to throw it open, but Lukas grabbed me.

No, don't, he told me. *The added oxygen could make the fire explode.*

I had no idea how fire behaved or if that was even possible, but I let go of the window, instead waving to try and attract Singh's attention. It took a moment or two, but he looked up, and before I knew it he was running towards the house.

'No!' I screamed. Why would he do something so stupid? There was no way he could reach us from the ground floor.

I don't care what you say, I'm opening the window, I told Lukas, grabbing the sash and hauling it upwards. It was old and it stuck on the way up, but I put my full strength behind it and it groaned as it eventually slid upwards, a bit of the old window frame splintering as I did. I felt the rush of cool air and took a deep breath, and when there was no answering rush of flame behind me I called out to Singh.

'Rav! You can't get in. The fire's in the front room.'

He looked up at me, over to the other officers, then back at me. 'Is there anything in there that you can throw down?'

'There's a mattress, but there's no way we can get it through this window.' I looked back at the room. There was an old armchair, but the cushions weren't big enough to provide any sort of platform for us to land on.

The street was filling up with people, as uniformed officers escorted neighbours out of their houses and along the street to wait at a safe distance. I could hear sirens in the distance, which told me there were fire engines on the way. A coughing fit overtook me and I doubled over, moving out of sight of the window.

'Paige? Paige!' I could hear the panic in Singh's voice

and I tried to hold up a hand to let him know I was okay, but I felt too dizzy. I tried to suppress the coughing, but that just made it worse, and in a moment I was on my knees. Lukas appeared beside me, trying to help me up to the window ledge so I could get some fresh air, but I felt like my limbs had been filled with lead.

Outside, I could hear Singh shouting my name, until the sound of the sirens drowned him out. I tried to move, but I was exhausted, and I curled up on the floor.

I have no idea how long I was lying there before I felt hands on my arms and legs, pulling me upwards and tipping me over something solid. As I drifted in and out of consciousness, I realised I was being held tightly over someone's shoulder as they carried me out of the house. Cool air was all around me, and faces drifted in and out of my vision. There was a pressure on my hand that remained constant, and on impulse I squeezed back against the hand that was gripping mine.

A mask had been placed over my nose and mouth, and I felt myself coming round a little bit. The coughing had subsided slightly, and I blinked tears out of my eyes. From the bright lights above me, and the man dressed in green to my side, I realised I was in the back of an ambulance.

'Where's Lukas?' I tried to say, but my tongue felt thick in my mouth, and the oxygen mask muffled my speech further. Moving it away from my face, I asked my question again, but the paramedic shushed me and replaced the mask.

I lay there for I don't know how long – minutes, maybe longer – staring at the roof and wondering what had happened to both Lukas and Paul, before Singh climbed up into the back of the ambulance. He took my hand, and something about the warmth of it made me realise he was the one who had been holding my hand as I was carried out of the house. I smiled at him, but he just shook his head, seemingly unsure of what to say.

'Is Lukas okay?' I asked. My voice was a lot croakier than I expected, and pain seared my throat. I tried to swallow, but the dryness made me cough again. Singh moved out of the way as the paramedic checked me over, and it was only once he gave the okay that Rav answered my question.

'As far as I know, yes. He's in another ambulance, being checked over. It looks like you inhaled more smoke than he did.'

I nodded, knowing I'd breathed in plenty while I was trying to fight Paul off me in the kitchen.

'Paul?' I asked, but Singh shook his head.

'We haven't found him yet.'

I squeezed my eyes shut. If Paul Ilford got away because I hadn't managed to stop him, I'd kick myself. I knew he would have set fire to the house and killed Lukas even if I hadn't knocked on the door, so that wasn't my fault, but I could have kept him occupied longer until the police arrived.

'I'm sorry,' I began, but he glared at me and shook his head. I wasn't going to be deterred, so I continued. 'I didn't know he'd be here. I spoke to Forest earlier and told her about Nadia thinking there was something suspicious about the death of Paul's mum. I wasn't going to go anywhere near him, but when I got here to speak to Lukas, it was Paul who answered the door.'

There were tears in my eyes, and I could hear the pleading in my own voice. Singh squeezed my hand a bit tighter and gave me a tight smile.

'It's okay, Paige. Please, don't worry about it.'

'But . . .'

'Don't. You're okay, and that's what matters right now.'

I looked at him closely. 'I keep screwing things up, but you're still here.'

He laughed gently and stroked my face. 'I was about to run into a burning building for you. I'm not great at talking about how I feel, but that should tell you something.'

Chapter 38

Friday 26th April

I had been discharged from hospital the previous night after being checked over by a doctor and given yet another list of signs to watch out for should my condition worsen. Singh had stayed with me the whole time, then taken me home and handed responsibility over to Anna, who had fussed constantly until I went to bed.

In the morning, my whole body ached as if I'd spent an hour in the ring in Worx gym with one of Roy Chapman's regular customers. I couldn't quite believe what had happened, and the idea that Paul was still out there somewhere, and knew where I lived, terrified me.

There was a knock on my bedroom door, and Anna came in with a cup of tea. She sat on the end of my bed and gave me a searching look.

How are you feeling?

Shit, I replied, truthfully.

You look it.

Thanks. I laughed, which set off a coughing fit.

Anna handed me a piece of paper. *Rav left this last night.*

It was a note asking me to come into the police station to give a statement this afternoon. I was glad he hadn't expected me to drag myself there this morning – it was already gone ten and I didn't feel like I had the energy to move yet.

He was very attentive last night, she commented lightly, giving me a sly look.

Don't, I signed with a firm shake of my head that made me wince. Rav and I hadn't had the opportunity to talk much, but I was looking forward to sitting down with him sometime soon and letting him know my real feelings as well as exploring his. Still, I didn't want to talk to Anna about it just yet; she didn't even know about the kiss.

Anna shrugged, but I knew from her expression that I hadn't heard the last of it.

So, tell me everything, she said, crossing her legs and settling herself at the foot of my bed.

Now the police knew what had happened, and would have enough evidence against Paul when it was coupled with my statement and Lukas's, I didn't see any harm in telling Anna. I was glad to be using sign language, because of the raging pain in my throat, and I kept having to stop to take sips of water to try and ease it.

What about the fires? she asked, once I'd finished explaining about Paul, and why he killed Nadia.

Singh told me about that while we were waiting at the hospital, I told her. *I was right; Mariusz has confessed to setting the fires. He got involved with the gang at a time when he was struggling emotionally at school and at home, making him an easy target for grooming, but once he* understood what they were doing he wanted to get out again. When he realised they'd been dealing from these houses, including his dad's house, he tried to think up a way to stop them. Apparently one of the houses they'd used in the past had accidentally caught fire and the gang moved on immediately to avoid being caught. The tenant was moved to a different area, so was no longer at risk from the gang. Mariusz panicked and took it to the extreme, thinking another fire was the only way to stop the gang using his dad's house. He was terrified the gang would find out it was him, so he set fire to another couple of houses to make it look like someone was targeting the drug dealer.

Couldn't he have reported them to the police? she asked.

I think he was too scared of the main dealer. That's one of the reasons he set fire to his dad's house first – he knew they wouldn't suspect him. Mariusz was recruited by the dealer and the other lads; he never realised that his mum's boss was in charge of it all. Neither did Lukas – he knew the gang had targeted other people in the area, but Nadia convinced him they were connected to Roy, and begged him to keep quiet about it in case the gang did something worse. She knew Mariusz was involved, so she wanted to protect him while she decided what to do about Paul.

And Lukas just believed that? she asked, incredulous.

I know, I agreed. I can't believe he didn't push any further either, but I think he never had a reason to doubt Nadia, and he wasn't surprised by the idea that Roy had gang contacts.

Anna rolled her eyes and I nodded.

364

So Mariusz set the other fires to try and stop the gang?

That's what he said. At first he was terrified and thought he'd killed Nadia; he'd thought the house was empty. She'd known he was mixed up with the gang and had tried to talk to him about it; he said she seemed to be the only one who noticed when he was feeling low and she always did her best to look out for him. The idea that he might have killed her left him absolutely devastated.

After that, he always checked that there was nobody in, so they didn't get hurt, and they were all council properties, so he thought the tenants would get somewhere else to live straight away. I shrugged. *He's only sixteen, and he's not a bad kid. Paul got one of the other kids to tempt him in, and luckily for them they caught him at a time when he was feeling particularly vulnerable.* I shook my head. *I think he nearly told me and Sasha about it all, when he came to see her a week ago, but in the end he was too scared to say anything. Sasha brushed it off, and now I know about the affair I think she was probably worried that Mariusz might have seen her meeting his dad, and thought she had something to do with Nadia's murder.*

Poor kid. What's going to happen to him?

I shook my head. *Singh wasn't sure. Hopefully nothing too bad, because he did come and hand himself in last night. When he found out his dad had nearly died in another fire he wanted to make sure the police knew he wasn't responsible for that one.*

She nodded, then looked at her watch. *Come on, you, let's get you in the shower and down to the police station. Then once you've given your statement we can choose some trashy films and stay on the sofa until Monday.*

Aren't you at work today?

No, I took the day off, compassionate leave. I figured you needed me more today.

I gave her a hug, then went off to try and wash some of the smoke out of my hair. There was a pleasant jittery feeling running through the whole of my body at the thought of seeing Rav, and I hummed to myself while I was in the shower. By the time I was finished, I'd made my mind up: it was time to seize the day, and once I'd given my statement I was going to ask him out for a drink.

Standing outside the police station, I realised there was still one question I didn't have the answer to, and I wouldn't feel like this was all over until I did. Before I went inside to give my statement, I made a call.

Hello? Lukas looked puzzled when he answered.

Hi, Lukas. Do you have a couple of minutes to talk?

He nodded. *You saved my life. I can always give you a few minutes.*

I thought back to the night Nadia had been killed, and our conversation in the hospital. *Do you remember telling me that you knew who was responsible for Nadia's death?*

I do. I was an idiot.

Did you know what Paul was up to? Had Nadia told you about any of it, about his mother, or the drug dealing?

Lukas shook his head hurriedly. *No, no, Paige, you must believe me. I didn't know about any of that, or I would have told the police.* He hung his head. *I should have talked to them. Maybe they would have found out about Paul sooner.*

You couldn't have saved Nadia, I told him gently. *She must have thought she could deal with Paul without getting you involved.*

I know, but . . . He shrugged. *Anyway, it doesn't matter now.*

I paused for a moment, wondering if I should leave it, but I wanted to know. *It matters to me,* I told him. *Who did you think had killed her?*

He grimaced before he replied. *I thought it was Roy. He'd already threatened me once that evening, when his thugs beat me up outside the pub, and then I got that text. I knew it was from him, but I assumed it referred to Nadia, not just the beating. But after a while, I began to wonder if it might have been Sasha. She is such a passionate woman, I believe there are a lot of things she would do to get what she wants. When she kept trying to see me I wondered if she was making sure I hadn't said anything to implicate her. I knew it was safest if I didn't say anything, and hoped to God that the police found out the truth.*

I nodded slowly. It made sense, and his reasons for not talking were ones I'd suggested myself – at first he was scared of Roy, but then when he started to suspect Sasha he stayed silent in order to protect her.

Thanks, Lukas. I appreciate you being honest with me.

He nodded. *Now I need to go and spend some time with my son,* he told me, so I said goodbye and hung up, then took a deep breath before going in to give my statement.

Something about the atmosphere in the police station felt different as I walked in. But it was as busy as ever, and as I was led through to an interview room there was the usual hustle and bustle of people coming and going that I was used to. I couldn't put my finger on what it was that might have changed.

I sat in the room and waited for about fifteen minutes. Rav hadn't specified a time to come in, so I didn't mind waiting until he was free. I used the time trying to get all the details straight in my head, knowing I would have to include as much information as possible.

The door opened and I felt a wave of disappointment when DI Forest walked in, alone.

'Good afternoon, Paige,' she said with a smile, which instantly threw me. I was so used to Forest scowling at me that I wondered what had happened to effect this change. 'Thank you for coming in. I'd like to take your statement about the events of yesterday, if that's okay?'

I agreed, but asked a question first.

'What about Paul?'

'Paul Ilford was arrested in the early hours of this morning. He was driving through Norfolk, and the automated number plate recognition cameras picked him up. I don't think he was expecting us to be looking for him quite so soon – he was going to stay in a cottage near Cromer for a while, until things had died down.'

'Did he realise that Lukas and I had survived?'

'I don't think so.'

I shuddered at the arrogance of the man, then Forest shuffled impatiently, and I knew she wanted to begin. We went through everything, from my conversation with the carer (whom Forest had managed to track down and take a statement from) to my decision to go into the house when I knew Paul Ilford was there. That was a difficult one to justify, because I couldn't quite explain why I'd done it. I had been fairly confident that he'd murdered Nadia and probably his mother, but it hadn't crossed my mind that he'd had similar plans for Lukas.

Once I'd finished describing my fight with Paul in the kitchen, finding Lukas, and our attempted escape, Forest sat back and turned off the tape recorder.

'Can I ask something?'

The DI nodded.

'Why did Paul kill his mother? That seems to have been the catalyst for this whole thing.'

Forest wrinkled her nose, and I wondered if she was going to refuse to reply, but she shuffled a couple of papers on the table then looked back at me. 'Mrs Ilford had given Paul the money he needed to start his business, over twenty years ago, and in return he'd given her a large share of it. This was back in the days when it was a legitimate care agency, without any other, illegal streams of income. Anyway, she still owned that part share and there was no legal way of Paul getting it back. When she died, it all reverted to him.'

Even though this was the man whom I had seen set a house on fire with two people inside it, I was stunned. 'Couldn't he have just waited for her to die naturally?'

'She was seventy-one, and in pretty good physical health, even if her memory was declining. The only reason he had a carer going in was to save himself from having to visit her. She might have lived for another fifteen or twenty years, and that was hindering the growth of the illegal branch of his business.'

I blew air out of my cheeks, trying to take it all in. At least I knew I was safe now, and so was Mariusz. I didn't know what would happen to the gang he'd been part of, but I knew Lukas would be keeping a much closer eye on his son now, and would make sure he knew what was happening in Mariusz's life.

Forest told me we'd finished, so I picked up my bag and stood up to leave.

'Is DS Singh around?' I asked, trying to keep my voice casual. She turned to me with a nasty smile.

'I'm sure he is, somewhere. He has a disciplinary meeting to attend, after all.'

I felt a swooping sensation, as if someone had just tilted the room. 'What do you mean?'

'Oh, didn't I mention? He's now on his final warning, for giving information about an ongoing inquiry to a civilian. Any other indiscretions and he'll be suspended.' With that she gave me one last smug look then swept out of the room.

I had to lean on the wall for support, or I thought I might be sick. What had I done? That was why Forest had been so pleasant to me, because she was waiting to drop that bombshell. She was the only one who had known that Rav told me about the cuckooing, so she must have reported him. How could she do that to one of her own team? Did she hate me that much, that she had to destroy the career of someone I cared about?

In a daze, I left the interview room and glanced around. I couldn't go hunting for him – I didn't know my way around the police station – so I went back out into the car park and looked for his car. Once I found it, I leant against it, sent him a text to let him know I was there, and waited.

It took about twenty minutes for him to come outside. When he saw me waiting by his car, he stopped and shook his head.

'Not now, Paige.'

'Rav, please. I'm so sorry. I don't know what I can do to make this better.'

He held up a hand. 'You can't. It's done now.'

'You'll be okay, won't you? She can't have you suspended because of this?'

He swallowed, and I realised he hadn't looked me in the eye yet. 'I don't know. Forest has been gunning for me for a while, and now she's got the perfect ammunition.'

Ammunition I had given her. He might not have said it out loud, but we both knew that was what he was thinking. After everything we'd been through together, after everything he'd done for me, I couldn't believe this was happening. I reached out to touch his arm, but he took a step back so he was out of my reach.

Again, I felt as if the ground had lurched beneath me. Throughout the last couple of weeks, I felt like he and I had been getting closer; I knew I hadn't imagined him kissing me back the other night. But suddenly a chasm had opened up between us, and what made it worse was that it was a chasm I had created.

'Rav, you know I never meant this. It was a stupid comment I made to Forest, and I am so sorry, but I didn't mean for this to happen.'

He pushed past me and opened the back door of his car, putting the bag he was carrying in there, then looked up at me.

'I know you didn't mean to do it. But that doesn't

change the fact that you did, and now I need to be careful. I can't be seen talking to you, Paige.' He was battling to keep his voice even, but I could see him almost shaking with the effort.

I squeezed my eyes shut, willing myself not to burst into tears. He was so angry, and it shook me that I was the cause of it.

'She can't make these things stick,' I said, not even convincing myself, and he let out a harsh laugh that felt like a stab to my heart.

'I'm glad you have confidence in that, because I don't.' He paused, then took a deep breath. 'Excuse me, I'd like to get in my car now.'

He reached past me to open the door and as he did, I grabbed his arm, forcing him to turn and look at me. The look in his eyes was a mixture of hurt and frustration, and I was about to step back when he closed the gap between us and kissed me. Before I had time to react, he'd pulled away again, shaking his head.

'I'm sorry, Paige. I can't lose my job. Try not to get in any more trouble.' He forced a smile but I could see the pain in his eyes as he got in the car.

I watched as he drove away, knowing there was nothing I could do to change what had happened, but also feeling certain of what I wanted. My lips still felt warm from his impulsive kiss, and I was in a daze as I walked up the road to where Anna was picking me up. I'd thought things were looking good between Rav and me, but what would the future hold for us now?

Acknowledgements

Writing the acknowledgements is nearly as difficult as writing the book itself, and if I wrote everything I'd like to say to everyone who's supported me it would also be nearly as long.

Firstly, huge thanks to my wonderful agent, Juliet Mushens. Even after two years I pinch myself when I remember she's the one who chose to represent me.

Also, much love and appreciation to editorial partners-in-crime Tilda McDonald and Beth Wickington, who together manage to figure out exactly what it was I was trying to say, and who always make me laugh on video calls.

Thank you to everyone else at Avon and Harper 360 who work so hard to make sure the books they publish are a success: Ellie Pilcher, Sabah Khan, Catriona Beamish, Caroline Bovey, Georgina Ugen, Alice Gomer, Charlotte Brown, Jean Marie Kelly, Emily Gerbner, Peter Borcsok and Helena Newton.

Thank you to Sarah Whittaker for yet another sensational cover – I love them so much, and I spend rather a lot of time looking at them when I should be doing something else.

I'm really lucky to have an amazing independent bookshop nearby – The Rabbit Hole, in Brigg. Nick and Mel Webb are hugely supportive of local authors and poets, and have continued to do their best to involve themselves in the local community during the challenges of 2020. I can't wait to hold a launch party there again in future, whenever it might be allowed.

Faye Robertson always deserves a special mention, for answering my complicated and confusing questions about police procedure, then forgiving me when I ignore her answers completely. All flights of fancy and drama are mine, please try to suspend your disbelief!

Thank you also to those people who have invited me onto their platforms to promote my books in the last year, whether on blogs or YouTube or via Zoom interviews for literary festivals. I've enjoyed taking part in all of these, but I can't wait to meet readers in person at events in the future!

Thank you to every single person who has read this book or the two that came before it, whether you already knew me, you saw something about the series online, or you picked it up at random in a bookshop, supermarket or library. Without readers, writers are pretty stuck. I also really appreciate all of the reviews online, whether they're from bloggers or seasoned reviewers, or just people who enjoyed the book.

The list of friends and family I want to thank for their

support is now getting so long I'm terrified of missing someone, so I might just have to pretend I'm on PopMaster on Radio 2 and go for 'anyone else who knows me'. Seriously, though, I've been absolutely blown away by the enthusiasm with which people have been talking about my books. I've reconnected with old friends who've seen something about me on social media and have then gone out to buy one of my books, as well as meeting many new people, both writers and readers. Most of all, though, I cannot put into words how much it means to me when I see my friends recommending my books to their friends again and again, tirelessly championing my work and going above and beyond what I would ever expect from them. I'm very lucky to be surrounded by these people.

Finally, as always, to Stuart and Albert. I love you both so much, and you make me the best version of myself.

If someone was in your house, you'd know . . .
Wouldn't you?

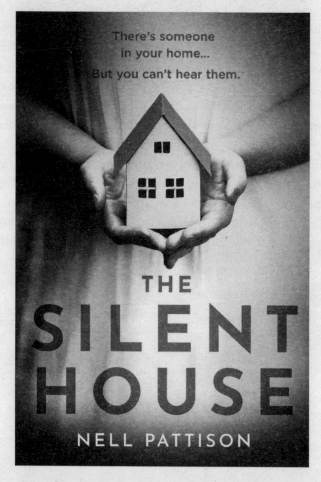

There's someone
in your home...
But you can't hear them.

THE
SILENT
HOUSE

NELL PATTISON

The first gripping Paige Northwood mystery.
Available in paperback, ebook and audio now.

What happened while they were sleeping? . . .

No one
saw them.

No one
heard them.

No one can find them…

SILENT
NIGHT

NELL PATTISON
USA TODAY BESTSELLING AUTHOR

The second gripping Paige Northwood mystery.
Available in paperback, ebook and audio now.